THE
NIGHTMARE

LARS KEPLER

Translated from the Swedish by Neil Smith

HarperCollins*Publishers*

HarperCollins*Publishers*
1 London Bridge Street
London SE1 9GF

www.harpercollins.co.uk

This paperback edition 2018
1

First published in Great Britain by HarperCollins*Publishers* 2012

Originally published in 2010 by Albert Bonniers Förlag, Sweden, as
Paganinikontraktet

Lars Kepler asserts the moral right to
be identified as the author of this work

A catalogue record for this book
is available from the British Library

ISBN: 978-0-00-824182-7

Set in Electra LT Std by Palimpsest Book Production Limited,
Falkirk, Stirlingshire

Printed and bound in Great Britain by
CPI Group (UK) Ltd, Croydon, CR0 4YY

MIX
Paper from
responsible sources

FSC
www.fsc.org

FSC™ C007454

There's no wind when the large leisure cruiser is found drifting in Jungfrufjärden in the southern part of the Stockholm archipelago one light evening. The water is a sleepy bluish-grey colour, and is moving as gently as fog.

The old man in a rowing boat calls out a couple of times even though he has a feeling he's not going to get any answer. He's been watching the boat from shore for almost an hour as it's been drifting slowly backwards on the offshore current.

The man angles his rowing boat so that the side butts up against the motor cruiser. He pulls the oars in, ties the rowing boat to the swimming platform, climbs up the metal steps and over the railing. In the middle of the aft-deck is a pink sun-lounger. When he can't hear anything he opens the glass door and goes down a few steps into the saloon. The large windows are casting a grey light across the polished teak interior and dark-blue upholstery of the sofa. He carries on down the steep wooden steps, past the dark galley and bathroom and into the large cabin. Pale light is filtering through the narrow windows up by the ceiling, illuminating the arrow-shaped double bed. Towards the top of the bed a young woman in a denim jacket is sitting against the wall in a limp, slumped posture with her legs wide apart and one hand resting on a pink cushion. She's looking the old man straight in the eye with a bemused, anxious smile on her face.

It takes a moment for the man to realise that the woman is dead.

In her long, dark hair there's a clasp in the shape of a dove, a peace dove.

When the old man goes over and touches her cheek, her head topples forward and a thin stream of water trickles out of her mouth and down her chin.

The word 'music' actually refers to the artistry of the muses, and comes from the Greek myth of the nine muses. All nine were the daughters of the great god Zeus and the titan Mnemosyne, goddess of memory. The muse of music itself, Euterpe, is usually depicted with a double-flute between her lips, and her name means 'bringer of joy'.

The talent known as musicality has no generally accepted definition. There are people who lack the ability to discern shifting frequencies of notes, and there are people who are born with an extensive musical memory and the sort of perfectly attuned hearing that enables them to identify any given note without any points of reference whatsoever.

Through the ages a number of exceptionally talented musical geniuses have emerged, some of whom have become extremely famous, such as Wolfgang Amadeus Mozart, who toured the courts of Europe from the age of six, and Ludwig van Beethoven, who composed many of his greatest works after he had become totally deaf.

The legendary Nicolò Paganini was born in 1782 in the Italian city of Genoa. He was a self-taught violinist and composer. To this day there have been very few violinists capable of playing Paganini's fast, complicated compositions. Up to his death Paganini was pursued by rumours that he had only acquired his unique talent by signing a contract with the devil.

1

A shiver runs down Penelope Fernandez's spine. Her heart suddenly starts to beat faster and she glances quickly over her shoulder. Perhaps at that moment she has a premonition of what is going to happen to her later that same day.

In spite of the heat in the studio Penelope's face feels cool. It's a lingering after-effect from the make-up room, where the cool cream-powder sponge was pressed to her skin, the clasp with the dove removed from her hair as the mousse was rubbed in to gather her hair into twining locks.

Penelope Fernandez is chairperson of the Swedish Peace and Arbitration Society. She is now being ushered silently into the news studio, and sits down in the spotlight opposite Pontus Salman, who is the managing director of Silencia Defence Ltd, an arms manufacturer.

The news anchor, Stefanie von Sydow, moves on to a new item, looks into the camera and starts to talk about the redundancies that have followed the purchase of the Swedish company Bofors by British defence manufacturer BAE Systems Ltd, then she turns to Penelope:

'Penelope Fernandez, in a number of debates now you have been highly critical of Swedish arms exports. Recently you drew a comparison with the Angolagate scandal in France, in which senior politicians and businessmen were accused of bribery and weapons smuggling, and have now been given long prison sentences. We haven't seen anything like that in Sweden, though, surely?'

'There are two ways of looking at that,' Penelope Fernandez replies. 'Either our politicians work differently, or our judicial system does.'

'As you're well aware,' Pontus Salman says, 'we have a long tradition of . . .'

'According to Swedish law,' Penelope interrupts. 'According to Swedish law, all manufacture and export of military equipment is illegal.'

'You're wrong, of course,' Salman says.

'Paragraphs 3 and 6 in the Military Equipment Act, 1992,' Penelope specifies.

'But Silencia Defence has been given positive advance notification,' he smiles.

'Yes, because otherwise we'd be talking about large-scale weapons offences, and . . .'

'Like I said, we have a permit,' he interrupts.

'Don't forget what military equipment is . . .'

'Hold on a moment, Penelope,' news anchor Stefanie von Sydow says, nodding to Pontus Salman who has raised a hand to indicate that he hasn't finished.

'Naturally, every deal is examined beforehand,' he explains. 'Either directly by the government, or by the Inspectorate for Strategic Products, if you're aware of them?'

'France has an equivalent body,' Penelope replies. 'Even so, military equipment worth eight billion kronor was able to reach Angola in spite of the UN arms embargo, and in spite of an absolutely binding ban on . . .'

'We're talking about Sweden now.'

'I understand that people don't want to lose their jobs, but I'd still be interested to hear how you can justify the export of huge quantities of ammunition to Kenya? A country which . . .'

'You haven't got anything,' he interrupts. 'Nothing, not a single instance of wrongdoing, have you?'

'Unfortunately I'm not in a position to . . .'

'Do you have any concrete evidence?' Stefanie von Sydow interrupts.

'No,' Penelope Fernandez replies, and lowers her gaze. 'But I . . .'

'In which case I think an apology is in order,' Pontus Salman says.

Penelope looks him in the eye, feels anger and frustration bubbling up inside her, but forces herself to stay quiet. Pontus Salman gives her a disappointed smile and then goes on to talk about their factory in Trollhättan. Two hundred jobs were created when Silencia Defence was given permission to start manufacture. He explains what positive advance notification means, and how far they have got with production. He slowly expands on his point to the extent that there's no time left for his co-interviewee.

Penelope listens and tries to suppress the pride in her heart. Instead she thinks about the fact that she and Björn will soon be setting off on his boat. They'll make up the arrow-shaped bed in the fore, fill the fridge and little freezer. In her mind's eye she can see the sparkle of the frosted vodka glasses when they're eating pickled herring, potatoes, boiled eggs and crisp-bread. They'll lay the table on the aft-deck, drop anchor by a small island in the archipelago and sit and eat for hours in the evening sun.

Penelope Fernandez leaves Swedish Television's studios and starts to walk towards Valhallavägen. She spent almost two hours waiting for a follow-up interview on a different programme before the producer said they were going to have to drop her to make room for five easy tips for a flat stomach this summer.

Over on the grassy expanse of Gärdet she can see the colourful tents of the Circus Maximum. One of the keepers is washing two elephants with a hose. One of them reaches into the air with its trunk to catch the hard jet of water in its mouth.

Penelope is only twenty-four, and she has dark, curly hair that reaches just past her shoulders. She has a short silver chain around her neck with a small crucifix from when she was confirmed. Her skin is a silky golden colour, like virgin olive oil or honey, as one boy wrote when they had to describe each other in a high-school exercise. Her eyes are large and serious. More than once she has been told that she bears a striking resemblance to film star Sophia Loren.

Penelope takes out her phone and calls Björn to say she's on her way, and is about to catch the underground from Karlaplan.

'Penny? Has something happened?' he asks, sounding stressed.

'No – why?'

'Everything's ready, I left you a message. You're the only thing missing.'

'There's no desperate rush, is there?'

As Penelope is standing on the long, steep escalator down to the underground platform her heart starts to beat faster with vague unease, and she closes her eyes. The escalator grows steeper and narrower, the air cooler and cooler.

Penelope Fernandez comes from La Libertad, which is one of the largest regions of El Salvador. Penelope's mother Claudia Fernandez was imprisoned during the civil war and Penelope was born in a cell where fifteen other interned women did their best to help. Claudia was a doctor, and had been active in the campaign to educate the population. The reason she ended up in one of the regime's notorious prisons was because she continued to campaign for the right of the indigenous people to form trades unions.

Penelope only opens her eyes when she reaches the bottom of the escalator. The feeling of being shut in vanishes. She thinks once more about Björn, waiting at the marina on Långholmen. She loves swimming naked from his boat, diving into the water and not being able to see anything but sea and sky.

The underground train shakes as it rushes through the tunnel, then sunlight streams through the windows when it reaches Gamla stan station.

Penelope Fernandez hates war and violence and military might. It's a burning conviction which led her to study for a master's degree at Uppsala University in Peace and Conflict Studies. She has worked for the French aid organisation Action Contre la Faim in Darfur alongside Jane Oduya. She wrote an acclaimed article for *Dagens Nyheter* about the women in the refugee camps and their attempts to recreate a semblance of normal life after every assault on them. Two years ago she succeeded Frida Blom as chair of the Swedish Peace and Arbitration Society.

Penelope gets off at Hornstull station and emerges into the sunshine. She suddenly feels inexplicably anxious, so runs down Pålsundsbacken to Söder Mälarstrand, hurries across the bridge to Långholmen and follows the road round to the left, towards the small boats harbour. Dust from the grit on the road hangs like a haze in the still air.

Björn's boat is moored in the shadow of the Western Bridge, the movements of the water forming a mesh of light reflected onto the grey steel beams high above.

She sees him at the back of the boat, wearing a cowboy hat. He's standing still, with his arms wrapped round him, his shoulders hunched.

Penelope puts two fingers in her mouth and wolf-whistles. Björn starts, and his face becomes completely unmasked, as if he were horribly afraid. He looks over towards the road and catches sight of her. He still has a worried look in his eyes as he walks to the gangplank.

'What is it?' she asks, walking down the steps to the jetty.

'Nothing,' Björn replies, then adjusts his hat and tries to smile.

They hug and she feels that his hands are ice-cold, and his shirt soaking wet on his back.

'You're really sweaty,' she says.

Björn looks away evasively.

'I'm just keen to get going.'

'Did you bring my bag?'

He nods and gestures towards the cabin. The boat is rocking gently beneath her feet, and she can smell sun-warmed plastic and polished wood.

'Hello?' she says breezily. 'Where are you right now?'

His straw-coloured hair is sticking out in all directions in small, matted dreads. His bright blue eyes are childlike, smiling.

'I'm here,' he replies, and lowers his eyes.

'What's on your mind?'

'I just want us to be together,' he says, and puts his arms round her waist. 'And have sex out in the open air.'

He nuzzles her hair with his lips.

'Is that what you're hoping?' she whispers.

'Yes,' he replies.

She laughs at him for being so upfront.

'Most people . . . well, most women, anyway, probably find that a bit overrated,' she says. 'Lying on the ground among loads of ants and stones and . . .'

'It's like swimming naked,' he maintains.

'You're just going to have to try to persuade me,' she says flirtatiously.

'I'll do my best.'

'How?' she laughs, as her phone starts to ring in her canvas bag.

Björn's smile seems to stiffen at the sound of the ringtone. The colour drains from his cheeks. She looks at the screen and sees that it's her younger sister.

'It's Viola,' she says quickly to Björn before she answers.

'*Hola*, little sister.'

A car blows its horn and her sister shouts something away from the phone.

'Bloody lunatic,' she mutters.

'What's going on?'

'It's over,' her sister says. 'I've dumped Sergey.'

'Again,' Penelope adds.

'Yes,' Viola says quietly.

'Sorry,' Penelope says. 'You must be upset.'

'It's not that bad, but . . . Mum said you were going out on the boat, and I was wondering . . . I'd love to come along, if that would be okay?'

Neither of them speaks for a moment.

'Sure, come along,' Penelope repeats, and hears the lack of enthusiasm in her own voice. 'Björn and I need a bit of time together, but . . .'

2

Penelope is standing at the helm with a light blue sarong wrapped round her hips and a white bikini top with a peace sign over the right breast. She is bathed in summer light coming through the windscreen. She carefully steers round Kungshamn light-house, then manoeuvres the large motor cruiser into the narrow strait.

Her sister Viola gets up from the pink sun-lounger on the aft-deck. She's spent the past hour lying there wearing Björn's cowboy hat and an enormous pair of mirror sunglasses, sleepily smoking a joint.

Viola makes five half-hearted attempts to pick up the box of matches with her toes before giving up. Penelope can't help smiling. Viola walks into the saloon through the glass door and asks if Penelope would like her to take over.

'If not, I'll go and make a margarita,' she says, and carries on down the steps.

Björn is lying out on the foredeck on a towel, using his paperback of Ovid's *Metamorphoses* as a pillow.

Penelope notices that the base of the railing by his feet has started to rust. Björn was given the boat by his father when he turned twenty, but he hasn't been able to afford to maintain it properly. The big motor cruiser is the only gift he ever got from his father, apart from a holiday. When his dad turned fifty he invited Björn and Penelope to one of his finest luxury hotels, the Kamaya Resort on the east coast of Kenya. Penelope only managed to put up with the hotel for two days before travelling to the refugee camp in Kubbum in Darfur in western Sudan, where the French aid organisation Action Contre la Faim was based.

Penelope decreases their cruising speed from eight to five knots as they approach the Skurusund Bridge. The heavy traffic high above on the bridge can't be heard at all on the water. Just as they're gliding into the shadow of the bridge she spots a black inflatable boat by one of the concrete foundations. It's the same sort used by the Special Boat Service: a RIB with a fibreglass hull and extremely powerful motors.

Penelope has almost passed the bridge when she realises that there's someone sitting in the boat. A man crouching in the gloom with his back to her. She doesn't know why her pulse quickens at the sight of him. There's something about the back of his head and his dark clothes. She feels as if she's being watched, even though he's facing the other way.

When she emerges into the sunshine again she shivers, and the goosebumps on her arms take a long time to go down.

She increases their speed to fifteen knots once she's past Duvnäs. The two on-board motors rumble, the water foams behind them and the boat takes off across the smooth sea.

Penelope's phone rings. She sees her mother's name on the screen. Perhaps she saw the discussion on television. Penelope wonders for a moment if her mum is calling to tell her she did well, but knows that's just a fantasy.

'Hi, Mum,' Penelope says when she answers.

'Ow,' her mother whispers.

'What's happened?'

'My back . . . I need to get to the chiropractor,' Claudia says. It sounds like she's filling a glass from the tap. 'I just wanted to find out if Viola's spoken to you?'

'She's here on the boat with us,' Penelope replies as she listens to her mother drink.

'Oh, good . . . I thought it would do her good.'

'I'm sure it will do her good,' Penelope says quietly.

'What food have you got?'

'Tonight we're having pickled herring, potatoes, eggs . . .'

'She doesn't like herring.'

'Mum, Viola called me just as . . .'

'I know you weren't expecting her to come with you,' Claudia interrupts. 'That's why I'm calling.'

'I've made some meatballs,' Penelope says patiently.

'Enough for everyone?' her mother asks.

'Everyone? That depends on . . .'

She tails off and stares out across the sparkling water.

'I don't have to have any,' Penelope says in a measured tone.

'If there aren't enough,' her mother says. 'That's all I meant.'

'I get it,' she says quietly.

'So it's poor you now, is it?' her mother asks with barely concealed irritation.

'It's just that . . . Viola is actually an adult, and . . .'

'I'm disappointed in you.'

'Sorry.'

'You always manage to eat my meatballs at Christmas and Midsummer and . . .'

'I can go without,' Penelope says quickly.

'Fine,' her mother says abruptly. 'That's that sorted.'

'I just mean . . .'

'Don't bother coming for Midsummer,' her mother interrupts crossly.

'Oh, Mum, why do you always have to . . .'

There's a click as her mother hangs up. Penelope stops talking and feels frustration bubbling inside her as she stares at the phone, then tosses it aside.

The boat passes slowly across the green reflection of the verdant slopes. The steps from the galley creak and Viola wobbles into view with a martini glass in her hand.

'Was that Mum?'

'Yes.'

'Is she worried I'm not going to get anything to eat?' Viola asks with a smile.

'There's food,' Penelope replies.

'Mum doesn't think I can take care of myself.'

'She's just worried,' Penelope replies.

'She never worries about you,' Viola says.

'I'm fine.'

Viola sips her cocktail and looks out through the windscreen.

'I saw the debate on television,' she says.

'This morning? With Pontus Salman?'

'No, this was . . . last week,' she says. 'You were talking to an arrogant man who . . . he had a fancy name, and . . .'

'Palmcrona,' Penelope says.

'That was it, Palmcrona . . .'

'I got angry, my cheeks turned red and I could feel tears in my eyes, I felt like reciting Bob Dylan's "Masters of War" or just running out and slamming the door behind me.'

Viola watches as Penelope stretches up and opens the roof hatch.

'I didn't think you shaved your armpits,' she says breezily.

'No, but I've been in the media so much that . . .'

'Vanity got the better of you,' Viola jokes.

'I didn't want to get written off as a troublemaker just because I had a bit of hair under my arms.'

'How's your bikini line going, then?'

'Well . . .'

Penelope lifts her sarong and Viola bursts out laughing.

'Björn likes it,' Penelope smiles.

'He can hardly talk, with his dreadlocks.'

'But you shave everywhere, just like you're supposed to,' Penelope says with a note of sharpness in her voice. 'For your married men and muscle-bound idiots and . . .'

'I know I have bad taste in men,' Viola interrupts.

'You don't have bad taste in anything else.'

'I've never really done anything properly, though.'

'You just have to improve your grades a bit, then . . .'

Viola shrugs her shoulders:

'I did actually sit the high-school paper.'

They're ploughing gently through the transparent water, followed high above by some gulls.

'How did it go?' Penelope eventually asks.

14

'I thought it was easy,' Viola says, licking salt from the rim of the glass.

'So it went well, then?' Penelope smiles.

Viola nods and puts her glass down.

'How well?' Penelope asks, nudging her in the side.

'Top marks,' Viola says, looking down.

Penelope lets out a shriek of joy and hugs her sister hard.

'You know what this means, don't you?' Penelope says excitedly. 'You can study anything you like, you can have your pick of the universities, you can chose whatever course you like, business studies, medicine, journalism.'

Her sister blushes and laughs, and Penelope hugs her again, knocking her hat off. She strokes Viola's head, then arranges her hair just as she always did when they were little, takes the clasp with the dove from her own hair and uses it to fasten her sister's, then looks at her and smiles happily.

3

A boat is left adrift in Jungfrufjärden

The fore cuts the smooth surface of the water like a knife, with a sticky, liquid sound. They're going very fast. Large waves hit the shore in their wake. They turn steeply and bounce across breaking waves, spraying water around them. Penelope heads out into the open water with the engines roaring. The fore lifts up and plumes of foaming white water spread out behind them.

'You're crazy, Madicken!' Viola shouts, pulling the clasp from her hair, just like she always did as a child when her hair was finally neat.

Björn wakes up when they stop at Gåsö. They buy ice-creams and have coffee. Then Viola wants to play mini-golf, and it's already late in the afternoon by the time they get going again.

The sea opens up on their port side, like a dizzyingly large stone floor.

The plan is to reach Kastskär, a long, narrow-waisted island that's uninhabited. There's a lush bay on the south side where they're going to drop anchor, swim, have a barbecue and spend the night.

'I think I'll go down and have a rest,' Viola says with a yawn.

'Go ahead,' Penelope smiles.

Viola goes down the steps and Penelope looks ahead of them. She lowers their speed and keeps an eye on the electronic depth sounder that will warn them of reefs as they approach Kastskär.

The water very quickly gets shallow, from forty metres to just five.

Björn comes into the cabin and kisses Penelope on the back of her neck.

'Shall I go and start the food?' he asks.

'Viola probably ought to sleep for an hour.'

'You sound like your mother,' he says gently. 'Has she phoned yet?'

'Yes.'

'To see if we let Viola come with us?'

'Yes.'

'Did you have an argument?'

She shakes her head.

'What is it?' he asks. 'Are you upset?'

'No, it's just that Mum . . .'

'What?'

Penelope smiles as she wipes the tears from her cheeks.

'She doesn't want me there for Midsummer,' she says.

Björn hugs her.

'Just ignore her.'

'I do,' she replies.

Very slowly, Penelope manoeuvres the boat as far into the bay as she can. The engines rumble softly. They're so close to the shore now that she can smell the plants.

They drop anchor, and the boat swings closer to the rocks. Björn jumps ashore onto the steep slope and ties the rope around a tree.

The ground is covered in moss. He stops and looks at Penelope. Some birds move in the treetops when the windlass rattles.

Penelope pulls on a pair of jogging bottoms and her white trainers, jumps ashore and takes his hand. He wraps his arms round her.

'Shall we go and take a look at the island?'

'Wasn't there something you were going to try to persuade me about?' she teases.

'The advantages of the Swedish "right to roam",' he says.

She nods and smiles, and he brushes her hair back and runs

a finger across her prominent cheekbone and thick, black eyebrow.

'How can you be so beautiful?'

He kisses her softly on the lips, then starts to walk towards the low-growing woods.

In the middle of the island is a small glade with dense clumps of tall meadow grass. Butterflies and small bumblebees are drifting about above the flowers. It's hot in the sun, and the water sparkles between the trees to the north. They stand still, hesitate, smiling as they look at each other, then turn serious.

'What if someone comes?' she says.

'We're the only people on the island.'

'Are you sure about that?'

'How many islands are there in the Stockholm archipelago? Thirty thousand? More, probably,' he says.

Penelope takes off her bikini top, kicks her shoes off and pulls down the rest of her bikini with her jogging bottoms, and is suddenly standing completely naked on the grass. Her initial feeling of embarrassment is replaced almost at once with sheer delight. She can't help finding the sea air on her skin and the heat radiating up from the ground intensely exciting.

Björn looks at her, mutters something about not being sexist, but that he just wants to look at her for a bit longer. She's tall, her arms simultaneously muscular and soft. Her narrow waist and powerful thighs make her look like a playful goddess.

Björn can feel his hands shaking as he pulls off his T-shirt and flowery, knee-length shorts. He's younger than her, his body is boyish, almost hairless, and his shoulders have already caught the sun.

'Now I want to look at you,' she says.

He blushes and walks over to her with a big smile.

'Can't I?'

He shakes his head and hides his face against her neck and hair.

They start to kiss, very gently, just stand close together kissing each other. Penelope feels his warm tongue in her mouth and a feeling of dizzy happiness courses through her. She forces herself to stop smiling so she can carry on kissing. They start to breathe faster. She feels Björn's erection growing as his heartbeat quickens. They lie down in the grass, finding a flat spot between the tussocks. His mouth traces its way down to her breasts and brown nipples, then he kisses her stomach and parts her thighs. When he looks at her it seems to him that their bodies are glowing with inner light in the evening sun. Suddenly everything is intensely intimate and sensitive. She's already wet and swollen when he starts to lick her, very softly and slowly, and she has to push his head away after a while. She presses her thighs together, smiles and blushes. She whispers to him to come closer, pulls him to her, guides him with her hand and lets him slide into her. He breathes heavily in her ear and she looks straight up at the pink sky.

Afterwards she stands naked in the warm grass, stretches, walks a few steps and stares off towards the trees.

'What is it?' Björn asks languidly.

She looks at him. He's sitting on the ground naked, smiling up at her.

'You've burned your shoulders.'

'Every summer.'

He gently touches the red skin on his shoulders.

'Let's go back – I'm hungry,' she says.

'I just need to go for a swim.'

She pulls her bikini bottoms and jogging pants back on, pulls her shoes on and stands there with her bikini top in her hand. She lets her eyes roam across his hairless chest, muscular arms, the tattoo on his shoulders, his careless sunburn and bright, playful eyes.

'Next time you get to lie underneath,' she smiles.

'Next time,' he repeats cheerfully. 'You're already a convert, I knew it.'

She laughs and waves at him dismissively. He lies back and stares up at the sky. She hears him whistling to himself as she walks through the trees towards the steep little beach where the boat is moored.

She stops to put her bikini top on before she goes down to the boat.

When Penelope goes on board she wonders if Viola is still

asleep in the aft-bunk. She decides to put a pan of new potatoes on to boil with some dill tops, then go and wash and get changed. Rather strangely the aft-deck is wet, as if it has been raining. Viola must have swabbed it down for some reason. The boat feels different. Penelope can't put her finger on what it is, but suddenly her skin comes out in goosebumps. It's almost completely silent, the birds have stopped singing. There's just a gentle lapping sound as the water hits the hull, and the faint creak of the rope around the tree. Penelope suddenly becomes very conscious of her own movements. She goes down the steps to the stern, and sees that the door to the guest cabin is open. The light is on, but Viola isn't there. Penelope notices that her hand is shaking when she knocks on the door of the little toilet. She opens it and looks inside, then goes back up on deck. Further along the bay she sees Björn on his way down to the water. She waves to him, but he doesn't see her.

Penelope opens the glass door to the saloon and walks past the blue sofas, teak table and helm.

'Viola?' she calls quietly.

She goes down to the galley and takes out a saucepan, but puts it down on the stove when her heart starts to beat even faster. She looks in the bathroom, then carries on to the cabin at the front where she and Björn always sleep. She opens the door and looks round in the gloom, and at first thinks she's looking at herself in the mirror.

Viola is sitting perfectly still at the top of the bed, her hand resting on the pink cushion from the Salvation Army.

'What are you doing in here?'

Penelope hears herself ask her sister what she's doing in the bedroom, even though she's already realised that something isn't right. Viola's face is oddly pale and wet, her hair hanging in damp clumps.

Penelope goes over and takes her sister's face in her hands, lets out a moan, then a scream, right close to her face.

'Viola? What is it? Viola?'

But she's already realised what's happened, what's wrong – her sister isn't breathing, there's no warmth in her skin, there's nothing left in her, the flame of life has been extinguished. The cramped room gets darker, closes in around Penelope. She hears herself whimpering in an unfamiliar voice and stumbles backwards, pulling clothes onto the floor, then hits her shoulder hard on the doorpost when she turns and runs up the steps.

When she emerges onto the aft-deck she gasps for breath as if she were close to suffocating. She coughs and looks round with a feeling of ice-cold terror in her body. A hundred metres away on the shore she can see a stranger dressed in black. Somehow Penelope realises how it all fits together. She knows it's the same man who was sitting in the military inflatable in the shadow under the bridge when they went past. She realises that the man in black killed Viola, and that he isn't finished yet.

The man is standing on the shore waving to Björn, who is swimming twenty metres out. He's shouting, holding his arm up. Björn hears him and stops, treading water, then turns to look back towards land.

Time almost stands still. Penelope rushes to the helm and digs about in the toolbox, finds a knife and runs back to the aft-deck.

She sees Björn's slow strokes, the rings spreading out across the water around him. He's looking curiously at the man. The man beckons him towards him. Björn smiles uncertainly and starts to swim back to shore.

'Björn!' Penelope screams as loudly as she can. 'Swim away from shore!'

The man on the shore turns towards her, then starts running towards the boat. Penelope cuts through the rope, slips over on the wet wooden deck, gets to her feet, hurries to the helm and starts the engine. Without looking she raises the anchor and puts the boat in reverse.

Björn must have heard her, because he's turned away from shore and has started to swim towards the boat instead. Penelope steers towards him as she sees the man in black change direction and start running up the slope towards the other side of the island. Without really thinking about it, she realises that the man has left his black inflatable in the bay to the north.

She knows there's no way they can outrun that.

She slowly turns the big boat and steers towards Björn. She yells at him as she gets closer, then slows down and holds a boathook out to him. The water's cold. He looks scared and exhausted. His head keeps disappearing below the surface. She manages to hit him with the point of the boathook, cutting his forehead and making it bleed.

'You have to hold on!' she shouts.

The black inflatable is already coming into view at the end of the island. She can hear its engine clearly. Björn is grimacing with pain. After several attempts he finally manages to wrap his arm around the boathook. She pulls him towards the swimming platform as fast as she can. He grabs hold of the edge and she lets go of the boathook and watches it drift off across the water.

'Viola's dead,' she screams, hearing the mixture of despair and panic in her voice.

As soon as Björn has climbed up onto the steps she runs back to the wheel and accelerates as hard as she can.

Björn clambers over the railing and she hears him yell at her to steer straight towards Ornäs.

The roar of the inflatable's motors is rapidly approaching from behind.

She swings the boat round in a tight curve, and the hull rumbles beneath them.

'He killed Viola,' Penelope whimpers.

'Mind the rocks,' Björn warns, his teeth chattering.

The inflatable has rounded Stora Kastskär and is speeding across the flat, open water.

Blood is running down Björn's face from the cut on his forehead.

They're rapidly approaching the large island. Björn turns to see the inflatable some three hundred metres behind them.

'Aim for the jetty!'

She turns and puts the engines in reverse, then switches them off when the fore hits the jetty with a creak. The whole side of the boat scrapes past some protruding wooden steps. The swell hisses as it hits the rocks and rolls back towards them. The boat rocks sideways and the wooden steps shatter as water washes over the railings. They leap off the boat and hurry across the jetty. Behind them they hear the hull scrape against the jetty on the waves. They race towards land as the black inflatable roars towards them. Penelope slips and puts her hand out, then clambers up the steep rocks towards the trees, gasping for breath. The inflatable's engines go quiet below them, and Penelope realises that they have barely any advantage at all. She and Björn rush through the trees, deeper into the forest, while her mind starts to panic as she looks around for somewhere they can hide.

4

Paragraph 21 of Swedish Police Law permits a police officer to gain entry to a house, room or other location if there is reason to believe that someone may have died, is unconscious or otherwise incapable of calling for help.

The reason why Police Constable John Bengtsson on this Saturday afternoon in June has been instructed to investigate the top flat at Grevgatan 2 is that the director general of the Inspectorate for Strategic Products, Carl Palmcrona, has been absent from work without any explanation and missed a scheduled meeting with the Foreign Minister.

It's far from the first time that John Bengtsson has had to break into someone's home to see if anyone is dead or injured. Mostly it's been because relatives have suspected suicide. Silent, frightened parents forced to wait in the stairwell while he goes in to check the rooms. Sometimes he finds young men with barely discernible pulses after a heroin overdose, and occasionally he has discovered a crime scene, women who have been beaten to death lying in the glow from the television in the living room.

John Bengtsson is carrying his house-breaking tools and an electric pick gun as he walks in through the imposing front entrance. He takes the lift up to the fifth floor and rings the doorbell. He waits a while, then puts his heavy bag down on the floor and inspects the lock. Suddenly he hears a shuffling sound in the stairwell, from the floor below. It sounds like someone is trying to creep silently down the stairs. Police Constable John Bengtsson listens for a while, then reaches out and tries the handle: the door isn't locked, and glides open softly on its four hinges.

'Is anyone home?' he calls.

John Bengtsson waits a few seconds, then pulls his bag into the hall and closes the door, wipes his shoes on the doormat and walks further into the large entrance hall.

Gentle music can be heard in a neighbouring room. He goes over, knocks and walks in. It's a spacious reception room, sparsely furnished with three Carl Malmsten sofas, a low glass table and a small painting of a ship in a storm on the wall. An ice-blue glow is coming from a flat, transparent music centre. Melancholic, almost tentative violin music is playing from the speakers.

John Bengtsson walks over to the double door and opens them, and finds himself looking into a sitting room with tall, art-nouveau windows. The summer light outside is refracted through the tiny panes of glass in the top sections of the windows.

A man is floating in the centre of the white room.

It looks supernatural.

John Bengtsson stands and stares at the dead man. It feels like an eternity before he spots the washing-line fixed to the lamp-hook.

The well-dressed man is perfectly still, as if he had been frozen in the middle of a big jump, with his ankles stretched and the toes of his shoes pointing down at the floor.

He's hanging – but there's something else, something that doesn't make sense, something wrong.

John Bengtsson mustn't enter the room. The scene needs to be left intact. His heart is beating fast, he can feel the heavy rhythm of his pulse, and swallows hard, but he can't tear his eyes from the man floating in the middle of the empty room.

A name has started to echo inside John Bengtsson's head, almost as a whisper: *Joona. I need to speak to Joona Linna.*

There's no furniture in the room, just a hanged man, who

in all likelihood is Carl Palmcrona, the director general of the Inspectorate for Strategic Products.

The cord has been fastened to the middle of the ceiling, from the lamp-hook in the middle of the ceiling-rose.

There was nothing for him to climb on, John Bengtsson thinks.

The height of the ceiling is at least three and a half metres.

John Bengtsson tries to calm down, gather his thoughts and register everything he can see. The hanged man's face is pale, like damp sugar, and he can see no more than a few spots of blood in his staring eyes. The man is wearing a thin overcoat on top of his pale grey suit, and a pair of low-heeled shoes. A black briefcase and a mobile phone are lying on the parquet floor a little way from the pool of urine that has formed immediately beneath the body.

The hanged man suddenly trembles.

John Bengtsson holds his breath.

There's a heavy thud from the ceiling, hammer-blows from the attic – someone is walking across the floor above. Another thud, and Palmcrona's body trembles again. Then comes the sound of a drill, which stops abruptly. A man shouts something. He needs more cable, the extension lead, he calls.

John Bengtsson notices his pulse settle down as he walks back through the sitting room. In the hall the front door is standing open. He stops, certain that he closed it properly, but perhaps he was mistaken. He leaves the flat and before he reports back to the station he takes out his mobile phone and calls Joona Linna of the National Crime Unit.

5

It's the first week of June. In Stockholm people have been waking up too early in the morning for weeks. The sun rises at half past three, and it's light almost all night through. It's been unusually warm for the time of year. The cherry trees were in blossom at the same time as the lilac. Heavy clusters of flowers spread their scent all the way from Kronoberg Park to the entrance to the National Police Committee.

The National Crime Unit is Sweden's only operative police department tasked with combatting serious crime on both a national and international level.

The head of the National Crime Unit, Carlos Eliasson, is standing at his low window on the eighth floor looking out at the steep slopes of Kronoberg Park. He's holding a phone, and dials Joona Linna's number, but once again his call goes straight to voicemail. He ends the call, puts the phone down on his desk and looks at his watch.

Petter Näslund comes into Carlos's office and clears his throat quietly, then stops and leans against a poster saying 'We watch, scrutinise and irritate.'

From the next room they can hear a weary telephone conversation about European arrest warrants and the exchange of information in the Schengen Zone.

'Pollock and his team will be here soon,' Petter says.

'I know how to tell the time,' Carlos replies gently.

'The sandwiches are ready, anyway,' Petter says.

Carlos suppresses a smile and asks:

'Have you heard that they're recruiting?'

Petter's cheeks go red and he lowers his eyes, then composes himself and looks up again.

'I'd . . . Can you think of anyone who'd be better suited to the National Homicide Commission?' he asks.

The National Homicide Commission consists of six experts who assist with murder cases throughout Sweden. The commission provides systematic support within a framework designed for serious crimes.

The workload of the permanent members of the National Homicide Commission is extreme. They're in such high demand that they very rarely have time to meet at Police Headquarters.

When Petter Näslund has left the room Carlos sits down behind his desk and looks over at the aquarium and his paradise fish. Just as he is reaching for the tub of fish-food his phone rings.

'Yes?' he says.

'They're on their way up,' says Magnus in reception.

'Thanks.'

Carlos makes one last attempt to get hold of Joona Linna before getting up from his chair, glancing at himself in the mirror and leaving the room. As he emerges into the corridor the lift pings and the door slides open without a sound. At the sight of the members of the National Homicide Commission an image flits quickly through his mind, a memory from a Rolling Stones concert he went to with a couple of colleagues a few years ago. As they walked out on stage, the group reminded him of laidback businessmen. Just like the members of the National Homicide Commission, they were all wearing dark suits and ties.

First is Nathan Pollock, with his grey hair in a ponytail, followed by Erik Eriksson with his diamond-studded glasses, which is why the rest of the team call him Elton. Behind him comes Niklas Dent, alongside P. G. Bondesson, and bringing up the rear is the forensic expert Tommy Kofoed, hunch-backed and staring morosely at the floor.

Carlos shows them into the conference room. Their operational boss, Benny Rubin, is already seated at the round table with a cup of black coffee, waiting for them. Tommy Kofoed takes an apple from the fruit-bowl and starts to eat it noisily. Nathan Pollock looks at him with a smile and shakes his head, and he stops mid-bite and looks back quizzically.

'Welcome,' Carlos says. 'I'm pleased you were all able to come, because we have a number of important issues to discuss on today's agenda.'

'Isn't Joona Linna supposed to be here?' Tommy Kofoed asks.

'Yes,' Carlos replies hesitantly.

'That guy tends to do as he likes,' Pollock adds quietly.

'Joona managed to clear up the Tumba murders a year or so back,' Tommy Kofoed says. 'I keep thinking about it, the way he was so certain . . . he knew in which order the murders had taken place.'

'Against all obvious logic,' Elton smiles.

'There's not much about forensic science that I don't know,' Tommy Kofoed goes on. 'But Joona just went in and looked at the footprints in the blood, I don't understand how . . .'

'He saw the whole picture,' Nathan Pollock says. 'The degree of violence, effort, agitation, and how listless the footprints in the row-house seemed in comparison to the changing room.'

'I still can't believe it,' Tommy Kofoed mumbles.

Carlos clears his throat and looks down at the informal agenda.

'The marine police have contacted us this morning,' he says. 'Apparently a fisherman has found a dead woman.'

'In his net?'

'No, he saw a large motor cruiser drifting off Dalarö, rowed out and went on board, and found her sitting on the bed in the front cabin.'

'That's hardly anything for the commission,' Petter Näslund says with a smile.

'Was she murdered?' Nathan Pollock asks.

'Probably suicide,' Petter replies quickly.

'Nothing urgent,' Carlos says, helping himself to a slice of cake. 'I just thought I'd mention it.'

'Anything else?' Tommy Kofoed says cheerfully.

'We've received a request from the police in West Götaland,' Carlos says. 'There's a summary on the table.'

'I won't be able to take it,' Pollock says.

'I know you've all got your hands full,' Carlos says, slowly brushing some crumbs from the table. 'Perhaps we should start at the other end and talk about recruitment to the National Homicide Commission.'

Benny Rubin looks around intently, then explains that the high-ups are aware of the heavy workload, and have therefore agreed as a first step to authorise the expansion of the commission by one permanent post.

'Thoughts, anyone?' Carlos says.

'Wouldn't it be helpful if Joona Linna was here for this discussion?' Tommy Kofoed asks, leaning across the table and looking through the wrapped sandwiches.

'It's not certain he's going to make it,' Carlos says.

'Maybe we could break for coffee first,' Erik Eriksson says, adjusting his sparkling glasses.

Tommy Kofoed removes the wrapper from a salmon sandwich, pulls out the sprig of dill, squeezes some lemon juice and unwraps the cutlery from the napkin they were rolled up in.

Suddenly the door to the big conference room opens and Joona Linna walks in with his blond hair on end.

'*Syö tilli, pojat,*' he says in Finnish with a grin.

'Exactly,' Nathan Pollock chuckles. 'Eat your dill, boys.'

Nathan and Joona smile as their eyes meet. Tommy Kofoed's cheeks turn red and he shakes his head with a smile.

'*Tilli,*' Nathan Pollock repeats, and bursts out laughing as Joona walks over and puts the sprig of dill back on Tommy Kofoed's sandwich.

'Perhaps we can continue the meeting?' Petter says.

Joona shakes Nathan Pollock's hand, then walks over to a spare chair, hangs his dark jacket on the back of it and sits down.

'Sorry,' Joona says quietly.

'Good to have you here,' Carlos says.

'Thanks.'

'We were just about to discuss the issue of recruitment,' Carlos explains.

He pinches his bottom lip and Petter Näslund begins to squirm on his chair.

'I think . . . I think I'll let Nathan speak first,' Carlos goes on.

'By all means,' Nathan Pollock says. 'I'm not just speaking for myself, here . . . Look, we all agree on this, we're hoping you might want to join us, Joona.'

The room falls silent. Niklas Dent and Erik Eriksson nod. Petter Näslund is sharply silhouetted in the light from the window.

'We'd like that very much,' Tommy Kofoed says.

'I appreciate the offer,' Joona says, running his fingers through his thick hair. 'You're a very smart team, you've proved that, and I respect your work . . .'

They smile.

'But as for me . . . I can't work to a specific framework,' he explains.

'We appreciate that,' Kofoed says quickly. 'It's a little rigid, but it can actually be helpful, because of course it's been proven that . . .'

He tails off.

'Well, we just wanted to extend the invitation,' Nathan Pollock says.

'I don't think it would suit me,' Joona replies.

They look down, someone nods, and Joona apologises when his phone rings. He gets up from the table and leaves the room. A minute or so later he comes back in and takes his jacket from the chair.

'I'm sorry,' he says. 'I'd have liked to stay for the meeting, but . . .'

'Has something serious happened?' Carlos asks.

'That call was from John Bengtsson, one of our uniforms,' Joona says. 'He's just found Carl Palmcrona.'

'Found?' Carlos says.

'Hanged,' Joona replies.

His symmetrical face becomes serious and his eyes shimmer like grey glass.

'Who's Palmcrona?' Nathan Pollock asks. 'I can't place the name.'

'Director general of the Inspectorate for Strategic Products,' Tommy Kofoed answers quickly. 'He takes the decisions about Swedish arms exports.'

'Isn't the identity of anyone working for the ISP confidential?' Carlos asks.

'It is,' Kofoed replies.

'So presumably the Security Police will be dealing with this?'

'I've already promised John Bengtsson that I'd take a look,' Joona replies. 'Apparently there was something that didn't make sense.'

'What?' Carlos asks.

'It was . . . No, I should probably take a look with my own eyes first.'

'Sounds exciting,' Tommy Kofoed says. 'Can I tag along?'

'If you like,' Joona replies.

'I'll come too, then,' Pollock says quickly.

Carlos tries to say something about the meeting, but realises that it's pointless. The three men leave the sun-drenched room and walk out into the cool corridor.

6

Twenty minutes later Detective Superintendent Joona Linna parks his black Volvo on Strandvägen. A silver-grey Lincoln Town Car pulls up behind him. Joona gets out of the car and waits for his two colleagues from the National Homicide Commission. They walk round the corner together and in through the door of Grevgatan 2.

In the creaking old lift up to the top floor Tommy Kofoed asks in his usual cheery voice what Joona has been told so far.

'The ISP reported that Carl Palmcrona had gone missing,' Joona says. 'He doesn't have any family and none of his colleagues know him privately. But when he didn't show up for work one of our patrols was asked to take a look. John Bengtsson went to the flat and found Palmcrona hanged, and called me. He said he suspected criminal activity and wanted me to come over at once.'

Nathan Pollock's craggy face frowns.

'What made him suspect criminal activity?'

The lift stops and Joona opens the grille. John Bengtsson is standing outside the door to Palmcrona's apartment. He tucks his notepad in his pocket and Joona shakes his hand.

'This is Tommy Kofoed and Nathan Pollock from the National Homicide Commission,' Joona says.

They shake hands briefly.

'The door was unlocked when I arrived,' John says. 'I could hear music, and found Palmcrona hanging in one of the big reception rooms. Over the years I've cut down a fair number of men, but this time, I mean . . . it can hardly be suicide, given Palmcrona's standing in society, so . . .'

'It's good that you called,' Joona says.

'Have you examined the body?' Tommy Kofoed says gloomily.

'I haven't even set foot inside the room,' John replies.

'Very good,' Kofoed mutters, and starts to lay down protective mats with John Bengtsson.

Shortly afterwards Joona and Nathan Pollock are able to enter the hall. John Bengtsson is waiting beside a blue sofa. He points towards the double doors leading to a brightly lit room. Joona walks over on the mats and pushes the doors wide open.

Warm sunlight is streaming in through the row of high windows. Carl Palmcrona is hanging in the middle of the spacious room. He's wearing a light suit, a summer overcoat and lightweight low-heeled shoes. There are flies crawling across his face, around his eyes and the corners of his mouth, laying tiny yellow eggs and buzzing around the pool of urine and smart briefcase on the floor. The thin washing-line has cut deep into Palmcrona's neck, the groove is dark red and blood has seeped out and run beneath his shirt.

'Execution,' Tommy Kofoed declares, pulling on a pair of protective gloves.

Every trace of moroseness suddenly vanishes from his face and voice. With a smile he gets down on his knees and starts to take photographs of the hanging body.

'I'd say we're going to find injuries to his cervical spine,' Pollock says, pointing.

Joona looks up at the ceiling, then down at the floor.

'He's been put on show,' Kofoed says eagerly as he photographs the dead man. 'I mean, the murderer isn't exactly trying to hide the crime. He wants to say something, wants to send a message.'

'Yes, that's what I was thinking,' John Bengtsson says keenly. 'The room's empty, there's no chair, no stepladder to climb on.'

'So what's the message?' Tommy Kofoed goes on, lowering

the camera and squinting at the body. 'Hanging is often associated with treachery, Judas Iscariot and . . .'

'Just hold on a moment,' Joona interrupts gently.

He gestures vaguely towards the floor.

'What is it?' Pollock asks.

'I think it was suicide,' Joona says.

'Typical suicide,' Tommy Kofoed says, and laughs a little too loudly. 'He flapped his wings and flew up . . .'

'The briefcase,' Joona goes on. 'If he stood the briefcase on its end he could have reached.'

'But not the ceiling,' Pollock points out.

'He could have fastened the rope earlier.'

'Yes, but I think you're wrong.'

Joona shrugs his shoulders and mutters:

'Together with the music and the knots, then . . .'

'Can we take a look at the briefcase, then?' Pollock asks tersely.

'I just need to secure the evidence first,' Kofoed says.

They look on in silence as Tommy Kofoed's hunched, short frame crawls across the floor unrolling black plastic film covered with a thin layer of gelatine on the floor. Then he carefully presses it down using a rubber roller.

'Can you take out a couple of bio-packs and a wrapper?' he asks, pointing at his bag.

'Cardboard?' Pollock wonders.

'Yes, please,' Kofoed replies, catching the bio-packs that Pollock throws him.

He secures the biological evidence from the floor, then beckons Nathan Pollock into the room.

'You'll find shoeprints on the far edge of the briefcase,' Joona says. 'It fell backwards and the body swung diagonally.'

Nathan Pollock says nothing, just goes over to the leather briefcase and kneels down. His silver ponytail falls forward over his shoulder as he leans down to lift the case onto one end. Clear, pale grey shoeprints are visible on the black leather.

'What did I tell you?' Joona asks.

'Damn,' Tommy Kofoed says, impressed, the whole of his tired face smiling at Joona.

'Suicide,' Pollock mutters.

'From a purely technical perspective, anyway,' Joona says.

They stand and look at the hanged body.

'So what have we actually got here?' Kofoed asks, still smiling. 'A man who makes the decisions about the supply of armaments has committed suicide.'

'Nothing for us,' Pollock sighs.

Tommy Kofoed takes his gloves off and gestures towards the hanging man.

'Joona? What did you mean about the music and the knots?' he asks.

'It's a double sheet bend,' Joona says, pointing to the knot around the lamp-hook. 'Which I assumed was linked to Palmcrona's long career in the navy.'

'And the music?'

Joona stops and looks thoughtfully at him.

'What do you make of the music?' he asks.

'I don't know. It's a sonata, for the violin,' Kofoed says. 'Early nineteenth-century or . . .'

He falls silent when the doorbell rings. The four men look at each other. Joona starts to walk towards the hall and the others follow him, but stop in the sitting room, out of sight of the front door.

Joona carries on across the hall, contemplates using the peep-hole and decides not to. He can feel the air blowing through the keyhole as he reaches out and pushes the handle down. The heavy door glides open. The landing is dark. The timed lamps have gone out and the light from the red-brown glass in the stairwell is weak. Joona suddenly hears slow breathing, very close to him. Laboured, almost heavy breathing from someone he can't see. Joona's hand goes to his pistol as he looks cautiously behind the open door. In the thin strip of light between the hinges he sees a tall woman with large hands. She looks like she's in her mid-sixties. She's standing perfectly still. There's a large, skin-coloured plaster on her cheek. Her grey hair is cut short in a girlish bob. She looks Joona straight in the eye without a trace of a smile.

'Have you taken him down?' she asks.

7

Joona had thought he was going to be on time for the meeting with the National Homicide Commission at one o'clock.

He was only going to have lunch with Disa at Rosendal Garden on Djurgården. Joona got there early and stood in the sunshine for a while watching the mist that lay over the little vineyard. Then he saw Disa walking towards him, her bag swinging over her shoulder. Her thin face with its intelligent features was covered with early-summer freckles, and her hair, usually gathered in two uneven plaits, was for once hanging loose over her shoulders. She had dressed up, and was wearing a floral-patterned dress and a pair of summery sandals with a stacked heel.

They hugged tenderly.

'Hello,' Joona said. 'You look lovely.'

'So do you,' Disa said.

They got food from the buffet and went and sat at one of the outdoor tables. Joona had noticed she was wearing nail varnish. As a senior archaeologist, Disa's fingernails were usually short and rather dirty. He looked away from her hands, across the fruit garden.

Disa started to eat, and said with her mouth full:

'Queen Christina was given a leopard by the Duke of Courland. She kept it out here on Djurgården.'

37

'I didn't know that,' Joona said calmly.

'I read in the palace accounts that the Treasury paid forty silver *riksdaler* to help cover the funeral costs of a maid who was killed by the leopard.'

She leaned back and picked up her glass.

'Joona Linna, stop talking so much,' she said sarcastically.

'Sorry,' Joona said. 'I . . .'

He tailed off and suddenly felt as if all the energy were draining from his body.

'What?'

'Please, keep talking about the leopard.'

'You look sad . . .'

'I was thinking about Mum . . . It was exactly a year ago yesterday that she died. I went and left a white iris on her grave.'

'I miss Ritva a lot,' Disa said.

She put her knife and fork down and sat quietly for a while.

'Do you know what she said the last time I saw her? She took my hand,' Disa said. 'And then she said I ought to seduce you, and make sure I got pregnant.'

'I can imagine,' Joona laughed.

The sun sparkled in their glasses and reflected off Disa's unusually dark eyes.

'I said I didn't think that would work, and then she told me to leave you and never look back, never come back.'

He nodded, but didn't know what to say.

'And then you'd be all alone,' Disa went on. 'A big, lonely Finn.'

He stroked her fingers.

'I don't want that.'

'What?'

'To be a big, lonely Finn,' he said softly. 'I want to be with you.'

'And I want to bite you, quite hard, actually. Can you explain that? My teeth always start to tingle when I see you,' Disa smiled.

Joona reached out his hand to touch her. He knew he was already late for the meeting with Carlos Eliasson and the National Homicide Commission, but went on sitting where he was, chatting and simultaneously thinking that he ought to go to the National Museum to look at the Sami bridal crown.

While he was waiting for Joona Linna, Carlos Eliasson had told the National Homicide Commission about the young woman who had been found dead in a motor cruiser in the Stockholm archipelago. In the minutes of the meeting Benny Rubin noted that the case wasn't urgent, and that they were going to wait for the marine police's own investigation.

Joona arrived late for the meeting, and barely had time to sit down before Police Constable John Bengtsson called him. They had known each other for years, and had played indoor hockey against each other for over a decade. John Bengtsson was a likeable man, but when he was diagnosed with prostate cancer almost all of his friends vanished. Nowadays John Bengtsson was completely well again, but, like many people who had felt death breathing down their neck, there was something sensitive and hesitant about him.

Joona stood in the corridor outside the conference room listening to John Bengtsson's protracted account of what he had found. His voice was full of the weariness that arises in the minutes following extreme stress. He described how he had just found the director general of the Inspectorate for Strategic Products hanging from the ceiling in his own home.

'Suicide?' Joona asked.

'No.'

'Murder?'

'Can't you just come over?' John asked. 'Because I can't make sense of this. The body's floating above the floor, Joona.'

Together with Nathan Pollock and Tommy Kofoed, Joona had just concluded that they were dealing with a case of suicide when the doorbell of Palmcrona's home rang. In the darkness of the landing stood a tall woman holding shopping bags in her large hands.

'Have you taken him down?' she asked.

'Taken down?' Joona repeated.

'Mr Palmcrona,' she said matter-of-factly.

'What do you mean, taken down?'

'I'm sorry, I'm only the housekeeper, I thought . . .'

The situation clearly troubled her, and she started to walk down the stairs, but stopped abruptly when Joona replied to her initial question:

'He's still hanging there.'

'Yes,' she said, and turned to him with a completely neutral expression on her face.

'Did you see him hanging there earlier today?'

'No,' she replied.

'What made you ask if we'd taken him down? Had something happened? Did you notice anything unusual?'

'A noose from the lamp-hook in the small drawing room,' she replied.

'You saw the noose?'

'Of course.'

'But you weren't worried that he might use it?' Joona asked.

'Dying isn't such a nightmare,' she replied with a restrained smile.

'What did you say?'

But the woman merely shook her head.

'What do you imagine his death looked like?' Joona asked.

'I imagine that the noose tightened round his throat,' she replied in a low voice.

'And how did the noose get to be round his neck?'

'I don't know . . . perhaps it needed help,' she said quizzically.

'What do you mean by help?'

Her eyes rolled back and Joona thought she was going to faint before she reached out for the wall with one hand and met his gaze again.

'There are helpful people everywhere,' she said weakly.

8

Nils Åhlén

The swimming pool at Police Headquarters is silent and empty, the glass wall dark and there's no one in the cafeteria. The large blue pool is almost perfectly still. The water is illuminated from below and the glow undulates gently across the walls and ceiling. Joona Linna swims length after length, maintaining a steady speed and controlling his breathing.

As he swims, memories tumble through his consciousness. Disa's face as she told him her teeth tingled when she looked at him.

Joona reaches the edge of the pool, turns beneath the water and kicks off. He isn't aware that he is swimming faster when his thoughts suddenly focus on Carl Palmcrona's apartment on Grevgatan. Once again he is looking at the hanging body, the pool of urine, the flies on the face. The dead man had been wearing his outdoor clothes, his coat and shoes, but had still taken the time to put some music on.

The whole thing had given Joona the impression of being both planned and impulsive, which is far from unusual with suicides.

He swims faster, turns and speeds up even more, and in his mind's eye sees himself crossing Palmcrona's hall to open the door when the bell rang. He sees the tall woman with big hands standing concealed behind the door, in the darkness of the stairwell.

Joona stops at the edge of the pool, breathing hard, and rests his arms on the plastic grille covering the overspill channel. His breathing soon calms down, but the heaviness of the lactic acid in his muscles is still increasing. A group of police officers in gym clothes come into the hall. They're carrying two life-saving dummies, one representing a child, the other someone badly overweight.

Dying isn't such a nightmare, the tall woman had said with a smile.

Joona climbs out of the pool with an odd feeling of unease. He doesn't know what it is, but the case of Carl Palmcrona's death won't leave him alone. For some reason he keeps seeing the bright, empty room, hearing the gentle violin music along with the dull buzzing of the flies.

Joona knows they're dealing with a suicide, and tries to tell himself that it's no concern of the National Crime Unit. But he still feels like running back to the scene of the discovery again and examining it more thoroughly, searching every room, just to see if he missed anything.

During his conversation with the housekeeper he had imagined that she was confused, that shock had settled around her like dense fog, making her answers opaque and incoherent. But now he tries to look at it the other way round. Perhaps she wasn't at all shocked or confused, and had answered his questions as accurately as she could. In which case the housekeeper, Edith Schwartz, was claiming that Carl Palmcrona had help with the noose, and there were helping hands, helpful people. In which case she was saying that his death wasn't a self-imposed act, and that he hadn't been alone when he died.

There's something that doesn't make sense.

He knows he's right, but he can't identify what the feeling is.

Joona goes through the door to the men's changing room, opens his locker, takes out his phone and calls senior pathologist Nils "The Needle" Åhlén.

'I'm not finished,' The Needle says when he answers.

'It's about Palmcrona. What are your first impressions, even if . . .?'

'I'm not finished,' The Needle repeats.

'Even if you're not finished,' Joona says, finishing his sentence. 'Call in on Monday.'

'I'm coming now,' Joona says.

'At five o'clock I'm going to look at a sofa with my wife.'

'I'll be with you in twenty-five minutes,' Joona says, and ends the call before The Needle can repeat that he isn't finished.

As Joona showers and gets dressed, he hears the sound of children laughing and talking, and realises that a swimming lesson is about to start.

He ponders the significance of the fact that the director general of the Inspectorate for Strategic Products has been found hanged. The person who, when it comes down to it, takes all the final decisions about Swedish arms manufacture and export, is dead.

What if I'm wrong, what if he was murdered after all? Joona asks himself. I need to talk to Pollock before I go and see The Needle, because he and Kofoed may have had a chance to look at the material from the crime scene investigation.

Joona strides along the corridor, runs down a flight of steps and calls his assistant, Anja Larsson, to find out if Nathan Pollock is still in Police Headquarters.

9

Joona's thick hair is still soaking wet when he opens the door to Lecture Room 11 where Nathan Pollock is giving a lecture to a select group of men and women who are training to handle hostage situations and rescues.

On the wall behind Pollock is a computer projection of an anatomical drawing of the human body. Several different types of handgun are laid out on a table, from a small, silver Sig Sauer P238 to a matt-black assault rifle from Heckler & Koch with a 40mm grenade launcher attachment.

One of the young officers is standing in front of Pollock, who pulls a knife, holds it concealed against his body, then rushes forward and pretends to cut the officer's throat. Then he turns to the group.

'The disadvantages of that sort of attack are that the enemy may have time to cry out, that the movement of the body can't be controlled, and it takes a while for them to bleed out because you've only opened one artery,' Pollock explains.

He goes over to the young officer again and wraps his arm around his face, so that the crook of his arm is covering his mouth.

'But if I do it this way instead, I can muffle any scream, manoeuvre his head and sever both arteries with a single cut,' he says.

Pollock lets go of the young officer and notices that Joona

44

Linna is standing just inside the door. He must have only just arrived, while he was demonstrating those two grips. The young police officer wipes his mouth and sits back down in his chair. Pollock smiles broadly and waves at Joona, beckoning him forward, but Joona shakes his head.

'I'd like a few words, Nathan,' he says quietly.

Some of the officers turn to look. Pollock walks over to him and they shake hands. Joona's jacket is dark where his wet hair has touched it.

'Tommy Kofoed secured shoeprints from Palmcrona's home,' Joona says. 'I need to know if he found anything unexpected.'

'I didn't think there was any urgency?' Nathan replies in a muted voice. 'Obviously we photographed all the impressions, but we haven't had time to analyse the results. I can't give you any sort of overall picture right now . . .'

'But you did see something,' Joona says.

'When I put the images into the computer . . . it could be a pattern, but it's too early to . . .'

'Just tell me – I have to go.'

'It looks like there were prints from two different set of shoes moving in two circles around the body,' Nathan says.

'Come with me to see Nils Åhlén,' Joona says.

'Now?'

'I'm supposed to be there in twenty minutes.'

'Damn, I can't,' Nathan replies, gesturing towards the room. 'But I'll have my phone on in case you need to ask anything.'

'Thanks,' Joona says, and turns to leave.

'You . . . you don't want to say hello to this lot?' Nathan asks.

They've all turned round now and Joona gives them a brief wave.

'So, this is Joona Linna, who I've told you about,' Nathan Pollock says, raising his voice. 'I'm trying to persuade him to come and give a lecture on close combat.'

The room falls silent as they all look at Joona.

'Most of you probably know more about martial arts than I do,' Joona says with a slight smile. 'The only thing I've learned is . . . when it's real, there are suddenly completely different rules. No art, just fighting.'

'Pay attention to this,' Pollock says keenly.

'In reality you only survive if you have the ability to adapt to changing circumstances and turn them to your advantage,' Joona goes on calmly. 'Practise making the most of the circumstances . . . you might be in a car, or on a balcony. The room might be full of teargas. Maybe the floor is covered with broken glass. There may be weapons, other implements. You don't know if you're at the start or the end of a chain of events. So you need to save your energy so you can keep working, so you can get through a whole night . . . So any flying kicks and cool round-house kicks are out of the question.'

A few of them laugh.

'In unarmed close combat,' Joona goes on, 'it's often a matter of accepting some pain in order to bring things to a rapid conclusion . . . but I don't really know much about this.'

Joona walks out of the lecture room. Two of the officers clap. The door closes and the room falls silent. Nathan Pollock smiles to himself as he walks back to the table.

'I was actually planning to save this for a later occasion,' he says, and clicks the computer. 'This recording is already a classic . . . from the hostage drama at the Nordea Bank on Hamngatan nine years ago. Two robbers. Joona Linna has already got the hostages out, and has incapacitated one of the men, who was armed with an Uzi. It was a fairly vicious fire-fight. The other guy is hiding, but only armed with a knife. They'd sprayed all the security cameras, but missed this one . . . We'll take it in slow motion because it only lasts a matter of seconds.'

Pollock hits play and the film starts. A grainy shot of a bank filmed from above comes into view. The seconds tick by on the timer at the bottom of the screen. The furniture has been thrown about, the floor is littered with paper and documents. Joona is moving smoothly sideways, his pistol raised, his arm straight. He's moving slowly, as if underwater. The bank robber is hiding behind the open vault door with a knife in his hand. Suddenly he darts forward with long, smooth strides. Joona turns the pistol on him, aiming straight at his chest, and fires.

'The pistol clicks,' Pollock says. 'Faulty bullet stuck in the chamber.'

The grainy footage flickers. Joona moves backwards as the man with the knife rushes at him. The whole thing is eerily silent and fluid. Joona ejects the cartridge, but realises that he's not going to have time. Instead he turns the useless pistol round, so that the barrel runs parallel to the bone in his lower arm.

'I don't get it,' one woman says.

'He turns the pistol into a tonfa,' Pollock explains.

'A what?'

'It's a sort of baton . . . like the ones the American police use, it extends your reach and increases the power of any blow because the area of impact is smaller.'

The man with the knife has reached Joona. He takes a long, hesitant step. The knife-blade glints as it describes a semi-circle, aimed at Joona's torso. The man's other hand is raised, and follows the rotation of his body. Joona isn't even looking at the knife, and moves forward instead, taking a long stride and striking hard as he does so. He hits the man on the neck, just below his Adam's apple, with the barrel of the pistol.

The knife spins as it falls towards the floor as if in a dream, and the man sinks to his knees, opens his mouth wide, clutches his neck and then collapses to the floor.

10

Joona Linna is sitting in his car on Fleminggatan, on his way to the Karolinska Institute in Solna, thinking about Carl Palmcrona's hanging body, the tense washing-line, the briefcase on the floor.

In his mind Joona tries adding the two circles of shoeprints on the floor around the dead man.

This case isn't over yet.

Joona turns onto Klarastrandsleden. He drives along the side of the canal where the trees have already woven their leafy baskets, leaning into the water, sinking their branches into the smooth, mirror-like surface.

In his mind's eye he sees the housekeeper, Edith Schwartz, again – every detail, the veins on the large hands holding the bags of shopping, and the way she said that there are helpful people everywhere.

The Department of Forensic Medicine is situated among the trees and neat lawns of the large Karolinska Hospital campus, a red-brick building at Retzius väg 5, surrounded by large buildings on all sides.

Joona pulls into the empty visitors' car park. He notes that senior pathologist Nils Åhlén has driven over the kerb and parked his white Jaguar in the middle of the lawn next to the main entrance.

Joona waves to the woman in reception, who responds by giving him the thumbs-up, and he carries on along the corridor, knocks on Nils Åhlén's door and walks in. As usual, The Needle's office is utterly free from superfluous objects.

The blinds are drawn, but the sunlight is still filtering in between the blades. The light reflects off all the white surfaces, but sinks into the expanses of brushed grey steel.

The Needle is wearing his white-framed aviator glasses and a white polo-neck under his white coat.

'I've just issued a parking ticket to a badly parked Jaguar outside,' Joona says.

'Good,' Nils says.

Joona stops in the middle of the floor and becomes serious. His eyes turn silvery dark.

'So, how did he die?' he asks.

'Palmcrona?'

'Yes.'

The phone rings and The Needle nudges the post-mortem report towards Joona.

'You didn't have to come all the way out here to get an answer to that,' he says before picking up the receiver.

Joona sits down opposite him on the chair with a white leather seat. The post-mortem on Carl Palmcrona's body is finished. Joona leafs through it, stopping to read different passages at random.

74. Kidneys weight a total of 290 grams. Smooth surface. Tissue grey-red. Consistency firm, elastic. Clear delineation.
75. Urinary ducts appear normal.
76. Bladder empty. Mucous membrane pale.
77. Prostate normal size. Tissue pale.

The Needle nudges his aviator glasses up his narrow, bent nose, then ends the phone call and looks up.

'As you can see,' he says with a yawn, 'there's nothing unexpected.

Cause of death is asphyxia . . . With a full-blown hanging, of course, it's rarely a matter of suffocation in the common sense, but of a blockage of the arteries.'

'The brain suffocates because the supply of oxygenated blood stops.'

The Needle nods.

'Arterial compression, bilateral constriction of the carotid arteries, and of course it happens very fast, he would have been unconscious within a matter of seconds . . .'

'But he was still alive before he was hanged?' Joona asks.

'Yes.'

The Needle's thin face is clean-shaven and gloomy.

'Can you estimate the height of the drop?' Joona asks.

'There are no fractures in the cervical spine or the base of the skull – so I'd guess ten, twenty centimetres.'

'Right . . .'

Joona thinks about the briefcase and the prints from Palmcrona's shoes. He opens the report again and leafs through to the external examination: the skin of the neck and the estimated angles.

'What are you thinking?' The Needle asks.

'I'm wondering if there's any chance he was strangled with the same cord, and then just strung up from the ceiling.'

'No,' Nils replies.

'Why not?' Joona asks quickly.

'Why not? There was only one groove, and it was in perfect condition.' Nils begins to explain, 'When a person is hanged, the rope or cord obviously cuts into the throat, and . . .'

'But a perpetrator could also know that,' Joona interrupts.

'It's practically impossible to reconstruct, though . . . you know, with a real hanging the groove around the neck forms the shape of an arrowhead, with the point uppermost, just by the knot . . .'

'Because the weight of the body tightens the noose.'

'Exactly . . . and for the same reason the deepest part of the groove should be exactly opposite the point.'

'So he died from being hanged,' Joona concludes.

'No question.'

The tall, thin pathologist bites his bottom lip gently.

'But could he have been forced to commit suicide?' Joona asks.

'Not by force – there's no sign of that.'

Joona closes the report and drums on it with both hands, thinking that the housekeeper's comment that other people were involved in Palmcrona's death must have been just confused talk. But he can't get away from the two different shoeprints Tommy Kofoed had found.

'So you're certain of the cause of death?' Joona says, looking The Needle in the eye.

'What were you expecting?'

'This,' Joona says, putting his finger in the post-mortem report. 'This is exactly what I was expecting, but at the same time there's something nagging at me.'

The Needle gives him a wry smile:

'Take the report away and read it at bedtime.'

'Yes,' Joona says.

'But I think you can probably let go of Palmcrona . . . suicide is about as exciting as this case gets.'

The Needle's smile fades and he lowers his gaze, but Joona's eyes are still sharp, focused.

'I daresay you're right,' he says.

'Yes,' Nils replies. 'I'm happy to speculate a bit, if you like . . . Carl Palmcrona was probably depressed, because his finger-nails were ragged and dirty, his teeth hadn't been brushed for a few days and he hadn't shaved.'

'I see,' Joona nods.

'You're welcome to take a look at him.'

'No need,' he replies, and gets heavily to his feet.

The Needle leans forward and says with great alacrity, as if he's been looking forward to this moment:

'But this morning I got something considerably more inter-esting. Have you got a few minutes?'

He gets up from his chair and gestures for Joona to follow him. Joona goes with him into the corridor. A pale blue butterfly has got lost and is fluttering in the air ahead of them.

'Has that young guy left?' Joona asks.

'Who?'

'The one who was here before, with the ponytail and . . .'

'Frippe? God, no. He's not allowed to leave. He's got the day off. Megadeth are playing in the Globe, with Entombed as the support act.'

They walk through a dimly lit room containing a stainless steel post-mortem table. There's a strong smell of disinfectant. They carry on into a cooler room where the bodies are kept in refrigerated drawers.

The Needle opens another door and turns the light on. The fluorescent tubes flicker and illuminate a white-tiled room with a long, plastic-covered examination table with a double rim and drainage channels.

On the table is an extremely beautiful young woman.

Her skin is suntanned, her long, dark hair lies glossy and curly across her forehead and shoulders. It looks as if she's gazing up at the room with a mixture of hesitancy and surprise.

There's something almost cheeky about the set of her mouth, like someone who laughs and smiles a lot.

But there's no sparkle in those big, dark eyes. Tiny dark-brown spots have already begun to appear.

Joona stops and looks at the woman on the table. He guesses she's nineteen, twenty at most. No time at all since she was a young child sleeping with her parents. Then she turned into a half-grown schoolgirl, and now she's dead.

Across the woman's chest, on the skin above her breastbone, is a faint curved line, like a smiley mouth drawn on in grey, some thirty centimetres long.

'What's that line?' Joona asks, pointing.

'No idea. An impression from a necklace, perhaps, or a low-cut top. I'll take a closer look later.'

Joona looks at the lifeless body, takes a deep breath, and – as usual when he is confronted by the absolute implacability of death – a gloom settles on him, a colourless loneliness.

Life is so terrifyingly fragile.

Her finger- and toenails are painted a pinkish-beige colour.

'What's so special about her, then?' he asks after a few moments.

The Needle looks at him seriously, and his glasses glint as he turns back towards the body again.

'The marine police brought her in,' he says. 'She was found sitting on the bed in the front cabin of a large motor cruiser that was drifting in the archipelago.'

'Dead?'

Nils meets his gaze and says, with a sudden lilt in his voice: 'She drowned, Joona.'

'Drowned?'

The Needle nods and smiles brightly.

'She drowned on board a boat that was still afloat,' he says.

'So someone found her in the water and brought her on board.'

'Well, if that had happened I wouldn't be taking up your valuable time,' Nils says.

'So what's this all about, then?'

'There's no trace of water on the rest of the body – I've sent her clothes for analysis, but the National Forensics Lab aren't going to find anything either.'

The Needle falls silent, glances through the preliminary external report, then glances at Joona to see if he's managed to pique his curiosity. Joona is standing completely still, and his face looks completely different now. He's looking at the dead body with an expression of intense concentration. Suddenly he takes a pair of latex gloves from the box and pulls them on. The Needle smiles happily to himself as Joona leans over the girl, then carefully lifts her arms and studies them.

'You won't find any signs of violence,' Nils says, almost inaudibly. 'It's incomprehensible.'

11

The large motor cruiser is moored at the marine police marina on Dalarö. It lies at anchor between two police boats, white and shiny.

The tall metal gates to the marina are open. Joona Linna drives slowly in along the gravel track, past a mauve van and a crane with a rusty winch. He parks, leaves the car and walks on.

A boat has been found abandoned, drifting in the archipelago, thinks Joona. On the bed in the front cabin sits a girl who has drowned. The boat is afloat, but the girl's lungs are full of brackish seawater.

From a distance Joona stops and looks at the boat. The front of the hull has been seriously damaged; long scratches run along the side, from a violent collision, damaging the paint and the fibreglass beneath.

He calls Lennart Johansson of the marine police.

'Lennart,' a voice answers brightly.

'Lennart Johansson?' Joona asks.

'Yes, that's me.'

'My name is Joona Linna, National Crime.'

The line goes quiet. Joona can hear what sounds like waves lapping.

'The motor cruiser that you brought in,' Joona says. 'I was wondering if it had taken on any water?'

'Water?'

'The hull is damaged.'

Joona takes a few steps closer to the boat as Lennart Johansson explains in a tone of heavy resignation:

'Dear Lord, if I had a penny for every drunk who crashed . . .'

'I need to look at the boat,' Joona interrupts.

'Look, here's a broad outline of what happened,' Lennart Johansson says. 'Some kids from . . . I don't know, let's say Södertälje. They steal a boat, pick up some girls, cruise about, listen to music, party, drink a lot. In the middle of everything they hit something, quite a hard collision, and the girl falls overboard. The guys stop the boat, drive back and find her, get her up on deck. When they realise she's dead they panic, so damn frightened that they just take off.'

Lennart stops and waits for a response.

'Not a bad theory,' Joona says slowly.

'It's not, is it?' Lennart says cheerfully. 'It's all yours. Might save you a trip to Dalarö.'

'Too late,' Joona says, as he starts to walk towards the marine police boat.

It's a Stridsbåt 90E, moored behind the motor cruiser. A tanned, bare-chested man in his mid-twenties is standing on deck holding a phone to his ear.

'Suit yourself,' he says. 'Feel free to book a sightseeing trip.'

'I'm here already – and I think I'm looking right at you, if you're standing on one of your shallow . . .'

'Do I look like a surfer?'

The suntanned man looks up with a smile and scratches his chest.

'Pretty much,' Joona says.

They end the call and walk towards each other. Lennart Johansson pulls on a short-sleeved uniform shirt and buttons it as he crosses the gangplank.

Joona holds up his thumb and little finger in a surfers' gesture. Lennart's white teeth flash in his suntanned face.

'I go surfing whenever there's enough swell – that's why I'm known as Lance.'

'I can see why,' Joona jokes drily.

'Right?' Lennart laughs.

They walk over to the boat and stop on the jetty beside the gangplank.

'A Storebro 36, Royal Cruiser,' Lennart says. 'Good boat, but it's seen better days. Registered to a Björn Almskog.'

'Have you contacted him?'

'Haven't had time.'

They take a closer look at the damage to the boat's hull. It looks recent, there's no algae among the glass fibres.

'I've asked a forensics specialist to come out – he should be here soon,' Joona says.

'She's taken a serious knock,' Lennart says.

'Who's been on board since the boat was found?'

'No one,' he replies quickly.

Joona smiles and waits with a patient expression on his face.

'Well, me, of course,' Lennart says hesitantly. 'And Sonny, my colleague. And the paramedics who removed the body. And our forensics guy, but he used floor mats and protective clothing.'

'Is that all?'

'Apart from the old boy who found the boat.'

Joona doesn't answer, just looks down at the sparkling water and thinks about the girl on the table in the Department of Forensic Medicine with The Needle.

'Do you know if your forensics guy secured all the surface evidence?' he asks after a while.

'He's done with the floor, and he's filmed the scene.'

'I'm going on board.'

A narrow, worn gangplank leads from the jetty to the boat. Joona climbs aboard and then stands on the aft-deck for a while. He looks around slowly, scanning everything carefully. This is the first and only time he will see the crime scene like this, as a first impression. Every detail he registers now could be vital. Shoes, an overturned sun-lounger, large towel, a paperback that has turned yellow in the sun, a knife with a red plastic handle, a bucket on a rope, beer tins, a bag of charcoal, a tub containing a wetsuit, bottles of sun cream and lotion.

He looks through the large window at the wooden furnishings

of the saloon and helm. From a certain angle fingerprints on the glass door stand out in the sunlight, impressions of hands that have pushed the door open, closed it again, reached for it when the boat rocked.

Joona enters the small saloon. The afternoon sun is glinting off the wood veneers and chrome. There's a cowboy hat and a pair of sunglasses on the navy-blue cushions on one of the sofas.

The water outside is lapping against the hull.

Joona's eyes roam across the worn floor of the saloon and down the narrow steps to the front of the boat. It's as dark as a deep well down there. He can't see anything until he turns his torch on. The cool, tightly focused beam illuminates the steep passageway. The red wood shimmers like the inside of a body. Joona goes down the creaking steps, thinking of the girl, toying with the idea that she was alone on the boat, dived from the foredeck, hit her head on a rock, breathed water into her lungs but somehow managed to get back on board, change out of her wet bikini into dry clothes. Perhaps she was already feeling tired and went down into the cabin, not realising that she was as badly hurt as she was, not realising that actually she had a serious concussion that was rapidly increasing the pressure on her brain.

But Nils would have found traces of brackish water on her body.

It doesn't make sense.

Joona goes down the steps, past the galley and bathroom, into the main cabin.

There's a lingering feeling from her death on the boat, even though her body has been moved to the Department of Forensic Medicine in Solna. It's the same feeling every time. Somehow the objects stare silently back at him, full of screams, cramps, silence.

Suddenly the boat creaks differently and seems to lean to one side. Joona waits and listens, then carries on into the cabin.

Summer light is streaming through the narrow windows by the ceiling, onto a double bed with its top end shaped to fit the bow of the boat. This was where she was found, in a seated position. There's an open sports bag on the floor, and a polka-dotted nightdress has been unpacked. On the back of the door are a pair of jeans and a thin cardigan. A shoulder bag is hanging from a hook.

The boat sways again and a glass bottle rolls across the deck above his head.

Joona photographs the bag from various angles with his mobile phone. The flash makes the little room shrink, as if the walls, floor and ceiling all took a step closer for an instant.

He carefully takes the bag down off the hook and carries it up on deck. The steps creak under his weight. He can hear a metallic clicking sound from outside. When he reaches the saloon an unexpected shadow crosses the glass door. Joona reacts and takes a step back, into the gloom of the stairwell.

12

Joona Linna stands completely still, just two steps down on the dark flight of steps leading to the galley and front cabin. From there he can see the bottom of the glass doors and some of the aft-deck. A shadow crosses the dusty glass, and suddenly a hand comes into view. Someone is creeping across the deck. The next moment he recognises Erixon's face. Drops of sweat are running down his cheeks as he rolls out his gelatine foil over the area around the door.

Joona takes the bag from the cabin up into the saloon with him. He carefully turns it upside down over the little hardwood table. Then he pokes the red wallet open with his pen. There's a driver's licence in the worn plastic pocket. He looks more closely and sees a beautiful, serious face caught in the flash of a photograph booth. She's leaning back slightly, as if looking up. Her hair is dark and curly. He recognises the girl from the table in the pathology lab, her straight nose, eyes, South American features.

'Penelope Fernandez,' he reads on the driver's licence, and thinks that he's heard that name before.

In his mind he goes back to the pathology lab, with the naked body on the table, the tiled roof, the smell of death, her slack features, a face beyond sleep.

Outside in the sunshine Erixon's bulky frame is moving very

slowly as he secures fingerprints from the railing, brushing them with magnetic powder and using tape to lift them. Slowly he wipes one wet area, adds some drops of SPR solution and photographs the imprint that appears.

Joona can hear him sighing deeply the whole time, as if every movement required painful effort, as if he'd just expended the last of his energy.

Joona looks out at the deck, and sees a bucket on a rope next to a training shoe. A faint smell of potatoes is coming from the galley.

He turns back at the driver's licence and the little photograph. He looks at the young woman's mouth, at the slightly parted lips, and suddenly realises that something is missing.

It feels like he's seen something, was on the point of saying something, but forgot what.

He starts when his phone begins to vibrate in his pocket. He takes it out, sees from the screen that it's The Needle, and answers.

'Joona.'

'My name is Nils Åhlén, and I'm a senior pathologist at the Department of Forensic Medicine in Stockholm.'

Joona smiles: they've known each other for twenty years, and he'd recognise The Needle's voice without any introduction.

'Did she hit her head?' Joona asks.

'No,' Nils replies, surprised.

'I thought maybe she hit a rock when she was diving.'

'No, nothing like that – she drowned, that was the cause of death.'

'You're sure?' Joona persists.

'I've found fungus inside her nostrils, perforations in the mucous membrane in her throat, probably the result of a severe vomit reflex, and there are bronchial secretions in both her trachea and bronchi. Her lungs look typical for a drowning: full of water, increased weight, and . . . well.'

They fall silent. Joona can hear a scraping sound, as if someone were pushing a metal trolley.

'You had a reason for calling,' Joona says.

'Yes.'

'Do you feel like telling me?'

'She had a high concentration of tetrahydrocannabinol in her urine.'

'Cannabis?'

'Yes.'

'But she didn't die of that,' Joona says.

'Hardly,' Nils says, sounding amused. 'I just assumed that you were probably busy reconstructing the sequence of events on the boat, and that this was one little detail of the puzzle that you may not have known about.'

'Her name is Penelope Fernandez,' Joona says.

'Good to know,' Nils mutters.

'Was there anything else?'

'No.'

Nils breathes down the phone.

'Say it anyway,' Joona says.

'It's just that this isn't an ordinary death.'

He falls silent.

'What have you spotted?'

'Nothing, it's just a feeling . . .'

'Great,' Joona says. 'Now you're starting to sound like me.'

'I know, but . . . Obviously it could be a case of *mors subita naturalis*, a swift but entirely natural death . . . There's nothing to contradict that, but if this is a natural death, it's a very unusual natural death.'

They end the call, but The Needle's words are echoing through Joona's head: *mors subita naturalis*. There's something mysterious about Penelope Fernandez's death. Her body wasn't just found in the water by someone and brought on board. Because then she would have been lying on deck. Okay, so whoever found her may have wanted to show the dead woman some respect. But in that case they would have carried her into the saloon and laid her on the sofa.

The last alternative, Joona thinks, is of course that she was taken care of by someone who loved her, who wanted to put her to bed in her own room, in her own bed.

But she was sitting on the bed. Sitting.

Maybe The Needle is wrong, maybe she was still alive when

she was helped back on board and shown to her room. Her lungs could have been badly damaged, beyond salvation. Maybe she felt ill, wanted to lie down and be left in peace.

But why was there no water on her clothes, or the rest of her body?

There's a fresh-water shower on board, Joona thinks, and tells himself that he's going to have to search the rest of the boat: check the aft-cabin, as well as the bathroom and galley. There's a lot left to look at before the whole picture starts to emerge.

When Erixon gets to his feet and takes a couple of steps, the whole boat rocks again.

Once more Joona looks out through the glass doors from the saloon, and for a second time finds himself staring at the bucket on a rope. It's standing next to a zinc wash-tub where someone had left a wetsuit. There are water-skis by the railing. Joona looks back at the bucket again. He looks at the rope tied to the handle. The curved zinc tub shimmers in the sun, shining like a new moon.

Suddenly it hits him: Joona can see the sequence of events with icy clarity. He waits, lets his heart settle down, and thinks through what happened once more, until he is now absolutely certain that he's right.

The woman now identified as Penelope Fernandez was drowned in the wash-tub.

Joona thinks back to the curved mark on her chest that he noticed in the pathology lab, which made him think of a smiling mouth.

She was murdered, then placed on the bed in her cabin.

His thoughts start to come faster now as adrenalin pumps through his body. She was drowned in brackish seawater and then placed on her bed.

This isn't an ordinary death, and this isn't an ordinary murderer.

A tentative voice starts to echo inside him, getting faster and more insistent. It keeps repeating the same five words, louder and louder: *Get off the boat now, get off the boat now.*

Joona looks at Erixon through the glass as he drops a swab in a small paper bag, seals it with tape and writes on it with a ballpoint pen.

'Peekaboo,' Erixon smiles.

'We're going ashore,' Joona says calmly.

'I don't like boats, they keep moving the whole time, but I've only just got . . .'

'Take a break,' Joona says sharply.

'What's got into you now?'

'Just follow me and don't touch your phone.'

They go ashore and Joona leads Erixon a short way from the boat before he stops. He can feel his cheeks flush as calmness spreads through his body, settling as a weight in his thighs and calves.

'There could be a bomb on board,' he says quietly.

Erixon sits down on the edge of a concrete plinth. Sweat is dripping from his forehead.

'What are you talking about?'

'This is no ordinary murder,' Joona says. 'There's a risk that . . .'

'Murder? There's nothing to suggest . . .'

'Hold on,' Joona interrupts. 'I'm certain that Penelope Fernandez was drowned in the wash-tub that was out on deck.'

'Drowned? What the hell are you saying?'

'She drowned in seawater in the tub, then was moved to the bed,' Joona goes on. 'And I think the plan was that the boat should sink.'

'But . . .'

'Because then . . . then she'd be found in her water-filled cabin with water in her lungs.'

'But the boat never sank,' Erixon says.

'That's what made me start to wonder if there is some sort of explosive device on board, a device that didn't go off, for whatever reason.'

'It's probably next to the fuel tank or the gas cylinders in the galley,' Erixon says slowly. 'We'll have to get the area evacuated and call in the Bomb Squad.'

13

Reconstruction

At seven o'clock that evening five very serious men meet in room 13 of the Department of Forensic Medicine at the Karolinska Institute. Detective Superintendent Joona Linna wants to take charge of the preliminary investigation into the case of the woman who was found dead on a boat in the Stockholm archipelago. Even though it's Saturday, he has summoned his immediate boss, Petter Näslund, and Chief Prosecutor Jens Svanehjälm to a reconstruction in order to try to convince them that they're actually dealing with a murder.

One of the fluorescent tubes in the ceiling keeps flickering. The cool lighting glints off the dazzling white tiled walls.

'Need to change the starter,' The Needle murmurs.

'Yes,' Frippe agrees.

Petter Näslund mutters something under his breath from where he's standing over by the wall. His wide, strong face looks like it's shaking in the flickering light. Beside him stands Chief Prosecutor Jens Svanehjälm with an irritable expression on his young face. He seems to be considering the risks of putting his leather briefcase down on the floor and leaning against the wall in his smart suit.

There's a strong smell of disinfectant in the room. Large, adjustable lamps hang from the ceiling above a free-standing stainless steel table, with a double tap and deep drainage channels. The floor is covered with pale grey linoleum. A zinc tub like the one on the boat is already half full of water. Joona Linna keeps fetching more water in a bucket from the tap on the wall above the drain, and then emptying it into the tub.

'It isn't actually against the law for someone to be found drowned on a boat,' Svanehjälm says impatiently.

'Quite,' Petter says.

'This could just be an accidental drowning that hasn't been reported yet,' Svanehjälm goes on.

'The water in her lungs is the same water the boat was floating in, but there's practically none of that water on her clothes or the rest of her body,' The Needle says.

'Strange,' Svanehjälm says.

'There's bound to be a rational explanation,' Petter says with a smile.

Joona empties one last bucket into the tub, then puts the bucket on the floor, looks up at the others and thanks them for coming.

'I know it's the weekend and everyone would rather be at home,' he says. 'But I think I've noticed something important.'

'Of course we're going to come if you tell us it's important,' Svanehjälm says amiably, and finally puts his briefcase down between his feet.

'The perpetrator made his way onto the leisure cruiser,' Joona says seriously. 'He went down the steps to the front cabin and saw Penelope Fernandez asleep, then went back up to the aft-deck, dropped the bucket on the rope into the water and started to fill the wash-tub that was standing on deck.'

'Five, six buckets,' Petter says.

'Then, when the tub was full, he went down to the cabin and woke Penelope. He took her up the steps and out onto the deck, where he drowned her in the tub.'

'Who would do something like that?' Svanehjälm asks.

'I don't know yet, maybe it was some sort of torture, like waterboarding . . .'

'Revenge? Jealousy?'

Joona tilts his head and says thoughtfully:

'This isn't any ordinary murderer. Maybe the perpetrator

wanted information from her, to get her to say or admit to something, before finally holding her underwater until she could no longer resist the urge to breathe in.'

'What does our pathologist say?' Svanehjälm asks.

The Needle shakes his head.

'If she was drowned,' he says, 'then I'd have found signs of violence on her body, bruises and . . .'

'Can we wait with the objections?' Joona interrupts. 'Because I'd like to start by showing what I think happened, the way it looks in my head. And then, once I'm done, I'd like us all to go and look at the body, and see if there's any basis for my theory.'

'Why can't you ever do anything the way it's supposed to be done?' Petter asks.

'I do need to go home soon,' the prosecutor warns.

Joona looks at him with an ice-grey glint in his pale eyes. There's a hint of a smile playing at the corners of his eyes, a smile that does nothing to detract from the seriousness of his look.

'Penelope Fernandez,' he begins. 'She had been sitting on deck just before, smoking a joint. It was a warm day and she felt tired, so went down to rest on her bed for a while, and fell asleep wearing her denim jacket.'

He gestures towards The Needle's young assistant, who is waiting in the doorway.

'Frippe has agreed to help with the reconstruction.'

Frippe smiles and takes a step forward. His dyed black hair is hanging in clumps down his back, and his worn leather trousers are studded with rivets. He carefully fastens his leather jacket over his black T-shirt with a picture of the pop-group Europe on it.

'Look,' Joona says quietly, and demonstrates how with one hand he can take a firm grip of both sleeves of the jacket to lock Frippe's arms behind his back, allowing him to grab hold of his long hair with the other hand.

'I've got complete control of Frippe now, and there won't be a single bruise on him.'

Joona raises the young man's arms behind his back. Frippe whimpers and leans forward.

'Take it easy,' he laughs.

'Obviously, you're much bigger than the victim, but I still think I could push your head down in the wash-tub.'

'Be careful with him,' The Needle says.

'I'm only going to spoil his hair.'

'Forget it,' Frippe says with a smile.

It's a silent tussle. The Needle looks worried, Svanehjälm uncomfortable. Petter swears. Without any great difficulty Joona manages to push Frippe's head down into the water and hold him there for a few moments before letting go and backing away. Frippe wobbles as he straightens up and Nils hurries forward with a towel.

'You could have just described it, surely?' he says irritably.

Once Frippe has finished drying himself they go silently into the next room, where the cool air is heavy with the stench of decay. One wall is covered with three layers of stainless steel fridge doors. Nils opens compartment 16 and pulls out the tray. The young woman is lying on the narrow bunk, naked and drained of colour, with brown, spidery veins around her neck. Joona points at the thin, curved line over her chest.

'Take your clothes off,' he says to Frippe.

Frippe unbuttons his jacket and pulls off his black T-shirt. Across his chest is a faint pink mark made by the edge of the wash-tub, a curved line, like a smiling mouth.

'Bloody hell,' Petter says.

The Needle goes over and inspects the roots of the dead woman's hair. He takes out a small torch and points it at the pale skin under her hair.

'I don't need a microscope for this. Someone's held her very tightly by her hair.'

He turns the torch off and puts it back in the pocket of his white coat.

'In other words . . .' Joona says.

'In other words, you're right, of course,' The Needle says, and claps his hands.

'Murder,' Svanehjälm sighs.

'Impressive,' Frippe says, wiping some eye-liner that has smeared across one cheek.

'Thanks,' Joona says distantly.

Nils looks at him quizzically:

'What is it, Joona? What have you seen?'

'It's not her,' he says.

'What?'

Joona meets Nils's gaze, then points at the body in front of them.

'This isn't Penelope Fernandez. It's someone else,' he says, and looks at the prosecutor. 'The dead woman isn't Penelope. I've seen her driver's licence, and I'm certain this isn't her.'

'But what . . .'

'Maybe Penelope Fernandez is dead too,' he says. 'But if she is, we haven't found her yet.'

14

Penelope's heart is still beating horribly fast – she's trying to breathe quietly, but the air shudders in her throat. She slides down the rough rocks, pulling the damp moss down with her, and ends up under cover of the branches of the fir tree. She's so terrified that she's shaking. She creeps closer to the trunk where the night's darkness is at its most dense. She hears herself start to whimper when she thinks of Viola. Björn is sitting motionless in the darkness under the branches with his arms wrapped tightly around him, muttering to himself over and over again.

They've been running in panic, not looking back, have stumbled and fallen and got back up, they've clambered over fallen trees, scraping their legs, knees and hands, but they've kept rushing on.

Penelope no longer has any sense of how close their pursuer is, if he's already caught sight of them again or if he's given up and decided to wait.

They've been running, but Penelope has no idea why. She can't understand why they're being hunted.

Maybe it's all a mistake, she thinks. A terrible mistake.

Her racing pulse starts to slow down.

She feels sick, and almost throws up, but swallows hard instead.

'Oh, God, oh, God,' she keeps whispering to herself. 'This is impossible, we have to get help, someone ought to find the boat soon and start looking for us . . .'

'Shhh,' Björn hisses with fear in his eyes.

Her hands are shaking. A series of rapid-fire images plays in her mind. She tries to blink them away, tries to look at her white trainers, at the brown fir needles on the ground, at Björn's dirty, bloody knees, but the images keep forcing their way through: Viola is dead, sitting on the bed with her eyes wide open, the look in them unreadable, her face blotchy and white and wet, her hair lank and dripping.

Somehow Penelope had understood that the man standing on the shore beckoning Björn to swim back to land was the person who had killed her sister. She could feel it. She put the few pieces she had together and interpreted the image in an instant. If she hadn't they would all be dead.

Penelope had screamed at Björn. They were losing time, it was going too slowly, and she hurt him with the end of the boathook before she managed to get him on board.

The black inflatable boat had appeared round the end of Kastskär and picked up speed on the flat, open water.

She had steered straight for an old wooden jetty, then hit reverse and switched the engine off as the hull hit a post. They'd slid sideways with a great creaking sound, then just fled from the boat in panic. They didn't take anything, not even a phone. Penelope slipped on the rocks and had to cling on with her hands, then turned and saw the man in black quickly tying the inflatable to the jetty.

Penelope and Björn ran into the forest, rushing along side by side, swerving round trees and dark rocks. Björn groaned when his bare feet trod on sharp twigs.

Penelope pulled him along after her, their pursuer wasn't far behind.

They had no thoughts, no plan, they were just rushing in panic, deep into dense ferns and blueberry bushes.

Penelope heard herself sob as she ran, sobbing in a voice she had never heard herself use before.

A thick branch caught her sharply in the thigh and she had

to stop. Her breathing was ragged as she pushed the branch away with trembling hands. Björn was running towards her. Her thigh muscle was throbbing painfully. She started running again, then speeded up. She could hear Björn behind her as she ran deeper and deeper into the dense forest without looking back.

Something happens to your mind when you're seized by panic. Because the panic isn't constant – every so often it shatters and is replaced by purely rational reasoning. It's like switching a horrible noise off and finding yourself surrounded by silence and a sudden overview of the situation. Then the fear comes back again, your thoughts go back to being one-track, chasing round in circles, and all you want to do is run, get away from whoever is chasing you.

Penelope thought plenty of times that they needed to find other people, there must be hundreds of them on Ornö that evening. They needed to find the inhabited parts of the island, further south, they had to get help, get hold of a phone and call the police.

They hid under cover of some fir trees, but after a while the fear became unbearable and they raced on.

As she was running Penelope could feel his presence again, thought she could hear his long, quick steps. She knew he hadn't stopped running. He'd catch up with them if they didn't get help soon, if they didn't reach the inhabited part of the island.

The ground was rising again, stones came loose beneath their feet and rolled down the slope.

They had to find some people, there must be some houses somewhere near. A wave of hysteria ran through her, a desire to just stand still and scream, call for help, but she forced herself to keep going, to keep climbing.

Björn coughed behind her, gasped for breath and then coughed again.

What if Viola wasn't dead, what if she just needed help? Fear chased through her head. On some level Penelope was aware that she was thinking things like that because the reality was so much worse. She knew Viola was dead, but it was incomprehensible, just a big, black void. She didn't want to understand, couldn't understand, didn't even want to try.

71

They scrambled up another steep cliff, past pines with scratchy branches, rocks and lingonberry bushes. Using her hands to support her, she made it to the top. Björn was right behind her, he tried to say something but was too out of breath, he just pulled her on – and down again – with him. On the other side of the ridge the forest sloped down towards the western shore of the island. Between the dark trees they could see the pale surface of the water. It wasn't far away. They carried on down the slope. Penelope slipped and slid part of the way, hitting the ground hard. She hit her mouth on her knees, got her breath back and started to cough.

She tried to get to her feet, wondering if she'd broken something, then suddenly she heard music, followed by loud voices and laughter. Leaning against the damp rock-face, she stood up, wiped her lips and looked at her bleeding hand.

Björn appeared beside her and pulled her along, pointing to where they should go: there was a party somewhere up ahead of them. Taking each other's hands they started to run. Between the dark trees they could see coloured garlands of lights wound through a wooden veranda overlooking the water.

They walked on warily.

There was a group of people sitting around a table in front of a beautiful rust-red summerhouse. Penelope realised it must be the middle of the night, but the sky was still bright. The meal was long since over, the table was strewn with glasses and coffee cups, napkins and empty bowls of crisps.

Some of the people at the table were singing, others were talking and topping up glasses from wine-boxes. The barbecue was still radiating heat. There were probably children asleep inside the house. To Björn and Penelope, they all looked like they were from a completely different world. Their faces were bright and calm. The obvious friendship between them sealed them off like a glass dome.

Only one person was outside the circle. He was standing off to one side with his face towards the forest, as if expecting visitors. Penelope stopped abruptly and clutched Björn's hand. They sank to the ground and crept behind a low fir tree. Björn looked frightened, uncomprehending. But she was sure of what she had seen. Their pursuer had figured out which way they were heading and had got to the house ahead of them. He had realised how irresistible the lights and sounds of the party would be to them. So he waited, watching for them among the dark trees, keen to head them off at the edge of the forest. He wasn't worried that the people at the party would hear their screams; he knew they wouldn't dare to enter the forest until it was too late.

When Penelope eventually risked a look up again he was gone. She was trembling from the adrenalin coursing through her blood. Maybe their pursuer thought he'd made a mistake, she wondered, looking around.

Perhaps he'd run off in a different direction.

She was just starting to think that their flight might finally be over, that she and Björn could go down to the party and alert the police, when she suddenly caught sight of him again.

He was standing beside a tree-trunk, not far away at all.

With measured movements their pursuer raised a pair of binoculars with pale green lenses.

Penelope huddled down next to Björn, trying to fight the urge to flee, to just run and run. She could see the man through the trees, raising the binoculars to his eyes, and realised that they probably had night vision, or heat-seeking sights.

Penelope took Björn by the hand and, crouching low, pulled him away from the house with her, away from the music, backwards into the forest. After a while she dared to straighten up. They started to run across a scree-slope formed by the kilometre-thick glaciers that once covered northern Europe. They carried on through thorny bushes, behind a large rock and across a sharp ridge. Björn grabbed hold of a thick branch and slowly started to slide down the other side. Penelope's heart was thudding hard in her chest, her thigh muscles were aching, and she was trying to breathe quietly, even though she was far too breathless. She slipped down the rough rocks, pulling damp moss and loose stones down with her until she reached the ground under the dense canopy of fir branches. Björn was wearing nothing but his knee-length board-shorts, his face was pale and his lips almost white.

It sounds like someone is repeatedly throwing a ball at the wall below senior pathologist Nils Åhlén's window. He and Joona Linna are waiting for Claudia Fernandez in silence. She's been asked to come to the Department of Forensic Medicine early this Sunday morning to help identify the dead woman.

When Joona called her to say that they feared her daughter Viola had died, Claudia's voice had sounded strangely calm.

'No, Viola's out in the archipelago with her sister,' she had said.

'On Björn Almskog's boat?' Joona asked.

'Yes, I was the one who suggested she call Penelope and ask if she could go with them, I thought it would do her good to get away for a bit.'

'Was anyone else going with them?'

'Well, Björn, obviously.'

Joona fell silent, and several seconds passed as he tried to shift the weight that had settled inside him. Then he cleared his throat and said very gently:

'Claudia, I'd like you to come to the Department of Forensic Medicine in Solna.'

'What for?' she asked.

Now Joona is sitting in an uncomfortable chair in the senior pathologist's room. The Needle has slipped a small picture of

Frippe into the bottom of his framed wedding photograph. They can hear the sound of the ball thudding against the wall, a hollow, lonely sound. Joona thinks back to how Claudia's breathing changed when she finally realised that it might actually be her daughter that they'd found dead. Joona had carefully explained the circumstances to her: that a woman they feared was her younger daughter had been found dead on an abandoned motor cruiser in the Stockholm archipelago.

He booked a taxi to collect Claudia Fernandez from her terraced house in Gustavsberg. She should be with them within the next few minutes.

The Needle makes a half-hearted attempt at small-talk, but gives up after a while when he realises Joona isn't going to respond.

They both just want this to be over. A positive identification is always a traumatic moment: any lacerating relief afforded by the end of uncertainty is mixed with the absolute agony of all hope being lost.

They can hear footsteps in the corridor. They both get to their feet at the same time.

Seeing the dead body of a family member is a merciless confirmation of all our worst fears. But at the same time it's an important, necessary part of the grieving process. Joona has read plenty of claims that identification also constitutes a form of liberation. There's no longer any opportunity for wild fantasies that the loved one is actually still alive, fantasies which can only bring emptiness and frustration.

Joona can't help thinking that's just hollow nonsense. Death is never anything but terrible, and never gives anything back.

Claudia Fernandez is standing in the doorway, a frightened-looking woman in her sixties. Her face bears traces of tears and anxiety, and her body looks frozen and hunched.

Joona gently introduces himself:

'Hello, my name is Joona Linna. I'm a detective superinten- dent – it was me you spoke to on the phone.'

The Needle introduces himself very quietly as he shakes hands with the woman, then immediately turns his back on her and pretends to sort through some files. He appears very brusque and dismissive, but Joona knows that he's really very upset.

'I've tried calling them, but I can't get hold of either of my girls,' Claudia whispers. 'They ought . . .'

'Shall we go?' Nils interrupts, as if he hasn't heard her.

They move silently through the familiar corridors. With each step Joona can't help thinking that the air is getting thinner. Claudia Fernandez is in no hurry to get to what lies ahead. She walks slowly, several metres behind Nils, whose tall, sharply defined figure hurries off ahead of them. Joona Linna turns and tries to smile at Claudia. But he has to steel himself against the look in her eyes: panic, pleading, prayer, desperate attempts to do a deal with God.

It feels like they're dragging her into the cold room where the bodies are kept.

Nils mutters something, sounding almost angry, then he bends over, unlocks one of the stainless steel doors and pulls out the drawer.

The young woman comes into view. Her body is covered with a white sheet. Her eyes are dull, half-closed, her cheeks sunken.

Her hair lies like a black wreath around her beautiful head.

A small, pale hand is visible beside her hip.

Claudia Fernandez is breathing fast. She reaches out and cautiously touches the hand, then lets out a whimpering moan. It comes from deep within her, as if she is breaking apart at that moment, her soul shattering.

Claudia's body starts to shake and she sinks to her knees, pressing her daughter's lifeless hand to her lips.

'No, no,' she sobs. 'Oh God, dear God, not Viola. Not Viola . . .'

Joona is standing a few steps behind Claudia, sees her back shake with weeping, hears her voice, as her desperate sobbing gets gradually louder, then slowly dies away.

She wipes the tears from her face, but is still breathing fitfully as she gets up from the floor.

'Can you confirm that this is her?' The Needle says curtly. 'Is this Viola Fernandez, your . . .'

His voice tails off and he clears his throat quickly and angrily.

Claudia shakes her head and gently strokes her daughter's cheek with her fingertips.

'Viola, Violita . . .'

Very shakily, she pulls her hand back, and Joona says gently: 'I'm so very, very sorry.'

Claudia almost falls, but reaches out to the wall for support, turns away and whispers to herself:

'We're going to the circus on Saturday, it's a surprise for Viola . . .'

They look at the dead woman, her pale lips, the veins on her neck.

'I've forgotten your name,' Claudia says helplessly, looking at Joona.

'Joona Linna,' he says.

'Joona Linna,' the woman repeats in a thick voice. 'I'll tell you about Viola. She's my little girl, my youngest, my happy little . . .'

Claudia glances over at Viola's white face and sways sideways. The Needle pulls up a chair, but she just shakes her head.

'Sorry,' she says. 'It's just that . . . my elder daughter, Penelope, she went through so many terrible things in El Salvador. When I think about what they did to me in that prison, when I remember how frightened Penelope was, she cried and called out for me . . . hour after hour, but I couldn't go to her, I couldn't protect her . . .'

Claudia looks Joona in the eye and takes a step towards him, and he gently puts his arm round her. She leans heavily against his chest, catches her breath, then pulls away and fumbles for the back of the chair without looking at her dead daughter, and sits down.

'My proudest achievement . . . was making sure that little Viola was born here in Sweden. She had a lovely room, with a pink lampshade, and lots of toys and dolls, she went to school, watched *Pippi Longstocking* . . . I don't suppose you can understand, but I was so proud that she never had to be hungry or afraid. Not like us . . . like Penelope and me, who still wake up in the middle of the night, ready for someone to break in and do terrible things . . .'

She falls silent, then whispers:

'Viola has known nothing but happiness and . . .'

Claudia leans forward and hides her face in her hands, and weeps softly. Joona very gently puts his hand on her back.

'I'll go now,' she says, still crying.

'There's no hurry.'

She calms down, but then her face contorts into another fit of tears.

'Have you spoken to Penelope?' she asks.

'We haven't been able to get hold of her,' Joona says quietly.

'Tell her I want her to call me, because . . .'

She stops herself, the colour drains from her face again and then she looks up.

'I just thought maybe she wasn't answering because she saw it was me calling, because I . . . I was . . . I said a horrible thing, but I didn't mean it, I didn't mean . . .'

'We've started to look for Penelope and Björn Almskog with a helicopter, but . . .'

'Please, tell me she's alive,' she whispers to Joona. 'Tell me that much, Joona Linna.'

Joona's jaw muscles tense as he strokes Claudia's back, then he says:

'I'm going to do everything I can to . . .'

'She's alive. Say it!' Claudia interrupts. 'She has to be alive.'

'I'm going to find her,' Joona says. 'I know I'm going to find her.'

'Say that Penelope's alive.'

Joona hesitates, then meets Claudia's clouded gaze, and different thoughts flash through his head, linked in fleeting combinations, and suddenly he hears himself say:

'She's alive.'

'Yes,' Claudia whispers.

Joona lowers his eyes; he can no longer grasp the thoughts that passed through his consciousness just moments before, which made him change his mind and tell Claudia that her eldest daughter is alive.

16

Joona goes with Claudia Fernandez to the waiting taxi, helps her in, and then waits by the turning circle until the car is out of sight before he starts to search his pockets for his phone. When he realises he must have put it down somewhere, he hurries back inside the Department of Forensic Medicine, walks straight into Nils Åhlén's office, picks up The Needle's phone as he sits down behind the desk, dials Erixon's number and waits as the call goes through.

'Let people sleep,' Erixon says when he answers. 'It's actually Sunday today.'

'Admit that you're on the boat.'

'I'm on the boat,' Erixon admits.

'So there weren't any explosives?' Joona says.

'Not in the usual sense – but you were still right. It could have exploded at any moment.'

'What do you mean?'

'The insulation on the cables is seriously damaged in one place, looks like they've been pinched . . . the metal's not touching, because that would trip the circuit, but it's uncovered . . . and when you start it up you can easily get an electrical surge . . . and arcing.'

'What happens then?'

'This arcing has a temperature of over three thousand degrees,

79

and they could easily set light to an old cushion someone has squeezed in there,' Erixon goes on. 'And then the fire would find its way along the tube from the fuel tank and . . .'

'Fast, then?'

'Well . . . the arcing might take ten minutes or so, maybe more . . . but after that it's fairly quick – fire, more fire, explosion – the boat would fill with water almost instantly and sink.'

'So there would have been a fire and an explosion if the engine had been left running?'

'Yes, but it hasn't necessarily been done on purpose,' Erixon says.

'So the cables could have been damaged by accident? And the cushion just ended up there?'

'Absolutely,' he replies.

'But you don't believe that?' Joona asks.

'No.'

Joona thinks about the fact that the boat was found drifting in Jungfrufjärden, then clears his throat and says thoughtfully:

'If the murderer did this . . .'

'Then he's no ordinary killer,' Erixon concludes.

Joona repeats the thought to himself, telling himself that they're not dealing with an ordinary murderer. Run-of-the-mill killers tend to react emotionally, even if they've planned the murder. There are always a lot of heightened emotions at play, and murders often have an element of hysteria about them. The plan usually emerges afterwards, in an effort to conceal the act and construct an alibi. But on this occasion the perpetrator appears to have followed a very specific strategy from the outset.

Even so, something still went wrong.

Joona stares into space for a while, then writes Viola Fernandez's name on the top page of The Needle's notepad. He circles it, then adds Penelope Fernandez and Björn Almskog's names underneath. The two women are sisters. Penelope and Björn are in a settled relationship. Björn owns the boat. Viola asked if she could go with them at the last minute.

Identifying the motive behind a murder is a long and winding road. Joona is aware that he only recently thought that Penelope Fernandez was alive. It hadn't just been a hope or an attempt to give comfort. It had been an intuition, but no more than that. He had caught the thought mid-flight, but lost his grip on it almost immediately.

If he were to follow the National Homicide Commission's template, his suspicions ought to be directed at Viola's boyfriend, and possibly Penelope and Björn seeing as they were on the boat. Alcohol and other drugs may have been involved. Perhaps there was a disagreement, a serious jealousy drama. Leif G. W. Persson would soon be giving his opinion on television, saying that the perpetrator was someone close to Viola, probably a boyfriend or former boyfriend.

Joona considers the intention behind making the fuel tank explode and tries to understand the logic behind the plan. Viola was drowned in the zinc wash-tub on the aft-deck and the perpetrator carried her down to the cabin and left her on the bunk.

Joona knows he's trying to think too many thoughts at the same time. He needs to stop himself and start to structure what he actually knows, and the questions that still need to be answered.

He draws another circle round Viola's name and starts again.

What he knows is that Viola Fernandez was drowned in a wash-tub and then placed on the bed in the front cabin, and that Penelope Fernandez and Björn Almskog haven't yet been found.

But that's not all, he tells himself, and turns to a new page. Details.

He writes the word 'calm' on the pad.

There was no wind, and the boat was found drifting near Storskär.

The front of the boat is damaged, from a fairly forceful collision. Forensics have presumably managed to secure evidence and taken imprints by now.

Joona throws Nils's notepad hard at the wall and closes his eyes.

'*Perkele*,' he whispers.

Something has slipped out of his grasp again, he had it, he knows he almost made a crucial observation. He was on the brink of making a breakthrough, but then he just lost it again.

Viola, Joona thinks. You died on the aft-deck of the boat. So why were you moved after you died? Who moved you? The murderer, or someone else?

If you find her apparently lifeless on deck, you probably try to resuscitate her, you call SOS Alarm, that's what you do. And if you realise that she's dead, that it's already too late, that you can't bring her back, maybe you don't just want to leave her lying there, you want to take her inside, cover her with a sheet. But a dead body is heavy and awkward to move, even if there are two of you. But it wouldn't have been too difficult to move her into the saloon. It's only five metres, through a pair of wide glass doors and down just one step.

That's perfectly possible, even without any specific intention.

But you don't drag her down a steep set of steps, through a narrow passageway, to put her on the bed in the cabin.

You only do that if you intend her to be found drowned in her room on the submerged boat.

'Exactly,' he mutters, and stands up.

He looks out of the window, spots an almost blue beetle crawling along the white sill, then looks up and sees a woman riding a bicycle disappear between the trees, and suddenly he realises what the missing component is.

Joona sits down again and drums his fingers on the desk.

It wasn't Penelope who was found dead on the boat, it was her sister Viola. But Viola wasn't found on her own bed, in her own cabin on the boat, but in the front cabin, on Penelope's bed.

The murderer could have made the same mistake as me, Joona thinks, and a shiver runs down his spine.

He thought he had killed Penelope Fernandez.

That's why he put her on the bed in the front cabin.

That's the only explanation.

And that explanation means that Penelope Fernandez and Björn Almskog aren't responsible for Viola's death, because they wouldn't have placed her on the wrong bed.

Joona starts when the door flies open. The Needle shoves it open with his back, then comes in backwards carrying a large, oblong box covered with red flames and the words 'Guitar Hero' on the front.

'Frippe and I are going to start . . .'

'Quiet,' Joona snaps.

'What's happened?' Nils asks.

'Nothing, I just need to think,' he replies quickly.

Joona gets up from the chair and walks out of the room without another word. He walks through the foyer without hearing what the twinkly-eyed woman at reception says to him. He just carries on, out into the early sunshine, and stops on the grass by the car park.

A fourth person who isn't well-acquainted with the two women killed Viola, Joona thinks. He killed Viola, but thought he had killed Penelope. That means that Penelope was still alive when Viola was killed, because otherwise he wouldn't have made that mistake.

Maybe she is still alive, Joona thinks. It's possible that she's lying dead somewhere out in the archipelago, on some island or deep underwater. But there's still every reason to hope that she's still alive, and if she is alive, then she'll be found before too much longer.

Joona strides off purposefully towards his car without actually knowing where he's going. His phone is on the roof of the car. He realises he must have left it there when he locked the car. When he picks it up to call Anja Larsson it's very hot. No answer. He opens the door, gets in, puts on his seat belt, then sits there and tries to find a flaw in his reasoning.

The air is stuffy, but the heavy scent of the lilac bushes by the car park eventually succeeds in driving the yeasty smell of the body in the mortuary from his nostrils.

His phone rings in his hand, and he looks at the screen before answering.

'I've just been talking to your doctor,' Anja says.

'Why were you talking to him?' Joona asks in surprise.

'Janush says you never show up,' she chides.

'I haven't had time.'

'But you're taking the medication?'

'It's disgusting,' Joona jokes.

'Seriously, though . . . he called because he's worried about you,' she says.

'I'll talk to him.'

'When you've solved this case, you mean?'

'Have you got a pen and paper handy?' Joona asks.

'Don't worry about me.'

'The woman who was found on the boat isn't Penelope Fernandez.'

'No, it was Viola. I know,' she says. 'Petter told me.'

'Good.'

'You were wrong, Joona.'

'Yes, I know . . .'

'Say it,' she jokes.

'I'm always wrong,' he says quietly.

Neither of them speaks for a moment.

'So we're not allowed to joke about that?' she asks tentatively.

'Have you managed to find out anything the boat and Viola Fernandez?'

'Viola and Penelope are sisters,' she says. 'Penelope and Björn have been in a relationship, or whatever you want to call it, for the past four years.'

'Yes, that's pretty much what I thought.'

'Right. Do you want me to go on, or is it all unnecessary?'

Joona doesn't answer, just leans his head back and notices that the windscreen is covered with pollen from a nearby tree.

'Viola wasn't supposed to be going out on the boat with them,' Anja goes on. 'She'd had a row with her boyfriend, Sergey Jarushenko, that morning, and had phoned her mother in tears. It was her mother's idea that she should ask Penelope if she could go with them.'

'What do you know about Penelope?'

'I've actually been prioritising the victim, Viola Fernandez, seeing as . . .'

'But the murderer thought he'd killed Penelope.'

'Hang on, what did you just say, Joona?'

'He made a mistake, he was planning to cover the murder up, make it look like an accident, but he put Viola on her sister's bed.'

'Because he thought Viola was Penelope.'

'I need to know everything about Penelope Fernandez and her . . .'

'She's one of my biggest idols,' Anja says, cutting him off. 'She's a peace campaigner, and she lives at Sankt Paulsgatan 3.'

'We've sent out an alert for her and Björn Almskog on the intranet,' Joona says. 'And the coastguard have got two helicopters searching the area around Dalarö, but they need to organise a proper search of the island with the marine police.'

'I'll find out what's going on,' she says.

'And someone needs to talk to Viola's boyfriend, and Bill Persson, the fisherman who found her on the boat. We need a comprehensive forensics report on the boat, and we need to speed up the results from the National Forensics Lab.'

'Do you want me to call Linköping?'

'I'll talk to Erixon, he knows them. I'll be seeing him shortly to take a look at Penelope's apartment.'

'Sounds like you're in charge of the preliminary investigation. Are you?'

17

A very dangerous man

The summer sky is still clear, but the air is getting more and more close, as if a storm were brewing.

Joona Linna and Erixon park outside the old fishermen's store, which always has pictures of the people who have caught the largest salmon in the centre of Stockholm each week.

Joona's phone rings and he sees that it's Claudia Fernandez. He walks over to the thin strip of shadow by the wall before answering.

'You said I could call you,' she says in a weak voice.

'Of course.'

'I realise that you probably say the same thing to everyone, but I was thinking . . . my daughter, Penelope. I mean . . . I need to know if you find anything, even if . . .'

Claudia's voice fades away.

'Hello? Claudia?'

'Yes, sorry,' she whispers.

'I'm a detective . . . I'm trying to find out if there's criminal activity behind these events. The coastguards are the people looking for Penelope,' Joona explains.

'When are they going to find her?'

'They usually start by searching the area with helicopters . . . and at the same time they organise a ground-search of any islands, but that takes longer . . . so they start with helicopters.'

Joona can hear that Claudia is trying to muffle her crying.

'I don't know what to do, I . . . I need to know if there's anything I can do, if I ought to carry on talking to her friends.'

'The best thing would be if you could stay at home,' Joona says. 'Because Penelope might try to contact you, and then . . .'

'She won't call me,' she interrupts.

'I think she . . .'

'I've always been too hard on Penelope, I get angry with her, I don't know why, I . . . I don't want to lose her, I can't lose Penelope, I . . .'

Claudia cries down the phone, tries to stop herself, quickly apologises and ends the call.

Opposite the fishing tackle shop is Sankt Paulsgatan 3, where Penelope Fernandez lives. Joona walks across to Erixon, who is waiting for him in front of a store window full of Japanese writing and manga pictures. The shelves are full of Hello Kitty, cat dolls with big, innocent faces. The entire shop is a surprising, garish contrast to the dirty brown façade of the building.

'Small body, big head,' Erixon says, pointing at one of the Hello Kitty dolls when Joona reaches him.

'Quite cute,' Joona mumbles.

'I got that the wrong way round, I'm stuck with a big body and a small head,' Erixon jokes.

Joona smiles as he gives him a sideways glance and opens the wide door for him. They walk up the steps and look at the list of names, the illuminated light-switches, the hatches to the garbage chute. The stairwell smells of sun and dust and detergent. Erixon grabs hold of the handrail, worn smooth with use, and it creaks as he heaves himself up behind Joona. They look at each other when they reach the third floor. Erixon's face is quivering from the exertion, and he nods and wipes the sweat from his brow as he whispers apologetically to Joona:

'Sorry.'

'It's very close today,' Joona says.

There are several stickers by the doorbell: a peace symbol, the Fairtrade logo, and anti-nuclear power. Joona glances at Erixon, and his grey eyes narrow when he puts his ear to the door and listens.

'What is it?' Erixon whispers.

Still listening, Joona rings the doorbell. He waits a few moments, then pulls a small case from his inside pocket.

'Probably nothing,' he says, and carefully picks the uncomplicated lock.

Joona opens the door, then seems to change his mind and closes it again. He gestures to Erixon to remain where he is, without really knowing why. They hear the melody of an ice-cream van outside. Erixon looks worried, and rubs his chin. A shiver runs through Joona's arms, but he still opens the door calmly and walks in. There are newspapers, adverts and a letter from the Left Party on the hall mat. The air is still, stale. A velvet curtain has been pulled across the closet. The pipes in the walls gush and then tick rapidly.

Joona doesn't know why, but his hand moves to his holstered pistol. He nudges it with his fingertips beneath his jacket, but doesn't draw it. He looks at the blood-red curtain, then the kitchen door. He is breathing quietly, trying to see through the textured pane of glass and the glass door to the living room.

Joona takes a step forward, but really he just wants to get out of the flat: a strong instinct is telling him to call for backup. Something goes dark behind the textured glass. A wind-chime with dangling brass weights is swaying, but without making any noise. Joona sees the motes of dust in the air change direction, following a new air-current.

He's not alone in Penelope's flat.

Joona's heart starts to beat faster. Someone is moving through the rooms. He can sense it, and turns to look at the kitchen door, and then everything happens very fast. The wooden floor creaks. He hears a rhythmic sound, like little clicks. The door to the kitchen is half open. Joona catches sight of movement in the crack between the hinges. He presses himself against the wall, as if in a railway tunnel. Someone moves quickly through the darkness of the long hallway. Just their back, a shoulder, an arm.

The figure approaches rapidly, then spins round. Joona catches just a glimpse of the knife, like a white tongue. It shoots up like a projectile, from below. The angle is so unexpected that he doesn't have time to parry the blow. The sharp blade cuts through his clothes and its tip hits his pistol. Joona strikes out at the figure, but misses. He hears the knife slash the air a second time and throws himself back. This time the blade comes from above. Joona hits his head on the bathroom door. He sees a long splinter of wood peel off as the knife cuts into the door-frame. Joona falls to the floor, rolls over, kicks out low, in an arc, and hits something, possibly one of his attacker's ankles. He rolls away, draws his pistol and removes the safety catch in the same fluid movement. The front door is open and he hears rapid footsteps going down the stairs. Joona gets to his feet, is about to set off after the man when he hears a rumbling sound behind him. He understands instantly what the noise is and rushes into the kitchen. The microwave oven has been switched on. It's crackling, and black sparks are visible through the glass door. The valves of the four burners on top of the old gas stove have been left open, and gas is streaming into the room.

With a feeling that time has become incredibly sluggish, Joona throws himself at the microwave. The timer is clicking anxiously. The crackling noise is getting louder. A can of insect spray is revolving on the glass plate inside. Joona pulls the plug from the wall and the noise stops. The only sound is the monotonous hiss of the open gas burners on the stove. Joona shuts the valves off. The chemical smell makes his stomach heave. He opens the kitchen window and then looks at the aerosol in the microwave. It's badly swollen, and could still explode at the slightest touch.

Joona leaves the kitchen and quickly searches the rest of the flat. The rooms are empty, untouched. The air is still thick with gas. On the landing outside the door Erixon is lying on the floor with a cigarette in his mouth.

'Don't light it,' Joona shouts.

Erixon smiles and waves his hand wearily.

'Chocolate cigarettes,' he whispers.

Erixon coughs weakly and Joona suddenly sees the pool of blood beneath him.

'You're bleeding.'

'Nothing too serious,' he says. 'I don't know how he did it, but he cut my Achilles' tendon.'

Joona calls for an ambulance, then sits down beside him. Erixon is pale and his cheeks are wet with sweat. He looks distinctly unwell.

'He cut me without even stopping, it was . . . it was like being attacked by a bloody spider.'

They fall silent and Joona thinks about the lightning-fast movements behind the door, and the way the knife moved with a speed and a purposefulness that was unlike anything he's ever experienced before.

'Is she in there?' Erixon pants.

'No.'

Erixon smiles with relief, then turns serious.

'But he was still planning to blow the place up?' he asks.

'Presumably to get rid of evidence, or some sort of connection,' Joona says.

Erixon tries to peel the paper from the chocolate cigarette but drops it and closes his eyes. His cheeks are greyish white now.

'I guess you didn't see his face either,' Joona says.

'No,' Erixon says weakly.

'But we saw something, people always see something . . .'

18

The fire

The paramedics reassure Erixon repeatedly that they're not going to drop him.

'I can walk,' Erixon says, as he shuts his eyes.

His chin trembles with every step they take.

Joona returns to Penelope Fernandez's flat. He opens all the windows, airing out the gas, and sits down on the comfortable, apricot-coloured sofa.

If the apartment had exploded, it would probably have been written off as an accident caused by a gas leak.

Joona reminds himself that no fragments of memory ever disappear, nothing you ever see is lost, it's all a matter of letting the memory drift up from the depths like flotsam.

So what did I see, then?

He didn't see anything, just rapid movements and a white knife-blade.

That was what I saw, Joona suddenly thinks. Nothing.

He tells himself that the very absence of observations supports the idea that they're not dealing with any ordinary murderer.

They could be dealing with a professional killer, a problem solver, a fixer.

He had already had his suspicions, but after his encounter he is convinced.

He's sure that the person he met in the hallway is the same

person who murdered Viola. His intention had been to kill Penelope, sink the motor cruiser and make the whole thing look like an accident. It was the same pattern here, before he was disturbed. He wants to remain invisible, he wants to get on with his business but hide it from the police.

Joona looks around slowly, trying to gather his observations into a coherent whole.

It sounds like some children are rolling balls across the floor in the flat upstairs. They would be trapped in an inferno of fire if Joona hadn't pulled the plug from the microwave in time.

He's never been subjected to such a deliberate and dangerous attack before. He's convinced that the person who was inside the home of peace campaigner Penelope Fernandez isn't some hate-filled enemy from the extreme right. Those groups may be guilty of carefully planned acts of violence, but this individual is a trained professional in a league far above the extreme right-wing groups in Sweden.

So what were you doing here? Joona asks himself. *What is a fixer doing with Penelope Fernandez, what has she got caught up in? What's going on under the surface?*

He thinks about the man's unpredictable movements, the knife-technique that was designed to get past any standard defensive manoeuvres, including those taught by the police and military.

He feels a shiver run through him when he realises that the first blow would have hit his liver if his pistol hadn't been hanging below his right arm, and the second would have hit his head if he hadn't thrown himself backward.

Joona gets up from the sofa and goes into the bedroom. He looks at the neatly made bed and the crucifix hanging above it.

A fixer thought he had murdered Penelope, and his intention was to make it look like an accident . . .

But the boat didn't sink.

Either the murderer was interrupted, or he left the scene of the crime intending to return later and finish the job. But he certainly couldn't have intended the boat to have been found drifting by the marine police with a drowned girl on board. Something went wrong along the way, or else his plans changed suddenly. Perhaps he received new orders, but a day and half after Viola's murder he was in Penelope's apartment.

You must have had very strong reasons for visiting her flat. What would motivate you to take a risk like that? Was there something in the flat that connects you or your employer to Penelope?

You did something here, removed fingerprints, erased a hard disk, erased a message on an answer-machine, or collected some-thing, Joona thinks.

That was what you were planning, anyway, but perhaps you got interrupted when I arrived.

Perhaps you were planning to use the fire to get rid of the evidence?

It's a possibility.

Joona thinks that he could have done with Erixon right now. He can't conduct a crime scene investigation without a forensics expert, he doesn't have the right equipment. And he could ruin evidence if he were to search the flat on his own, possibly contaminate DNA and miss invisible clues.

Joona goes over to the window and looks down at the street, and the empty tables outside a café.

He realises he's going to have to go to Police Headquarters and talk to his boss, Carlos Eliasson, and ask to be put in charge of the preliminary investigation: that's the only way to get access to another forensics expert, the only way to get any help while Erixon is off work injured.

Joona's phone rings just as he makes up his mind to follow the correct procedures and go and talk to Carlos and Jens Svanehjälm, and put together a small investigative team.

'Hi, Anja,' he says.

'I'd like to have a sauna with you.'

'A sauna?'

'Yes, can't the two of us have a sauna together? You could show me what a proper Finnish sauna is like.'

'Anja,' he says slowly. 'I've lived almost my whole life here in Stockholm.'

He goes out into the hallway, then carries on towards the front door.

'You're a Swedish Finn, I know,' Anja goes on. 'Could there be anything more boring? Why can't you be from El Salvador? Have you read any of Penelope Fernandez's articles? You should see her – the other day when she went on the attack against Swedish arms exports on television.'

Joona can hear Anja's breathing down the phone as he leaves Penelope Fernandez's flat. He sees the paramedics' bloody footprints on the stairs and feels his scalp prickle when he thinks of his colleague sitting in the stairwell with his legs wide apart, his face getting paler and paler.

Joona thinks again about the fact that the fixer thought he had killed Penelope Fernandez. That part of his job was done. The second part involved him breaking into her apartment, for some reason. If she's still alive, finding her has to be a priority, because it won't be long before the fixer realises his mistake and takes up the chase again.

'Björn and Penelope don't live together,' Anja says.

'Yes, I've worked that out,' he replies.

'People can still love each other – just like you and me.'

'Yes.'

Joona emerges into the strong sunshine. The air is heavy and even more close than it had been earlier.

'Can you give me Björn's address?'

Anja's fingers fly over the key of her computer with tiny clicking sounds.

'Almskog, Pontonjärgatan 47, second floor . . .'

'I'll head over there before . . .'

'Hang on,' Anja says abruptly. 'Not possible . . . Listen to this, I've just double-checked the address . . . There was a fire in the building on Friday.'

'And Björn's flat?'

'That entire floor was destroyed,' she replies.

19

An undulating landscape of ash

Detective Superintendent Joona Linna goes up the steps, stops, and stands absolutely still as he gazes into a black room. The floor, walls and ceiling are badly burned. The smell is still strongly acrid. There's practically nothing left of those internal walls that aren't load-bearing. Black stalactites hang from the ceiling. Charred stumps of posts rise up from an undulating landscape of ash. In places you can see right through between the beams to the rooms below. It's no longer possible to tell which parts of that floor of the building belonged to Björn's flat.

Grey plastic has been hung over the empty windows, blocking off the summer's day and a green building on the other side of the street.

The only reason no one was injured in the fire at Pontonjärgatan 47 was that most people were at work when it broke out.

At five minutes past eleven o'clock the first call was received by the emergency control centre, but even though Kungsholmen fire station is very close to the building, the fire spread so rapidly that four flats were completely destroyed.

Joona thinks about his conversation with fire investigator Hassan Sükür. He used the second-highest level on the National Forensic Laboratory's scale when he explained that their findings indicated that the fire had started in the home of Björn Almskog's eighty-year-old neighbour Lisbet Wirén. She had gone down to

95

the corner shop to exchange a small win on a lottery scratchcard for two new cards, and couldn't remember if she'd left the iron on. The fire had spread rapidly, and all the indications were that it had started in her living room where the remains of an iron and ironing-board were found.

Joona looks round at the charred remains of the apartments on that floor. All that remains of the furniture are a few twisted metal shapes, part of a fridge, a bedstead and a sooty bath.

Joona goes back downstairs. The walls and ceiling of the stairwell have been damaged by smoke. He stops at the police cordon, turns round and looks up towards the blackness again.

As he bends down to pass under the cordon tape he sees that the fire investigators had dropped a few zip-lock bags on the ground – bags used to secure fluids. Joona walks through the green marble hall and out onto the street. He starts to walk towards Police Headquarters as he takes his phone out and calls Hassan Sükür again. Hassan answers at once and lowers the volume of a radio in the background.

'Have you found any traces of flammable liquids?' Joona asks. 'You dropped some zip-lock bags in the stairwell, and I was wondering . . .'

'Look, if someone uses any sort of flammable liquid to start a fire, then obviously that burns first . . .'

'I know, but . . .'

'But I . . . I usually manage to find evidence anyway,' he goes on. 'Because often it runs between cracks in the floorboards, ends up in the insulation or in the cavity between floors.'

'But not this time?' Joona asks as he walks down Hantverkargatan.

'Nothing,' Hassan says.

'But if someone knew where traces of flammable liquids often get found, it would be possible to avoid detection.'

'Of course . . . I'd never make a mistake like that if I was a pyromaniac,' Hassan replies brightly.

'But you're convinced that the iron was the cause of this particular fire?'

'Yes, it was an accident.'

'So you've dropped the investigation?' Joona asks.

20

Penelope feels terror seize hold of her again. It's as if it had only paused for breath before continuing to scream inside her. She wipes the tears from her cheeks and tries to stand up. Cold sweat runs down between her breasts, and down her sides from her armpits. Her body aches and trembles from the effort. Blood seeps through the dirt on her hands.

'We can't stay here,' she whispers, pulling Björn after her.

It's dark in the forest, but night is slowly turning to morning. Together they walk quickly down towards the shore again, but far to the south of the house where the party was.

As far away from their pursuer as they can get.

They're still all too aware that they need help, that they have to get hold of a phone.

The forest opens up gradually towards the water, and they start running again. Between the trees they see another house, perhaps half a kilometre away, maybe less. They can hear a helicopter rumbling somewhere in the distance, moving away.

Björn seems dazed, and whenever she sees him lean on the ground or against a tree she starts to worry that he won't be able to run any more.

A branch creaks somewhere behind them, as if snapped by someone standing on it.

Penelope starts to run through the forest as fast as she can. She can hear Björn breathing heavily behind her.

The trees begin to thin out and she can see the house again, just a hundred metres away. The lights in the window are reflecting off the red paint of a Ford parked outside.

A hare darts off across the moss and undergrowth.

Panting and wary, they emerge onto the gravel drive.

Their calves are stinging with exertion as they stop and look round. They walk up the front steps, open the door to the porch and go in.

'Hello? We need help!' Penelope calls.

The house is warm inside from the sun. Björn is limping, and his bare feet leave bloody prints on the hall floor.

Penelope hurries through the rooms, but the house is empty. The inhabitants probably slept over at their neighbours' after the party, she thinks, and stands at the window and looks out, hidden behind the curtain. She waits for a while, but can't detect any movement in the forest or on the lawn or drive. Maybe their pursuer has finally lost track of them, maybe he's still waiting at the other house. She goes back to the hall, where Björn is sitting on the floor looking at the wounds on his feet.

'We need to find you a pair of shoes,' she says.

He looks up at her with a blank expression, as though he doesn't speak the language.

'This isn't over yet,' she says. 'You need to put something on your feet.'

Björn starts to hunt through the hall cupboard, pulling out flip-flops, wellington boots and old bags.

Avoiding all the windows, Penelope hunts as quickly as she can for a phone, checking the hall table, the briefcase on the sofa, the bowl on the coffee table, and among the keys and paperwork on the kitchen counter.

There's a sound outside and she stops to listen.

Perhaps it was nothing.

The first of the morning sun is shining in through the windows.

Crouching, she hurries into the main bedroom and pulls out the drawers in an old chest. She finds a framed family photograph lying among the underwear. A portrait taken in a studio, a husband and wife and two teenage daughters. The other drawers are empty. Penelope opens the wardrobe, pulls the few items of clothing from their metal hangers, and takes a knitted jumper and a hooded jacket that looks like it would suit a fifteen-year-old.

She hears a tap running in the kitchen and hurries in there. Björn is leaning over the sink drinking from the tap. He's wearing a pair of old trainers on his feet, a couple of sizes too big.

We have to find someone who can help us, she thinks. This is getting ridiculous, there must be people everywhere.

Penelope goes over to Björn and hands him the knitted jumper. Suddenly there's a knock at the door. Björn smiles in surprise, pulls the sweater on and mutters about them finally having a bit of luck. Penelope walks towards the hall, brushing her hair from her face. She's almost there when she sees the silhouette through the frosted glass.

She stops abruptly and looks at the shadow through the glass. Suddenly she can't bring herself to reach out her hand and open the door. She recognises his posture, the shape of his head and shoulders.

The air feels like it's running out.

Slowly she backs away into the kitchen. Her body is twitching, she wants to run, her whole body wants to run. She stares at the glass window, at the indistinct face, the narrow chin. She feels dizzy as she moves backwards, trampling on bags and boots, reaching out to the wall for support, running her fingers across the wallpaper, knocking the hall mirror askew.

Björn stops beside her, he's clutching a broad-bladed kitchen knife in his hand. His cheeks are white, his mouth half open, his eyes staring at the window in the door.

Penelope backs into a table as she sees the door-handle slowly being pushed down. Quickly she goes into the bathroom and turns the taps on, then calls out in a loud voice:

'Come in! The door's open!' Björn starts, his pulse is thudding in his head, he's holding the knife in front of him, ready to defend himself, to attack, as he sees their pursuer slowly let go of the door-handle. The silhouette disappears from the window, and a few seconds later he hears footsteps on the gravel path beside the house. Björn glances to his right. Penelope comes out of the bathroom. He points to the window in the television room and they move away into the kitchen as they hear the man walk across the wooden terrace. Penelope tries to figure out what their pursuer can see, wondering if the angles and light will reveal the shoes scattered across the hall, Björn's bloody footprints on the floor. The wooden terrace creaks again. He's making his way round the house, towards the kitchen window. Björn and Penelope huddle up on the floor, pressing against the wall beneath the window. They try to lie still and breathe quietly. They hear him reach the window, his hands slide across the sill and they realise he's looking into the kitchen.

Penelope notices that the glass door of the oven reflects the window, and in the reflection she sees their pursuer looking around the room. It occurs to her that he'd be looking her right in the eye if he happened to look at the oven door. It won't be long before he realises that they're hiding in there.

The face in the window disappears, they hear footsteps across the terrace again, then along the gravel path leading to the front of the house. When the front door opens Björn walks quickly over to the kitchen door, puts the knife down, turns the key that's sitting in the lock, pushes the door open and rushes out.

Penelope follows him, out into the coolness of the garden. They run across the grass, past the compost heap and into the forest. It's still fairly dark, but the first light of dawn is pressing between the trees. Penelope's fear is chasing her, driving her on, churning up the panic in her chest again. She dodges thick branches, jumps over low bushes and rocks. Just behind her she can hear Björn, breathing hard. And behind him she can sense the other man the whole time, the man who feels like a shadow. He's following them, and she knows he's going to kill them when he finds them. She remembers something she once read somewhere. There was a woman in Rwanda who survived the Hutus' genocide of the Tutsis by hiding in the marshes and running every day, running for all the months the genocide lasted. Her former neighbours and friends came after her with machetes. *We imitated the antelope*, the woman explained in the book. *Those of us who survived in the jungle imitated the antelope's flight from its predators. We ran, we chose unexpected paths, we split up and changed direction to confuse our pursuers.*

Penelope knows that the way that she and Björn are running is completely wrong. They have no plan, no ideas, and that's only going to benefit the man chasing them. There's no guile to the way they're running. They want to go home, they want to find help, they want to call the police. And their pursuer knows all this, he understands that they're going to try to find people who can help them, that they're going to try to find inhabited areas, heading towards the mainland and home.

Penelope tears a hole in her jogging bottoms on a fallen branch. She staggers a few steps but keeps going, only noting the pain as a burning snare round her leg.

They mustn't stop. She can taste blood in her mouth. Björn stumbles through a thicket, they change direction at a fallen tree with a pool of water in the hole left by its roots.

As she runs alongside Björn, her fear suddenly brings to mind an unexpected memory, a memory of a time when she was just as frightened as she is now. It was when she was in Darfur. There was something about people's eyes there, a difference in the eyes of those who had been traumatised, who couldn't go on, and those who were still fighting, who refused to give up. She will never forget the children who came to Kubbum one night with a loaded revolver. She will never forget the fear she felt then.

21

The main offices of the Security Police are on the third floor of the main block at Police Headquarters, with its entrance on Polhemsgatan. The sound of a whistle can be heard from the exercise yard of the prison, which is situated at the top of the same building. The head of the department for security measures is called Verner Zandén. He is a tall man with a pointed nose, dark, jet-black eyes and a very deep voice. He's sitting with his legs wide apart on the chair behind his desk, holding up a calming hand. Weak light is coming in through the little window facing the inner courtyard. The room smells of dust and hot light-bulbs. In this unusually drab room stands a young woman named Saga Bauer. She is a superintendent, and has specialised in counter-terrorism. Saga Bauer is only twenty-five years old, and has green, yellow and red ribbons threaded through her long, blonde hair. She looks like a wood-nymph, always in the middle of a beam of light in a forest glade. She is wearing a large-calibre pistol in a shoulder holster beneath an open hooded jacket with the logo of Narva Boxing Club on it.

'I've led the operation for more than a year,' she pleads. 'I've done the surveillance, I've spent whole nights and weekends . . .'

'But this is something different,' her boss interrupts with a smile.

'Please . . . You can't just ignore me again.'

'Ignore you? A forensics expert from National Crime has been seriously injured, a detective superintendent has been attacked, the apartment could have exploded, and . . .'

'I know all that. I'm on my way there now . . .'

'I've already sent Göran Stone.'

'Göran Stone? I've worked here for three years, and I haven't been allowed to finish a single case. This is my area of expertise. Göran doesn't know anything about . . .'

'He did well in the tunnels.'

Saga swallows hard before replying:

'That was my case too, I found the link between . . .'

Verner says seriously:

'But it got dangerous, and I still consider that I made the right decision.'

She blushes and looks down, composes herself and then says calmly:

'I can do this. It's what I've been trained to . . .'

'Yes, but I've already made my decision.'

He rubs his nose, sighs, then puts his feet up on the waste-paper basket under the desk.

'You know I'm not here because of some equal opportunities programme,' Saga says slowly. 'I'm not part of any quota, I came top of my group in all the tests, I was the best ever at sniper fire, I've investigated two hundred and ten different . . .'

'I'm just worried about you,' he says weakly, looking into her clear blue eyes.

'I'm not a doll, I'm not some princess or fairy.'

'But you're so . . . so . . .'

Verner turns bright red and then he holds his hands up helplessly.

'Okay, what the hell, you can be in charge of the preliminary investigation, but Göran Stone is part of the team, so he can keep an eye on you.'

'Thanks,' she says with a relieved smile.

'This isn't a game, remember that,' he says in his deep voice. 'Penelope Fernandez's sister is dead, executed, and she herself is missing . . .'

'And I've noticed an increase in activity among a number of

extreme left-wing groups,' Saga says. 'We're investigating whether the Revolutionary Front are behind the theft of explosives in Vaxholm.'

'Obviously the most important thing is to find out if there's any immediate threat,' Verner explains.

'Right now there's a lot of radicalisation going on,' she says, a little too keenly. 'I've just been in touch with Dante Larsson at the Military Intelligence and Security Service, and he says they're expecting acts of sabotage during the summer.'

'But for the time being we're concentrating on Penelope Fernandez,' Verner smiles.

'Of course,' Saga says quickly. 'Of course.'

'The forensic examination is a collaboration with National Crime, but apart from that they're to be kept out of it.'

Saga Bauer nods and waits a few moments before asking:

'Am I going to be allowed to conclude this investigation? It's very important to me, so that . . .'

'As long as you're still sitting in the saddle,' he interrupts. 'But we have no idea where this is going to end. We don't even know where it starts.'

22

Incomprehensible

On Rekylgatan in Västerås there's a very long, and very white, housing block. The people who live there have easy access to Lillhags School, the football pitch and tennis courts.

Out of door number 11 comes a young man carrying a motorcycle helmet in one hand. His name is Stefan Bergkvist, and he's almost seventeen years old, he attends the technical college and lives with his mum and her partner.

He has long fair hair and a silver ring in his bottom lip, and he's wearing a black T-shirt and baggy jeans whose cuffs have been trodden to pieces.

Without any hurry he walks down to the car park, hangs the helmet on the handlebars of his motocross bike and rides slowly down onto the path around the building, carries on beside the double railway track, under the Norrleden viaduct, into the big industrial estate and stops beside a wooden shack covered with blue and silver graffiti.

Stefan and his friends usually meet here to race on the motocross circuit they've made along the railway embankment, riding up and down the various tracks before returning to Terminalvägen.

They started coming here four years ago when they found the keys to the shack hidden on a nail at the back among the thistles. The building had stood untouched for almost ten years.

For some reason it had been left behind after a large building project.

Stefan gets off his bike, unlocks the padlock, lowers the steel bar and opens the wooden door. He goes inside the shack, looks at the time on his phone, and sees that his mum's called.

He doesn't notice that he's being watched by a man of about sixty wearing a grey suede jacket and light-brown shoes. The man is standing behind a skip by the low industrial building on the other side of the railway line.

Stefan goes over to the little kitchen corner, picks up the packet of crisps from the sink, tips the last few crumbs into his hand and eats them.

The light inside the shack comes from two dirty windows with bars across them.

Stefan waits for his friends, leafing through one of the old magazines that were left on top of the map cabinet, a copy of a soft porn magazine with the words 'Imagine being licked and getting paid for it!' on the front beside a young woman with bare breasts.

The man in the suede jacket calmly leaves his hiding place, passes the gantry holding the overhead power lines and crosses the brown embankment with its double tracks. He goes over to Stefan's motorcycle, folds the support away and wheels it over to the door of the shack.

The man looks round, then leans the motorbike on the ground and pushes it with his foot so that it's wedged tightly against the door. He opens the fuel tank and lets the petrol run out beneath the shack.

Stefan goes on looking through the old magazine, looking at faded photographs of women taken in a prison setting. One blonde woman is sitting in a cell with her legs wide apart, showing her genitals to a prison guard. Stefan stares at the picture, then jumps when he thinks he hears a rustling sound from outside. He listens, thinks he can hear footsteps and quickly closes the magazine.

The man in the suede jacket has pulled out the red petrol can the boys had hidden among the bushes behind the shack, and is emptying it around the shack. Only when he reaches the back wall does he hear the first shouts from inside. The boy is banging on the door, trying to push it open. His footsteps thud across the floor, and his worried face appears at one of the dirty windows.

'Open the door, this isn't funny,' he shouts loudly.

The man in the suede jacket carries on around the shack, empties the last of the petrol, then puts the can down.

'What are you doing?' the boy cries.

He throws himself at the door, trying to kick it open, but it won't budge. He calls his mum, but her phone is switched off. His heart is beating hard as he tries to look through the grey-streaked windows, moving from one to the other.

'Are you mad?'

When he suddenly notices the acrid smell of petrol, fear rises up inside him and his stomach clenches.

'Hello?' he shouts in a frightened voice. 'I know you're still there!'

The man pulls a box of matches from his pocket.

'What do you want? Please, just tell me what you want . . .'

'It isn't your fault, but a nightmare needs to be reaped,' the man says without raising his voice, and lights a match.

'Let me out!' the boy screams.

The man drops the match in the wet grass. There's a sucking sound, like a big sail suddenly filling with air. Pale blue flames fly up with such ferocity that the man is forced to take several steps back. The boy cries for help. The flames spread to surround the shack. The man keeps backing away as he feels the heat on his face and hears the terrified screams.

The shack is ablaze in a matter of seconds, and the glass shatters behind the bars in the heat.

The boy shrieks when the flames set light to his hair.

The man walks across the railway lines, stands beside the industrial building and watches as the old shack burns like a torch.

A few minutes later a goods train approaches from the north. It comes rolling slowly down the track, and with a scraping, rattling sound the row of brown wagons passes the dancing flames as the man in the suede jacket vanishes along Stenbygatan.

23

Forensics

Even though it's the weekend the head of the National Crime Unit, Carlos Eliasson, is in his office. His gradually increasing introversion means that he's becoming more and more averse to spontaneous visits. The door is closed and he's got the 'engaged' light on. Joona knocks and opens the door in the same gesture.

'I need to know if the marine police find anything,' he says.

Carlos puts his book down on the desk and replies calmly:

'You and Erixon were attacked. That's a traumatic experience and you need to look after yourselves.'

'We will,' Joona says.

'The helicopter search has been concluded.'

Joona stiffens.

'Concluded? How large an area did . . .'

'I don't know,' Carlos interrupts.

'Who's in charge of the operation?'

'It's nothing to do with National Crime,' Carlos explains. 'The marine police are . . .'

'But it would be very useful to us to know if we're investigating one or three murders,' Joona says sharply.

'Joona, right now you're not investigating anything. I've discussed the matter with Jens Svanehjälm. We're putting

108

together a joint team with the Security Police. Petter Näslund will represent National Crime, Tommy Kofoed the National Homicide Commission, and . . .'

'What's my role?'

'Take a week off.'

'No.'

'Then you can go out to Police Academy and give some lectures.'

'No.'

'Don't be stubborn,' Carlos says. 'That obstinacy of yours isn't as charming as . . .'

'I don't give a damn what you think,' Joona says. 'Penelope . . .'

'You don't give a damn about me,' Carlos says in astonishment. 'I'm head of . . .'

'Penelope Fernandez and Björn Almskog could still be alive,' Joona goes on in a hard voice. 'His flat has been burned out and hers would have been if I hadn't got there in time. I think the murderer is looking for something that they've got, I think he tried to get Viola to talk before he drowned her . . .'

'Thank you very much,' Carlos interrupts, raising his voice. 'Thank you for your interesting ideas, but we've . . . No, let me finish. I know you have trouble accepting this, Joona, but you're not the only police officer in the country. And most of the others are actually very good, you know.'

'Agreed,' Joona says slowly, with a degree of sharpness in his voice. 'And you ought to take care of them, Carlos.'

Joona looks at the brown stains on his cuffs made by Erixon's blood.

'What do you mean?'

'I've encountered the perpetrator, and I think we need to be prepared for police fatalities in this case.'

'You were taken by surprise, I understand it was unpleasant . . .'

'Okay,' Joona says harshly.

'Tommy Kofoed is in charge of the crime scene investigation, and I'll call Britta at Police Academy and tell her you'll be calling in today, and will be a guest-lecturer next week,' Carlos says.

*　*　*

The heat hits Joona when he emerges from Police Headquarters. As he takes his jacket off he realises that someone is approaching him from behind, stepping out between the parked cars in the street from the shadows of the park. He turns round and sees that it's Penelope's mother, Claudia Fernandez.

'Joona Linna,' she says in a tense voice.

'Claudia, how are you?' he asks seriously.

She just shakes her head. Her eyes are bloodshot and her face looks anguished.

'Find her, you have to find my little girl,' she says, and hands him a thick envelope.

Joona opens the envelope and sees that it's full of banknotes. He tries to give it back, but she won't take it.

'Please, take the money. It's all I've got,' she says. 'But I can get more, I'll sell the house, as long as you find her.'

'Claudia, I can't take your money,' he says.

Her tormented face crumples:

'Please . . .'

'We're already doing everything we can.'

Joona gives the envelope back to Claudia, and she holds it stiffly in her hand, then mumbles that she'll go home and wait by the phone. Then she stops him and tries to explain again:

'I told her not to come to mine . . . she's never going to call me.'

'You had an argument, Claudia, but that's not the end of the world.'

'But how could I say that? Can you imagine?' she asks, and raps her knuckles against her forehead. 'Who says a thing like that to their own child?'

'It's so easy to just . . .'

Joona's voice tails off, he feels his back sweating and forces himself to suppress the fragments of memory that are starting to stir.

'I can't bear it,' Claudia says quietly.

Joona takes hold of Claudia's hands, and tells her he's doing all he can.

'You have to get my daughter back,' she whispers.

He nods, and they go their separate ways. Joona hurries down

Bergsgatan, and peers up at the sky as he walks to his car. It's sunny but a little hazy, and still very close. Last summer he was sitting in the hospital holding his mother's hand. As usual, they spoke Finnish to each other. He told her they'd go to Karelia together as soon as she felt better. She was born there, in a little village which, unlike so many others, wasn't burned down by the Russians during the Second World War. His mum had said it would be better if he went to Karelia with one of the people who were waiting for him.

Joona buys a bottle of Pellegrino from Il Caffè and drinks it before getting in the warm car. The steering wheel is hot and the seat burns his back. Instead of driving to Police Academy, he drives back to Sankt Paulsgatan 3, the flat of the missing Penelope Fernandez. He thinks about the man he encountered in the flat. There had been a remarkable speed and precision to his movements, as if the knife itself had been alive.

Blue and white tape has been strung up across the door, with the words 'Police' and 'No entry' on it.

Joona shows his ID to the uniformed officer on guard, and shakes his hand. They've met before, but never worked together.

'Hot today,' Joona says.

'Just a bit,' the police officer says.

'How many forensics people have we got here?' he asks, nodding towards the stairwell.

'One of ours and three from the Security Police,' the officer says brightly. 'They want to get hold of DNA as quickly as possible.'

'They won't find any,' Joona says, almost to himself as he starts to walk towards the stairs.

An older police officer, Melker Janos, is standing outside the door to the flat on the third floor. Joona remembers him from his training as a stressed and unpleasant senior officer. Back then Melker's career was on the up, but an acrimonious divorce and sporadic alcohol abuse gradually saw him demoted to a beat officer again. When he sees Joona he greets him curtly and irritably, then opens the door for him with a sarcastic servile gesture.

'Thanks,' Joona says, without expecting any response.

Inside the door he finds Tommy Kofoed, the forensics coordinator from the National Homicide Commission. Kofoed is scuttling about sullenly. He reaches no higher than Joona's chest. When their eyes meet he opens his mouth in an almost childishly happy grin.

'Joona, great to see you. I thought you were going off to Police Academy.'

'I got the directions wrong.'

'Good.'

'Have you found anything?' Joona asks.

'We're secured all the shoeprints from the hall,' he says.

'Yes, they probably match my shoes,' Joona says as he shakes Kofoed's hand.

'And the attacker's,' Kofoed says with an even broader smile. 'We've got four prints. He moved in a bloody weird way, didn't he?'

'Yes,' Joona replies curtly.

There are protective mats laid out in the hall so that any evidence isn't contaminated before it's been secured. There's a camera on a stand with its lens pointing at the floor. A sturdy lamp with an aluminium shade is lying in the corner with its cord wrapped round it. The forensics team have looked for invisible shoeprints by shining light almost parallel to the floor. Then they've secured the prints electrostatically and identified the perpetrator's steps through the hall from the kitchen.

Joona can't help thinking that their precision is a waste of effort, seeing as the attacker's shoes, gloves and clothes have almost certainly already been destroyed and burned.

'How exactly did he run through here?' Kofoed asks, pointing at the marks. 'There, there . . . and then across to there, then there's nothing until here and here.'

'You've missed one,' Joona smiles.

'Like hell we have.'

'There,' Joona points.

'Where?'

'On the wall.'

'Bloody hell.'

Some seventy centimetres above the floor there's a faint shoeprint on the pale grey wallpaper. Tommy Kofoed calls one of his colleagues and asks him to take a gelatine print.

'Is it okay to walk on the floor now?' Joona asks.

'As long as you don't walk on the walls,' Kofoed grunts.

24

The object

In the kitchen stands a man in jeans and a pale brown blazer with leather patches on the elbows. He strokes his blond moustache as he talks loudly and points at the microwave oven. Joona walks in and watches as a forensics officer in a protective mask and gloves packs the buckled aerosol can in a paper bag, folds it over twice, then tapes and labels the bag.

'You're Joona Linna, aren't you?' the man with the blond moustache says. 'If you're as good as everyone says, you ought to come over to us.'

They shake hands.

'Göran Stone, Security Police,' the man says proudly.

'Are you in charge of the preliminary investigation?'

'Yes, I am . . . well, formally Saga Bauer is – for the sake of the statistics,' he grins.

'I've met Saga Bauer,' Joona says. 'She seems capable of . . .'

'Doesn't she just?' Göran Stone says, then bursts out laughing before covering his mouth.

Joona looks out of the window, thinking about the boat that was found adrift, and trying to figure out who the murderer had been tasked with liquidating. He is aware that the investigation is at far too early a stage to be able to draw any conclusions, but at the same time it's always useful to consider different hypotheses. The only person the perpetrator was almost certainly after was Penelope, Joona thinks. And the only person he probably didn't mean to kill was Viola, seeing as he couldn't have known that she was going to be on the boat – her presence was the result of an unfortunate quirk of fate, Joona tells himself as he leaves the kitchen and walks over to the bedroom.

The bed is neatly made, the cream-coloured bedspread smooth. Saga Bauer from the Security Police is standing in front of a laptop that she's placed on the windowsill as she talks on her phone. Joona remembers her from a seminar about counter-terrorism.

Joona sits down on the bed and tries to gather his thoughts again. He imagines Viola and Penelope standing in front of him, then puts Penelope's boyfriend Björn next to them. They can't all have been on the boat when Viola was murdered, he tells himself. Because then the perpetrator wouldn't have made his mistake. If he had got on board when they were out at sea he would have murdered all three, put them on the right beds and sunk the boat. So his mistake means that Penelope can't have been on the boat. Which means that they must have moored somewhere.

Joona gets up again, leaves the bedroom and walks into the living room. He looks at the wall-mounted television, the red sofa, the modern table with piles of left-wing magazines and newspapers. He walks over to the bookcase covering a whole wall, stops, and thinks about the pinched cables in the machine room which would have arced within a matter of minutes, igniting the cushion which had been stuffed next to the pipe from the fuel tank. But the boat didn't sink. The engine can't have been running for long enough.

There's no such thing as coincidence any more.

Björn's flat was destroyed by fire, Viola was murdered the same day, and if the boat hadn't been abandoned the fuel tank would have exploded.

Then the murderer attempted to set off a gas explosion in Penelope's flat.

Björn's flat, the boat, Penelope's flat.

He's after something that Björn and Penelope have got. He started by searching through Björn's apartment, and when he didn't find what he was looking for he burned it, then when he'd searched the boat and not found anything he tried to force Viola to talk, and when she couldn't give him any answers he went to Penelope's flat.

Joona helps himself to a pair of protective gloves from a box, then goes back to the bookcase and looks at the thin layer of dust in front of the books. He notes that there's no dust in front of some of the spines, suggesting that someone has looked at those books at some point in the past few weeks.

'I don't want you here,' Saga Bauer says behind him. 'This is my investigation.'

'I'll go in a minute, I just need to find something first,' Joona replies quietly.

'Five minutes,' she says.

He turns round.

'Can you photograph the books?'

'Already done,' she says curtly.

'From a certain angle you can see the dust,' he goes on, unconcerned.

She realises what he means but her expression doesn't change, she just borrows a camera from one of the forensics officers, photographs all the shelves she can reach, then tells him he can look at the books on the bottom five shelves.

Joona pulls out Karl Marx's *Capital*, leafs through it and notices that it's full of underlined passages and notes in the margins. He peers into the gap between the books but can't see anything. He puts the book back. He moves on to a biography of Ulrike Meinhof, and worn anthology entitled *Key Texts of Political Feminism*, and the collected works of Bertolt Brecht.

On the second shelf up he suddenly spots three books that have evidently been pulled out from the bookcase recently.

There's no dust in front of them.

The Strategy of Antelopes, a book about the genocide in Rwanda, *Cien Sonetos de Amor*, a collection of Pablo Neruda's poetry, and *The Intellectual Roots of Swedish Eugenics*.

Joona flicks through them one at a time, and when he reaches the last one a photograph falls out. He picks it up from the floor. It's a black and white photograph of a serious-looking girl with tightly plaited hair. He recognises Claudia Fernandez at once. She can't be more than fifteen in the photograph, and is strikingly like her daughters.

But who would put a photograph of their mother in a book about eugenics? he asks himself, and turns the picture over.

On the back of the photograph someone has written *No estés lejos de mí un solo día* in pencil.

It's clearly a line from a poem: *Don't go far off, not even for a day.*

Joona pulls out the volume of Neruda's poetry again, leafs through it and soon finds the whole verse: *No estés lejos de mí un solo día, porque cómo, porque, no sé decirlo, es largo el día, y te estaré esperando como en las estaciones cuando en alguna parte se durmieron los trenes.*

This is where the photograph should have been, in the book by Neruda.

This is the right place, Joona thinks.

But if the murderer searched the books for something, the picture could have fallen out.

He stood here, Joona thinks, and looked at the dust on the shelves, just like me, and quickly leafed through the books that have been pulled out in the past few weeks. Suddenly the murderer notices that a photograph has fallen out onto the floor, and puts it back, but in the wrong book.

Joona closes his eyes.

That must be what happened, he thinks.

The fixer searched these books.

If he knew what he was looking for, that means the object can fit between the pages of a book.

So what could it be?

A letter, a will, a photograph, a confession. Possibly even a CD or DVD, a memory chip or SIM-card.

117

25

The child on the stairs

Joona leaves the living room and looks into the bathroom, which is in the process of being photographed in detail. He carries on to the hall and out through the open front door to the landing, and stops in front of the mesh covering the lift-shaft.

The name Nilsson is on the door beside the lift. He raises his hand and knocks, then waits. After a while he hears footsteps inside. A rotund woman in her sixties opens the door slightly and peers out.

'Yes?'

'Hello, my name is Joona Linna, I'm a detective superintendent, and I . . .'

'I've already said, I didn't see his face,' she interrupts.

'Have the police already spoken to you? I didn't know that.'

She opens the door and two cats lying on the telephone table jump down and disappear into the flat.

'He was wearing a Dracula mask,' the woman says impatiently, as if she's already explained this numerous times.

'Who?'

'Who,' she mutters, and walks into the flat.

She returns shortly afterwards with a yellowing newspaper cutting.

Joona glances at the article, which is twenty years old, about a flasher who dressed up as Dracula when he exposed himself to women on Södermalm.

'He didn't have a stitch on down below . . .'

'I was actually . . .'

'Not that I looked,' she goes on. 'But I've already told your people all about it.'

Joona looks at her and smiles.

'I was actually thinking about something completely different.'

The woman opens her eyes wide.

'Then why didn't you say so at once?'

'I was wondering if you know Penelope Fernandez, your neighbour, who . . .'

'She's like a granddaughter to me,' the woman interrupts. 'Such a sweet girl, so kind and pretty and . . .'

She stops abruptly, then asks quietly:

'Is she dead?'

'Why do you ask?'

'Because the police have been here asking horrid questions,' she says.

'I was just wondering if she'd had any unusual visitors in the past few days.'

'Just because I'm old doesn't mean I poke my nose into other people's business and keep charts of what they get up to.'

'No, but I was thinking that you might just have happened to notice something.'

'Well, I haven't.'

'Has anything else out of the ordinary happened?'

'Definitely not. She's a very clever, well-behaved girl.'

Joona thanks her for her time and says that he may come back if he has further questions, then stands aside so the woman can close the door.

There are no other flats on the third floor. He starts to walk up the stairs to the next floor. Halfway up he sees a child sitting on one of the steps. It looks like an eight-year-old boy: short hair, dressed in jeans and a washed-out Helly Hansen T-shirt, and clutching a plastic bag with a Ramlösa water-bottle with its label almost rubbed off, and half a loaf of bread.

Joona stops in front of the child, who looks up at him warily.

'Hello,' he says. 'What's your name?'

'Mia.'

'Mine's Joona.'

He notices the dirt on the girl's thin neck.

'Have you got a gun?' she asks.

'Why do you ask?'

'You told Ella that you're a policeman.'

'That's right – I'm a superintendent.'

'Have you got a gun?'

'Yes, I have,' Joona says in a neutral voice. 'Do you want to practise shooting it?'

The child looks at him in astonishment.

'You're kidding?'

'Yeah,' Joona says with a smile.

The child laughs.

'Why are you sitting on the stairs?' he asks.

'I like it, you get to hear stuff.'

Joona sits down beside the child.

'What sort of stuff have you heard?' he asks calmly.

'I just heard that you're a policeman, and I heard Ella lie to you.'

'What did she lie to me about?'

'When she said she likes Penelope,' Mia says.

'Doesn't she?'

'She puts cat poo through her letterbox.'

'Why does she do that?'

The girl shrugs and fiddles with the plastic bag.

'I don't know.'

'What do you think of Penelope?'

'She usually says hello.'

'But you don't really know her?'

'No.'

Joona looks round.

'Do you live on the stairs?'

The girl tries not to smile.

'No, I live on the first floor with my mum.'

'But you hang out on the stairs.'

Mia shrugs again.

'Most of the time.'

'Do you sleep here?'

The girl picks at the label on the bottle and says quickly:

'Sometimes.'

'On Friday,' Joona says slowly, 'very early in the morning, Penelope left her flat. She took a taxi.'

'She was really unlucky,' the child says quickly. 'She missed Björn by just a few seconds, he arrived just after she left. I told him she'd just gone.'

'What did he say?'

'That it didn't matter, because he was only going to collect something.'

'Collect something?'

Mia nods.

'He usually lets me borrow his phone to play games, but he didn't have time that visit, he just went into the flat and came back out again straight away, then he locked the door and ran down the stairs.'

'Did you see what it was that he collected?'

'No.'

'What happened after that?'

'Nothing, I went to school at quarter to nine.'

'What about after school, later that day? Did anything happen then?'

Mia shrugged once more.

'Mum was out, so I stayed at home, had some macaroni and watched TV.'

'How about yesterday?'

'She was gone yesterday too, so I was home.'

'So you didn't see anyone coming and going?'

'No.'

Joona pulls out his card and writes a phone number on it.

'Take this, Mia,' he says. 'These are two really good phone numbers. One of them's mine.'

He points at the number printed on the card beside the police logo.

'Call me if you ever need help, if anyone's mean to you. And the other number, the one I've just written, 0200-230230, that's the number for Childline. You can call them any time and talk about whatever you like.'

'Okay,' Mia says, taking the card.

'And don't throw it away as soon as I've gone,' Joona says. 'Because even if you don't want to call now, you might want to another time.'

'Björn was holding his hand like this when he left,' Mia says, holding her hand to her stomach.

'As if he had tummy-ache?'

'Yes.'

26

The palm of a hand

Joona knocks on the other doors in the building but doesn't learn anything else, beyond the fact that Penelope is a fairly quiet, almost shy neighbour who took part in annual cleaning days and meetings of the residents' committee, but not much else. When he's finished he walks slowly back down the stairs to the third floor.

The door to Penelope's flat is open. One of the Security Police's forensics experts has just dismantled the lock and placed it in a plastic bag.

Joona goes in and stands in the background, watching the forensic examination. He's always liked seeing the experts at work – how systematically they photograph everything, securing all the evidence and making careful notes about each part of the process. A crime scene investigation destroys evidence as it proceeds: things get contaminated as the layers are stripped back. The important thing is to wreck the crime scene in the correct order, so that no evidence or vital clues are lost.

Joona looks around at Penelope Fernandez's neat flat. What was Björn Almskog doing here? He showed up as soon as Penelope had left. It feels almost as if he'd been hiding outside the building waiting for her to go.

It could just be a coincidence, but it could also be because he didn't want to see her.

Björn hurried inside, bumped into the little girl sitting on the stairs, didn't have time to talk to her, explained that he was going to collect something, and was only in the flat for a few minutes.

Presumably he did collect something, like he told the child. Perhaps he'd hidden the key to the boat there, or something else he could slip in his pocket.

But perhaps he'd left something else there. What if he just needed to look at something, check some information, a phone number?

Joona goes into the kitchen and looks round.

'You've checked the fridge?'

A young man with a full beard looks at him.

'Hungry?' he asks in a broad Dalarna accent.

'It's a good place to hide things,' Joona says drily.

'We haven't got there yet,' the man says.

Joona goes back to the living room and notes that Saga is still talking into a Dictaphone in one corner of the room.

Tommy Kofoed presses a strip of tape containing fibres onto transparent film then looks up.

'Have you found anything unexpected?' Joona asks.

'Unexpected? Well, there was a shoeprint on the wall . . .'

'Anything else?'

'The important information usually comes from the National Forensics Lab in Linköping.'

'So we should have results within a week?' Joona asks.

'If we nag the hell out of them,' he replies, then shrugs his shoulders. 'I'm just about to take a look at the doorframe where the knife went in, to make an impression of the blade.'

'Don't bother,' Joona mutters.

Kofoed interprets this as a joke and laughs, then turns serious.

'Did you get a glimpse of the knife? Steel?'

'No, the blade was lighter, maybe tungsten carbide – some people prefer that. But none of it will get us anywhere.'

'What?'

'This whole crime scene investigation,' Joona replies. 'We won't manage to find any DNA or fingerprints that will help identify the perpetrator.'

'So what should we be doing?'

'I think the perpetrator came here to look for something, and I think he was interrupted before he had time to find it.'

'You mean whatever he was looking for is still here?' Kofoed asks.

'It's possible,' Joona replies.

'But you've got no idea what it is?'

'Small enough to fit inside a book.'

Joona's granite-grey eyes stare into Kofoed's brown eyes for a moment. Göran Stone from the Security Police is photographing both sides of the bathroom door, the frame, sill and hinges. Then he sits down on the floor to photograph the white ceiling. Joona is about to open the living room door to ask him to take some pictures of the journals on the coffee table when a camera flash goes off. The glare takes him by surprise and he has to stop, as his vision flares. Four white dots slide across his vision, then an oily pale blue hand. Joona looks round; he can't understand where the hand came from.

'Göran,' Joona calls loudly through the glass door to the hall. 'Take another picture!'

Everyone in the flat stops. The man from Dalarna looks out from the kitchen, and the man by the front door looks round at Joona with interest. Tommy Kofoed takes his breathing mask off and scratches his neck. Göran Stone is still sitting on the floor with a curious look on his face.

'Just like you did a few moments ago,' Joona says, pointing. 'Take another picture of the bathroom ceiling.'

Göran Stone shrugs, raises his camera and takes another photograph of the ceiling. The flash goes off, and Joona feels his pupils contract as his eyes start to water. He closes his eyes and once again sees a black square. He realises it's the glass panel in the door. Because of the flash he's seeing it in negative.

In the middle of the square are four white dots, and beside them a pale blue hand.

He knew he'd seen it.

Joona blinks, his vision returns to normal and he walks straight over to the glass door. The remnants of four pieces of tape form an empty rectangle, and there's a handprint on the glass beside them.

Tommy Kofoed comes over to stand next to Joona.

'A handprint,' he says.

'Can you get it?' Joona says.

'Göran,' Kofoed says. 'We need a picture of this.'

Göran Stone gets up from the floor and hums to himself and he brings his camera over and looks at the handprint.

'Yes, someone's been a bit messy here,' he says happily, and takes four pictures.

He moves out of the way and waits as Tommy Kofoed treats the print with cyanoacrylate to bind the salts and moisture, then Basic Yellow 40.

Göran waits a few seconds, then takes two more pictures.

'Now we've got you,' Kofoed whispers to the print, as he carefully lifts it off onto transparent plastic.

'Can you check it at once?' Joona asks.

Tommy Kofoed takes the print out into the kitchen. Joona stays where he is, staring at the four pieces of tape on the pane of glass. Behind one of them is the torn-off corner of a sheet of paper. Whoever left the handprint didn't have time to remove the tape carefully, just tugged the paper from the door leaving one corner behind.

Joona looks more closely at the torn-off corner. He sees straight away that it isn't ordinary paper. It's photographic printing paper, used for colour photographs.

A photograph which had been stuck on the glass door to be looked at and studied. And then there's a sudden rush, there's no time to remove the photograph carefully – instead someone rushed up to the door, put their hand on the glass to steady it, and pulled the photograph from the tape.

'Björn,' Joona says quietly.

This photograph must be what Björn came to collect. He wasn't holding his hand to his stomach because it hurt, but because he was hiding a photograph under his jacket.

Joona moves his head slightly so he can see the impression of the handprint in the light, the narrow lines of the palm.

A human being's papillary lines never change, never age. And, unlike DNA, even identical twins don't share the same fingerprints.

Joona hears quick footsteps behind him and turns round.

'Okay, that's more than fucking enough!' Saga Bauer yells. 'This is my investigation. Christ, you're not even supposed to be here!'

'I just wanted . . .'

'Shut up!' she snaps. 'I've just spoken to Petter Näslund. You're nothing to do with this, you're not supposed to be here – you're not allowed to be here!'

'I know, I'm about to go,' he says, and looks back at the pane of glass.

'Fucking Joona Linna,' she says slowly. 'You can't just show up here and pick at little bits of tape . . .'

'There was a photograph stuck to the glass,' he replies calmly. 'Someone tore it off, they leaned over this chair, rested their hand on the glass, and pulled it off.'

She looks at him reluctantly and he notices a white scar running across her left eyebrow.

'I'm perfectly capable of running this investigation,' she says firmly.

'The handprint is probably Björn Almskog's,' Joona says, and starts to walk to the kitchen.

'Wrong way, Joona.'

He ignores her and walks into the kitchen.

'This is my investigation,' she shouts.

The forensics team have set up a small work-station in the middle of the floor. Two chairs and a table with a computer, scanner and printer. Tommy Kofoed is standing behind Göran Stone, who has connected his camera to the computer. They've imported the handprint and are running an initial test for a fingerprint match.

Saga follows Joona.

'What have you got?' Joona asks, without bothering about Saga.

'Don't talk to Joona,' she says sharply.

Tommy Kofoed looks up.

'Don't be silly, Saga,' he says, then turns to Joona. 'No luck this time, the print's from Björn Almskog, Penelope's boyfriend.'

'He's in the database of suspects,' Göran Stone says.

'What was he suspected of?' Joona asks.

'Violent riot and threatening a public servant,' Göran replies.

'They're the worst,' Kofoed jokes. 'He probably took part in a march.'

'Funny,' Göran says sourly. 'Not everyone in the force is quite so entertained by the rioting and sabotage of the extreme left-wing, and . . .'

'Speak for yourself,' Kofoed interrupts.

'The rescue operation speaks for itself,' Göran grins.

'What?' Joona asks. 'What do you mean? I haven't had time to keep up with the operation – what's happened?'

27

Carlos Eliasson, head of the National Crime Unit, jumps, and spills a load of fish-food into the aquarium when Joona Linna throws his door open.

'Why is there no ground-search?' he asks in a hard voice. 'There are two lives at stake, and we can't get hold of any boats.'

'The marine police have made their own evaluation, you know that perfectly well,' Carlos replies. 'They've searched the entire area by helicopter and everyone agrees that Penelope Fernandez and Björn Almskog are either dead or they don't want to be found . . . and neither of those options suggests that there's any urgency to conduct a ground-search.'

'They've got something the killer wants, and I honestly believe . . .'

'There's no point guessing . . . We don't know what happened, Joona. The Security Police seem to think these youngsters have gone underground, they may well be sitting on the train to Amsterdam by . . .'

'Stop that,' Joona interrupts sharply. 'You can't rely on the Security Police when it comes to . . .'

'This is their case.'

'Why? Why is it their case? Björn Almskog was once suspected of taking part in a riot. That doesn't mean anything. Anything at all.'

'I spoke to Verner Zandén, and he was quick to point out that Penelope Fernandez has links to extreme left-wing groups.'

'Maybe, but I'm convinced that this murder is about something else entirely,' Joona says stubbornly.

'Of course you are! Of course you're convinced,' Carlos shouts.

'I don't know what, but the person I encountered in Penelope's flat was a professional killer, not just . . .'

'The Security Police seem to think that Penelope and Björn were planning an attack.'

'Is Penelope Fernandez supposed to be a terrorist now?' Joona asks in astonishment. 'Have you read any of her articles? She's a pacifist, and always condemns . . .'

'Yesterday,' Carlos says, cutting him off. 'Yesterday someone from the Brigade was arrested by the Security Police, just as he was on his way into her flat.'

'I don't even know what the Brigade is.'

'A militant left-wing organisation . . . They're loosely connected to Anti-Fascist Action and the Revolutionary Front, but are independent . . . They're close to the Red Army Faction ideologically, and they want to become as operative as Mossad.'

'That doesn't make sense,' Joona says.

'You don't want it to make sense, which is a different matter,' Carlos says. 'There'll be a ground-search in the fullness of time, and we'll check the currents and see how the boat drifted so that we can start dragging and maybe send some divers down.'

'Good,' Joona says.

'What remains is trying to figure out why they were killed . . . or why and where they're hiding.'

Joona opens the door to the corridor, but stops and turns back towards Carlos again.

'What happened to the guy from the Brigade who tried to get into Penelope's flat?'

'He was released,' Carlos replies.

'Did they find out what he was doing there?' Joona asks.

'He was just visiting.'

'Visiting,' Joona sighs. 'That's all the Security Police managed to get?'

'You're not to investigate the Brigade,' Carlos says with sudden anxiety in his voice. 'I hope that's understood?'

Joona leaves the room and takes his phone out as soon as he's in the corridor. He hears Carlos shout that that's an order, and that he doesn't have permission to trespass on Security Police territory. As Joona walks away he looks up Nathan Pollock's number and calls him.

'Pollock,' Nathan says when he answers.

'What do you know about the Brigade?' Joona says as the lift doors open.

'The Security Police have spent several years trying to infiltrate and map the militant left-wing groups in Stockholm, Gothenburg and Malmö. I don't know if the Brigade are particularly dangerous, but the Security Police seem to believe that they've got weapons and explosives. Several of the members were in youth custody centres and have previous convictions for violent offences.'

The lift glides downwards.

'I understand that the Security Police arrested someone with direct links to the Brigade outside Penelope Fernandez's flat.'

'His name's Daniel Marklund, he's part of the inner circle,' Nathan replies.

'What do you know about him?'

'Not much,' Pollock replies. 'He's got a suspended sentence for vandalism and unlawful hacking.'

'What was he doing at Penelope's?' Joona asks.

The lift stops and the doors open.

'He was unarmed,' Nathan says. 'Demanded legal representation at the start of the preliminary interview, refused to answer any questions at all and was released the same day.'

'So they don't know anything?'

'No.'

'Where can I get hold of him?' Joona asks.

'He's got no home address,' Nathan explains. 'According to the Security Police he lives with the other key members of the group in the Brigade's premises at Zinkensdamm.'

28

The Brigade

As Joona Linna strides towards the car park beneath Rådhusparken he finds himself thinking about Disa, and a sudden longing for her courses through him. He wishes he could touch her slender arms, feel the scent of her soft hair. It makes him feel oddly calm to hear her talk about her archaeological finds, about fragments of bone with no connection to any crime, about the remains of people who lived their lives so long ago.

Joona thinks to himself that he must talk to Disa, that he's been far too busy for far too long. He carries on into the garage and is walking between the parked cars when he detects movement behind one of the concrete pillars. There's someone waiting next to his Volvo. He can see a figure, almost hidden by a van. There's no sound but the roar of the large ventilation units.

'That was quick,' Joona calls.

'Teleport,' Pollock replies.

Joona stops and closes his eyes, and presses his temple with one finger.

'Headache?' Pollock asks.

'I haven't had much time for sleep.'

They get in the car and close the doors. Joona turns the key in the ignition and an Astor Piazzolla tango starts to play from the speakers. Pollock turns the volume up slightly: it sounds like two violins are circling each other.

'Obviously you know you haven't heard any of this from me,' Nathan says.

'Of course,' Joona replies.

'I've just found out that the Security Police are planning to use Daniel Marklund's attempt to get into Penelope's flat as a pretext for mounting a raid on the Brigade's premises.'

'I have to talk to him before then.'

'You'd better hurry, then,' Nathan says.

Joona reverses, turns and drives out of the garage.

'How much of a hurry?' Joona asks as he turns right onto Kungsholmsgatan.

'I think they're on their way now.'

'Show me where the entrance to the Brigade is and you can get back to Police Headquarters and pretend you don't know anything,' Joona says.

'What's your plan?'

'Plan?' Joona asks playfully.

Nathan laughs.

'No, the plan's just to find out what Daniel Marklund was doing in Penelope's flat,' Joona explains. 'There's a chance he might know what's going on.'

'But . . .'

'It's no coincidence that the Brigade tried to get into her flat right now, I really can't believe that it is. The Security Police seem convinced that the extreme left-wing are planning some sort of attack, but . . .'

'They always think that. It's their job to think that,' Nathan smiles.

'Well, I need to talk to Daniel Marklund before I let go of this case.'

'Even if you do get there before the Security Police, there's no guarantee the Brigade are going to want to talk to you.'

29

Saga Bauer inserts thirteen rounds into the magazine, then slides it into her big, black pistol, a .45 calibre Glock 21.

The Security Police are going to storm the Brigade's headquarters on Södermalm.

She's sitting with three colleagues inside a minibus on Hornsgatan, outside Folkoperan. They're all in plain clothes, and are going to head into Nagham Fast Food in fifteen minutes to wait for the SWAT team.

In recent months the Security Police have reported an increase in activity among left-wing extremists in Stockholm. It could be a coincidence, but the Security Police's best strategists believe that several of the militant groups have come together to carry out a large act of sabotage. There's even been a warning of a terrorist attack, bearing in mind the theft of explosives from a military store in Vaxholm.

The strategists have also linked the murder of Viola Fernandez and the attempt to blow up Penelope Fernandez's flat to the impending attack.

The Brigade is regarded as the most dangerous and most militant group on the extreme left. Daniel Marklund is a member of the Brigade's inner circle. He was arrested trying to get into Penelope Fernandez's flat, and according to the strategists he could very well be the same person who attacked

Detective Superintendent Joona Linna and his forensics colleague.

Göran Stone smiles as he puts on his heavy protective vest:

'Now we're going to get those cowardly bastards.'

Anders Westlund laughs, but doesn't manage to conceal his nerves.

'Fuck, I really hope they resist, so I get to sterilise at least one Commie.'

Saga Bauer thinks about the fact that Daniel Marklund was caught outside Penelope Fernandez's flat. Her boss, Verner Zandén, decided that Göran Stone should conduct the interview. He went in aggressively in order to provoke a reaction, which only led to Marklund demanding legal representation and refusing to say another word.

The minibus door opens and Roland Eriksson climbs in with a can of Coca-Cola and a bag of foam banana sweets and sits down.

'Christ, I'm going to shoot if I so much as see a gun,' Roland says, sounding stressed. 'It all goes so damn fast, you just shoot . . .'

'We do as we discussed,' Göran Stone says. 'But if there's a fire-fight, you don't have to aim for their legs . . .'

'Right in their mouths!' Roland cries.

'Take it easy now,' Göran says.

'My brother's face is . . .'

'What the fuck, Roland? We know,' Anders interrupts anxiously.

'A fucking firebomb in his face,' Roland goes on. 'After eleven operations he still . . .'

'Are you going to be able to keep it together?' Göran asks sharply.

'Fuck, yes,' Roland replies quickly.

'Really?'

'No problem.'

Roland looks out of the window and scrapes the top of a tub of chewing tobacco with his thumb.

Saga Bauer opens the door to let some air into the minibus. She agrees that it's a good time to mount a raid. There's no reason to wait. But at the same time, she'd like to understand the connection to Penelope Fernandez. She can't see what Penelope's role among the left-wing extremists would be, or why her sister was murdered. Too many details are unclear. She would have liked to question Daniel Marklund before the raid, look him in the eye and ask some direct questions. She's tried to explain this to her boss, saying that there might not be anything left to interview after the raid.

This is still my investigation, Saga thinks as she gets out of the minibus to stand on the pavement in the sweltering heat.

'The SWAT team goes in here, here, and here, and we wait here,' Göran Stone repeats, pointing at the plan of the building. 'We might have to enter via the theatre . . .'

'Where the hell has Saga Bauer gone?' Roland asks.

'Probably chickened out, or got her period,' Anders grins.

30

Pain

Joona Linna and Nathan Pollock park on Hornsgatan and glance at the poor-quality printout of Daniel Marklund's picture. They get out of the car, hurry across the busy road and in through the door of a small theatre.

The Tribunal Theatre is an independent theatrical group that lets people pay what they can afford, which has put on performances of everything from *The Oresteia* to *The Communist Manifesto*.

Joona and Nathan hurry down the broad staircase to the combined bar and ticket desk. A woman with straight, dyed black hair and a silver ring in her nose smiles at them. They both give her a friendly nod but carry on walking past without a word.

'Are you looking for someone?' she calls as they start to head up the metal staircase.

'Yes,' Pollock replies almost inaudibly.

They reach a messy office containing a photocopier, desk and noticeboard covered with newspaper cuttings. A thin man with scruffy hair and an unlit cigarette in his mouth is sitting in front of a computer.

'Hello, Richard,' Pollock says.

'Who are you?' the man asks distractedly, then looks back at the screen.

They continue into the actors' dressing rooms, with neatly arranged costumes, make-up tables and bathrooms.

There's a bouquet of roses in a vase on one table.

Pollock looks round, then indicates where they should go. They hurry towards a steel door labelled 'Electricity'.

'Should be through here,' Pollock says.

'In the electrical cabinet inside a theatre?'

Pollock doesn't answer as he deftly picks the lock. They find themselves looking at a cramped space with electricity meter, fuse-boxes and a lot of removal boxes. The light in the ceiling doesn't work, but Joona climbs in past the boxes, trampling on bags of old clothes, and discovers another behind a jumble of extension leads. He opens the door and hurries through a narrow passageway with bare concrete walls. Nathan Pollock follows him. The air is stale, and smells of garbage and damp soil. They can hear distant music, an elusive backbeat. On the floor there's a poster of Marxist guerrilla leader Che Guevara with a burning fuse sticking out of his head.

'The Brigade has been hiding out here for a couple of years,' Pollock says quietly.

'I should have brought cake.'

'Promise me you'll be careful.'

'I'm just worried Daniel Marklund isn't going to be here.'

'He will be. He seems to spend most of his time here.'

'Thanks for your help, Nathan.'

'Maybe it would be best if I came in with you?' Pollock says. 'You'll only have a couple of minutes, and when the Security Police storm in things could get dangerous.'

Joona's grey eyes narrow but his voice is calm when he says:

'I'm only paying a social call.'

Nathan goes back to the theatre, and coughs as he pulls the doors closed behind him. Joona stands still for a moment, alone in the empty passageway, then draws his pistol, checks that the magazine is full and slips it back into its holster. He walks towards the steel door at the other end of the corridor. It's locked, and he wastes valuable seconds picking the lock.

Someone has scratched 'the brigade' into the blue paint on

the door in very small letters. The words are no more than two centimetres across.

Joona pushes the handle down and cautiously opens the door. He is met by loud, discordant music.

It sounds like a digitally manipulated version of Jimi Hendrix's track 'Machine Gun'. The music drowns out all other sounds. The shrieking guitars have a dreamlike, rolling rhythm.

Joona closes the door behind him and runs at a jog into a room full of clutter. The piles of books and old newspapers reach all the way to the ceiling.

It's almost completely dark, but Joona realises that the stacks form a system of passageways in the room, a labyrinth that leads to more doors.

He walks quickly along the passageway until he reaches a more brightly lit area, then carries on. The path divides, and he turns right, then quickly spins round.

He thought he saw something, a flash of movement.

A shadow that vanished out of the corner of his eye.

He's not sure.

Joona moves on, but stops at the corner and tries to look around. A bare light-bulb is swinging from the ceiling. Through the music Joona suddenly hears a roar, someone screaming in another room. He stops and retraces his steps, and peers into a passageway where a stack of magazines has toppled over onto the floor.

Joona's head is starting to ache. It occurs to him that he ought to eat something; he should have brought something with him – a few pieces of dark chocolate would be enough.

He clambers over the toppled magazines and reaches a spiral staircase leading to the floor below. There's a sweet smell of smoke in the air. Holding onto the handrail, he tries to creep down as quickly as he can, but the metal steps still make a noise. On the bottom step he stops in front of a black velvet curtain and puts his hand on his pistol.

The music isn't as loud here.

Red light reaches him through the gap in the curtains, along with a heavy smell of cannabis and sweat. Joona tries to see through the gap, but his field of vision is limited. In one corner there's a plastic clown with a red nose. Joona hesitates for a couple of seconds, then steps into the room through the black velvet curtain. His pulse speeds up and his headache worsens as he glances around the room. On the polished concrete floor he can see a double-barrelled shotgun and an open box of slugs – heavy, solid lead bullets which can cause serious injury. A naked man is sitting on an office chair. He's smoking with his eyes closed. It isn't Daniel Marklund, Joona notes. A bare-breasted blonde woman is half-sitting against the wall on a mattress with a military-issue blanket over her hips. She meets Joona's gaze, blows him a kiss, then takes a careless swig from a can of beer.

Another scream echoes from the only doorway.

Without taking his eyes off the pair, he picks up the shotgun, aims it at the floor, and stands on it to bend the barrel.

The woman puts the beer can down and absent-mindedly scratches her armpit.

Joona carefully puts the shotgun down, then carries on across the floor, past the woman on the mattress, into a passageway with a low ceiling made of chicken-wire over yellow glass-fibre insulation. Heavy cigar smoke hangs in the air. A strong light is shining at him and he tries to block it with his hand. The end of the passageway is covered by wide strips of industrial plastic. Joona is dazzled, and can't really see what's going on. He can only vaguely discern movements, and hears an echoing voice full of fear. Suddenly someone screams loudly, very close to him. The scream comes from deep in the person's throat and is followed by quick, gasped breathing. Joona creeps quickly forward, goes past the blinding light and can suddenly see into the room behind the thick plastic.

The room is veiled in smoke, drifting slowly through the still air.

A short, muscular woman wearing a balaclava, black jeans and a brown T-shirt is standing in front of a man in his socks and underpants. His head is shaved, and he has the words 'White power' tattooed on his forehead. He's bitten his tongue. Blood is running down his chin, neck and fat stomach.

'Please,' he whispers, and shakes his head.

Joona looks at the smoking cigarette the woman is holding in her dangling hand. Suddenly she walks up to the man and presses the lit end of the cigarette against the tattoo on his forehead, making him scream out loud. His fat stomach and saggy breasts shake. He wets himself, and a dark stain spreads across his blue underpants as urine trickles down his bare legs.

Joona draws his pistol and moves closer to the gap in the thick plastic curtain, trying to figure out if there are other people in the room. He can't see anyone else, and is opening his mouth to shout when suddenly he sees his pistol fall to the floor.

It clatters on the bare concrete and comes to rest by the plastic screen. He looks in confusion at his own hand, sees it shake, and then comes the pain. Joona's vision fades, and he feels a heavy thumping behind his forehead. He can't hold back a groan, and has to reach for the wall for support with one hand. He can feel that he's on the point of passing out as he hears the voices of the people on the other side of the plastic.

'Fuck it!' the woman with the cigarette shouts. 'Just tell me what the fuck you did!'

'I don't remember,' the neo-Nazi sobs.

'What did you do?'

'I was just giving a guy a hard time.'

'In detail!'

'I burned him in the eye.'

'With a cigarette,' she says. 'A ten-year-old boy . . .'

'Yes, but I . . .'

'Why? What had he done?'

'We followed him from the synagogue and down to . . .'

Joona doesn't notice when he pulls a heavy fire extinguisher off the wall. He loses all sense of time. The whole room vanishes. All that exists is the pain inside his head and a loud ringing tone in his ears.

31

Joona leans against the wall, blinking to get his sight back, and realises that there's someone in front of him, someone's come after him from the room with the naked couple in. He feels a hand on his back, and can make out a face through the dark veils of pain.

'What's happened?' Saga Bauer says quietly. 'Are you injured?'

He tries to shake his head but is in too much pain to speak. It feels like someone is dragging a hook right through this head, his skull, cerebral cortex and brain fluid.

Joona sinks to his knees.

'You have to get out of here,' she says.

He feels Saga raise his face. But he can't see anything. His whole body is covered with beads of sweat, he can feel it running from his armpits, down his neck and back, he can feel the sweat on his face, in his hair.

Saga is patting his clothes, she's assuming it's an epileptic fit and is trying to find some sort of medication in his pockets. He realises that she's taken his wallet and is looking for the symbol to show that he suffers from epilepsy.

After a while the pain eases. Joona moistens his mouth with his tongue and looks up. His jaw muscles feel tight and his whole body is aching from the migraine attack.

'You can't come yet,' he whispers. 'I need to . . .'

'What the hell happened?'

'Nothing,' Joona replies, picking his pistol up off the floor.

He stands up and walks as quickly as he can past the hanging plastic strips and into the room. It's empty. There's an illuminated emergency exit sign on the far wall. Saga follows him, and shoots him a questioning glance. Joona opens the emergency exit and sees a steep flight of steps leading up to a metal door facing the street.

'*Perkele*,' he mutters.

'Talk to me,' Saga says angrily.

Joona always tries to keep the direct cause of his illness at arm's length, he refuses to think about what happened many years ago: the reason why his brain sometimes throbs with pain which for a minute or so almost knocks him out completely. According to his doctor, it's an extreme form of migraine brought on by physical trauma.

The only thing that helps at all is the preventive epilepsy medication Topiramate. Joona is supposed to take it all the time, but when he has to work and think clearly he refuses to because it makes him tired, because it feels like it takes the edge off his thoughts. He knows it's a balancing act, that he can cope most of the time without medication and not have any migraines, but he's also aware that he can suffer one after just a few days without the drug, as on this occasion.

'They were torturing a guy, a neo-Nazi, I think, but . . .'

'Torturing?'

'Yes, with a cigar,' he replies, and starts to walk back along the passageway.

'What happened?'

'I couldn't . . .'

'Look,' she interrupts calmly. 'Maybe you shouldn't, I mean . . . be on operative duty, if you're ill.'

She rubs her face.

'What a fucking mess,' she whispers.

Joona walks into the room containing the clown, and hears Saga following him.

'What the hell are you doing here anyway?' she asks behind him. 'The Security Police SWAT team are about to storm in here. If they see you're armed they'll shoot, you know that, it'll be dark, there'll be tear gas, and . . .'

'I have to talk to Daniel Marklund,' Joona interrupts.

'You shouldn't even know about him,' she says, following him up the spiral staircase. 'Who told you this?'

Joona starts walking through one of the passageways but stops when he sees Saga gesturing in a different direction. He follows her, sees that she's started to run, draws his pistol and goes round a corner as he hears her call out.

Saga has stopped in the doorway of a room containing five computers. In one corner stands a young man with a beard and dirty hair. It's Daniel Marklund. His lips are moist and nervous. In his hand he's clutching a Russian bayonet.

'We're police officers, and we're asking you to put the knife down,' she says calmly, holding up her ID.

The young man shakes his head, and moves the knife through the air in front of him, rapidly changing the angle of the blade.

'We only need to talk to you,' Joona says, putting his pistol back in its holster.

'So talk,' Daniel says in a tense voice.

Joona walks towards him and looks into his worried eyes. He ignores the knife sweeping through the air in front of him.

'Daniel, you're really not very good at that,' Joona says with a smile.

He can smell gun-grease from the shiny blade. Daniel Marklund waves the knife faster, and there's a look of concentration in his eyes as he says:

'Finns aren't the only ones who can . . .'

Joona darts forward and grabs the young man's hand, twists the knife free with a fluid movement and puts it down heavily on the table.

The room falls silent, they look at each other and then Daniel Marklund shrugs his shoulders.

'I mostly do IT,' he says by way of excuse.

'We're going to be interrupted any time now,' Joona says. 'Just tell me what you were doing round at Penelope Fernandez's flat.'

'I was visiting.'

'Daniel,' Joona says darkly. 'You'd get a guaranteed prison sentence for that business with the knife, but I've got more important things to do than haul you in, so I'm giving you a chance to save me some time.'

'Is Penelope a member of the Brigade?' Saga asks quickly.

'Penelope Fernandez?' Daniel Marklund smiles. 'She's come out strongly against us.'

'So what were you doing with her?' Joona wonders.

'What do you mean, she's "come out strongly against you"?' Saga asks. 'Is there some sort of power struggle . . .'

'Don't the Security Police know anything?' Daniel asks with a weary smile. 'Penelope Fernandez is a total pacifist, she's a committed democrat. So she doesn't like our methods . . . but we like her.'

He sits down on a chair in front of two computers.

'Like?'

'She has our respect,' he says.

'Why?' Saga asks, surprised. 'Why would . . .'

'You have no idea how much people hate her . . . I mean, just try googling her name, the results are pretty brutal . . . and now it looks like someone's crossed the line.'

'What do you mean, crossed the line?'

Daniel looks at them carefully.

'You must know she's missing, right?'

'Yes,' Saga replies.

'Good,' he says. 'That's good, but for some reason I don't really believe the police are going to go to that much effort to find Penelope. That was why I went round there, I needed to check her computer to see who was behind it. I mean, the Swedish Resistance Movement sent out an unofficial message to their members back in April, encouraging them to kidnap "Communist bitch Penelope Fernandez" and turn her into a sex-slave for the whole organisation. But check this out . . .'

Daniel Marklund types on one of the computers, then turns the screen towards Joona.

'This site has direct links to the Aryan Brotherhood,' he says.

Joona scans the online chat-room, full of horrifically vulgar threats about Aryan cocks and how they're going to kill Penelope.

'But these groups have nothing to do with Penelope's disappearance,' Joona says.

'Haven't they? Who was it, then? The Nordic Association?' Daniel asks eagerly. 'Come on! It's not too late yet!'

'What do you mean, it's not too late?' Joona asks.

'Isn't it usually too late by the time anyone actually reacts . . .? But I managed to catch a message from her mum's voicemail. I mean, it seemed pretty fucking urgent, but still not too late, so I had to check her computer and . . .'

'Managed to catch?' Joona interrupts.

'She tried to call her mother yesterday morning,' the young man replies, scratching his messy hair nervously.

'Penelope?'

'Yes.'

'What did she say?' Saga asks quickly.

'That she's being hunted,' Daniel Marklund says tersely.

'What did she say, exactly?' Joona asks.

Daniel glances at Saga Bauer, then asks:

'How long have we got before your lot storm the building?'

Saga looks at her watch.

'Between three and four minutes,' she replies.

'Then you've got time to listen to this,' Daniel Marklund says, typing a couple of quick commands on the other computer and then playing an audio-file.

The speaker crackles, then there's a click as Claudia Fernandez's voicemail message plays. They hear three short bleeps, then a lot of hissing and crackling as a result of a very poor signal. Somewhere behind the static there's a faint voice. It's a woman, but her words are unintelligible. After just a few seconds a male voice can be heard, saying 'Get a job!' then there's a click, followed by silence.

'Sorry,' Daniel mutters. 'I need to run it through some filters.'

'The clock's ticking,' Saga murmurs.

He taps at the computer, adjusts the settings, looks at the audio-waves, changes some figures, then plays the recording again:

You've reached Claudia – I can't answer right now, but if you leave a message I'll get back to you as soon as I can.

The three bleeps sound different this time, and the crackling is more like gentle metallic tinkling.

Suddenly they hear Penelope Fernandez's voice very clearly: 'Mum, I need help, I'm being hunted by . . .'

'Get a job!' a man says. Then the line goes silent.

32

Proper police work

Saga Bauer looks at the time and says that they have to leave. Daniel Marklund mutters a joke about staying to mount the barricades, but there's a frightened look in his eyes.

'We're going to hit you hard. Put the knife down, don't resist, surrender at once, no rapid movements,' Saga says quickly before she and Joona leave the little office.

Daniel Marklund remains seated on the office chair and watches them go, then he picks up the bayonet and tosses it in the waste-paper basket.

Joona and Saga Bauer leave the Brigade's labyrinthine premises and emerge onto Hornsgatan. Saga goes back to Göran Stone's group of plain-clothed officers sitting in Nagham Fast Food, and eats some fries in silence. Their eyes are shining and empty as they await orders from operational command.

Two minutes later fifteen heavily armed officers in full gear rush out of four black vans. The SWAT team break down all the entrances, and tear gas spreads through the rooms. Five young people, including Daniel Marklund, are found sitting on the floor with their hands on their heads. They're dragged out onto the street, coughing, with their arms fastened behind their backs with cable-ties.

The arms seized by the Security Police really only demonstrate the Brigade's low-level militancy: an old Colt army pistol, a rifle, a shotgun with a bent barrel, a box of slugs, four knives and two shurikens.

As he drives along Söder Mälarstrand Joona takes out his phone and calls the head of the National Crime Unit. After two rings Carlos Eliasson answers by clicking the speaker-function with a pen.

'How are you enjoying Police Academy, Joona?' he asks.

'I'm not there.'

'I know that, because . . .'

'Penelope Fernandez is alive,' Joona interrupts. 'She's being hunted, and is running for her life.'

'Says who?'

'She left a message on her mother's voicemail.'

The line goes quiet, then Carlos takes a deep breath.

'Okay, she's alive, great . . . What else do we know? She's alive, but . . .'

'We know she was alive thirty hours ago when she made the call,' Joona says. 'And that someone's after her.'

'Who?'

'She didn't have time to say, but . . . if it's the same man I ran into, then there really is no time to lose,' Joona says.

'You think we're dealing with a professional?'

'I'm certain that the person who attached me and Erixon is a professional fixer, a grob.'

'A grob?'

'The Serbian word for grave. They're expensive, they pretty much work alone, but they do what they're paid for.'

'That sounds extremely unlikely.'

'I'm right,' Joona says tersely.

'You always say that, but if we really are dealing with a professional killer, Penelope shouldn't have lasted this long . . . it's been almost two days,' Carlos says.

'If she's alive, that means the fixer has other priorities.'

'You still think he's looking for something?'

'Yes,' Joona replies.

'What?'

'I'm not sure, but it could be a photograph . . .'

'Why do you think that?'

'It's the best theory I've got right now . . .'

Joona quickly explains about the books that had been pulled from Penelope's bookcase, the picture with the line of poetry on the back, Björn's brief visit, the way he was holding his hand when he left, the palm-print on the glass door, the scraps of tape and the torn corner of the photograph.

'You think the killer was looking for a photograph that Björn had already collected?'

'My guess is that he began by searching Björn's flat, and when he didn't find it he poured out a load of petrol and turned the neighbour's iron on full. The fire brigade received the call at 11.05, and that whole floor of the building was burned out before they got the fire under control.'

'And that same evening he kills Viola.'

'He probably assumed that Björn had taken the photograph onto the boat with him, made his way on board, drowned Viola, searched the boat and planned to sink it when something made him change his mind, leave the archipelago and return to Stockholm, where he started searching Penelope's flat . . .'

'But you don't think he found the photograph?' Carlos asks.

'Either Björn has it with him, or he's hidden it with a friend or in a storage locker – anywhere, really.'

The line goes silent. Joona hears Carlos breathing heavily.

'But if we manage to find this photograph first,' Carlos says thoughtfully, 'then presumably this would all be over.'

'Yes,' Joona replies.

'I mean . . . if we've seen the photograph, if the police have seen it, then it would hardly be a secret any more, hardly the sort of thing worth killing for.'

'I hope it's as simple as that.'

'Joona, I . . . I can't take the preliminary investigation away from Petter, but I assume . . .'

'That I'm going to go out to Police Academy and give some lectures,' Joona interrupts.

'That's all I need to know,' Carlos laughs.

On his way back to Kungsholmen Joona listens to his

voicemail, which includes a number of messages from Erixon. First he explained that he could work perfectly well from hospital. Thirteen minutes later he demanded to be included in the work, and twenty-seven minutes after that he was yelling that not having anything to do was driving him mad. Joona calls him, and Erixon answers in a tired voice:

'Quack, quack . . .'

'Am I too late?' Joona asks. 'Have you gone mad already?'

Erixon merely hiccoughs in response.

'I don't know how much you can understand,' Joona says. 'But things are getting urgent. Yesterday morning Penelope Fernandez left a voicemail message for her mother.'

'Yesterday?' Erixon repeats, suddenly alert.

'She said she was being hunted.'

'Are you on your way here?'

Joona can hear Erixon breathing hard through his nose as he explains that Penelope and Björn didn't spend Thursday night together. She was picked up by taxi at 06.40 and driven to the television studio to take part in a debate. Just a minute or so after the taxi had left Sankt Paulsgatan, Björn arrived at the flat. Joona tells Erixon about the handprint on the door, the tape and torn corner, and goes on to say that he at least is convinced that Björn had been waiting outside the building for Penelope to leave her flat so he could pick up the photograph quickly without her knowledge.

'And I think the person who attacked us is a fixer, and that he was looking for the photograph when we caught him by surprise,' Joona says.

'Maybe,' Erixon whispers.

'He just wanted to get away from the flat, and chose to prioritise that over killing us,' Joona says.

'Because if he hadn't, we'd be dead,' Erixon replies.

The line crackles and Erixon asks someone to leave him alone. Joona hears a woman repeat that it's time for physiotherapy, then Erixon snaps that this is a private conversation.

'One conclusion we can agree on is that the fixer hasn't found the photograph,' Joona goes on. 'Because if he'd found it on the boat, he wouldn't have been searching Penelope's flat.'

'And it wasn't in her flat because Björn had already taken it.'

'I think the attempt to set fire to the flat shows that the fixer isn't really interested in getting hold of the photograph, he just wants to destroy it.'

'So why was it fixed to Penelope Fernandez's living room door if it was that damn important?' Erixon wonders.

'I can think of several explanations,' Joona says. 'The most likely is that Björn and Penelope took a photograph that proves something, without them actually realising its significance.'

'That could well be the case,' Erixon says animatedly.

'To them, the photograph is nothing to hide, and certainly not worth killing anyone for.'

'But Björn suddenly changes his mind.'

'Maybe he found something out, maybe he realised it was dangerous and that's why he took it,' Joona says. 'There's a lot we don't know, and the only way we're going to get any answers is through good, honest police work.'

'Exactly!' Erixon says, almost shouting.

'Can you get hold of all their phone calls in the past week, as well as text messages, bank withdrawals and so on? Receipts, bus tickets, meetings, work . . .'

'Of course I can.'

'Actually, forget I asked.'

'Forget? What do you mean, forget it?'

'Your physiotherapy,' Joona says with a smile. 'You've got an appointment with the physiotherapist.'

'Very funny,' Erixon says, with suppressed anger. 'Physiotherapists? What sort of a fucking job is that?'

'But you do need to rest,' Joona teases. 'There's another forensics expert . . .'

'Just lying here doing nothing is driving me mad.'

'You've been off work for sixteen hours.'

'I'm climbing the walls here,' Erixon moans.

33

Joona is driving east towards Gustavsberg. A white dog is sitting completely still by the side of the road, staring laconically at the car. Joona thinks about phoning Disa, but instead he calls Anja's number.

'I need Claudia Fernandez's address.'

'Mariagatan 5,' she says instantly. 'Not far from the old porcelain factory.'

'Thanks,' Joona replies.

Anja doesn't hang up.

'I'm waiting,' she says in a sing-song voice.

'What are you waiting for?' he asks softly.

'For you to say we're going to Turku on the *Silja Galaxy*, and that you've rented a little cottage with a wood-fired sauna beside the water.'

'Sounds lovely,' Joona says slowly.

The weather is that special type of summery grey, hazy and close. He parks outside Claudia Fernandez's house and gets out of the car to the bitter scent of boxwood and blackberry bushes. He stands completely still for a moment, caught in a memory. The face that came to mind gradually fades when he rings on the door bearing a name-plate with the name *Fernandez* branded into it in childish lettering, the product of school woodwork classes.

The bell rings inside the house. He waits. After a while he hears slow footsteps.

Claudia opens the door with a worried look on her face. When she sees Joona she retreats backwards into the hall. A coat comes loose from its hanger and falls to the floor.

'No,' she whispers. 'Not Penny . . .'

'Claudia, it's nothing bad,' he says quickly.

She can't stand up, and sinks to the floor among the shoes under the coats on the rack, breathing like a frightened animal.

'What's happened?' she asks in a scared voice.

'We don't know much, but yesterday morning Penelope tried to phone you.'

'She's alive,' Claudia says.

'Yes, she is,' Joona replies.

'Oh, dear God, thank you,' she whispers. 'Thank God . . .'

'We picked up the message from your voicemail.'

'From my . . . no,' she says, getting to her feet.

'There was so much interference that it required specialist equipment to hear her voice,' Joona explains.

'The only . . . there was just a man telling me to get a job.'

'Yes, that's right,' Joona says. 'Penelope spoke before that, but she's very hard to hear . . .'

'What does she say?'

'She says she needs help. The marine police are on their way to organise a ground-search.'

'What about tracing the phone, though? Surely . . .'

'Claudia,' Joona says calmly. 'I need to ask you a few questions.'

'What sort of questions?'

'Shall we sit down?'

They go through the hall and into the kitchen.

'Joona Linna, can I ask you something?'

'You can ask, but I might not know the answer.'

Claudia Fernandez gets cups out for them. Her hand is shaking. She sits down opposite him and looks at him intently.

'You've got family, haven't you?' she asks.

The bright, yellow kitchen is very quiet.

'Do you remember the last time you were in Penelope's flat?' Joona asks after a while.

'It was last week, on Tuesday. She helped me take up a pair of trousers for Viola.'

Joona nods and sees Claudia's mouth tremble with suppressed sobs.

'I want you to think carefully now, Claudia,' he says, leaning forward. 'Did you see a photograph stuck to the living room door?'

'Yes.'

'What was it of?' Joona asks, trying to keep his voice calm.

'I don't know, I didn't look.'

'But you do remember that there was a photograph there, you're sure about that?'

'Yes,' Claudia nods.

'Were there any people in the picture?'

'I don't know, I suppose I thought it was to do with her work.'

'Was it taken indoors or outside?'

'No idea.'

'Try to see it in your mind's eye.'

Claudia closes her eyes, but then shakes her head.

'I can't.'

'Try, it's important.'

She lowers her eyes and thinks, but shakes her head again.

'All I can remember is that I thought it was odd that she'd stuck a picture to the door, it didn't look good at all.'

'Why did you think it was to do with her work?'

'I don't know,' Claudia whispers.

Joona excuses himself when his phone rings in his jacket. He takes it out, sees that it's Carlos and answers.

'Yes?'

'I just spoke to Lance at the marine police out on Dalarö, and he says they're organising a ground-search tomorrow. Three hundred people, and almost fifty boats.'

'Good,' Joona says, as he watches Claudia walk into the hall.

'And then I called Erixon to see how he was doing,' Carlos says.

'He seems to be on the mend,' Joona says in a neutral tone of voice.

'Joona, I don't want to know what you're doing . . . but

Erixon warned me that I'm going to have to admit that you were right.'

After the call Joona goes out into the hall and sees that Claudia has put on a jacket and a pair of wellington boots.

'I heard what he said over the phone,' she says. 'And I can help look, I can go on looking all night . . .'

She opens the door.

'Claudia, you need to let the police do their job.'

'My daughter called me, asking for help.'

'I know it's terrible having to wait . . .'

'Please, can't I come with you? I won't get in the way, I can make food and answer the phone so you don't have to think about it.'

'Isn't there anyone who could be here with you? A relative or a friend, or . . .'

'I don't want anyone here, I just want Penny,' she interrupts.

34

In his lap Erixon is holding a folder and a large envelope that has been couriered to his hospital room. He's holding a small, whirring fan in front of his face as Joona pushes him along the hospital corridor in a wheelchair.

His Achilles' tendon has been repaired, and instead of plaster his foot is fixed to a special type of shoe that keeps his toes pointing downward. He's been muttering that he's going to need a tap-dance shoe for the other foot if they want to see his Swan Lake.

Joona nods amiably at two old women sitting on a sofa holding each other's hands. They giggle, look at one another, and then wave at him like schoolgirls.

'The same morning they set out in the boat Björn bought an envelope and two stamps at the Central Station,' Erixon says. 'He had the receipt in his wallet on the boat, and I got the security company to email me the footage from the surveillance cameras. It's definitely a photograph, just as you've been saying all along.'

'So he sends the photograph to someone?' Joona asks.

'It's not possible to see what he writes on the envelope.'

'Perhaps he sent it to himself.'

'But his apartment is burned out, there isn't even a door any more,' Erixon says.

'Ring and check with the post office.'

When they reach the lift Erixon starts to make weird swimming

157

movements with his arms. Joona looks at him placidly without asking what he's doing.

'Jasmin says it's good for me,' Erixon explains.

'Jasmin?'

'My physiotherapist . . . she's a tiny little thing, but wonderfully strict: *Shut up, sit up straight, stop whining*. She even called me lard-arse,' Erixon says with a shy smile. 'Do you know how long they have to train?'

They get out of the lift and go into a chapel adorned with a plain wooden cross on a metre-high stand and a simple altar. On the wall is a tapestry of Jesus depicted in a number of coloured triangles.

Joona goes out into the corridor, opens a cupboard and takes out an easel with a large pad of paper, and some marker pens. When he returns to the chapel he sees Erixon nonchalantly pull down the tapestry and drape it over the cross, which he has moved to the corner.

'What we know is that, to someone, this photograph is worth killing people for,' Joona says.

'Yes, but why?'

Erixon fixes the printout of Björn Almskog's bank statement to the wall with safety-pins, then the list of calls, copies of underground tickets, receipts from his and Penelope's wallets and transcripts of voicemail.

'The photograph must reveal something someone wants to keep secret. It has to contain important information, maybe confidential industrial material,' Joona says, as he starts to construct a timeline on the pad of paper.

'Yes,' Erixon says.

'Let's find this photograph so we can put an end to this,' Joona says.

He picks up one of the marker pens and writes on the large pad:

06.40 Penelope collected from her flat by taxi.
06.45 Björn arrives at Penelope's flat.
06.48 Björn leaves the flat with the photograph.

07.07 Björn posts the photograph at the Central Station.

Erixon rolls over and looks at the times as he unwraps a bar of chocolate.

'Penelope Fernandez leaves the television studios and calls Björn five minutes later,' he says, pointing to the list of phone calls. 'Her underground ticket was stamped at 10.30. She gets a call from her sister Viola at 10.45. By then Penelope is probably already with Björn at the small boat marina on Långholmen.'

'So what was Björn doing?'

'That's what we're going to figure out,' Erixon says happily, wiping his fingers on a white handkerchief.

He moves along the wall and points to one of the local transport tickets:

'Björn leaves Penelope's flat with the photograph. He gets straight on the underground and at 07.07 he buys the envelope and two stamps at the Central Station.'

'And posts the envelope,' Joona says.

Erixon clears his throat and continues:

'The next fixed point is a transaction on his Visa card, twenty kronor at the Dreambow internet café on Vattugatan at 07.35.'

'Twenty-five to eight,' Joona says, adding it to the timeline.

'Remind me, where the hell is Vattugatan?'

'It's pretty small,' Joona replies. 'It's tucked away in the old Klara district.'

Erixon nods and goes on:

'I'm guessing Björn Almskog got the underground to Fridhemsplan before the stamp on his ticket expired. Because then we have a call made from the landline in his flat at Pontonjärgatan 47, to his father, Greger Almskog, but his dad didn't answer.'

'We'll have to talk to his father.'

'The next timing is another stamp on his bus ticket, at 09.00. Looks like he caught the number 4 bus from Fridhemsplan to Högalidsgatan on Södermalm, then walked to the boat on Långholmen.'

159

Joona adds these latest timings to the timeline, then moves it back and looks at their plan of that morning.

'Björn was in a hurry to fetch the photograph,' he says. 'But he didn't want to run into Penelope that morning, so he waited until she'd gone off in the taxi, then rushes in, takes the photo off the door, leaves the flat and goes to the Central Station.'

'I want to look at the security camera footage.'

'Then Björn goes to an internet café nearby,' Erixon goes on. 'He spends about half an hour there, then goes . . .'

'That's it!' Joona says, and starts walking towards the door.

'What?'

'Penelope and Björn both have broadband at home.'

'So why use an internet café?' Erixon asks.

'I'll head over there,' Joona says, and leaves the room.

35

Detective Superintendent Joona Linna turns into Vattugatan from Brunkebergstorg, behind the City Theatre. He stops and gets out of the car, hurries through an anonymous-looking metal gate and walks down a sloping concrete path.

There's not much going on in the Dreambow internet café. The floor has been freshly cleaned, and the room smells of lemon and plastic. Shiny transparent chairs are lined up at small computer tables. The only movement is from the slow patterns of the screen-savers.

An overweight man with a black, pointed beard is leaning on a tall counter sipping coffee from a mug saying 'Lennart means lion' on it. His jeans are baggy and one of the laces is dangling from his Reeboks.

'I need a computer,' Joona says before he gets to the counter.

'Get to the back of the queue,' the man jokes, making a sweeping gesture towards all the empty desks.

'One computer in particular,' Joona goes on with a glint in his eye. 'A friend of mine was here last Friday, and I'd like the same computer he used.'

'I don't know if I can let . . .'

He falls silent when Joona goes down on one knee and ties his shoelace for him.

'It's important.'

'I'll check Friday's list,' the man says, as two red circles appear on his cheeks. 'What's his name?'

'Björn Almskog,' Joona replies, standing up.

'Number five, over in the corner,' he says. 'I just need to see some ID.'

Joona hands the man his police ID and the man looks confused as he makes a note of Joona's name and date of birth in the register.

'Okay, all yours.'

'Thanks,' Joona says warmly, and goes over to the computer.

He takes out his mobile and calls Johan Jönson, a young technician in National Crime's department for IT-related offences.

'Hang on a moment,' a croaky voice says. 'I've swallowed some paper, a bit of a paper handkerchief, I was blowing my nose, then breathed in before I sneezed . . . Okay, there's no point trying to explain. Who am I talking to, anyway?'

'Joona Linna, National Crime.'

'Damn, Joona, hi!'

'You sound better already,' Joona says.

'Yes, got rid of it now.'

'I need to see what a guy was doing on a computer last Friday.'

'Say no more!'

'I'm in a hurry, I'm sitting in an internet café.'

'And you've got access to the computer?'

'It's right in front of me.'

'That makes things easier. Try looking at the internet history. It's probably been deleted, they're supposed to reset the computers after each user, but things are usually still there on the hard drive, you just have to . . . Actually, the easiest and most thorough way to do this is if you can bring it in so I can run through the hard drive using a program I designed to . . .'

'Meet me in fifteen minutes in the chapel of Sankt Göran's Hospital,' Joona says, then disconnects the computer, tucks it under his arm and starts to walk towards the door.

The man with the mug of coffee looks at him in astonishment and tries to block his path.

'The computer's not allowed to leave . . .'

'It's been arrested,' Joona says obligingly.

'So I can see – but what's it been arrested for?'

The man turns pale as he watches Joona walk out into the sunshine and wave back at him with his free hand.

36

The car park in front of Sankt Göran's Hospital is hot, and the air unpleasantly humid.

Erixon is manoeuvring his wheelchair around the chapel. He's set up a functional base-station and three different phones are ringing non-stop.

Joona comes in with the computer in his arms and puts it on a chair. Johan Jönson is already sitting on a small sofa. He's twenty-five years old, dressed in a black, ill-fitting tracksuit. He has a shaved head and thick eyebrows that grow together over his nose. He stands up and walks over to Joona, glances at him bashfully, shakes hands and puts his red computer bag down.

'Ei saa peittää,' he says, taking out a thin laptop.

Erixon pours Fanta from a flask into some small, fragile paper cups.

'I usually put the hard drive in the freezer for a few hours if it's playing up,' Johan says. 'And then just hook up an ATA/SATA lead. Everyone has a different way of doing this, I mean, I've got a friend at IBAS Computing who works with remote data recovery and he doesn't even meet his clients, he just does the whole thing over an encrypted phone-line. That usually retrieves most things, but I don't want most of it, I want it all, that's my thing, every last crumb of information, and for that you need a program called Hangar 18 . . .'

He throws his head back and pretends to laugh like a mad scientist.

'Mwah-ha-ha! I designed it myself,' he goes on. 'It works like a digital vacuum cleaner, it sucks up absolutely everything and reconstructs it in date order, down to the micro-second.'

He sits down on the altar-rail and connects the computers. His laptop whirrs quietly. He types commands at an astonishing speed, reads the screen, scrolls down, reads some more and then types more commands.

'Will it take long?' Joona asks after a while.

'I don't know,' Johan Jönson mutters. 'No more than a month.'

He swears quietly to himself, types another command, then looks at the digits flickering past.

'I'm kidding,' he says.

'So I realised,' Joona replies patiently.

'I'll know how much can be retrieved within fifteen minutes,' Jönson says, then looks at the pad where Joona wrote down the date and time of Björn Almskog's visit to the internet café.

'The internet history seems to have been deleted several different times, which is a bit of a nuisance . . .'

Fragments of old graphics flit across the sun-dappled screen. Johan Jönson inserts a portion of chewing tobacco under his lip, wipes his fingers on his trousers and waits, with half an eye on the screen.

'They've done their housekeeping,' he says languidly. 'But you can't ever erase anything, there are no secrets . . . Hangar 18 can find rooms that don't even exist.'

His laptop suddenly starts to bleep, and he types something, then reads a long list of numbers. He types some more, and the bleeping stops abruptly.

'What's happening?' Joona asks.

'Not much,' Johan Jönson says. 'The latest firewalls, sandboxes and fake virus protection just make it all a bit chewier, that's all . . . It's a miracle that computers work at all these days with all the barriers set up inside them.'

He shakes his head and licks a bit of tobacco from his top lip.

'I've never had a single virus program, and . . . Okay, shut up,' he suddenly tells himself, breaking off mid-flow.

Joona comes closer and looks over his shoulder.

'What have we got here?' Jönson whispers. 'What have we got here?'

He leans back and rubs his neck, then types something with one hand, presses Enter and smiles to himself.

'Here it is,' he says.

Joona and Erixon stare at the screen.

'Give me a moment . . . It's not that easy, it's coming in tiny little pieces . . .'

He shades the screen with his hand and waits. Slowly letters and fragments of graphics start to appear.

'Look, the door's slowly opening now . . . Let's see what Björn Almskog was doing on this computer.'

Erixon has put the brakes on his wheelchair and is leaning forward to see the screen.

'That's just a few random lines,' he says.

'Look at the corner.'

At the bottom right of the screen is a colourful little flag.

'He was using Windows,' Erixon says. 'Highly original . . .'

'Hotmail,' Joona says.

'Logging in,' Johan Jönson replies.

'Now things might get interesting,' Erixon says.

'Can you see a name?' Joona asks.

'It doesn't work like that . . . we can only change the time of the image,' Johan Jönson says, scrolling down.

'What was that?' Joona asks, pointing.

'We're inside the folder of sent emails,' he replies.

'Did he send something?' Joona asks in a tense voice.

Fragments of adverts for cheap flights to Milan, New Y k, Lo d n and P ris appear on the screen. And at the bottom is a pale grey number, a time: 07.44.42 PM.

'We've got something here,' Johan Jönson says.

More fragments appear on the screen:

orge I   contact d y

'Personal ads,' Erixon grins. 'They don't work, I've . . .'

He cuts himself off abruptly. Johan Jönson scrolls carefully past incomprehensible shreds of graphics, then stops suddenly. He moves away from the laptop with a big smile.

Joona takes his place, squints against the sunlight and reads what it says in the middle of the screen:

Carl Palmcr
ent t e   graph.   orget I   contact d you

Joona feels the hairs on the back of his neck stand up, and a shiver runs down his arms and back. Palmcrona, he thinks over and over again as he writes down the fragments the way they appear on the screen, then he runs his fingers through his hair and goes over to the window. He tries to think clearly and breathe calmly. A tiny glimmer of a migraine attack flits past. Erixon is still staring at the screen, swearing to himself repeatedly.

'Are you sure it was Björn Almskog who wrote this?' Joona asks.

'No doubt,' Johan Jönson replies.

'Completely sure?'

'If he was sitting at this computer at that time, then this is his email.'

'Then it's his email,' Joona concludes, his mind already elsewhere.

'Bloody hell,' Erixon whispers.

Johan Jönson looks at the fragments in the address box – 'crona@isp.se'– and drinks some Fanta straight from the flask. Erixon leans back in his wheelchair and closes his eyes for a while.

'Palmcrona,' Joona says intently, mostly to himself.

'This is crazy,' Erixon says. 'What's Carl Palmcrona got to do with this?'

Joona walks towards the door, immersed in thought. He says nothing as he goes down the steps from the chapel, and leaves the hospital and his colleagues behind. He just strides across the car park in the bright sunlight towards his black car.

37

Joona Linna walks quickly along the corridor towards the head of the National Crime Unit's office to tell him about Björn Almskog's email to Carl Palmcrona. To his surprise, the door is wide open. Carlos Eliasson is looking out through the window, then sits back down behind his desk again.

'She's still there,' he says.

'Who?'

'The girls' mother.'

'Claudia?' Joona says, and goes over to the window.

'She's been standing there for the past hour.'

Joona looks but can't see her. A father in a dark-blue suit with a crown on his head walks past with a little girl dressed in a princess costume.

Then, almost exactly opposite the main entrance to the National Police Committee, he sees a hunched woman next to a dirty Mazda pickup. Claudia Fernandez. She's standing perfectly still, staring intently at the entrance.

'I went out and asked if she was waiting for anyone in particular, I thought you might have forgotten that you were going to see her . . .'

'No,' Joona says quietly.

'She said she was waiting for her daughter, Penelope.'

'Carlos, we need to talk . . .'

Before Joona gets a chance to tell him about Björn Almskog's email, there's a knock on the door and Verner Zandén, head of the department for security measures at the Security Police, comes in.

'Good to see you,' the tall man says as he shakes Carlos's hand.

'Welcome.'

Verner shakes Joona's hand, then looks round the room and behind him.

'Where the hell has Saga got to?' he asks in his very deep voice.

She walks in slowly through the door. Her slim, slight figure almost seems to reflect the silvery shimmer of the aquarium.

'I didn't notice you were right behind me,' he smiles.

Carlos turns to Saga but doesn't seem to know what to do, and whether it's appropriate to shake hands with an elf or not. He chooses instead to take a step back and gesture invitingly towards the room.

'Come in, come in,' he says in an oddly shrill tone of voice.

'Thanks,' she says.

'You've already met Joona Linna.'

Saga stands there with her glossy, mid-length hair, but her eyes are hard, her jaw clenched determinedly. The scar running through one of her eyebrows shimmers chalk-white.

'Make yourselves at home,' Carlos says, and manages to sound almost jolly.

Saga sits down stiffly on the sofa beside Joona. Carlos puts a shiny folder on the table bearing the title 'Strategies for Collaboration'. Verner jokily raises his hand like a schoolboy before speaking:

'From a formal perspective, the entire investigation comes under the Security Police's remit,' he says. 'But without National Crime and Joona Linna we wouldn't have made the breakthrough in the case.'

Verner gestures towards the folder, and Saga Bauer's face turns bright red.

'Perhaps we shouldn't call it a breakthrough,' she murmurs.

'What?' Verner asks loudly.

'Joona just managed to find a handprint and the remains of a photograph.'

'And you – together with him – discovered that Penelope Fernandez is alive and being hunted. I'm not saying that's entirely down to him, but . . .'

'This is fucking ridiculous,' Saga yells, sweeping all the papers onto the floor. 'How the hell can you sit here heaping praise on him when he wasn't even supposed to be there, he wasn't even supposed to know that Daniel Marklund was . . .?'

'But he was, and he did,' Verner interrupts.

'The whole damn lot's supposed to be confidential,' she goes on loudly.

'Saga,' Verner says sternly. 'You weren't supposed to be there either!'

'No, but if I hadn't been, then . . .'

She stops abruptly.

'Can we carry on now?' Verner asks.

She looks at her boss for a moment before turning to Carlos and saying:

'Sorry, I didn't mean to get angry.'

She bends over and starts to pick the papers up from the floor. Her forehead is still flushed with frustration. Carlos tells her not to bother, but she picks them all up, arranges them and puts them back on the table.

'I really am very sorry,' she repeats.

Carlos clears his throat, then turns to her tentatively:

'We're still hoping that Joona Linna's contribution, or whatever we should call it, will make you willing to let him join the investigation,' he says.

'Seriously, though,' Saga says to her boss. 'I don't want to be negative, but I don't understand why we should let Joona into our investigation, we don't need him. You talk of a breakthrough, but I don't think . . .'

'I agree with Saga,' Joona says slowly. 'I'm sure you would have found that handprint and the corner of the photograph without my help.'

'Maybe,' Verner says.

'Can I go now?' Saga asks her boss in a composed voice, and gets to her feet.

'But what you don't know,' Joona goes on steadily, 'is that Björn Almskog secretly contacted Carl Palmcrona the same day Viola was murdered.'

Silence descends on the room. Saga slowly sits down again. Verner leans forward, lets his thoughts settle, and then he clears his throat.

'Are you suggesting that Carl Palmcrona's and Viola Fernandez's deaths are connected?' he asks in his deep, bass voice.

'Joona?' Carlos says, prompting him to answer.

'Yes, the two murders are linked,' he confirms.

'This is bigger than we thought,' Verner says, almost in a whisper. 'This is big . . .'

'Good work,' Carlos says with an anxious smile.

Saga Bauer has folded her arms and is staring at the floor, and the frustrated rash spreads across her forehead again.

'Joona,' Carlos says, and clears his throat cautiously. 'I can't override Petter, he's still in charge of our preliminary investigation, but I would be prepared to second you to the Security Police.'

'What do you say, Saga?' Joona asks.

'That would be perfect,' Verner replies quickly.

'I'm leading this preliminary investigation,' Saga says, then gets up and walks out of the room.

Verner excuses himself and follows her.

Joona's grey eyes glint icily. Carlos remains seated, clears his throat and says:

'She's young, you're going to have to try . . . I mean, be nice, look after her.'

'I think she's more than capable of looking after herself,' Joona replies curtly.

38

Saga Bauer

Saga Bauer is thinking about Carl Palmcrona, and only manages to turn her head away a fraction. She sees the punch a little too late. It comes from the side. A low hook that passes over her left shoulder and hits her ear and cheek. She staggers. Her helmet is off-balance again and she can barely see, but realises that a second blow is coming, so lowers her chin and protects her face with both hands. It's a hard punch, followed up by another to the top of her ribs. She stumbles backwards into the ropes. The referee hurries over, but Saga has already slipped out of the trap. She moves sideways, towards the centre of the ring, and takes stock of her opponent: Svetlana Krantz from Falköping, a thickset woman in her forties, with sloping shoulders and a Guns N' Roses tattoo on her shoulder. Svetlana is breathing through her mouth, moving after her with heavy footsteps, confident of winning by a knockout. Saga skips gently backwards, swirling like an autumn leaf across the ground. Boxing is easy, she thinks, and feels a sudden joy fill her chest. Saga Bauer stops and smiles so broadly she almost loses her mouth-shield. She knows she's the better boxer, but hadn't been planning to knock Svetlana out. She had decided to win on points. But when she heard Svetlana's boyfriend calling to her to smash the little blonde cunt's face in, she changed her mind.

Svetlana moves quickly across the ring, her right hand is

eager, too eager. She's so keen to beat Saga that she's no longer following their movements and has decided to finish things off with one or more heavy right hooks. She thinks Saga is sufficiently shaken that she'll be able to hammer the blows in, straight through her guard. But Saga Bauer hasn't been weakened, and is extremely focused. She dances on the spot, waiting for her opponent to rush her, holds her hands up in front of her face as if she only wants to protect herself. But at precisely the right moment she performs a surprising movement with her shoulders and feet, and with one forward step slips out of her opponent's line of attack. Saga ends up beside her, but manages to put all her momentum into a body blow, right at the other woman's solar plexus.

She feels the edge of Svetlana's chest protection through her glove as her body folds forward. The next blow doesn't connect as well, she only hits the padding, but the third is almost perfect, from below, right in the mouth and extremely hard.

Svetlana's head jolts backward. Sweat and snot fly out. Her dark-blue mouth-guard falls out. Svetlana's knees buckle and she thuds helplessly to the canvas, rolls over and lies there for a moment before starting to move again.

After the match Saga Bauer stands in the women's changing room and feels her body slowly relax. There's a strange taste in her mouth, a mixture of blood and adhesive. She had to use her teeth to remove the tape covering the laces of her gloves. The door of her locker is open, the padlock is on the bench. She looks in the mirror and quickly wipes away a few tears. Her nose is throbbing and sore after that hard punch her opponent managed to land. Her mind was elsewhere at the start of the match, on the conversation with her boss and the head of National Crime, and the decision that she should work together with Joona Linna.

There's a sticker on the door of the locker, from the 'Södertälje Rockets', with a picture of a rocket that looks more like an angry shark.

Saga's hands are shaking as she pulls off her shorts, jockstrap and underpants, her black vest and the bra with protective pads. Shivering, she walks into the tiled shower room and stands in one of the cubicles. The water runs down her neck and back. She forces herself to stop thinking about Joona as she spots some blood-streaked saliva by the drain in the floor.

When she walks back into the changing room there are about twenty other women there. They've just finished a Ki exercise session. Saga doesn't notice the other women stop and almost glaze over at the sight of her. Saga Bauer is very beautiful, in a way that makes people looking at her go weak inside. Perhaps it's the fact that she's related to fairytale artist John Bauer that makes people think of an elf or fairy. Her face is neat and symmetrical, with no make-up, and her eyes are big and blue as a summer sky. Saga Bauer is one metre seventy centimetres tall, and finely proportioned, even though her limbs are muscly and covered in bruises. Most people would probably guess she was a ballet dancer if they saw her now, not an elite boxer and superintendent with the Security Police.

John Bauer, a legendary figure in the fantasy art-world, had two brothers, Hjalmar and Ernst. Ernst, the younger brother, is Saga's great-grandfather. She can still remember her grandfather talking about his father, and his grief when his big brother John drowned with his wife Esther and their little son one November night on Lake Vättern, just a few hundred metres from the harbour in Hästholmen.

Three generations later, John Bauer's paintings found a remarkable reflection in reality. Saga resembles the fairytale princess Tuvstarr standing in front of the big, gloomy troll without any trace of fear.

Saga knows she's a good superintendent, even though she has never been allowed to complete an investigation on her own. She's used to having her work taken away from her, she's used to being shut out after many weeks of dedicated effort, she's used to being overprotected and sidelined on operations.

She's used to it, but that doesn't mean she likes it.

Saga Bauer did her initial training at Police Academy, where she got extremely good grades, then received specialist tuition in counter-terrorism within the Security Police. She is already a superintendent, involved in both investigative and operational duties. She has taken care to keep her skills updated, while simultaneously doing a lot of physical exercise. She goes running every day, spars or fights matches at least twice a week, and she practises shooting with her Glock 21 and the police's sniper rifle 90 every week.

Saga lives with Stefan Johansson, who plays piano in a jazz group called the Red Bop Label. They've released seven albums with ACT Music, and won a Swedish Grammy for their melancholic improvisation, 'A Year Without Esbjörn'. When Saga gets home from work or training she usually lies on the sofa eating sweets and watching a film with the sound turned down while Stefan plays his piano for hours at a time.

Saga emerges from the sports club and sees that her opponent is waiting for her by one of the concrete plinths.

'I just wanted to say thanks and congratulate you,' Svetlana says.

Saga stops.

'Well, thank you.'

Svetlana flushes slightly.

'You're really good.'

'So are you.'

Svetlana looks down and smiles. There's some rubbish among the sharply trimmed shrubs surrounding the car park in front of the entrance.

'Are you getting the train?' Saga asks.

'Yes, I should probably get going.'

Svetlana picks up her bag, then stops. She seems to want to say something, but hesitates for a moment.

'Saga . . . I'm sorry about my boyfriend,' she says eventually. 'I don't know if you heard what he was shouting. It's the last time I'm going to let him come.'

Svetlana clears her throat, then starts to walk.

'Hang on,' Saga says. 'I can drive you to the station if you like.'

39

Further away

Penelope runs up diagonally across the slope, slipping on loose stones and sliding down. She puts her hands out to steady herself and jolts her shoulder and back, cuts herself and gasps. Pain shoots up from her wrist. She's out of breath, coughs and looks back, down between the trees, into the darkness among the trunks, scared that she's going to see their pursuer again.

Björn comes over to her. His face is pouring with sweat, his eyes are bloodshot and hunted. He mutters something and helps her up.

'We can't stop,' he whispers.

They no longer know where their pursuer is, if he's close or if he's lost the trail. Only a few hours ago they were hiding on the floor of someone's kitchen while he stared in through the window.

They run up, force their way through a thicket, feel the warm smell of the branches, and keep going, hand in hand.

There's a rustling sound nearby and Björn lets out a frightened whimper, takes an abrupt step sideways and gets a branch in his face.

'I don't know how much longer I can keep going,' he gasps.

'Don't think about it,' Penelope says.

They walk for a while. Their feet and knees ache. They carry on through the leafy undergrowth, down into a ditch, wade through some weeds and emerge onto a gravel track. Björn looks round, whispers to her to follow him, then starts running south, towards the more populated area around Skinnardal. It can't be far. She limps a few steps, then follows him. There's a ridge of gravel with a few clumps of grass between the smooth tyre-tracks. The road curves round a group of birches. They run side by side, and when they get past the white tree-trunks they suddenly see two people. A woman in her twenties in a short tennis dress, and a man with a red motorbike. Penelope zips up her hooded jacket and tries to breathe more calmly.

'Hi,' she says.

They look at her and she can understand the looks on their faces. She and Björn are both filthy and streaked with blood.

'We've been in an accident,' she says quickly between breaths. 'We really need to borrow a phone.'

Tortoiseshell butterflies drift across the fat-hen and horsetail in the ditch.

'Okay,' the young man says, pulling his phone out and handing it to Penelope.

'Thanks,' Björn says, then looks along the road and into the forest.

'What happened?' the young man asks.

Penelope doesn't know what to say, and swallows as tears start to run down her dirty cheeks.

'An accident,' Björn replies.

'I recognise her,' the girl in the tennis dress says to her boyfriend. 'She's that stupid bitch we saw on TV.'

'Which one?'

'The one talking shit about Swedish arms exports.'

Penelope tries to smile at her while she keys in her mother's number. Her hands are shaking too much and she gets it wrong and has to start again. The young woman whispers something in the man's ears.

There's a rustling sound in the forest and Penelope suddenly imagines she can see something among the trees. Before she realises she's mistaken, she thinks the man following them has managed to find them, that he's tracked them from the house. Her hand is shaking so badly when she raises the phone to her ear that she's worried she's going to drop it.

'Tell me something,' the woman says to Penelope in a tight voice. 'Do you think people who work hard, maybe sixty hours a week, ought to pay for people who don't want to work, who just sit around in front of the television?'

Penelope doesn't understand what the young woman is getting at, why she's angry, she can't bring herself to concentrate on the question, can't understand why it's remotely relevant. Her mind is racing as she glances back at the trees and hears the phone ring, a distant, crackling ringtone.

'Don't you think working should be worthwhile?' the woman says in an agitated voice.

Penelope looks at Björn, hoping he can come to her rescue, say something to the young woman to keep her happy. She sighs when she hears her mother's voicemail message.

You've reached Claudia – I can't answer right now, but if you leave a message I'll get back to you as soon as I can . . .

Tears are running down her cheeks and her knees are ready to give way, she's so incredibly tired. She holds one hand up to the woman to indicate that she can't speak right now.

'We bought our phones with money we earned,' the young woman says. 'Maybe you should try earning some money and buying a phone of your own . . .'

The phone crackles, the reception is bad and she moves, but that only makes it worse – the line goes silent, and she doesn't know it but the connection has been broken when she says:

'Mum, I need help, I'm being hunted by . . .'

Suddenly the girl swears, snatches the phone from her and gives it back to the young man.

'Get a job!' he says.

Penelope staggers and looks at the young couple in surprise, as the young woman gets on the motorbike behind her boyfriend and wraps her arms round his waist.

'Please,' Penelope begs. 'We really do need . . .'

Her voice is drowned out when the motorbike starts up. The back wheel spins and kicks up gravel before it drives off. Björn calls out to them to stop. They start to run after them, but the motorbike disappears in the direction of Skinnardal.

'Björn,' Penelope says, stopping.

'Run!' he cries.

She's out of breath and looks back along the road, thinking that they're making a mistake. He stops, looks at her, gasping for breath, leans his hands on his thighs for a while, then starts walking.

'Wait, he knows what we're thinking,' she says seriously. 'We need to do something different.'

Björn slows down, turns round and looks at her, still backing away.

'We have to find help,' Björn says.

'Not now.'

He walks back to her and takes hold of her shoulders.

'Penny, it's probably no more than ten minutes to the nearest house. You can manage that, I'll help . . .'

'We have to get back into the forest again,' she says, cutting him off. 'I know I'm right about this.'

She pulls off her hairband and throws it onto the road, then turns off and walks straight into the forest, away from the settlement.

Björn looks at the road, then follows Penelope, taking a long stride across the ditch and carrying on into the forest. He catches up with her and takes her hand.

They run side by side, not very fast, but with each minute they get further from the road, further away from other people and help.

Suddenly their path is blocked by a patch of water. Panting for breath, they wade through some forty metres of thigh-deep water.

They reach the other side and carry on running through the forest with wet shoes.

After ten minutes Penelope slows down again. She stops, tries to catch her breath, then looks up to see where they are. For the first time she can't feel the chilly presence of their pursuer. Björn wipes his mouth with the back of his hand and walks up to her.

'When we were in the house,' he says. 'Why did you call out to him to come in?'

'Because otherwise he would have opened the door and come straight in – it was the only thing he wasn't expecting.'

'But . . .'

'He's been one step ahead of us the whole time,' she goes on. 'We've been frightened, and he knows how frightened people behave.'

'They don't tell him to come in,' Björn says, and a weary smile spreads across his face.

'That's why we couldn't stay on the road to Skinnardal. We need to keep changing direction, the whole time, running deeper into the forest, not heading towards anything.'

'Right.'

She looks at his exhausted face, his dry, white lips.

'I think we have carry on like that if we're going to make it. We need to think differently. I think . . . instead of trying to get from this island to the mainland, we should make our way further out into the archipelago, away from the mainland.'

'No one would do that.'

'Can you go on for a bit longer?' she asks quietly.

He nods, and they start to run deeper into the forest, further and further away from roads, houses and people.

40

Axel Riessen slowly removes the cufflinks from the starched sleeves of his shirt. He puts them in the bronze bowl on his gentleman's dresser. He inherited the cufflinks from his grandfather, Admiral Riessen. But the motif is civilian, two crossed palm leaves.

Axel Riessen looks at himself in the mirror beside the door of his dressing room. He loosens his tie, then walks to the other end of the room and sits down on the edge of the bed. The radiator is making a rushing sound, and through the walls he can hear fragments of notes.

The music is coming from his younger brother's apartment next door. A lone violin, he thinks, and immediately pieces the fragments together in his imagination. In his mind he can hear Bach's first violin sonata in G minor, the opening movement, the adagio, but far slower than most interpretations. Axel can't just hear the intended notes, but also enjoys each squeak and accidental knock of the frame.

His fingers tingle as the music changes tempo, and his hands yearn to pick up a violin. It's been a long time since he let his fingers merge with the music, running across the strings and up the neck.

The music in Axel's head falls silent when his phone rings. He gets off the bed and rubs his eyes. He's very tired, has hardly slept in the past week.

The screen says he's being called by someone in the main government offices. Axel clears his throat before answering in a calm voice:

'Axel Riessen.'

'My name is Jörgen Grünlicht, I'm chair of the government's Foreign Affairs Committee, as you might be aware.'

'Good evening.'

'Sorry to call so late.'

'I was awake.'

'I was told that you would be,' Jörgen Grünlicht says, then pauses before he goes on. 'We've just had an extraordinary committee meeting at which it was agreed that we should try to recruit you as the director general of the Inspectorate for Strategic Products.'

'I see.'

Neither of them speaks for a moment.

'I assume you know what happened to Carl Palmcrona.'

'Only what I've read in the paper.'

Grünlicht clears his throat weakly and says something Axel can't hear before raising his voice again.

'You're familiar with our work and in theory – if you accept our proposal – would be able to get to work very quickly.'

'I have to complete my duties with the UN,' Axel replies.

'Is that a problem?' Grünlicht asks, with a trace of anxiety in his voice.

'No.'

'Take a look at the suggested terms . . . there's nothing that isn't open to discussion,' Grünlicht says. 'As you can appreciate, we'd very much like to have you on board, so there's no need to make a big secret out of this.'

'Let me think about it.'

'Have you got time to meet first thing tomorrow morning?'

'Is there any particular urgency?'

'We always take the time we need,' Grünlicht replies. 'But obviously, bearing in mind what's happened . . . the Trade Minister is eager for us to reach a resolution regarding one specific issue that has already started to drag out.'

'What's that?'

'Nothing unusual . . . just an export licence. The advance notification was positive, and the Export Control Committee has done its job, the report is ready, but Palmcrona didn't have time to sign it.'

'And he needed to do that?' Axel asks.

'Only the director general can authorise the export of military equipment or dual-use products,' Jörgen Grünlicht explains.

'But surely the government authorises some deals?'

'Only if the ISP's director general takes the decision to refer the case to the government.'

'I see.'

Axel Riessen spent eleven years working as an arms inspector under the old system, for the Foreign Ministry, before he moved to the United Nations body UNODA, the United Nations Office for Disarmament Affairs. He is now a senior advisor in the Division of Analysis and Assessment. Riessen is only fifty-one years old, and his greying hair is still thick. His features are regular and attractive. He's got a suntan from his holiday in Cape Town, where he hired a yacht and made his way along the magnificent coast on his own.

Axel goes into his library, sits down in his reading chair, closes his stinging eyelids and considers the fact that Carl Palmcrona is dead: he read the short report of his death in *Dagens Nyheter*. It was hard to get any real idea of what had happened, but there was something about the article that suggested it had come out of the blue. He evidently hadn't been ill, because they usually mention that. Axel thinks back to the many times they've met over the years. They had both been consulted as experts on the proposal that led to the government's decision to combine the Military Equipment Inspectorate and the Cabinet Office's strategic export controls in a single body, the Inspectorate for Strategic Products.

And now Palmcrona is dead. In his mind's eye Axel can see the tall, pale man with his military cropped hair and an air of loneliness.

He feels suddenly anxious. The apartment is too quiet. Axel stands up and looks out into the other room, listening for noises.

'Beverly?' he calls quietly. 'Beverly?'

She doesn't answer. He starts to feel scared. He walks quickly through the other rooms, then down into the hall to grab his coat and go out to look for her, when he suddenly hears her humming to herself. She pads barefoot across the carpet from the kitchen. When she sees the worried look on his face her eyes widen.

'Axel,' she says in her high voice. 'What is it?'

'I just got worried that you might have gone out,' he mumbles.

'Into the big, bad world,' she smiles.

'I just mean you can't always trust everyone.'

'I don't, I look at them, at their auras,' she explains. 'If they've got a bright aura I know they're kind.'

Axel doesn't know how to respond, and just says that he's bought her some crisps and a big bottle of Fanta.

She doesn't even seem to hear him. He tries to read her face, see if she's starting to become restless or depressed or withdrawn.

'Do you think we should still get married?' she asks.

'Yes,' he lies.

'It's just that flowers make me think of Mum's funeral, and Dad's face when . . .'

'We don't have to have flowers,' he says.

'But I like lily-of-the-valley.'

'Me too,' he says weakly.

'I'm so sleepy,' she says, and leaves the room. 'Are you ready for bed?'

'No,' Axel Riessen says to himself, but gets up and follows her.

He walks through the apartment with a strong sense that parts of his body are trying to stop him. He feels clumsy and oddly slow as he follows her through the corridor, across the marble floor and up the stairs, through two sitting rooms and into the suite of rooms he usually withdraws to in the evenings.

The girl is slender and short, she only reaches his chest. Her hair has started to grow again after she shaved it off last week. She gives him a quick hug, and he has time to detect the smell of caramels from her mouth.

41

No sleep

It's now ten months since Axel Riessen met Beverly Andersson for the first time. It was all because of his acute insomnia. Ever since an event thirty-four years ago he has had trouble sleeping. His life functioned as long as he took sleeping pills, and he would sleep a chemical sleep without dreams, and perhaps without real rest.

But he slept.

He kept having to increase the dose in order to sleep. The tablets created a soporific buzz that drowned out his thoughts. He loved his medication, and would mix it with expensive single-malt whisky. But after twenty years of high consumption his brother found him in the hallway, unconscious and with blood pouring from his nostrils.

At the Karolinska Hospital he was diagnosed with severe cirrhosis of the liver.

The damage was so extreme that he was placed on the list for a liver transplant after the compulsory evaluation period. But because he was blood group O and his tissue type was extremely unusual, the number of potential donors was vanishingly small.

His younger brother could have donated part of his liver if he hadn't been suffering from severe arrhythmia that meant his heart wouldn't be able to cope with such a serious operation.

The chances of finding a donor were almost non-existent,

but as long as Axel kept away from alcohol and sleeping pills, he wouldn't die. With regular doses of Konaktion, Inderal and Spironolactone, his liver was at least able to function and he could lead a relatively normal life.

The problem was that sleep was as good as gone, he slept for no more than an hour each night. He was admitted to a sleep clinic in Gothenburg, underwent polysomnography and had his insomnia diagnosed. But because medication was out of the question, he was given advice on different sleep strategies – meditation, hypnosis, auto-suggestion – but nothing helped.

Four months after his liver gave out he spent nine days awake and suffered something approaching a psychotic breakdown.

At his own request he was admitted to a private psychiatric clinic, Sankta Maria Hjärta.

That was where he met Beverly. She was only fourteen years old at the time.

As usual, Axel was lying awake in his room, it was something like three o'clock at night and completely dark when she opened his door. She was an unquiet spirit, a walker, wandering the corridors of the clinic at night.

Perhaps she was just looking for someone to be with.

He lay there sleepless and confused when the girl came in. She stopped in front of him, with her long nightdress dragging on the floor.

'I saw the light in here,' she whispered. 'You're glowing.'

Then she just walked over to him and curled up on his bed. He was still ill from lack of sleep, didn't know what he was doing, he grabbed hold of her tightly, too tightly, and held her to him.

She said nothing, just lay there.

He clung onto her small body, pressing his face against her neck, and suddenly fell asleep.

He fell into dreams, into liquid sleep.

It was only a few minutes the first time, but after that she came to him every night.

He held her tight, and fell asleep, wet with sweat.

His mental instability faded like mist on glass, and Beverly stopped wandering the corridors.

Axel Riessen and Beverly Andersson both chose to leave the clinic, and what happened after that was a silent agreement between the two of them born of desperation.

They understood that the true nature of the relationship must remain secret, but outwardly Beverly got permission from her father to lodge in a self-contained set of rooms in Axel Riessen's apartment while she waited to be given a student flat.

Beverly Andersson is now fifteen years old, and has been diagnosed with a borderline personality disorder. She has no barriers in her behaviour towards other people, and lacks the ability to impose them. She lacks the usual instinct for self-preservation.

Girls like Beverly used to be locked away in institutions, forcibly sterilised or lobotomised out of anxiety about sexual promiscuity and immorality.

Girls like Beverly still go home with the wrong people, placing all their trust in people who don't always wish them well.

But Beverly has been lucky to find Axel Riessen. He often tells himself that he isn't a paedophile, he has no intention of harming her or making money from her. He just needs her so he can sleep, so he can stay afloat.

She often says he's going to marry her when she's old enough.

Axel Riessen lets her weave her fantasies about the wedding, because it seems to make her happy and calm. He tells himself that it's a way of protecting her from the outside world, but he's still aware that he's exploiting her. He feels ashamed, but can't think of any way out: he's terrified of finding himself back in the horrors of perpetual insomnia again.

Beverly comes out with her toothbrush in her mouth. She nods towards the three violins hanging on the wall.

'Why don't you ever play them?' she asks.

'I can't,' he replies with a smile.

'So they're just going to hang there? Give them to someone who plays instead.'

'I like the violins because Robert gave them to me.'

'You hardly ever talk about your brother.'

'It's complicated . . .'

'He makes violins in his workshop,' she says.

'Yes, Robert makes violins . . . and plays in a chamber orchestra.'

'Can he play at our wedding?' she asks, wiping toothpaste from the corners of her mouth.

Axel looks at her and hopes she doesn't notice the stiffness in his face when he says:

'That's a good idea.'

He feels tiredness washing over him, through his body and brain. He walks past her, into the bedroom, and sinks down on the edge of the bed.

'I feel quite sleepy, I . . .'

'Poor you,' she says seriously.

Axel shakes his head.

'I just need to sleep,' he says, and suddenly feels like he's about to cry.

He stands up and gets out a pink cotton nightdress.

'Please, Beverly, put this on.'

'If you like.'

She stops and looks at the big oil-painting by Ernst Billgren, of a fox dressed up and sitting in an armchair in a very smart home.

'Creepy picture,' she says.

'Do you think?'

She nods and starts to get undressed.

'Can't you get changed in the bathroom?'

She shrugs and when she pulls her pink top up he turns away so he doesn't see her naked. He walks over to the painting of the fox, looks at it, then takes it down and puts it on the floor facing the wall.

Axel sleeps stiffly and heavily, with his face scrunched up and his jaw clenched. He holds the girl tight. Suddenly he wakes up, lets go of her and gasps for breath, as if he were drowning. He's sweating and his heart is thudding anxiously. He switches the bedside light on. Beverly is sleeping like a small child, completely relaxed, with her mouth open.

Axel finds himself thinking about Carl Palmcrona again. The

last time they met was in the House of Nobility. Palmcrona had been drunk, and behaved rather aggressively, complaining about the UN's various arms embargoes, and concluded with the remarkable words: *If it all goes to hell I suppose one can always do an Algernon to avoid reaping the nightmare.*

Axel turns the light out again and makes himself comfortable as he thinks about Palmcrona's phrase, 'doing an Algernon'. What had he meant? And what was the nightmare he referred to? Was that really what he had said?

Avoid reaping the nightmare.

Carl-Fredrik Algernon's fate was a mystery in Sweden. Up until his death he had been a weapons inspector for the Foreign Ministry. One January day he had a meeting with the head of Nobel Industries, Anders Carlberg, during which he told him that their investigation indicated that one of the group's subsidiaries had been smuggling arms to countries in the Persian Gulf. Later that day Carl-Fredrik Algernon fell in front of an underground train at the Central Station in Stockholm.

Axel's thoughts wander off, circling with increasing vagueness around the allegations of arms smuggling and bribery that had been directed at the Bofors company. In his mind's eye he sees a man in a trenchcoat fall backwards in front of a speeding underground train.

The man falls slowly, his coat fluttering behind him.

Beverly's gentle breathing captures Axel and makes him calm. He turns towards her and puts his arm around her slender frame.

She sighs as he pulls her to him.

Axel holds her tightly. Sleep gathers in cloudlike shapes, and his thoughts spread out and dissipate.

He sleeps fitfully for the rest of the night, and wakes up at five o'clock to find himself holding her thin upper arms in a cramp-like grip. He feels her cropped hair tickle his lips, and wishes desperately that he was still able to take his pills.

42

The Inspectorate for Strategic Products

At seven o'clock in the morning, Axel goes out onto the terrace that he shares with his brother. At eight o'clock he's going to meet Jörgen Grünlicht in Carl Palmcrona's office at the Inspectorate for Strategic Products.

The air on the terrace is already warm, but not yet humid. His younger brother Robert has opened the doors to his apartment and is sitting on a sun-lounger. He hasn't shaved yet, and is just sitting with his arms hanging limply as he stares up into the dew-covered foliage of the chestnut tree. He's wearing his old silk dressing-gown. It's the same one their father used to wear on Saturday mornings.

'Good morning,' Robert says.

Axel nods, without looking at his brother.

'I've finished repairing a Fiorini for Charles Greendirk,' Robert says, in an attempt to start a conversation.

'I'm sure he'll be pleased,' Axel replies quietly.

Robert looks up at him.

'Are you feeling stressed?'

'A bit, to be honest,' Axel replies. 'It looks like I'm going to be changing job.'

'Well, why not?' Robert says absent-mindedly.

Axel looks at his brother's friendly face, his deep wrinkles, bald head. He thinks how different things could have been between them.

'How's your heart these days?' he asks. 'It hasn't stopped yet?'

Robert puts his hand to his chest before replying:

'Not quite . . .'

'Good.'

'How about your poor liver?'

Axel shrugs and starts to walk back towards his apartment.

'We're playing Schubert tonight,' Robert says.

'That's nice.'

'I thought maybe you . . .'

Robert falls silent, looks at his brother, then changes the subject.

'That girl who's got the room up there . . .'

'Yes . . . Beverly,' Axel says.

'How long is she going to be living here?' Robert asks, squinting towards Axel.

'I don't know,' he replies. 'I've promised her she can stay here until she gets a student flat.'

'Yes, you always did like to look after exhausted bumblebees and frogs that . . .'

'She's a human being,' Axel interrupts.

He opens the tall terrace door and watches his face slide across the uneven glass as it swings open. Hidden behind the curtain he watches his brother as he gets up from the sun-lounger, scratches his stomach, then walks down the steps that lead from the terrace to the little garden and studio. As soon as Robert has gone, Axel returns to his room and gently wakes Beverly, who is lying asleep with her mouth open.

The Inspectorate for Strategic Products is an official body that was established in 1996. The ISP took over responsibility for all matters concerning arms exports and dual-use equipment.

The ISP is based on the fifth floor of a salmon-pink building at Klarabergsviadukten 90.

When Axel emerges from the lift he sees Jörgen Grünlicht from the Foreign Ministry waiting for him inside the big glass doors. He nods impatiently, even though there are still two minutes to go before eight o'clock, then runs a card through a reader and taps in a code to let Axel through the doors. Grünlicht is a tall man with uneven pigmentation on the skin of his face, large white patches that stand out against his otherwise ruddy complexion.

They walk to Carl Palmcrona's office, a corner room with two huge windows and a view of the network of southbound roads behind the Central Station, and, beyond them, Klara sjö and the dark, regular outline of the City Hall.

Despite the smart address, there's something spartan about the ISP's premises. The floors are lined with linoleum, the furniture is simple and neutral, white and pine. As if trying to point out that all arms exports are morally dubious, Axel thinks with a shiver.

It feels rather macabre to be in Carl Palmcrona's office so soon after his death.

Axel notes that the ceiling light is making a loud buzzing sound, like an undertone from an untuned piano. Suddenly Axel remembers that he once heard the same note in a recording of composer John Cage's first sonata.

Grünlicht closes the door, and when he invites Axel Riessen to sit down he seems tense, in spite of his friendly smile.

'Good that you could come so quickly,' he says, and hands him a folder containing the suggested contract.

'Don't mention it,' Axel says with a smile.

'Sit yourself down and look through it,' Grünlicht says, gesturing towards the desk.

Axel sits down on the unfussy chair, puts the folder on the desk, then looks up.

'I'll take a look and be in touch next week.'

'It's a very advantageous contract, but the offer can't remain open indefinitely,' Grünlicht says.

'I appreciate that you're keen to move on this.'

'The committee are extremely keen to have you, given your career, your reputation – there's no better candidate, but at the same time we can't let the organisation sit idle.'

Axel opens the folder and tries to suppress a feeling of unease inside him, a suspicion that he's being lured into a trap. There's something forced about Grünlicht's manner, something mysterious and impatient.

If he signs the contract, he'll be director general of the ISP. He alone would be responsible for Swedish arms exports. Axel has spent his years at the UN trying to disarm regions where there's been armed conflict, limit the flow of conventional weaponry, and would like to think of this appointment as a continuation of that work.

He very carefully reads through the agreement: it really is very generous, almost too generous. He flushes several times as he reads it.

'Welcome on board,' Grünlicht smiles, handing him a pen.

Axel thanks him, signs his name on the contract, then stands up, turns his back on Grünlicht and looks out of the window. He can only just make out the three crowns at the top of the tower of the City Hall through the hazy sunlight.

'Not a bad view from here,' Grünlicht murmurs. 'Better than from my room in the Foreign Ministry.'

Axel turns towards him.

'You've got three cases on your desk at the moment, of which Kenya is the most pressing. It's a big, important deal. I'd advise you to look at that one first, preferably immediately. Carl has already done a lot of the preliminary work, so . . .'

He tails off, pushes the document towards Axel and then looks at him with an odd twinkle in his eye. Axel gets the feeling that Grünlicht would really just like to force a pen in his hand and make him sign.

'I'm sure you're going to be a very worthy successor to Carl.'

Without waiting for a response, he pats Axel's arm, then strides quickly across the floor. At the door he turns back and says curtly:

'Meeting with the committee at 15.00 today.'

Axel is left standing on his own in the room. A mute silence settles around him. He sits down at the desk again and looks through the document Carl Palmcrona had left unsigned. The preliminary work is careful and thorough. The case concerns the export of 1.25 million rounds of 5.56 x 45 mm ammunition to Kenya. The Export Control Board voted in favour, Palmcrona's advance notification was positive, and Silencia Defence Ltd is an established and reputable company.

But the deal can't go ahead before this final step, when the director general of the ISP takes the decision to grant an export licence.

Axel leans back and thinks about Palmcrona's words about 'doing an Algernon', and dying without reaping the nightmare.

43

A cloned computer

Göran Stone smiles at Joona Linna, then pulls an envelope from his bag, opens it and tips the requisitioned key into his cupped hand. Saga Bauer is still standing outside the closed lift door with her eyes downcast. The three of them are standing on the landing outside Carl Palmcrona's apartment at Grevgatan 2.

'Our forensics team will be here tomorrow,' Grünlicht says.

'Do you know what time?' Joona asks.

'What time, Saga?' Göran asks.

'I think we . . .'

'Think?' he interrupts. 'You're supposed to know what time.'

'Ten,' she replies in a low voice.

'You told them that I personally want them to start with IT and telephones?'

'Yes, I said . . .'

Göran silences her with a gesture when his phone rings. He answers it and walks a few steps down the staircase, stopping in the alcove containing the window with the reddish-brown glass.

Joona turns to Saga and asks in a subdued voice:

'Aren't you in charge of the preliminary investigation?'

Saga shakes her head.

'What's happened?' he asks.

'I don't know,' she replies wearily. 'It's always the same. This isn't even Göran's area, he's never worked in counter-terrorism.'

'What are you going to do about it?'

'There's nothing . . .'

She falls silent when Göran Stone ends his call and comes back up to join them. Saga holds out her hand for the key to Palmcrona's door.

'The key,' she says.

'What?'

'I'm in charge of this preliminary investigation.'

'What do you say about that?' Göran Stone says with a laugh, looking at Joona.

'I'm sure there's nothing wrong with you, Göran,' Joona says. 'But I've just come from a meeting with our bosses, where I agreed to work with Saga Bauer . . .'

'She's allowed to come along,' he says quickly.

'As head of the preliminary investigation,' Saga says.

'So you want to get rid of me? What the hell is going on here?' Göran Stone asks with a surprised, affronted smile.

'You're allowed to come along, if you like,' Joona says calmly.

Saga takes the key from Göran's hand.

'I'm calling Verner,' he says, and starts to walk down the stairs.

They hear his footsteps in the stairwell, then his conversation with his boss, and his voice gets more and more agitated until he finally exclaims 'Bunch of cunts!' so loudly that it echoes up the stairs.

Saga forces the smile from her face, composes herself, then inserts the key in the lock, turns it twice and opens the heavy door.

The police cordon was lifted once any suspicions of wrongdoing had been dismissed. The preliminary investigation was dropped as soon as The Needle submitted his post-mortem report: all of his findings supported what Joona Linna had said about the suicide. Carl Palmcrona took his own life by hanging a washing-line with a running noose from the lamp-hook in the ceiling of his home. The crime scene investigation was called off and the analysis of the samples that were sent to the National Forensics Laboratory in Linköping was never carried out.

But now it has emerged that the day before Carl Palmcrona was found hanged in his home, Björn Almskog sent him an email.

Later that day Viola Fernandez was murdered on board Björn Almskog's boat.

Björn is the link, the connection between the two deaths. Two deaths that would have been written off respectively as a suicide and a drowning, entirely unconnected, if the boat had sunk at sea.

Saga and Joona walk into the hall and note that there hasn't been any post. A smell of strong floor-cleaner hangs in the air. They walk through the large rooms. Sunlight is flooding through the windows. The red roof of the building on the other side of Grevgatan glints in the sun. From the bay window there's a view of the sparkling water of Nybroviken.

The forensics experts' protective mats are gone, and the floor beneath the lamp-hook in the large drawing room has been mopped clean.

They walk slowly across the creaking parquet floor. Oddly enough, there's no sense of Palmcrona's suicide lingering in the apartment. It doesn't feel uninhabited at all. Joona and Saga both sense it. The large, almost unfurnished rooms are full of a feeling of comfortable tranquillity.

'She hasn't stopped coming,' Saga suddenly says.

'Exactly,' Joona replies quickly with a smile. The housekeeper has kept coming, cleaning, opening the windows, picking up the post, changing the beds and so on.

They're both thinking that this isn't particularly unusual in a case of sudden death. There's a reluctance to admit that life has changed, and instead of accepting the new state of affairs, things carry on much as before.

The doorbell rings. Saga looks slightly alarmed, but follows Joona out into the hall.

The front door is opened by a man with a shaved head, wearing a baggy black tracksuit.

'Joona told me to throw my hamburger away and come straight away,' Johan says.

'This is Johan Jönson, from IT,' Joona explains.

Johan makes a lame attempt to imitate Joona's Finnish accent.

'And Saga Bauer is a superintendent with the Security Police,' Joona says.

'So are we here to talk or work?' Johan Jönson asks, still in a Finnish accent.

'Stop that,' Saga says.

'We need to look at Palmcrona's computer,' Joona says. 'How long will it take?'

They walk towards the study.

'Will it be used in evidence?' Johan Jönson asks.

'Yes,' Joona replies.

'So you want me to clone the computer?' he asks.

'How long will it take?' Joona asks.

'You'll have time to tell the Security Police some jokes,' he replies, without moving.

'What's the matter with you?' Saga says irritably.

'Can I ask, are you seeing anyone?' Johan Jönson asks with an embarrassed smile.

She looks him in the eye and nods seriously. He looks down, mutters something, then disappears into Carl Palmcrona's study.

Joona takes a pair of protective gloves from Saga, pulls them on and then checks the post on the shelf, but doesn't find anything special. There isn't much, just a few letters from the bank and an accountant, some information from the Cabinet Office, test results from the Sophia Clinic's orthopaedic department, and the minutes of the spring meeting of the residents' committee.

They return to the room where the music was playing when Palmcrona was found dead. Joona sits down on one of the Carl Malmsten sofas and gently moves his hand in front of the thin, ice-blue beam of light coming from the music centre. Music starts to play from the loudspeakers, a solo violin. A virtuoso is conjuring forth a fragile melody in the highest part of the instrument's register, but in the manner of a nervous bird.

Joona looks at his watch, leaves Saga by the music centre and goes out to the study. Johan Jönson isn't there. He's sitting in the kitchen with his thin laptop on the table in front of him.

'Did it go okay?' Joona asks.

'What?'

'Did you manage to copy Palmcrona's computer?'

'All done – this is an exact clone,' he replies, as if he doesn't really understand the question.

Joona goes round the table and looks at the screen.

'Can you get into his emails?'

Johan Jönson opens the program.

'Ta-dah,' he says.

'We'll look at his mail from the past week,' Joona goes on.

'Starting with the inbox?'

'Yes, starting there.'

'Do you think Saga likes me?' Johan Jönson suddenly asks out of the blue.

'No,' Joona replies.

'Love often starts with arguments.'

'Try tugging her plait,' Joona says, and points at the screen.

Johan Jönson opens the inbox and grins.

'*Jackpot-voitto*,' he says in Finnish.

Joona sees three emails from the address *skunk@hotmail.com*.

'Open them,' Joona whispers.

Johan Jönson clicks on the first one, and Björn Almskog's email suddenly fills the whole screen.

'Jesus Christ, Superstar,' Johan whispers, and moves out of the way.

44

The emails

Joona reads the email, stands still for a moment, then opens the other emails and reads them through twice. He goes to find Saga Bauer, who is still standing in the music room.

'Did you find anything?' she asks.

'Yes . . .' Joona says. 'On the second of June, Carl Palmcrona received a blackmail email from Björn Almskog, from an anonymous address.'

'So it's all about blackmail,' she sighs.

'I'm not so sure about that,' Joona replies.

He goes on to give an account of Carl Palmcrona's final days. Together with Gerald James from the Technology and Science Council, Palmcrona paid a visit to Silencia Defence's arms factory in Trollhättan. In all likelihood, he didn't read Björn Almskog's email until he got home, seeing as his response to his blackmailer was sent at 18.25. In his reply Palmcrona warned the blackmailer of serious consequences. At lunchtime the following day Palmcrona sent a second email to the black-mailer expressing complete capitulation. After that, he presumably fastened the cord to the ceiling and asked his housekeeper to leave him alone. Once she had left he turned on some music, went into the sitting room, placed his briefcase on end, climbed up on it, put the noose round his neck and kicked the briefcase away. Immediately after his death Björn

Almskog's second email to Palmcrona arrived, and the third the following day.

Joona places printouts of the five emails in the right order on the table, and Saga comes and stands next to him and reads the entire exchange.

The first email from Björn Almskog, on Wednesday 2 June, at 11.37:

Dear Carl Palmcrona,

I am writing to inform you that I am in possession of an original photograph of a sensitive nature. The picture shows you sitting in a private box drinking champagne with Raphael Guidi. Seeing as I fully understand the troubling nature of this documentary evidence, I am prepared to sell the photograph to you for one million kronor. As soon as you have transferred the money to transit account 837-9 222701730 the picture will be sent to you and all evidence of this correspondence destroyed.

Sincerely, a skunk.

Carl Palmcrona's reply, on Wednesday 2 June, at 18.25:

I don't know who you are, but one thing I do know is that you don't understand what you are getting yourself into. You have absolutely no idea.

So I am warning you: this is extremely serious, and I beg you, give me the photograph before it's too late.

Carl Palmcrona's second reply, Thursday 3 June, at 14.02:

It's too late now, you and I are both going to die.

Björn Almskog's second email, Thursday 3 June, at 16.02:

I give up, I'll do as you say.

Björn Almskog's third email, Friday 4 June, at 07.47:

Dear Carl Palmcrona,
   I have sent the photograph. Forget I ever contacted you.
   Sincerely, a skunk.

After reading the emails through twice Saga Bauer looks very serious, then says that the exchange contains the core of the entire tragedy:

'Björn Almskog wanted to sell a compromising photograph to Palmcrona. It's clear that Palmcrona believed the photograph existed, and it's clear that the content of the photograph was far more serious than Björn imagined. Palmcrona warned Björn, there's no suggestion of him paying anything for the picture, he seemed to think its very existence was dangerous to the pair of them.'

'So what do you think happened?' Joona asks.

'Palmcrona waited for a reply, either by email or post,' Saga says. 'When he didn't get an answer, he sent the second email in which he said they were both going to die, both him and Björn.'

'And then he hanged himself,' Joona says.

'When Björn got to the internet café and read Palmcrona's second email, "It's too late now, you and I are both going to die", he got scared and replied that he was going to do what Palmcrona suggested.'

'Without knowing that Palmcrona was already dead.'

'Exactly,' she says. 'It was already too late, and everything he did after that was pretty much in vain . . .'

'He seems to have panicked after Palmcrona's second email,'

Joona says. 'He dropped any thought of blackmail and just wanted to get out of the situation.'

'But the problem was that the photograph was taped to the door in Penelope's flat.'

'He didn't get a chance to get hold of the picture until she went off to the television studio for that debate,' Joona goes on. 'He waited outside and watched her go off in a taxi, rushed in, met the little girl on the stairs, hurried into the flat, grabbed the photograph from the door, took the underground to the Central Station, posted the photograph to Palmcrona, emailed him, went back to his flat on Pontonjärgatan, got his bags, caught the bus to Södermalm and hurried to his boat on Långholmen.'

'So what makes you think this is anything more than ordinary extortion?'

'Björn's flat was completely destroyed by fire about three hours after he left it,' Joona says. 'The fire brigade's experts are convinced it was caused by an iron being left on in the next flat, but . . .'

'I've stopped believing in coincidences when it comes to this case,' Saga says.

'Me too,' Joona smiles.

They look at the email exchange again, and Joona points at Palmcrona's two messages.

'Palmcrona must have been in contact with someone between his first and second emails,' he says.

'The first includes a warning,' Saga says. 'The second says it's too late, and that they're both going to die.'

'I think Palmcrona called someone when he got the blackmail email. He was scared, but was hoping to get help,' Joona says. 'Then, when he realised there was no way out, he sent his second email where he simply stated that they were both going to die.'

'We can put someone to work examining his phone records,' Saga says.

'Erixon's already started.'

'What else?'

'We need to check the person mentioned in Björn's first email,' Joona says.

'Raphael Guidi?' Saga wonders.

'Do you know him?'

'Everyone calls him Raphael, after the archangel,' Saga says. 'He's an Italian businessman who puts together arms deals in the Middle East and Africa.'

'The arms trade,' Joona says.

'Raphael has been active for thirty years, and has built up a private empire, but I doubt he's involved. Interpol have never been able to get anything on him. There have been suspicions, but nothing more.'

'Is it strange for Carl Palmcrona to meet Raphael?' Joona asks.

'On the contrary,' she replies. 'It's part of his job, even if we might think it pretty inappropriate to drink champagne with him.'

'But still not the sort of thing you commit suicide over, or the sort of thing you kill anyone for,' Joona says.

'No,' she smiles.

'So the photograph must have revealed something else, something dangerous.'

'If Björn sent the photograph to Palmcrona, it ought to be here in his apartment,' Saga says.

'I looked through the post, and . . .'

He stops abruptly and Saga stares at him.

'What is it? What are you thinking?' she asks.

'There were only letters addressed directly to him in the box, no adverts, no bills,' he says. 'The post is already sorted by the time it gets here.'

45

The motorway

The housekeeper, Edith Schwartz, doesn't have a phone. She lives approximately seventy kilometres north of Stockholm, outside Knivsta. Joona is sitting quietly beside Saga. She drives steadily up the entire length of Sveavägen, then they leave the centre of the city at Norrtull and carry on along the motorway, past the turning to the Karolinska Hospital.

'The Security Police's investigation of Penelope's flat is finished,' she says. 'I've been through all the material, and it doesn't look like she had any connections to any extreme left-wing groups. Quite the contrary, in fact – she distances herself from them, is an outspoken pacifist and campaigns against their methods. I've also looked at what little we've got on Björn Almskog. He works at Debaser at Medborgarplatsen, isn't polit-ically active, but he was arrested once in connection to a street-party that was organised by Reclaim the City.'

They drive past the flickering railings of the Northern Cemetery and the tall trees of Hagaparken.

'I've been through our archives,' Saga says slowly. 'Everything we've got on extremist groups in Stockholm, on both left and right . . . it took most of the night. Obviously it's all classified, but you need to know that the Security Police made a mistake: Penelope and Björn aren't involved in any sort of sabotage, nothing like that at all. They're almost ridiculously innocent.'

'So you've dropped that line of inquiry?'

'Just like you, I'm convinced we're investigating something in an entirely different league altogether, way above left- or right-wing extremists . . . probably a league way above the Security Police and National Crime,' she says. 'I mean, Palmcrona's death, the fire in Björn's flat, Viola's murder and so on . . . this is about something else entirely.'

They fall silent and Joona thinks back to his encounter with the housekeeper, the way she looked him in the eyes and asked if they had taken Palmcrona down yet:

'What do you mean, taken down?'

'I'm sorry, I'm only the housekeeper, I thought . . .'

He had asked her if she had noticed anything unusual.

'A noose from the lamp-hook in the small drawing room,' she had replied.

'You saw the noose?'

'Of course.'

Of course, Joona thinks, and looks out at the motorway. There's a red noise-suppressing fence to their right, screening a residential area and some football pitches. The sharp way the housekeeper said the words 'Of course' linger in Joona's mind. He thinks back to the look on her face when he explained that she might have to come to Police Headquarters and talk to a police officer. She didn't react anxiously, as he had expected, but merely nodded.

Joona calls Nathan Pollock at the National Homicide Commission and hears his slightly nasal voice after just two rings.

'Nathan.'

'You and Tommy Kofoed looked at the circles of prints beneath Palmcrona's body.'

'The preliminary investigation was dropped,' Pollock replies, and Joona hears him typing on a keyboard.

'Yes, but now . . .'

'I know,' he interrupts. 'I've spoken to Carlos, he's told me about the latest developments.'

'Can you take another look?'

'That's what I'm doing right now,' Pollock replies.

'Sounds good,' Joona says. 'When do you think you'll be done?'

'Now,' he says. 'The shoeprints come from Palmcrona and his housekeeper, Edith Schwartz.'

'No one else?'

'No.'

Saga is maintaining a steady speed of 140 kilometres per hour as they head ever further north on the E4.

Joona and Saga have sat together in Police Headquarters, listening to the recording of the interview with Edith Schwartz, simultaneously following John Bengtsson's handwritten comments.

Now Joona goes through the interview again in his head: after the introductory formalities John Bengtsson explains that there are no suspicions that a crime has been committed, but that he hopes she might be able to shed some light on the circumstances surrounding Carl Palmcrona's death. Then there's silence, a vague hum from the ventilation system, and a chair creaking, a pen scratching on paper. John Bengtsson's notes record that he chose to wait for Edith Schwartz to speak because she seemed so completely indifferent.

It took a little more than two minutes for her to say something. That's a long time to sit at a desk opposite a police officer, while nothing but the slow silence is recorded.

'Had Mr Palmcrona taken his coat off?' she eventually asks.

'Why do you wonder that?' John Bengtsson asks amiably.

She falls silent again, for another thirty seconds or so, before John speaks again:

'Was he wearing his coat the last time you saw him?' he asks.

'Yes.'

'Earlier you told Detective Superintendent Linna that you'd seen a noose hanging from the ceiling.'

'Yes.'

'What did you think it was going to be used for?'

She doesn't answer.

'How long had it been hanging there?' John asks.

'Since Wednesday,' she replies calmly.

'So you saw the noose hanging from the ceiling on the evening of second of June, went home, returned the following morning, third of June, saw the noose again, met Palmcrona, left the apartment, then returned again at 14.30 on the fifth of June . . . and that was when you met Superintendent Linna.'

The notes indicate that Edith shrugged her shoulders at this.

'Can you tell me about those days in your own words?' John Bengtsson asks.

'I arrived at Mr Palmcrona's apartment at six o'clock in the morning of the Wednesday. I'm only allowed to use my key in the morning because Mr Palmcrona sleeps until half past six. He's careful to stick to a regular schedule, so there are no lie-ins, not even on Sundays. I grind coffee beans in the manual grinder, cut two slices of bread, spread them with extra salted spreadable butter, put two slices of liver pâté with truffle on them, then sliced pickled gherkin, and a slice of Cheddar cheese on the side. I laid the table with starched linen and the summer china. The morning paper should be empty of loose adverts and the sport section, and lie to the right of the chair, folded.'

She goes on to relate in exemplary detail the preparation of Wednesday's evening meal, minced beef patties in cream sauce, then lunch on Thursday.

When she reaches the moment on Saturday when she returned with the shopping for the weekend and rang on the door, she falls silent.

'I appreciate that this is difficult,' John Bengtsson says after a brief silence. 'But I've sat here and listened to you describe what happened on Wednesday and Thursday, in great detail, but you haven't mentioned anything about Carl Palmcrona's sudden demise, not once.'

She remains silent, and makes no attempt to offer an explanation.

'I have to ask you to search your memories again,' John Bengtsson goes on patiently. 'Did you know that Carl Palmcrona was dead when you rang on the door?'

'No,' she replies.

'Didn't you ask Superintendent Linna if we had taken him down yet?' John asks, with a degree of impatience in his voice.

'Yes,' she replies.

'Had you already seen that he was dead?'

'No.'

'What the hell?' John says irritably. 'Can you not just tell me what you know? What made you ask if we had taken him down? You asked, after all! Why did you do that if you didn't know he was dead?'

In his report, John Bengtsson wrote that he had unfortunately made the mistake of allowing himself to be provoked by her evasive manner, and that she had clammed up completely after his outburst.

'Am I under suspicion for anything?' she asks coolly.

'No.'

'Then we're done.'

'It would be a great help if . . .'

'I don't remember anything else,' she says, cutting him off and getting up from her chair.

Joona looks at Saga. Her eyes are focused on the motorway and the lorry ahead of them.

'I've been thinking about the interview with the housekeeper,' Joona says.

'Me too,' she replies.

'John got annoyed with her, thought she was contradicting herself. He claimed she knew Palmcrona was dead when she rang the doorbell,' Joona says.

'Yes,' Saga replies, without looking at him.

'But she was telling the truth, because she didn't know he was dead. She thought he probably was, but she didn't know,' he goes on. 'That's why she said no when he asked.'

'Edith Schwartz seems to be an unusual woman.'

'I think she's trying to hide something from us, without actually having to lie,' Joona says.

46

Both Joona and Saga doubt that they're going to be able to get the housekeeper, Edith Schwartz, to say anything conclusive, but she might be able to lead them to the photograph, and that in turn could help bring the entire case to a close.

Saga indicates right, leaves the motorway and slows down, then turns left onto highway 77, drives under the motorway towards Knivsta, but soon turns off onto a narrow gravel track that runs parallel to the motorway.

Low pine forest is interspersed with fields that have been cropped. The brick wall of a manure heap has given way, and the tin roof is hanging crookedly.

'We should be there now,' Saga says, glancing at the satnav.

They roll slowly towards a rusty barrier and stop. When Joona gets out of the car he can hear the traffic on the motorway as a rolling, lifeless roar.

Twenty metres away is a single-storey building made of dirty yellow brick, with shuttered windows and mossy cement tiles on the roof.

They hear a peculiar whirring sound as they approach the house.

Saga looks at Joona. They move cautiously towards the front door, suddenly very alert. There's a rustling sound behind the house, then the metallic whirring again.

The sound is rapidly coming closer, and a large dog throws itself at them. It stops on its hind legs with its mouth open just a metre away from Saga. Then it is yanked backwards before it puts its front legs down and starts to bark. It's a large Alsatian with a matted coat. It's barking aggressively, tossing its head and running from side to side. Only now do they see that the dog is attached to a long leash. The wire rattles and whirrs as it runs.

The dog turns and rushes at Joona, but the leash stops it and it gets yanked back again. It's still barking uncontrollably, but stops at the sound of a voice through the wall.

'Nils!' a woman shouts.

The dog whines and walks round in a circle with its tail between its legs. The floor creaks and a few moments later the door opens. The dog runs into the house, dragging the leash behind it. Edith comes onto the steps dressed in a pilled, purple dressing-gown and looks at them.

'We need to talk to you,' Joona says.

'I've already told you all I know,' she replies.

'Can we come in?'

'No.'

Joona looks past her into the gloomy house. The hall is full of saucepans and plates, a grey vacuum-cleaner hose, clothes, shoes and rusty crayfish cages.

'Out here will do fine,' Saga says cheerfully.

Joona looks at his notes and starts by checking the details of what she said in her previous interview. It's a routine method of uncovering any lies or inconsistencies, seeing as it's often hard to remember details that aren't true, details you came up with on the spur of the moment.

'What did Palmcrona have to eat on Wednesday?'

'Minced beef patties in cream sauce,' she replies.

'With rice?' Joona asks.

'Potatoes. Always boiled potatoes.'

'What time did you arrive at Palmcrona's apartment on Thursday?'

'Six o'clock.'

'What did you do when you left Palmcrona's apartment on Thursday?'

'He'd given me the evening off.'

Joona looks into her eyes and concludes that there's no point skirting round the important questions.

'Had Palmcrona hung the noose from the ceiling on Wednesday?'

'No,' Edith replies.

'That's what you told our colleague, John Bengtsson,' Saga says.

'No.'

'We've got a recording of the entire interview,' Saga says with suppressed irritation, then stops herself abruptly.

'Did you say anything to Palmcrona about the noose?' Joona asks.

'We didn't talk about personal matters with each other.'

'But isn't it a little odd to leave a man alone with a noose hanging from the ceiling?' Saga asks.

'I could hardly stand and watch,' Edith replies with a trace of a smile.

'I suppose not,' Saga says calmly.

For the first time Edith seems to take a proper look at Saga. Without any sign of embarrassment she lets her gaze wander from Saga's blonde hair and colourful ribbons, her unmade-up face, to her faded jeans and trainers.

'I still can't quite make sense of it, though,' Saga says wearily. 'You told our colleague that you saw the noose on Wednesday, but when I asked just now you said the opposite.'

Joona looks in his notebook at what he wrote a minute or so before, when Saga asked if Palmcrona had hung the noose up on Wednesday.

'Edith,' Joona says. 'I think I understand what you're saying.'

'Good,' she replies in a low voice.

'When you were asked if Palmcrona hung the noose up on Wednesday, you said no, because it wasn't him who hung it up.'

The old woman raises her head and gives him a hard stare, then says stiffly:

'He tried, but he couldn't do it, his back was far too bad after the operation last winter . . . So he asked me to do it.'

They fall silent. The trees stand motionless in the static sunshine.

'So you were the person who tied the noose to the lamp-hook on Wednesday?' Joona asks.

'He made the noose, and held the stepladder while I went up it.'

'Then you put the stepladder away, returned to your usual duties and went home on Wednesday evening once you had done the washing-up after dinner,' Joona says.

'Yes.'

'You returned the following morning,' he goes on. 'You let yourself in as usual, and set about making his breakfast.'

'Did you know that he wasn't hanging from the noose then?' Saga asks.

'I'd checked in the small drawing room,' Edith replies.

Something approaching a snide smile flits quickly across her otherwise impassive face.

'You've already said that Palmcrona ate breakfast at exactly the same time as usual, but he didn't go to work that morning.'

'He sat in the music room for at least an hour.'

'Listening to music?'

'Yes,' she replies.

'Just before lunchtime he made a short phone-call,' Saga says.

'I don't know about that, he was in his study with the door closed, but before he sat down to have his poached salmon he asked me to phone and book a taxi for two o'clock.'

'He was going to Arlanda Airport,' Joona says.

'Yes.'

'And at ten minutes to two he received a phone-call?'

'Yes, he'd already put his coat on and answered the call in the hall.'

'Did you hear what he said?' Saga asks.

Edith stands still, scratches the plaster on her face and then puts her hand on the door-handle.

'Dying isn't such a nightmare,' she says quietly.

'I asked if you heard what he said,' Saga says.

'Now you'll have to excuse me,' Edith says curtly, and starts to close the door.

'Wait,' Joona says.

213

The door stops abruptly and she looks at him through the gap without opening it again.

'Have you had time to sort out Palmcrona's post today?' Joona asks.

'Of course.'

'Fetch everything that isn't adverts,' Joona says.

She nods, goes into the house, closing the door behind her, then returns a short while later with a blue plastic tray full of post.

'Thank you,' Joona says, taking the tray.

She shuts and locks the door. After a few moments the dog's leash starts to rattle again. They hear it barking aggressively behind them as they go back to the car and get in.

Saga starts the engine, puts the car in gear and turns it round. Joona puts on a pair of protective gloves, looks through the post in the tray, takes out a white envelope with a handwritten address, opens it and carefully pulls out the photograph that at least two people have died for.

47

The fourth person

Saga Bauer pulls over to the side of the road and stops. The tall grass in the ditch brushes the windows. Joona Linna is sitting absolutely still, staring at the photograph.

The top of the image is obscured by something, but apart from that it's extremely sharp. Presumably the camera was hidden and the picture taken without anyone knowing.

The photograph shows four people in a spacious box in a concert hall. Three men and a woman. Their faces are visible, and very clear. Only one of them is turned away, but not completely.

There's an ice-bucket with champagne, and the table is laid so that they can eat, talk and listen to the music at the same time.

Joona immediately recognises Carl Palmcrona holding a tall champagne glass in his hand, and Saga identifies two of the others.

'That's Raphael Guidi, the arms dealer mentioned in the blackmail email,' she says, pointing at a man with thinning hair. 'And that one who's half-turned away is Pontus Salman, the boss of Silencia Defence.'

'Weapons,' Joona says in a low voice.

'Silencia Defence is a reputable company.'

On stage behind the men in the private box is a string quartet, two violins, a viola and a cello. The musicians are all men. They're sitting in a semi-circle, facing each other, with looks of calm concentration on their faces. It's not possible to tell if their eyes are open or closed, if they're looking at their scores or if they've got their eyes closed and are listening to the other instruments.

'Who's the fourth person, the woman?' Joona asks.

'It's on the tip of my tongue,' Saga says thoughtfully. 'I recognise her, but . . . Damn . . .'

Saga falls silent and stares at the woman's face.

'We have to find out who she is,' Joona says.

'Yes.'

Saga starts the car, and just as she pulls away she remembers:

'Agathe al-Haji,' she says quickly. 'She's a military advisor to President Omar al-Bashir.'

'Sudan,' Joona says.

'Yes.'

'How long has she been his advisor?' Joona asks.

'Fifteen years, maybe more, I don't remember.'

'So what's so special about this picture?'

'I don't know. Nothing, I mean . . . it's not at all strange for these four to meet and discuss the possibility of doing business,' Saga says. 'Quite the contrary. Meetings like this are part of the job. It could be a first point of contact. They meet, discuss their intentions, maybe request an advance evaluation from Carl Palmcrona.'

'And positive advance notification means that the ISP will probably award an export licence?'

'Precisely. It's an initial indication.'

'Does Sweden usually export military equipment to Sudan?' Joona asks.

'No, I don't think so,' she replies. 'We'll have to talk to someone who specialises in that part of the world. I have a feeling that China and Russia are the main suppliers, but that isn't necessarily still the case, because of course Sudan's civil war ended in 2005, so I presume the market opened up after that.'

'So what does this picture actually mean? Why did it lead Carl Palmcrona to commit suicide? I mean, the only thing it proves is that he met these people in a box at a concert hall.'

They drive south on the dusty motorway in silence while Joona looks at the photograph, turns it over, looks at the torn corner and thinks.

'So the picture itself isn't remotely dangerous?' he asks.

'No, not to my eyes.'

'Did Palmcrona kill himself because he realised that whoever took the picture was going to reveal some secret? Maybe the picture was just a warning. Maybe Penelope and Björn are more important than the photograph?'

'We don't know a damn thing.'

'Yes, we do,' Joona says. 'The problem is that we haven't managed to put together the pieces we've found. We can still do nothing but guess at the fixer's mission, but it looks like he was trying to find this photograph so he could destroy it, and that he killed Viola Fernandez in the mistaken belief that she was Penelope.'

'Penelope could be the photographer,' Saga says. 'That's probably the case, but he wasn't content with just killing her.'

'Precisely, that's just what I've been wondering about. We don't know what came first . . . Is the picture the link to the photographer, who is perceived to be the real threat? Or is the photographer the link to the photograph, which is seen as the real threat?'

'The fixer's first target was Björn's flat.'

They sit in silence for half an hour, and have almost reached Police Headquarters on Kungsholmen when Joona looks at the photograph again. The four people in the box, the food, the four musicians on stage behind them, the instruments, the heavy curtain, the champagne bottle, the tall glasses.

'I'm looking at this picture,' Joona says. 'I see four faces . . . and I'm thinking that one of them is behind Viola Fernandez's murder.'

'Yes,' Saga says. 'Palmcrona is dead, so we can pretty much rule him out. Which leaves three . . . and we aren't going to be able to talk to two of them, they're far beyond our reach.'

'We need to get Pontus Salman to talk,' Joona says tersely.

'Shall we bring him in for questioning?'

48

It's hard to get hold of anyone at Silencia Defence Ltd. All the phone numbers they can find lead to the same labyrinth of automated options and pre-recorded messages. Eventually Saga finds an opening by pressing nine plus the asterisk to speak to a member of the sales team. She gets put through to the secretary of the sales department, ignores her questions and explains why she's calling. At first the secretary goes quiet, then she explains that Saga's got the wrong number and that their telephone time is already over.

'I'll have to ask you to call back tomorrow, between nine and eleven, and . . .'

'Just make sure Pontus Salman is expecting a visit from the Security Police at 14.00 today,' Saga interrupts loudly.

She hears cautious tapping at a keyboard.

'I'm sorry,' the secretary says after a pause. 'He's in meetings all day.'

'Not at 14.00,' Saga says softly.

'Yes, it says here that . . .'

'Because that's when he's going to be talking to me,' she interrupts again.

'I'll pass on your message.'

'Thanks very much,' Saga says and ends the call, and meets Joona's gaze across the table.

'Two o'clock?' he asks.

'Yes.'

'Tommy Kofoed wants to look at the photograph,' Joona says. 'I'll meet you in his room after lunch before we set off.'

While Joona has lunch with Disa, the National Crime Unit's forensics experts ruin the photograph.

The face of one of the four people in the box is blurred to the point where it is unrecognisable.

Disa smiles to herself as she removes the container from the rice cooker. She passes it to Joona and watches as he wets his hands to see if the rice is cool enough for him to start making little parcels with it.

'Did you know that Södermalm had its own Calvary?' she asks.

'Calvary? Isn't that . . .'

'Golgotha,' Disa nods, opens Joona's fridge, finds two glasses and pours wine in one, water in the other.

Disa's face looks relaxed. Her early summer freckles have got darker, and her unruly hair is tied back in a loose plait. Joona rinses his hands and takes out a clean tea-towel. Disa stands in front of him and wraps her arms round his neck. Joona returns the embrace. He leans his face against her head and breathes in her scent as he feels her hands caress his neck and back.

'Can't we try?' she whispers. 'We can, can't we?'

'Yes,' he replies quietly.

She holds him tight, then pulls free from his embrace.

'Sometimes I get so angry with you,' she mumbles, and turns her back on him.

'Disa, I am who I am. I mean . . .'

'It's a good thing we don't live together,' she interrupts, and walks out of the kitchen.

He hears her lock herself in the bathroom, wonders if he ought to go after her and knock on the door, but knows that she really just wants to be alone for a while. He carries on with the food instead. He takes a piece of fish, places it gently in the palm of his hand, then rubs some strong wasabi on it.

After a few minutes the bathroom door opens and Disa comes back to the kitchen, stands in the doorway and looks on as he prepares the sushi.

'Do you remember,' Disa says with laughter in her voice, 'that your mum always removed the salmon from the sushi and fried it before putting it back on the rice again?'

'Yes.'

'Shall I lay the table?' Disa asks.

'If you like.'

Disa takes plates and chopsticks into the living room, then stops at the window and looks down at Wallingatan. A clump of trees stand out, their summer leaves bright green. She looks off towards Norra Bantorget, across the pleasant neighbourhood where Joona Linna has lived for the past year.

She lays the white glass dining table, returns to the kitchen and drinks a sip of wine. It's lost the crispness that really only comes from being chilled. She suppresses a strong urge to sit down on the polished wooden floor and ask if they can eat on the floor with their hands, like children, under the table.

'You've been outbid,' she says instead.

'Outbid?'

She nods, with a fleeting feeling of wanting to be a bit mean, but not quite.

'Tell me,' Joona says calmly, carrying the dish of sushi to the table.

Disa picks up her glass again and says brightly:

'It's just that someone at the museum has been asking if I'd like to have dinner with him one evening for the past six months.'

'Is that what people do these days? Ask ladies out to dinner?'

Disa gives him a wry smile.

'Jealous?'

'I don't know. A bit, maybe,' Joona says, and walks over to her. 'It's nice to be asked out to dinner.'

'Yes.'

Disa runs her fingers hard through his thick hair.

'Is he handsome?' Joona asks.

'Yes, actually.'

'That's good.'

'But I don't want to go out with him,' Disa smiles.

He doesn't answer, just stands there completely still with his face turned away.

'You know what I want,' Disa says softly.

His face is suddenly oddly pale, and she can see tiny beads of sweat on his forehead. Slowly he looks up at her, and there's something about his eyes; they're black, hard, bottomless.

'Joona, forget it,' she says hastily. 'Sorry . . .'

Joona opens his mouth to say something, he takes a step towards her but his legs suddenly give way.

'Joona!' Disa cries, knocking her glass off the table.

She sinks down onto the floor beside him, holds him and whispers that it will soon pass.

After a while the expression on Joona's face changes, as the pain slowly eases, little by little.

Disa sweeps up the pieces of her glass and then they sit down at the table in silence.

'You're not taking your medication,' she says after a while.

'It makes me sleepy. I have to be able to think, it's really important that I can think completely clearly right now.'

'You promised you'd take it.'

'I will,' he says.

'It's dangerous, you know that,' she whispers.

'I'll start again as soon as I've solved this case.'

'And if you don't solve it?'

From a distance the Nordic Museum looks like an ornament carved from ivory, but it's actually built of sandstone and limestone. An ornate fantasy renaissance palace with masses of towers and turrets, the museum was intended to sing the praises of the sovereignty of the Nordic peoples, but by the time it was inaugurated one rainy day in the summer of 1907, the union with Norway had been dissolved and the king was dying.

Joona walks quickly through the vast museum hall and only stops when he's reached the top of the stairs, where he composes himself, looks down at the floor for a long time, then carries on slowly past the illuminated display cases. Nothing catches his eye. Joona merely carries on, absorbed in memories and loss.

The security guard has already placed a chair in front of the display case for him.

Joona Linna sits down and looks at the Sami bridal crown with its eight points, like two interwoven hands. It's glowing gently behind the thin glass. Joona hears a voice inside him, sees a face smile at him as he sits behind the wheel driving that day after it had been raining, and the sun was shining off the puddles on the road as if lit up from below. He glances round at the back seat to check that Lumi has got her seat belt on properly.

The bridal crown looks like it's made of thin branches, leather, or plaited hair. He stares at its promise of love and happiness, and thinks about the serious set of his wife's mouth, the sand-coloured hair falling across her face.

'How are you doing?'

Joona looks up at the security guard in surprise. He's worked here for many years, a middle-aged man with stubble and eyes worn with rubbing.

'I honestly don't know,' he mumbles, and gets up from the chair.

The memory of Lumi's small hand lingers like an absence in his body as he leaves the museum. All he had done was look back to make sure she was sitting properly, and had suddenly felt her hand touch his fingers.

49

The indistinct face

Joona and Saga are sitting in the car on the way to Silencia Defence's head office to talk to Pontus Salman. They're taking with them the photograph that the National Crime Unit's technicians ruined. They head south in silence along highway 73, which runs like a dirty trail down to Nynäshamn.

Two hours ago Joona had been looking at a sharp photograph of the four people in the box: Raphael's calm face and thin hair; Palmcrona's slack smile and steel-rimmed glasses; Pontus Salman with his handsome, boyish looks, and Agathe al-Haji, with her wrinkled cheeks and heavy, intelligent eyes.

'I had a thought,' Joona said slowly, meeting Saga's gaze. 'If we could make the quality of the photo worse, and treat it in some way so that it's no longer possible to identify Pontus Salman . . .'

He fell silent and carried on thinking to himself.

'What do we achieve by that?' Saga asked.

'He wouldn't know we've got a high-resolution original, would he?'

'There's no way he'd know. He'd probably assume we'd done everything we could to improve the sharpness, not make it worse.'

'Exactly. We've done all we could to identify the four people in the picture, but have only succeeded with three of them, because the fourth is facing away slightly and is far too unclear.'

'You mean we give him the chance to lie?' Saga said quickly.

'To lie and say he wasn't there, that he didn't meet Palmcrona, Agathe al-Haji and Raphael.'

'Because if he denies being there, then maybe it's the meeting itself which is sensitive.'

'And if he starts to lie, we've trapped him.'

Just beyond Handen they turn off the Jordbro link road and roll into an industrial area surrounded by peaceful forest.

Silencia Defence's head office is an impersonal, dull grey concrete building, with a sterile, almost chaste appearance.

Joona looks at the huge building, slowly scanning the dark windows and tinted glass, thinking once again about the photograph of the four people in the concert-hall box, the photograph that had unleashed a chain of violence, leaving one dead girl and a grieving mother in its wake. And perhaps Penelope Fernandez and Björn Almskog are also dead because of the picture. He gets out of the car and his jaw tenses when he thinks about the fact that Pontus Salman, one of the people in the mysterious photograph, is inside this building right now.

The photograph has been copied and the original sent to the National Forensics Laboratory in Linköping. Tommy Kofoed has digitally manipulated one copy so that it looks old and battered. One corner is missing and fragments of tape are visible on the others. Kofoed has blurred Pontus Salman's face and hand to make it look as if he was moving when the picture was taken.

Salman will believe that he – and he alone – had the good fortune to be blurred and unrecognisable on the picture, Joona thinks. Meaning that there's nothing to link him to the meeting with Raphael Guidi, Carl Palmcrona and Agathe al-Haji. All he has to do to distance himself from it is to deny ever being there. It isn't a criminal offence not to recognise yourself in a blurred picture, or to not remember meeting certain people.

Joona starts to walk towards the entrance.

But if Salman does deny it, we'll know he's lying, that he wants to keep something secret.

The air is oppressively hot and humid.

Saga nods seriously at Joona as they walk through the heavy, shining doors.

And if he does start lying, Joona thinks, we'll see to it that he carries on lying, digging himself deeper into a hole until we've got him.

They find themselves in a large, chilly reception area.

When Pontus Salman looks at the picture and says he can't identify the fourth person, we'll lament the fact that he's unable to help us, Joona tells himself. We'll get ready to leave, but will stop and ask him to look at the photograph one last time through a magnifying glass. Kofoed has left a signet ring visible on Salman's hand. We'll ask him if he recognises the clothes, the shoes, or the ring on the man's little finger. He'll be forced to deny this too, and his blatant lie will be reason enough to take him to Police Headquarters for questioning, reason enough to put him under pressure.

Behind the desk in reception is the illuminated logo with the company's name and a snakelike design filled with runes.

'*He fought as long as he had a weapon,*' Joona says.

'Can you read runes?' Saga asks sceptically.

Joona points at the sign bearing the translation, then looks back at the desk. Behind it sits a pale man with thin, dry lips.

'Pontus Salman,' Joona says tersely.

'Have you arranged a meeting with him?'

'Two o'clock,' Saga says.

The receptionist looks at his papers, leafs through them and reads something.

'Ah, yes,' he says quietly, then looks up. 'Pontus Salman has had to cancel.'

'The message didn't reach us,' Saga says. 'We need his help to . . .'

'I'm very sorry.'

'Call him and explain the misunderstanding,' Saga says.

'I can try, but I don't think . . . Because he's in a meeting.'

'On the fourth floor,' Joona says.

'Fifth,' the receptionist replies automatically.

Saga sits down in one of the armchairs. The sun is shining through the large windows, spreading like fire through her hair.

Joona remains standing by the desk as the receptionist puts the phone to his ear and clicks a number on his computer. The phone rings for a long time before the receptionist shakes his head apologetically.

'Don't worry,' Joona suddenly says. 'We'll surprise him instead.'

'Surprise him?' the receptionist says, looking unsettled.

Joona merely walks over to the glass door leading to the corridor and opens it.

'No need to let him know we're on our way,' he says with a smile.

The young receptionist's cheeks flush bright red. Saga gets up from the armchair and follows Joona.

'Wait,' the man says. 'I'll try . . .'

They walk along the corridor, into the waiting lift and press the button for the fifth floor. The doors close and they are carried silently upwards.

Pontus Salman is standing waiting for them when the lift doors open. He's in his forties, and there's something haggard about his face, about the way his features move.

'Welcome,' he says in a subdued voice.

'Thanks,' Joona says.

Pontus Salman looks them up and down.

'A detective and a fairytale princess,' he concludes.

As they follow him down a long corridor Joona thinks through the trap in his mind again, and how they have agreed to present the blurred photograph.

Joona feels a cold shiver run down his spine – as if Viola Fernandez has suddenly opened the door of her compartment in the cold-store of the pathology lab and is watching him expectantly.

The windows in the corridor are tinted, and give a sense of timelessness. The office is very big, with an elm desk and a pale grey suite of sofas and armchairs arranged around a black glass table.

They sit down in the armchairs. Pontus Salman smiles at them joylessly, steeples his fingers and asks:

'What's this about?'

'Are you aware that Carl Palmcrona from the ISP is dead?' Saga asks.

Salman nods twice.

'Suicide, I heard.'

'The investigation is ongoing,' Saga says amiably. 'We're looking into a photograph that we've found, we're very keen to identify the people with Palmcrona.'

'Three of them are clear enough, but the fourth is badly blurred,' Joona says.

'We'd like you to let your staff look at the picture, someone might recognise him. One of his hands is relatively sharp, for instance.'

'I see,' Salman says, pursing his lips.

'Perhaps someone might be able to tell from the context who it could be,' Saga goes on. 'It's worth a try, anyway.'

'We've been to see Patria and Saab Bofors Dynamics,' Joona says. 'But no one there recognised the man.'

Pontus Salman's haggard face is giving absolutely nothing away. Joona wonders if he's on medication to keep himself calm and confident. There's something remarkably lifeless about the look in his eyes, a lack of connection between expression and emotion, an evasive core that gives the impression of complete indifference.

'You must think it's important,' Salman says, crossing one leg over the other.

'Yes,' Saga says.

'May I see this remarkable photograph?' Pontus Salman asks in an easy, impersonal tone of voice.

'Apart from Carl Palmcrona,' Joona says, 'we've been able to identify Raphael Guidi, the arms dealer, and Agathe al-Haji, a military advisor to President al-Bashir . . . but no one has been able to identify the fourth person.'

Joona picks up his folder and holds out the plastic sleeve containing the photograph. Saga points at the blurred figure at the edge of the concert-hall box. Joona can see the concentration in her face, ready to register every nervous twitch, every tiny movement in Salman when he starts lying.

Salman moistens his lips again, his cheeks turn pale, then he smiles, taps the photograph and says:

'But that's me!'

227

'You?'

'Yes,' he says, laughing in a way that reveals his childish front teeth.

'But . . .'

'We met in Frankfurt,' he goes on with a happy smile. 'Listened to a wonderful performance of . . . I can't remember what they played now, Beethoven, I think it was . . .'

Joona tries to understand this abrupt confession, and clears his throat.

'You're quite sure?'

'Yes,' Salman says.

'Then that's that mystery solved,' Saga says, in a warm tone of voice that betrays nothing of their miscalculation.

'Maybe I should come and work for the Security Police,' Salman jokes.

'What was the meeting about?' Joona asks. 'If it's okay to ask?'

'Of course,' Salman laughs, looking at Joona. 'This photograph was taken in the spring of 2008, we were discussing sending ammunition to Sudan. Agathe al-Haji was negotiating on behalf of their government. The region needed to be stabilised after 2005. The negotiations were fairly well-advanced, but all that work went up in smoke after what happened in the spring of 2009. We were shaken, of course, as you can understand . . . Naturally, since then we haven't had any contact with Sudan.'

Joona looks at Saga, seeing as he has no idea what happened in the spring of 2009. Her face is perfectly neutral, and he decides not to ask.

'How many times did you meet?' Joona asks.

'Just this once,' he replies. 'So one might think it a little surprising that the director of the ISP accepted a glass of champagne.'

'Is that what you think?' Saga asks.

'There was nothing to celebrate . . . but perhaps he was just thirsty,' Salman says with a smile.

50

The hiding place

Penelope and Björn don't know how long they've been hiding in silence in a deep crevice in the rock. Until the second night they just sat curled up in the shadow of a broken pine.

They didn't have the energy to run any more, their bodies were way beyond tired, and they took turns keeping watch while the other slept.

Up until then their pursuer had predicted every step they had taken, but now the sense of his immediate presence has faded, he's been peculiarly quiet for a long time. The chilling, lurching sensation that he was right behind them disappeared the moment they left the road that led towards the more densely inhabited part of the island, when they made the unpredictable choice to head into the forest again, away from other people and the mainland.

Penelope isn't sure if she managed to leave a message on her mum's voicemail.

But someone ought to find Björn's boat soon, she thinks. And then the police will start looking.

All they have to do is stay hidden so that their pursuer doesn't find them.

The rounded rock-face is covered in green moss, but inside the crevice the stone is bare, and in several places clear water seeps out.

They've lapped up the water and then gone back to hiding in the shadows. The day has been hot, and they've sat completely still, panting, but towards evening, when the hot sun descends behind the trees, they fall asleep again.

Dreams and memories merge inside Penelope's mind. She hears Viola playing 'Twinkle, Twinkle, Little Star' on her miniature violin with coloured stickers to mark where she should put her fingers, then sees her put pink eye-shadow on and suck in her cheeks in front of the mirror.

Penelope gasps for breath as she wakes up.

Björn is sitting with his arms round his knees, shaking.

When the third night starts to fade they can't bear it any longer, they're so hungry and weak that they leave their hiding place and start to walk.

It's almost morning by the time Björn and Penelope reach the shore. The first red rays of sunlight are already tinting the edges of the long veils of cloud. The water is still and calm. Two swans are gliding on the surface side by side. They move gently on, slowly paddling their feet.

Björn holds Penelope's hand as they climb down to the water. His knees suddenly buckle with exhaustion and he staggers, slips, and reaches out one hand to the rocks to steady himself.

Penelope stares vacantly ahead of her as she takes her shoes off, ties them together and hangs them round her neck.

'Come on,' Björn whispers. 'We're just swimming, don't think about it, just do it.'

Penelope wants to tell him to wait, she isn't sure she's going to be able to make it, but he's already on his way into the water. She shivers and looks over at the other side of the island further out in the Stockholm archipelago.

She wades out behind him, feels the chilly water caress her calves and thighs. The bottom is stony and slippery, and soon gets deep beneath her. She doesn't have time to think about it, and slips into the water behind Björn.

With her arms aching and her clothes weighing her down, she starts to swim towards the other shore. Björn is already a long way ahead of her.

It takes a lot of effort, every stroke feels unbearable, her muscles are screaming for rest.

Kymmendö lies like a sandy bank in front of them. She kicks with her tired legs, struggles on and stays afloat. Suddenly the first rays of sunlight above the treetops dazzle her, her eyes prick and she stops swimming. She mustn't get cramp, but her arms can't take any more, they just give up. It's only a few seconds, but her wet clothes drag Penelope under the water before her arms start to obey her again. When she breaks the surface and breathes, she's extremely frightened, adrenalin is pumping round her body, she's breathing quickly and has lost her sense of direction and can see nothing but sea around her. She treads water desperately and spins round, managing to stop herself crying out. Then she catches sight of Björn's bobbing head, just above the surface of the water fifty metres away. Penelope goes on swimming, but isn't sure if she's going to be able to make it to the other island.

The shoes around her neck are impeding her swimming and she tries to get rid of them, but they've got tangled in her crucifix. The thin clasp breaks and her crucifix sinks into the water along with her shoes.

She swims on, feeling her heart pounding hard in her body, and far in front of her she can just make out Björn crawling ashore.

She gets water in her eyes, then sees Björn standing up on the shore. He's looking back for her when he ought to be hiding. Their pursuer could be at the north shore of Ornö at this very moment, he could be standing somewhere behind them searching the area with binoculars.

Penelope's movements are getting slower and weaker. She can feel how tired and sluggish her legs become as the lactic acid spreads through her thigh muscles. Swimming is hard, the last bit feels insurmountable. Björn looks worried, and he wades out into the water towards her as she gets closer to the shore. She's on the point of giving up again, but takes a few more strokes, then a few more, and then she feels the bottom below her. Björn is in the water now, he takes her hand and pulls her to him, and drags her onto the stony foreshore.

'We have to get under cover,' she gasps.

He helps her in amongst the pine trees. She can't feel her legs and feet, and is so cold she's shaking. They move deeper into the forest, only stopping when the sea is no longer in sight. Exhausted, they sink onto the moss and blueberry bushes and hold each other until their breathing calms down.

'We can't go on like this,' she whimpers.

'We can help each other.'

'I'm freezing, we have to get hold of dry clothes,' Penelope says with her teeth chattering, pressing her face against the goosebumps on Björn's chest.

They stand up and Björn supports her as they walk on through the forest on stiff legs. Björn's wet trainers squelch with every step. Penelope's bare feet shine out white against the ground. Her tracksuit is hanging from her body, wet and cold. They make their way east in silence, away from Ornö. After twenty minutes they reach the other side of the island. The sun is already high in the sky, sparkling on the calm sea. The air is starting to heat up. Penelope stops in front of a tennis ball lying in the tall meadow grass. Yellow-green, and almost alien to her. Almost completely hidden behind a dense lilac hedge is a little red cottage with a veranda facing the water. The curtains in all the windows are drawn, and there are no cushions on the swing-seat in the arbour. The lawn is overgrown and a broken branch from an old apple tree is lying right across the pale grey stone path.

'There's no one home,' Penelope whispers.

They creep closer to the house, ready for the sound of dogs barking or angry voices. They peer through the gaps between the curtains, then walk round and try the front door. It's locked, and Penelope starts to look round.

'We have to get inside, we need to rest,' Björn says. 'We'll have to break a window.'

Beside the door is a terracotta pot containing a small bush with narrow, grey-green leaves. Penelope can smell the lavender as she bends over and picks up one of the stones on top of the soil. It's made of plastic, and underneath is a small compartment. She opens it, removes the key and puts the stone back.

They unlock the door and walk into a pine-floored hallway. Penelope can feel her legs shaking, they're on the verge of giving way beneath her. She reaches out her hand to support her. The walls are covered with plush textured wallpaper. Penelope is so tired and hungry that the house feels unreal, like a gingerbread house. There are framed photographs everywhere, with signatures written in gold pen or black ink. They recognise the row of faces from old Swedish television programmes.

They carry on, further into the house, through a living room and into the kitchen, looking around anxiously.

'We can't stay here,' Penelope whispers.

Björn goes over to the fridge and opens the door. The shelves are full of fresh groceries. The house isn't deserted, as they thought. Björn looks round, then takes out some cheese, half a salami and the carton of milk. Penelope finds a baguette in the larder, and a packet of cornflakes. They eat the food greedily with their hands, passing the cheese between them and biting off chunks to chew with the bread. Björn drinks large swigs of milk from the carton, and it dribbles from the corners of his mouth and down his neck. Penelope eats some salami with the cornflakes, takes the milk from Björn, chokes, coughs and drinks some more. They smile nervously at each other, move away from the window and eat some more, before finally calming down.

'We need to find some clothes before we move on,' Penelope says.

As they look through the house they experience a strange, tingling sensation as the food warms them up. Their bodies wake up, their hearts beat faster, their stomachs ache, their blood flows more quickly through their veins.

In the largest bedroom, with a glass door facing the lilac arbour, is a built-in wardrobe with mirror doors. Penelope hurries over and pulls it open.

'What's all this?'

The big cupboard is full of peculiar clothes. Gold jackets, sparkling black sequined girdles, a yellow tuxedo and a fluffy waist-length fur-coat. Taken aback, Penelope hunts through a load of skimpy bikinis, transparent, leopard-skin print, camouflage-patterned, even some crocheted briefs.

She opens the other door and finds some simpler clothes: tops, jackets and trousers. She searches through them quickly and pulls out several garments. Unsteadily she pulls off her wet clothes.

She suddenly catches sight of herself in the mirror. She has big bruises all over her body, her hair is hanging in black clumps, she has scratches on her face, cuts and bruises on her shins, she's still bleeding from a small wound on her thigh, and her hip has been scraped from when she slid down the rock.

She pulls on a pair of crumpled bathing trunks, a T-shirt with the words 'Eat more porridge' and a knitted top. The sweater is big and almost reaches her knees. She starts to get even warmer, and her body wants nothing more than to rest. Suddenly she starts to cry, but quickly calms down, wipes the tears from her cheeks, and goes out into the hall to look for shoes. She finds a pair of blue wellington boots and returns to the bedroom. Björn is muddy and wet, but is pulling a pair of purple velour trousers over the dirt. His feet look terrible, filthy and covered in cuts, and he leaves bloody footprints on the floor when he walks. He pulls on a blue T-shirt and a slim bright blue leather jacket with wide lapels.

Penelope's tears start to run again, and she starts to cry in great, heaving sobs, wracking her whole body. She's too tired, she's got nothing left to hold back the tears. Her tears encompass all the terror of their frantic flight.

'What's going on?' she whimpers.

'I don't know,' Björn whispers.

'We haven't even seen his face. What does he want? What the hell does he want? I don't understand. Why is he hunting us? Why does he want to hurt us?'

She wipes her tears on the sleeve of the sweater.

'I've been thinking,' she goes on. 'I mean . . . what if Viola did something, something really stupid? Because you know, her guy, Sergey, she finished with him, he could be dodgy, I know he used to work as a bouncer.'

'Penny . . .'

'I just mean, Viola, she's so . . . Maybe she did something you're not supposed to do.'

'No,' Björn whispers.

'What do you mean, no? We don't know anything, you don't have to try to comfort me.'

'I have . . .'

'He . . . the man chasing us . . . maybe he just wants to talk to us. I know that isn't true, I just mean . . . I don't know what I mean.'

'Penny,' Björn says seriously. 'Everything that's happened is my fault.'

He looks at her. His eyes are bloodshot, his cheeks flushing brightly against his pale skin.

'What are you saying? What the hell are you saying?' she asks in a low voice.

He swallows slowly, then tries to explain.

'I've done something really stupid, Penny.'

'What have you done?'

'It's the photograph,' he replies. 'It's all because of the photograph.'

'What photograph? The one of Palmcrona and Raphael Guidi?'

'Yes. I contacted Palmcrona,' Björn replies bluntly. 'I told him about the picture, and said I wanted money, but . . .'

'No,' she whispers abruptly.

Penelope stares at him and moves away, backwards, away from him, knocking over the bedside table holding a glass of water and a clock-radio.

'Penny . . .'

'No, shut up,' she says loudly. 'I don't get it. What are you saying? What the fuck are you saying? You can't . . . you can't . . . Are you mad, trying to blackmail Palmcrona? Have you really tried to . . .'

'Just let me finish! I changed my mind, it was wrong, I know it was wrong, he's got the picture, I sent it back to him.'

They fall silent. Penelope tries to make sense of what he's said. Thoughts are swirling helplessly around her head. She's struggling to understand what Björn has just admitted.

'It's my picture,' she says slowly, trying to gather her thoughts. 'It could be important. It could have been an important picture.

I was given it in confidence, someone might know something that . . .'

'I just didn't want to have to sell the boat,' he whispers, looking as if he might cry.

'I don't get it . . . You sent the picture to Palmcrona?'

'I had to, Penny, I realised I'd done the wrong thing . . . I had to give him the picture.'

'But . . . I have to get it back,' she says. 'Don't you understand? What if the person who sent me the picture gets in touch and wants it back? This is about serious stuff, Swedish arms exports. This isn't about you and your money problems, it isn't about us, this is real, Björn.'

Penelope looks at him in despair and her voice becomes shrill as she raises it:

'This is about people, about people's lives. I'm disappointed,' she says heavily. 'I'm so fucking angry with you I could hit you, but I haven't got the strength.'

'Penny, I didn't know,' he says. 'How was I supposed to know? You didn't tell me anything, you said the picture was embarrassing for Palmcrona, you didn't say . . .'

'What difference does that make?' she says, cutting him off.

'I just thought . . .'

'Shut up!' she shouts. 'I don't want to hear your excuses, you're an extortionist, a greedy little extortionist. I don't know you, and you don't know me.'

She falls silent and they stand facing each other for a while. A seagull cries above the water, and others join in as plaintive echoes.

'We need to get moving,' Björn says limply.

Penelope nods, but a moment later they hear the front door open. Without looking at each other, they move backwards, further into the bedroom. They hear someone come in, one step at a time. Björn tries to open the terrace door, but it's locked. Penelope loosens the catch on the window with trembling hands, but it's too late to try to escape.

51

Penelope takes a deep breath. A man is standing in the doorway of the bedroom. Björn looks round for something to defend them with, some sort of weapon.

'And what the hell are you doing here?' the man asks in a hoarse voice.

Penelope realises that he isn't their pursuer, but presumably the owner of the house. He's a short man, broad and a little overweight. His face looks familiar somehow, as if she used to know him many years ago.

'Junkies?' he asks with genuine interest.

Suddenly she figures out who he is. They've broken into Ossian Wallenberg's house. He was a popular television presenter ten years ago, mostly light-entertainment shows at the weekends – *Golden Friday, Climbing the Walls, Live from the Göta Lejon*. Ossian Wallenberg used to host glitzy quiz-shows, with mystery prizes and celebrity guests. Every edition of *Golden Friday* ended the same way, with Ossian trying to pick his guest up, smiling and red-faced. Penelope remembers watching as a child as he picked up Mother Teresa. The frail old woman had looked terrified. Ossian Wallenberg was famous for his golden hair, his extravagant clothes, and also for his barbed sense of humour.

'We've been in an accident,' Björn says. 'We really need to contact the police.'

'Oh,' Ossian says disinterestedly. 'I've only got a mobile phone.'

'Can we borrow it? It's urgent.'

Ossian takes out his phone, looks at it, then switches it off.

'What are you doing?' Penelope asks.

'Whatever the hell I like,' he replies.

'We really need to use your phone,' she says.

'Then you're going to need my pin-code,' Ossian smiles.

'What are you doing?'

He leans against the doorpost and looks at them for a few moments.

'Imagine that a couple of junkies have found their way here, to my humble abode.'

'We're not . . .'

'Who cares?' Ossian snaps.

'Okay, I've had enough of this,' Penelope says to Björn.

She wants to leave, but Björn looks exhausted, his cheeks and lips are pale, and he's leaning against the wall with one hand.

'We're sorry we broke into your house,' Björn says. 'And we'll pay for what we've taken, but right now we really need to borrow your phone, this really is a desperate situation and . . .'

'And your name is?' Ossian interrupts with a smile.

'Björn.'

'You look good in that jacket, but didn't you see the tie? There's a tie that goes with it.'

Ossian goes over to the wardrobe and takes out a thin leather tie, the same shade of blue as the jacket, and slowly knots it round Björn's neck.

'Call the police yourself,' Penelope says. 'Tell them you've caught two burglars red-handed.'

'Not nice,' Ossian says sullenly.

'What do you want?' she asks through clenched teeth.

He takes a few steps back and looks at the intruders.

'I don't like her,' Ossian says to Björn. 'But you're very stylish, and my jacket suits you. She can have that ugly sweater, don't you think? Like an old owl. She doesn't look Swedish, she looks like . . .'

'Stop it,' Björn says.

Ossian walks up to Björn with an angry look on his face and raises his clenched fist in front of his face.

'I know who you are,' Penelope says.

'Good,' Ossian says with a thin smile.

Björn looks at her curiously, then at the man. Penelope feels sick, and sits down on the bed and tries to breathe normally.

'Hang on,' Ossian says. 'You too . . . I've seen you on television, I recognise you.'

'I've been in a few televised debates . . .'

'And now you're dead,' he says with a smile.

Her whole body grows tense and alert at his bizarre words. She tries to understand what he means, and her eyes dart about, trying to find an escape route. Björn is standing against the wall, and slides down towards the floor. All the colour has drained from his face, and he can't get a single word out.

'If you don't want to help us,' Penelope says, 'we'll go and ask someone else who . . .'

'I want to, of course I want to,' he interrupts.

Ossian goes out into the hall and comes back with a plastic bag. He pulls out a carton of cigarettes and a newspaper, tosses the newspaper on the bed and takes the bag and cigarettes out to the kitchen. Penelope sees a photograph of herself on the front of the paper, alongside one of Björn, and a larger one of Viola. Above Viola's picture is the word 'Dead', and above the other two 'Missing'.

Boat Drama – Three Feared Dead runs the headline.

Penelope thinks of her mother, she can see her in her mind's eye, distraught and exhausted from crying. Sitting quietly with her arms wrapped tightly around her, as if she were in prison.

The floor creaks and Ossian Wallenberg comes back into the bedroom again.

'Let's have a competition,' he says eagerly.

'What do you mean . . .?'

'Hell, I feel like a competition!'

'A competition?' Björn says with an uncertain smile.

'You don't know what a competition is?'

'Yes, but . . .'

Penelope looks at Ossian, and realises how vulnerable they

are as long as no one knows they're alive, as long as no one knows what's happened. He could kill them, because everyone already thinks they're dead.

'He wants to show how much power he has over us,' Penelope says.

'Will you let us use your phone if we join in?' Björn asks.

'If you win,' Ossian replies, looking at them with a glint in his eyes.

'And what if we lose?' Penelope asks.

52

Axel Riessen walks across the floor of his dining room to the window, where he stops to look at the roses growing against the metal railings, then along the street to the steps leading to Engelbrekt Church.

The moment he signed the contract he assumed all of the late Carl Palmcrona's duties and responsibilities.

He smiles to himself at the unexpected turn his life has taken, then suddenly remembers that he's forgotten about Beverly. Anxiety begins to flutter in his stomach. One time she told him she was just going to the shop, but when she hadn't returned four hours later he set out to look for her. Two hours after that he found her in a bicycle shed outside the Observatory Museum. She was extremely confused, smelled of drink and her underpants had gone missing. Someone had stuck chewing gum in her hair.

She said she had met some boys in the park.

'They were throwing stones at a wounded pigeon,' Beverly explained. 'So I thought that if I gave them my money they'd stop. But I only had twelve kronor. That wasn't enough. They wanted me to do something instead. They said they'd stamp on the pigeon if I didn't do it.'

She tailed off. Tears welled up in her eyes.

'I didn't want to,' she whispered. 'But I was so sad about the poor little bird.'

He takes out his phone and calls her.

As the call goes through he looks down the street, past the building that once housed the Chinese Embassy and over to the gloomy building that is the Swedish headquarters of the Catholic network Opus Dei.

Axel Riessen and his brother Robert share one of the large townhouses on Bragevägen. The building is at the heart of the area known as Lärkstaden, an exclusive district between Östermalm and Vasastan, where the buildings bear an external resemblance to each other, as if they belonged to the same family.

The Riessen family residence consists of two large, separate apartments, each spread over three floors.

The brothers' father, Erloff Riessen, who died twenty years ago, was Sweden's ambassador in Paris, and later London, while their uncle Torleif Riessen was a renowned pianist who performed at the Symphony Hall in Boston and the Grosser Musikvereinssaal in Vienna, amongst other places. The noble Riessen family consisted largely of diplomats and musicians, professions that have a lot in common – they both demand a sensitive ear and a lot of dedication.

As a couple, Alice and Erloff Riessen had an unusual but logical agreement: they decided early on that their eldest son Axel should become a musician, and their younger son Robert should follow his father into the diplomatic corps. But that arrangement was suddenly turned upside down when Axel made his fateful mistake. He was seventeen years old when he was forced to abandon music. He was sent to a military school and Robert was left to take over the musical career. Axel accepted his punishment, found it reasonable, and hasn't played the violin since then.

After what happened, that dark day thirty-four years ago, Axel's mother cut off all contact with her son. She didn't even want to speak to him when she was on her deathbed.

After nine rings Beverly finally answers, coughing.

'Hello?'

'Where are you?'

'I'm . . .'

She turns away from the phone and he doesn't hear the end of the sentence.

'I can't hear,' he says, anxiety making his voice sharp and strained.

'Why are you angry?'

'Just tell me where you are,' he pleads.

'What's the matter with you?' she says, laughing. 'I'm here, in my flat. Isn't that a good thing?'

'I was just worried.'

'Don't be silly. I'm just going to watch that programme about Princess Victoria.'

She clicks to end the call and he feels a lingering concern at the vagueness in her voice.

He looks at the phone and wonders if he ought to call her again. Suddenly it rings in his hand and he jumps, then answers:

'Riessen.'

'Jörgen Grünlicht here.'

'Hello,' Axel says in a slightly curious tone of voice.

'How was your meeting with the reference group?'

'I thought it was very worthwhile,' Axel replies.

'You prioritised Kenya, I hope?'

'And the end-user certificate from the Netherlands,' Axel says. 'There was a lot to get through, so I'm withholding my judgement until I've had time to familiarise . . .'

'But Kenya,' he interrupts. 'You haven't signed the export licence yet? Pontus Salman is on my back wondering why the hell you're dragging the whole thing out. It's a bloody big deal, and it's already been delayed. The ISP gave them such positive indications that they started production. The consignment is ready, it's being moved from Trollhättan to Gothenburg, and the shipping company is bringing in a container vessel from Panama tomorrow. They'll spend the day unloading their cargo, and will be ready to load the ammunition the day after tomorrow.'

'Jörgen, I realise all of that, I've looked at the documentation and . . . obviously I'm going to give authorisation, but I've only just taken up the post and it's important for me to be thorough.'

'I've looked through the deal myself,' Jörgen says in a brusque tone of voice. 'And I haven't noticed any lack of clarity on any points.'

'No, but . . .'

'Where are you right now?'

'I'm at home,' Axel says, slightly bemused.

'I'll get the paperwork couriered to you,' Jörgen says curtly. 'The courier can wait while you sign it so we don't lose any more time.'

'No, I'll look at it tomorrow.'

Twenty minutes later Axel goes into the hall to meet the courier sent by Jörgen Grünlicht. He finds the pushiness troubling, but can see no reason to delay the deal.

53

Axel opens the door to the courier. The mild evening air spills in, along with the thunderous music from the graduation party at the School of Architecture.

He takes the folder, and for some reason feels awkward about signing the contract in front of the courier, as if he were the sort of man who can be made to do anything if you put a bit of pressure on him.

'Give me a minute,' Axel says, leaving the courier in the hall.

He walks through the corridor on the left, past the downstairs library to the kitchen. He passes the shiny, dark stone worktops and black cupboards and walks over to the double fridge and ice-machine. He takes out a small bottle of mineral water and drinks some, loosens his tie and sits down on one of the high bar stools and opens the folder.

It's all very neat, and seems to be in order: all the appendixes are there, the declaration of the Export Control Council, the classification, the advance notification, the copies for the Foreign Affairs Committee and the submission of tender.

He looks at the documents relating to the export licence, the final authorisation, and leafs through to the page where the director general of the Inspectorate for Strategic Products has to sign his name.

A shiver runs through his body.

This is a big deal, with consequences for the nation's balance of trade, a routine transaction which has been delayed because of Carl Palmcrona's suicide. He understands that Pontus Salman is in a difficult position: there's always a chance that the deal will fall through if the process drags out any longer.

But at the same time he recognises that he's being pressured into authorising the export of ammunition to Kenya, without personally being able to vouch for the correctness of the decision.

Axel takes his own decision, and immediately feels more comfortable.

He'll devote all his time to this particular deal over the next few days, and then he'll sign the export licence.

He's going to sign, he knows that, but not right now. He doesn't care if they get upset and angry. He's the one who makes the decisions, he's the one who's the director general of the Inspectorate for Strategic Products.

He picks up his pen and on the line that's waiting for his signature he draws a smiling stick-figure with a speech bubble coming out of his mouth.

Axel returns to the hall with a serious expression on his face and hands the folder to the courier, then goes upstairs to the sitting room. He wonders if Beverly really is upstairs in her rooms, or if she didn't dare tell him she'd crept out.

What if she sneaks out and disappears?

Axel picks up the remote from a sideboard and puts on a compilation of David Bowie's early work.

The wireless music centre is a sleek, glass contraption. The speakers are set into the walls, and are completely invisible.

He goes over to the glass-fronted cabinet, opens the curved door and looks at the array of bottles.

He hesitates briefly before pulling out a numbered bottle of Hazelburn from the Springbank Distillery. The distillery is in Campbeltown in Scotland. Axel has been there, and remembers the more than hundred-year-old mash tun that was still in use. It was worn, and painted a bright red colour, and didn't even have a lid.

Axel Riessen pulls out the cork and inhales the smell of the whisky: peaty and dark as a stormy sky. He puts the cork back in, then slowly puts the bottle back on the shelf as he hears the music centre play a track from the *Hunky Dory* album.

But her friend is nowhere to be seen. Now she walks through her sunken dream, to the seat with the clearest view, and she's hooked to the silver screen, David Bowie sings.

The door to his brother's apartment slams shut. Axel looks out through the big picture window that overlooks the compact garden. He wonders if Robert is going to call in, and at that moment there's a knock at the door.

'Come in,' he calls to his brother.

Robert opens the door and walks into the sitting room with a troubled expression on his face.

'I know you only listen to rubbish to annoy me, but . . .'

Axel smiles and sings along:

Take a look at the Lawman, beating up the wrong guy. Oh man! Wonder if he'll ever know: he's in the best selling show . . .

His brother takes a few dance-steps and goes over to the glass-fronted cabinet and looks at all the bottles.

'Help yourself,' Axel says drily.

'Do you want to see my Strosser? Can I turn this off for a bit?'

Axel shrugs his shoulders, Robert presses pause and the music gently fades to silence.

'Have you finished it already?'

'I sat up all night,' Robert replies with a broad smile. 'Put the strings on this morning.'

They fall silent. A long time ago their mother had been certain that Axel was going to become a famous violinist. Alice Riessen had herself been a professional musician, and played second violin in the orchestra of the Stockholm Opera for ten years, and openly favoured her eldest son.

It all went wrong when Axel was studying at the Royal College of Music and was one of three finalists for the Johan Fredrick Berwald Award for young soloists, which was regarded as a ticket to the international elite.

After the contest Axel gave up music altogether and switched schools to the Military Academy in Karlsborg. His brother Robert was left to take up the mantle of the musician of the family.

Like most of the students at the Royal College of Music, Robert never became a virtuoso violinist. But he does play with a chamber orchestra and has, above all, built a reputation as a violin-maker, with clients all over the world.

'Show me the violin,' Axel says after a brief pause.

Robert nods and goes to get the instrument, a charming violin with fiery red varnish and a base of tiger-striped maple.

He stops in front of his brother and starts to play a tremulous passage from a piece by Béla Bartók. Axel has always liked him. Bartók was an outspoken critic of Nazism and was forced to leave his country. As a composer he was a worrier who occasionally managed to convey a few short moment of happiness. A sort of melancholic folk-music among the rubble after a catastrophe, Axel thinks as Robert reaches the end of the piece.

'That sounds pretty good,' Axel says. 'But you need to move the sound-post, because there's a slightly muffled . . .'

His brother's face closes up.

'Daniel Strosser has said that . . . that he wants that sound,' he explains tersely. 'He wants the violin to sound like a young Birgit Nilsson.'

'You really should move the sound-post,' Axel smiles.

'You're not an expert, I just wanted . . .'

'Otherwise it's really great,' Axel says hurriedly.

'You can hear the tone, though? Dry and sharp and . . .'

'I'm not saying anything bad about it,' Axel goes on blithely. 'I'm just saying there a tiny fraction of the sound that doesn't sound alive, and which . . .'

'Alive? This instrument's for someone who really knows his Bartók – that's not the same thing as Bowie.'

'Maybe I heard wrong,' Axel says quietly.

Robert opens his mouth to reply, but changes his mind as he hears his wife Anette knock on the door.

She comes in, and smiles when she sees him sitting there with the violin.

'Have you tried the Strosser, then?' she asks expectantly.

'Yes,' Robert says curtly. 'But Axel doesn't like it.'

'That's not true,' Axel says. 'I'm sure your customer is going to be delighted. That thing I mentioned, it's probably just in my head, and . . .'

'Don't listen to him, he doesn't know anything,' Anette interrupts irritably.

Robert wants to leave, wants to take his wife with him, doesn't want a scene, but she walks over to Axel.

'Admit that you just pretended to find fault with it,' she says in a shrill voice.

'There's no fault, it's just the sound-post which . . .'

'And when did you last play? Thirty, forty years ago? You were only a child then. I think you should apologise.'

'Let it go,' Robert says.

'Say sorry,' she demands.

'Okay, sorry,' Axel says, and feels himself blush.

'For lying,' she goes on. 'For lying, because you couldn't bear to give Robert the praise his new violin deserves.'

'Sorry for that.'

Axel turns his music on again, fairly loud. At first it sounds like gentle strumming from two untuned guitars, and a singer trying to find the right note in a weak voice: *Goodbye love, goodbye love . . .*

Anette mutters something about Axel's lack of talent and Robert tells her to stop as he pulls her out of the room. Axel turns the volume up further and the drums and electric bass make the inside-out music sound right: *Didn't know what time it was, the lights were low oh oh. I leaned back on my radio oh oh.*

Axel closes his eyes and feels them sting in the darkness. He's already very tired. Sometimes he sleeps for half an hour, and sometimes he doesn't get any sleep at all, even when Beverly is lying beside him. On nights like that, he usually wraps a blanket round him and goes to sit on the veranda, gazing out at the beautiful trees in the garden in the damp dawn light. Axel Riessen has a reasonable idea what's causing his problems, of course. He keeps his eyes shut and returns in his thoughts to the day that changed his life.

54

The competition

Penelope and Björn look at each other with tired, serious eyes. Through the closed door they can hear Ossian Wallenberg singing as he rearranges the furniture.

'We can overpower him,' Penelope whispers.

'Maybe.'

'We have to try.'

'And then what? What do we do then? Torture him until he tells us the code to his phone?'

'I think he'll let us have it if the balance of power shifts,' Penelope says.

'And if he doesn't?'

She sways with exhaustion as she walks over to the window to loosen the catch. Her fingers are sore and weak. She stops and looks at her hands in the daylight, sees the dirt under her brown nails, her fingers, grey with mud and clay, covered in congealed blood from any number of cuts.

'We won't get any help here, we have to go on,' she says. 'If we keep going along the shore, we'll . . .'

She tails off and looks at Björn, who is sitting huddled up on the edge of the bed in his blue leather jacket.

'Fine,' he says quietly. 'You go.'

'I'm not leaving you.'

'I can't do it, Penny,' he says without looking at her. 'My feet,

I won't be able to run, I might manage to walk for half an hour, but my feet are still bleeding.'

'I'll help you.'

'There may not be any more phones on the island, we don't know, we've got no idea.'

'I'm not going to take part in his disgusting . . .'

'Penny, we . . . we have to talk to the police, we have to borrow his phone.'

With a big smile on his face, Ossian throws the door open. He's wearing a leopard-skin print jacket and a sarong. He beckons them towards the huge sofa with extravagant gestures. The curtains are closed and he's pushed the furniture against the walls so that he can move freely in the room. Ossian walks into the glare of the two standard lamps, stops and turns round.

'Friday night, people! Time flies when you're having fun!' he says with a wink. 'We've reached the competition already, so let's welcome tonight's celebrity guest, a shitty little columnist and her underage lover. A really odd couple, if you ask me. A scruffy hag and a young man with a finely chiselled torso.'

Ossian laughs and flexes his muscles towards the imaginary camera.

'Come on, now!' Ossian cries, and jogs on the spot. 'Climbing the walls! Have you all got your buttons ready? I give you . . . "Truth or Dare!" Ossian Wallenberg challenges – the Hag and the Studmuffin!'

Ossian places an empty wine bottle on the floor and spins it. It rotates several times, then comes to a stop with the neck pointing at Björn.

'Studmuffin!' Ossian cries with a smile. 'First off the blocks! Here comes your question. Are you ready to tell the truth, and nothing but the truth?'

'Absolutely,' Björn sighs.

A drop of sweat falls from Ossian's nose as he opens an envelope and reads:

'What do you think about when you're having sex with the Hag?'

'Funny,' Penelope mutters.

'Do I get the phone if I answer?' Björn asks as calmly as he can.

Ossian purses his lips and shakes his head.

'No, but if the audience believe your answer, you get the first number of the code.'

'And if I choose dare?'

'Then you'll be competing against me, and the audience will choose,' Ossian says. 'But the clock's ticking, tick, tock, tick, tock. Five, four, three, two . . .'

Penelope looks at Björn in the harsh glare from the lamps: his dirty face, stubble, his matted hair. His nostrils are black with caked blood, and his eyes are tired and bloodshot.

'I think about Penelope when we're having sex,' Björn replies quietly.

Ossian boos, pulls a disgusted face and jogs into the spotlight.

'You were supposed to tell the truth,' he shouts. 'And that was nowhere near it. No one in the audience believes you think about the Hag when you have sex with her. That's one, two, three minus points to Studmuffin!'

He spins the bottle again, and this time it stops almost at once, pointing at Penelope.

'What's this?' Ossian cries. 'A forfeit! And what does that mean? That's right! Automatic dare! No pickle on your burger! Straight to go! I'll open the hatch and see what the hippopotamus whispers.'

Ossian picks up a small hippopotamus made of dark, polished wood from the table, holds it to his ear, listens and nods.

'You mean the Hag?' he asks, and listens again. 'I see, Mr Hippopotamus. Yes, thank you very much.'

Ossian carefully puts the hippopotamus down and turns to Penelope with a smile.

'The Hag has to compete against Ossian! And the category is striptease! If you can turn the audience on better than Ossian, you get all the numbers to the code – otherwise Studmuffin has to kick you up the arse as hard as he can.'

Ossian bounces over to the stereo, presses a button and 'Teach Me, Tiger' starts to play.

'I lost this round to Michael Douglas once,' Ossian says in a stage whisper as he sways his hips in time to the music.

Penelope gets up from the sofa, takes a step forward and stops in her wellington boots, stripy bathing suit and big, knitted sweater.

'You want me to take my clothes off?' she asks. 'Is that what this is all about? Getting to see me naked?'

Ossian stops singing and comes to a halt with a look of disappointment on his face, and looks at her coolly before replying:

'If I was interested in seeing a refugee whore's cunt I'd use the internet.'

'So what the hell do you want, then?'

Ossian gives her a hard slap. She staggers and almost falls, but manages to stay on her feet.

'You need to be nice to me,' he says seriously.

'Okay,' she mutters.

A trace of a smile crosses his face before he goes on:

'I'm someone who competes against television celebrities – and I've seen you on telly before I've had time to change the channel.'

She looks at his flushed, excited face.

'You're not going to give us your phone, are you?'

'I promise, rules are rules, you'll get it, as long as I get what I want,' he replies quickly.

'You know we're in a desperate situation, and you're exploiting that to . . .'

'Yes! I am!' he screams.

'Okay, what the fuck, why not? We'll do some stripping and then I get the phone.'

She turns her back on Ossian and pulls off the sweater and T-shirt. In the harsh light the scratches on her shoulder-blades and hip stand out vividly, as well as the bruises and dirt. She turns round, covering her breasts with both hands.

Björn claps his hands and whistles, with a sad look in his eyes. Ossian's face is sweating, he glances at Penelope and then stands in the glare of the lights in front of Björn. He rolls his hips, then suddenly pulls off the sarong, swirls it round, passes it between his legs, then tosses it at Björn.

Ossian blows him a kiss and gestures to him to phone him.

Björn claps his hands again, whistles louder, and goes on clapping and whistling as he sees Penelope pick up the wrought-iron poker from the fireplace.

The little shovel sways and tinkles against the tongs.

Ossian is skipping and dancing in his sparkly gold sequined underpants.

Holding the poker in both hands, Penelope approaches Ossian from behind. He's rolling his hips in front of Björn now.

'Down on your knees,' he whispers to Björn. 'Go on, get down, Studmuffin!'

Penelope swings the heavy poker and hits him across the thigh as hard as she can. Ossian lets out a scream and collapses to the floor, clutching his thigh and rolling around in agony as he roars with pain. Penelope marches over to the stereo and smashes it with four heavy blows, until it finally shuts up.

Ossian is lying still now, breathing very fast and whimpering. She walks over to him, and he looks up at her with frightened eyes. She stands there for a moment. The heavy poker swings slowly in her right hand.

'Mr Hippopotamus whispered that he wants you to give me your phone and code,' she says calmly.

55

The police

It's very warm and oppressively stuffy inside Ossian Wallenberg's cottage. Björn gets up from the sofa time and time again, goes over to the window and looks down towards the water and the jetty. Penelope is lying on the sofa with the phone in her hand waiting for the police to call back. When they took her call they promised to get back to her when the marine police boat was approaching. Ossian is sitting in an armchair with a large glass of whisky in front of him, watching them. He's taken some painkillers, and has told them in a subdued voice that he'll survive.

Penelope looks at the phone, sees that the signal is weaker now, but still good enough. The police will phone back any time now. She leans back on the sofa. It's horribly humid. Her T-shirt is wet with sweat. She closes her eyes and thinks about Darfur, the heat in the bus when she travelled to Kubbum to join up with Jane Oduya and Action Contre la Faim.

She had been on her way to the barracks that acted as the organisation's admin block when she suddenly stopped. She had caught sight of some children playing a strange game. They seemed to be placing little clay figures in the road, hoping that they'd be squashed by the vehicles. She went cautiously closer to see what they were doing. They laughed whenever one of their clay figures was run over:

'I killed another one! It was an old man!'

'I've killed a Fur!'

One of the children ran out onto the road again and quickly put two more clay figures down, one big, one small. When a barrow knocked over and squashed the small one, the children were delighted:

'The kid died! The whore's kid died!'

Penelope went over to the children and asked what they were doing, but they didn't answer, just ran off. She stood there staring at the pieces of clay on the baked red road.

The Fur are the people who give their name to Darfur. This ancient African tribe is facing extinction because of the persecution of the Janjaweed.

Because the African tribes have traditionally been farmers, there has been trouble between them and the nomadic part of the population from time immemorial. But the real cause of the genocide is oil. Oil has been found on land inhabited by ancient African tribes, and the violence is an attempt to clear the villages from the area.

Even though the civil war is officially over, the Janjaweed have continued their systematic raids, raping women, killing men and boys, then burning their homes.

Penelope watched the Arab children rush off, and was just picking one of the last intact clay figures from the road when she heard someone call out:

'Penny! Penny!'

She started with fear, turned and saw Jane Oduya standing there waving at her. Jane was a short, rotund woman, dressed in faded jeans and a yellow jacket. Penelope hardly recognised her. Jane's face had become wrinkled and aged in just a few years.

'Jane!'

They hugged each other hard.

'Don't talk to those children,' Jane muttered. 'They're like all the rest, they hate us because we're black, I can't understand it. They hate black skin.'

Jane and Penelope started to walk towards the refugee camp. Here and there people had begun to gather to eat and drink.

The smell of burned milk mingled with the stench of the latrines. The UN's blue plastic sheeting was everywhere, used for all manner of things: curtains, windbreaks, sheets. Hundreds of the Red Cross's white tents jerked in the wind that was sweeping across the plains.

Penelope followed Jane into the main hospital tent. The sunlight turned grey through the white fabric. Jane looked in through the plastic window of the surgical section.

'My nurses have become talented surgeons,' she said softly. 'They carry out amputations and simple operations all on their own.'

Two young boys, no more than thirteen years old, were carrying a large box of bandages into the tent, and carefully put it down beside some other boxes. They came over to Jane, she thanked them and told them to help the women who had just arrived, they needed water to wash their wounds with.

The boys went off, and soon returned with large plastic bottles of water.

'They used to belong to the Arab militia,' Jane explained, nodding towards the boys. 'But things are quiet now. Because of the shortage of ammunition and parts for weapons, a sort of equilibrium has been reached. People don't really know what to do, and a lot of them have started to help out here instead. We've got a boys' school, with several young men from the militia in the class.'

A woman let out a moan from a bunk, and Jane hurried over to her and stroked her forehead and cheeks. She looked no more than fifteen, but was heavily pregnant, and one of her feet had been amputated.

Penelope spent all day working at Jane's side, doing everything she said, asking no questions, not talking about anything, just doing all she could to help Jane make the most of her medical training, so that as many people as possible could get help.

An African man in his thirties with a beautiful face and muscular arms hurried up to Jane with a little white box.

'Thirty new doses of antibiotics,' he said, beaming.

'Really?'

He nodded, still smiling.

'Good work.'

'I'll go and put a bit more pressure on Ross, he said we might be able to get a box of blood-pressure monitors this week.'

'This is Grey,' Jane said. 'He's really a teacher, but I couldn't manage without him.'

Penelope held out her hand and met the man's playful gaze. 'Penelope Fernandez,' she said.

'Tarzan,' he said, shaking her hand.

'He wanted to be called Tarzan when he arrived,' Jane laughed.

'Tarzan and Jane,' he smiled. 'I'm her Tarzan.'

'In the end I agreed that he could be called Greystoke,' Jane said. 'But everyone finds that too much of a mouthful, so he has to make do with Grey.'

A truck suddenly sounded its horn outside the tent, and the three of them ran outside. Red dust was swirling around the rusty vehicle. Seven men with gunshot wounds were lying on the open bed of the truck. They came from the west, from a village where an argument about a well had developed into a fire-fight.

The rest of the day was spent performing emergency operations. One of the men died. At one point Penelope was stopped by Grey. He held a bottle of water out to her. Stressed, Penelope just shook her head, but he smiled back calmly and said:

'You've got time to drink.'

She thanked him, drank the water, then helped him lift one of the injured men onto a bunk.

That evening Penelope and Jane sat exhausted on the veranda of one of the barracks and ate a late meal. It was still very warm. They chatted and looked out at the road between the buildings and the tents, at the people carrying out their last chores of the evening as it got dark.

Just as quickly as darkness fell, an ominous silence spread. At first Penelope heard people withdrawing, then noises from the latrines, and a few people hurrying about. But soon everything was quiet, there weren't even any children crying.

'Everyone's still scared the Janjaweed troops will come through,' Jane said, gathering their dishes.

They went inside, locked and barred the door, then did the

washing-up together. They said goodnight and Penelope went to the guestroom at the end of the corridor.

Penelope woke up two hours later with a start. She had fallen asleep in her clothes, and now lay there listening to the heavy Darfur night. She couldn't say what woke her. Her heartbeat was slowing down again when she heard a sudden cry outside. Penelope got up and went over to the small, barred window, and looked out. The road was lit up in the moonlight. She could hear an agitated conversation somewhere. Three teenage boys were walking down the middle of the road. There was no doubt that they belonged to the Janjaweed militia. One of them was holding a revolver in his hand. Penelope heard them shouting something about killing slaves. An old African man who usually grilled sweet potatoes on a fire and sold them for two piasters was already sitting on his blanket outside one of the UN stores. The boys went over to the old man and spat at him. The skinny boy raised the revolver and shot the old man right in the face. The shot echoed eerily between the buildings. The boys shrieked, took some sweet potatoes, ate some and trod the rest into the dust on the road beside the dead man.

They walked back onto the street, looked around, pointed, then walked straight towards the barracks where Penelope and Jane were staying. Penelope remembers how she held her breath as she heard them stomp about on the veranda, talking excitedly to each other and banging on the door.

Penelope suddenly gasps for breath and opens her eyes. She must have dozed off on Ossian Wallenberg's sofa.

A rumble of thunder fades away, dull and threatening. The sky has got darker.

Björn is standing at the window, and Ossian is sipping his whisky.

Penelope looks at the phone – no one has called.

The marine police should be there soon.

The thunder is getting closer very quickly. The lamp in the ceiling goes out, the fan in the kitchen falls silent: power cut. The first drops of rain hit the roof and windowsills, then suddenly it's pouring down.

The mobile signal disappears completely.

A flash of lightning lights up the room, followed by a heavy rumble of thunder.

Penelope leans back and listens to the rain, feels the cooler air stream in through the windows, falls asleep again, but wakes up when Björn says something.

'What?' she asks.

'A boat,' he repeats. 'A police boat.'

She quickly gets to her feet and looks out. The water looks like it's boiling in the heavy downpour. The big boat is already close, heading towards the jetty. Penelope looks at the phone. There's still no coverage.

'Hurry up!' Björn says.

He tries to insert the key into the lock of the terrace door. His hands are trembling. The police boat glides in beside the jetty and sounds its siren.

'It won't fit,' Björn says loudly. 'It's the wrong key!'

'Oh dear,' Ossian laughs, taking out his keyring. 'It must be this one, then.'

Björn takes the key, manages to get it into the lock, turns it, and hears a metallic click inside the mechanism.

It's hard to see the police boat through the rain. It's already started to slip away from the jetty when Björn gets the door open.

'Björn!' Penelope shouts.

The engine is roaring and white foam is kicking up behind the boat. Björn waves and runs through the rain as fast as he can on the gravel path that leads down the slope.

'Up here!' he cries. 'We're over here!'

Björn's shoulders and thighs are drenched. He gets down to the jetty and sees the boat's engines go into reverse. There's a first-aid box on the aft-deck. Through the windscreen he can see a policeman. Another flash of lightning lights up the sky. The noise is deafening. The policeman behind the wheel looks like he's talking into a comms radio. Rain is bouncing off the roof of the boat. Waves lap up onto the shore. Björn is shouting and waving his arms. The boat glides back and its port side bumps against the jetty.

Björn grabs hold of the wet railing and clambers aboard, and climbs down to a metal door. The boat is rolling on its own swell. He sways, opens the metal door and goes in.

The cabin is full of a cloying metallic smell, of oil and sweat.

The first thing Björn sees is a suntanned police officer lying on the floor with his head smashed in. His eyes are wide open. An almost black pool of blood is spreading out beneath him. Björn is breathing hard, looking round the dark space among the police equipment, raincoats and surfing magazines. He hears a voice over the noise of the engine. It's Ossian Wallenberg, calling from the path. He's limping towards the jetty with a yellow umbrella above his head. Björn feels his pulse thudding in his temples and realises his mistake: he's walked straight into the trap. He sees the blood spattered across the inside of the windscreen and fumbles for the door-handle. The steps down to the cabin creak and he turns round and sees his pursuer emerge from the gloom. He's wearing a police uniform and his face is alert, almost curious.

Björn realises that it's too late to run. He grabs a screwdriver from the shelf above the instrument panel to defend himself. His pursuer holds onto the railing and reaches the top of the steps, blinks in the bright light, then glances at the windscreen and shore. Rain is beating against the glass. Björn moves quickly. He aims for the man's heart with the screwdriver, thrusts and then doesn't really understand what happens next. He feels his shoulder shake. Björn loses the feeling in his arm when the man parries his attack with a heavy sideswipe. It's as if his arm isn't there any more. The screwdriver falls to the deck and rolls behind an aluminium toolbox. The man is still holding him by his numb arm, yanks him forward, angles his body and sweeps his legs out from under him with a kick. He directs the angle of Björn's fall, and pushes him harder as his face crashes down onto the footrest below the wheel. His neck breaks on impact with a muffled crunching sound. He doesn't feel anything, but sees strange sparks, tiny glimmers dancing in the darkness, ever more slowly and oddly soothing. Björn's face twitches slightly, then just moments later he's dead.

56

The helicopter

Penelope is standing at the window. The sky lights up with a flash of lightning, and thunder rolls across the sea. The rain is pouring hard. Björn has gone on board the police boat and has disappeared into the cabin. The surface of the sea is foaming in the heavy downpour. She watches Ossian limp down to the jetty with a yellow umbrella over his head. The metal door to the cabin opens and a uniformed policeman emerges onto the foredeck, jumps onto the jetty and makes the boat fast.

Only when the policeman starts to walk up the gravel path does Penelope see who it is.

Their pursuer doesn't bother to return Ossian's greeting, he just reaches out his left hand and takes a firm grip of Ossian's chin.

Penelope doesn't notice when she drops the phone on the floor.

With business-like brusqueness, the uniformed man turns Ossian's face to the side. The yellow umbrella falls to the ground and rolls part of the way down the slope. The whole thing is over in a matter of seconds. The man has barely stopped walking before he draws a short dagger with his free hand. He turns Ossian's face a little more, then with lightning speed stabs him in the neck just above his atlas vertebra, right in the brainstem. Like a bite from a snake. Ossian is dead before he hits the ground.

The man in police uniform carries on up the path towards the cottage with long strides. The glare of a flash of lightning suddenly lights up his face and Penelope meets his gaze through the rain. Before it fades she has time to see the troubled look on his face. The tired, sad eyes and the mouth with the deep scar. The thunder rumbles. The man keeps walking towards the house. Penelope just stands there in the window. She's breathing fast, but feels paralysed, unable to run.

The rain beats against the windowpane and sill. The world outside seems strangely distant to her, but suddenly a different, bright yellow light flares up behind the man. The jetty, water and sky are all lit up. A great plume of flame rises from the police boat, like an oak tree made of fire. Fragments of metal are thrown into the air. The cloud of fire grows and pulsates in shades of fiery yellow. The heat sets light to the reeds and jetty as the pressure wave and roar of the explosion reach the house.

Penelope only reacts when the windowpane in front of her face starts to shake, then cracks from one side to the other. The rain is still falling torrentially, meeting the black smoke billowing from the remains of the boat behind the man. He's marching towards the house. Penelope turns and rushes through the rooms, climbing over the moved armchair into the hallway with the signed photographs, opens the front door and runs across the wet, overgrown lawn.

She slips but carries on, out into the rain, away from the house along the path, round a clump of birches and out onto a meadow. There she meets a family with young children dressed in raincoats, clutching fishing rods and bright orange life-jackets. She runs straight through the little group, down towards a sandy beach. She's out of breath, panting uncontrollably, it feels like she's about to pass out. She has to stop, has no idea what to do, and crawls behind a small shed where she throws up on the nettles and whispers the Lord's Prayer. A rumble of thunder echoes in the distance. Her whole body is shaking, but she gets to her feet again and wipes the rain from her face with the sleeve of her sweater. She leans cautiously forward and looks round the corner, back across the meadow. Her pursuer is just emerging round the clump of birch trees, and stops next to the family, who immediately point in the direction she ran off in.

She pulls back, slides down the rocks and starts to run along the shore until she reaches the sandy beach. Her footsteps stand out white behind her as she disturbs the wet sand. She carries on, out onto a long pontoon jetty, further and further out. Suddenly she hears the heavy clatter of a helicopter's rotor-blades. Penelope keeps running along the jetty, and sees her pursuer running between the trees, down towards the beach. A man in bright yellow clothing is being winched down from the rescue helicopter, and lands at the far end of the jetty. The water around him is churned up in choppy circles. Penelope runs straight towards him on the slippery jetty, he shouts instructions about how she should stand, then attaches the harness to her and signals to the helicopter pilot. Together they rise up from the jetty, flying close above the water, then get winched upward. The last thing Penelope sees of the beach before it disappears behind the trees is her pursuer crouching down with one knee on the ground. His black rucksack is lying in front of him. With practised gestures he is putting together a rifle. Then she can't see him any more. Just dense green trees. The surface of the water rushes away beneath her. Suddenly she hears a sharp crack and there's a crunching sound up above. The wire jerks hard and her stomach clenches. The man behind her shouts something to the helicopter pilot. They suddenly lurch the other way as the helicopter banks steeply, and Penelope realises what has happened. Her pursuer has shot the helicopter pilot from the beach. Without any conscious thought Penelope loosens the safety catch on the harness, pulls free of the straps and drops straight down. She rushes through the air as the helicopter loses altitude and tips sideways as it starts to spin. The cable holding her rescuer gets caught in the main rotor. There's a deafening roar and then two distinct cracking sounds as the huge rotor-blades are torn off. Penelope falls twenty metres before she hits the water. She sinks deep into the cold water before slowly starting to rise again.

She kicks her legs, breaks the surface and gasps for air, then looks round and starts to swim away from the island, straight out to sea.

57

Joona Linna and Saga Bauer leave Silencia Defence after their short meeting with director Pontus Salman.

They had prepared a trap for him. But Pontus Salman had surprised them by immediately identifying himself and explaining the circumstances. The photograph was taken in the spring of 2008, at a concert hall in Frankfurt.

Pontus Salman had explained that they had been discussing a shipment of ammunition to Sudan when the picture was taken. The deal was at an advanced stage when something happened in the spring of 2009 which rendered it impossible. Salman appeared to assume that both Joona and Saga understood what he was referring to.

He said it was their only meeting with Sudan, and that any possibility of continuing negotiations had been ruled out.

'Do you know what Salman was talking about?' Joona asks. 'What happened in the spring of 2009?'

Before they pull out onto Nynäsvägen, Saga Bauer takes out her phone and calls Simon Lawrence at the Security Police.

'I presume you're calling to ask me out on a date,' Simon says slowly.

'Africa north of the Sahara is your area, isn't it? So presumably you'll know what happened in Sudan in the spring of 2009?'

'What are you referring to?'

'For some reason, Sweden wasn't able to export arms to Sudan after then.'

'Don't you read the papers?'

'Yes,' she says quietly.

'In March 2009 the International Criminal Court in the Hague issued a warrant for the arrest of the Sudanese president, Omar al-Bashir.'

'The president?'

'Yes.'

'Quite a big deal, then.'

'The warrant indicted the president on five counts of crimes against humanity, murder, extermination, forcible transfer, torture and rape, and two of war crimes, pillaging and targeting civilians, against three ethnic groups in Darfur.'

'I see,' Saga says.

Before they end the call Simon Lawrence gives her a short summary of the situation in Sudan.

'What was it?' Joona asks.

'The International Criminal Court in the Hague issued a warrant for the arrest of President al-Bashir,' she says, fixing her gaze on Joona.

'I didn't know that,' Joona says.

'The UN imposed an arms embargo against the Janjaweed and other armed groups in Darfur in 2004.'

They head north on Nynäsvägen. The summer sky is getting darker and lower.

'Go on,' Joona says.

'President al-Bashir has always denied any links with the militia,' she says. 'And after the UN embargo arms could only be exported directly to the Sudanese government.'

'Because they weren't connected to the militia in Darfur.'

'Exactly,' Saga says. 'And in 2005 a comprehensive peace agreement was reached, bringing the longest-running civil war in Africa to an end. After that there were no fundamental obstacles to Swedish arms exports to the Sudanese military. Carl Palmcrona's role was therefore to determine whether it was suitable in terms of security policy.'

'But the ICC evidently came to a different conclusion,' Joona says bluntly.

'Yes, totally . . . they saw a direct connection between the president and the armed militia, and issued a warrant for his arrest on the grounds of rape, torture and genocide.'

'So what's happened since then?'

'There was an election in April and al-Bashir is still president, and of course Sudan has no intention of complying with the arrest warrant. But today it's obviously out of the question to export arms to Sudan and do deals with Omar al-Bashir and Agathe al-Haji.'

'Just as Pontus Salman said,' Joona says.

'That's why they stopped the deal.'

'We have to find Penelope Fernandez,' Joona says as the first drops of rain hit the windscreen.

They drive into a heavy rainstorm and visibility becomes very poor. The rain thunders on the roof of the car. Joona is forced to lower his speed to fifty kilometres an hour on the motorway. It's very dark, but sometimes the sky lights up with flashes of lightning. The windscreen-wipers sweep rapidly back and forth.

Suddenly Joona's phone rings. It's Petter Näslund, his immediate superior, who explains in a stressed voice that Penelope Fernandez called SOS Alarm twenty minutes ago.

'Why wasn't I told before now?'

'I prioritised the despatch of the marine police, they're already on their way. But I've also requisitioned a helicopter from the coastguard to bring them home quickly.'

'Good work, Petter,' Joona says, and sees Saga shoot him a quizzical glance.

'I know you'll want to talk to Penelope Fernandez and Björn Almskog as soon as possible.'

'Yes,' Joona says.

'I'll call you when I know what condition they're in.'

'Thanks.'

'Our colleagues from the marine police ought to reach Kymmendö in a matter of . . . Hang on, something's happened, can you wait a moment?'

Petter puts the phone down and Joona hears him talking to

someone. He hears Petter getting more and more agitated, until he eventually yells 'Just keep trying!' before he picks the phone up again.

'I've got to go,' Petter says tersely.

'What's happening?' Joona asks.

A rumble of thunder goes off overhead and slowly echoes away.

'We can't contact our colleagues on the boat, they're not answering. It's that bloody Lance, he's probably spotted a wave he needs to try out.'

'Petter,' Joona says in a loud and serious voice. 'Listen to me, you need to act very quickly now. I think the boat has been hijacked and that . . .'

'Oh, come off . . .'

'Shut up and listen,' Joona interrupts. 'In all likelihood our colleagues from the marine police are already dead. You've got a few minutes to put together a team and take charge of the operation. Call the National Communications Centre on one phone and Bengt Olofsson on the other, try to get two patrols from National Response Unit, and ask for helicopter backup from the nearest naval base.'

58

The beneficiary

A storm sweeps in across Stockholm, the thunder rumbles, lightning flashes across the sky and the rain pours down. The water patters against the windows of Carl Palmcrona's large apartment. Tommy Kofoed and Nathan Pollock have resumed the abandoned forensic examination.

It's so dark that they have had to switch on the lights.

In one of the full-height closets in Palmcrona's dressing room, beneath a row of grey, blue and black suits, Pollock finds a blue leather folder.

'Tommy,' he calls.

Kofoed comes in, hunched and morose.

Nathan Pollock taps the leather folder with his gloved fingers.

'I think I've found something,' he says simply.

They go over to the tall, deep window alcove and Pollock carefully undoes the catch and opens the leather folder.

'Go on,' Kofoed whispers.

Pollock gently removes the covering page bearing the words: *Carl Palmcrona's last will and testament.*

They read in silence. The document is dated 1 March three years ago. Palmcrona has left all his assets to one single person: Stefan Bergkvist.

'Who the hell is Stefan Bergkvist?' Kofoed asks once they've

269

finished reading. 'Palmcrona had no family, no friends as far as I can see, he didn't have anyone.'

'Stefan Bergkvist lives in Västerås . . . at the time this was signed, anyway,' Pollock says. 'Rekylgatan 11 in Västerås, and . . .'

Pollock breaks off and looks up.

'He's a child. According to his ID number, he's only sixteen years old.'

The will was drawn up by Palmcrona's solicitor at the law firm Wieselgreen & Sons. Pollock leafs through the updated appendix listing all of Palmcrona's assets. There are four pension funds, some forest, just two hectares, a farm in Södermanland that's on a long-term lease, and the mortgaged apartment on Grevgatan. His biggest asset appears to be an account at the Standard Chartered Bank in Jersey, whose balance Palmcrona estimated at nine million euros.

'It looks like Stefan's just inherited a fortune,' Pollock says.

'Yes.'

'But why?'

Tommy shrugs his shoulders.

'Some people leave all they have to their dog, or their personal trainer.'

'I'll call him.'

'The boy?'

'What else are we going to do?'

Nathan Pollock takes out his phone and dials a number, and asks to be put through to Stefan Bergkvist of Rekylgatan 11 in Västerås, and is told that there's a Siv Bergkvist at that address. He thinks that she's probably the boy's mother. Nathan looks out at the heavy rain, and the overflowing gutters.

'Siv Bergkvist,' a woman answers in a shaky voice.

'My name is Nathan Bergkvist, I'm a detective superintendent . . . Are you Stefan Bergkvist's mother?'

'Yes,' she whispers.

'Can I talk to him?'

'What?'

'There's no cause for alarm, I just need to ask . . .'

'Go to hell!' she screams, and ends the call.

Pollock calls the same number again, but gets no answer. He looks down at the wet street and calls the number again.

'Micke,' a male voice answers warily.

'My name is Nathan Pollock, and I . . .'

'What the hell do you want?'

Nathan can hear the woman crying in the background, she says something to the man and he tells her he can take care of this.

'No,' she says. 'I'll do it . . .'

The phone gets passed over and Nathan hears footsteps walking away.

'Hello,' the woman says quietly.

'I really do need . . .'

'Stefan's dead,' she interrupts in a shrill voice. 'Why are you doing this, why are you calling and telling me you need to talk to him, I can't bear it . . .'

She sobs down the phone, and something falls to the floor with a clatter.

'I'm sorry,' Pollock says. 'I didn't know, I . . .'

'I can't bear it,' she weeps. 'I can't bear it any more . . .'

He hears footsteps again, then the man's voice comes back.

'That's more than enough now,' he says.

'Wait,' Pollock says quickly. 'Can you tell me what's happened? It's important . . .'

Tommy Kofoed has been following the conversation, and watches as Nathan listens to someone at the other end of the line, turns pale and strokes his silvery ponytail.

59

When life gets new meaning

A large number of police officers have gathered in the corridors of Police Headquarters. There's a nervous atmosphere. They're all waiting impatiently for fresh reports. First the Coordination Centre lost contact with the police boat, then all radio contact with the rescue helicopter disappeared as well.

Up in the National Crime Unit Joona is sitting in his office reading the postcard Disa has sent him from a conference on Gotland. 'I'm forwarding a love letter from your secret admirer. Hugs, Disa.' He guesses she had to spend a lot of time looking for a card that was bound to make him shudder. He steels himself, then turns the card over. On the front the words 'Sex on the beach' are printed across a picture of a white poodle in sunglasses and a white bikini. The dog is sitting on a sun-lounger with a red drink in a tall glass beside it.

There's a knock on the door and Joona's smile vanishes when he sees the sombre expression on Nathan Pollock's face.

'Carl Palmcrona left all he had to his son,' Nathan says.

'I didn't think he had any family.'

'The son's dead, only sixteen. Died in an accident yesterday.'

'Yesterday?' Joona repeats.

'Stefan Bergkvist survived Carl Palmcrona by three days,' Nathan says slowly.

'What happened?'

'I didn't quite understand, something about his motorbike,' Pollock says. 'I've asked to get the preliminary report . . .'

'What do you know?'

The tall man with the silver ponytail sits down on the office chair.

'I've spoken to his mother, Siv Bergkvist, and her partner Micke Johansson several times . . . It appears that Siv worked as Palmcrona's secretary when she was attached to No.4 Naval Squadron. They had a brief relationship. She got pregnant. When she told him, he said he assumed she would be getting an abortion. Siv returned to Västerås, gave birth to the child and has claimed ever since that she didn't know who the father was.'

'Did Stefan know that Carl Palmcrona was his father?'

Nathan shakes his head, and thinks about what the boy's mother said: 'I told him his dad was dead, that he died before he was born.'

There's a knock on the door and Anja Larsson comes in and puts a report, still warm from the printer, on the desk.

'An accident,' Anja says without further elaboration, and leaves the room again.

Joona picks up the plastic sleeve and starts to read the report from the preliminary forensic investigation. Because of the rapid spread of the fire, the cause of death wasn't carbon dioxide poisoning but burns. Before the boy died his skin had split wide open, then all his muscles had withered away. The heat had fractured his skull and the bones in his limbs. The pathologist had diagnosed fire-related haematoma, a clotting of the blood between the skull and the brain tissue which is caused by the blood starting to boil.

'Nasty,' Joona mutters.

The investigation of the fire had been exacerbated by the fact that there was basically nothing left of the shack where Stefan Bergkvist's remains were found. Just a smouldering heap of ash, twisted metal and the scarred remains of a body in a contorted position behind where the door had been. The police's preliminary theory is based upon the testimony of a single witness, the train driver who called the fire brigade. He had seen the burning motorcycle lying like a wedge against the door. Everything suggested that sixteen-year-old Stefan Bergkvist had been inside the shack when his motorbike toppled over in such a way that it blocked the door. The lid of the petrol tank wasn't properly secured and the petrol poured out. What set light to the petrol wasn't clear when this report was written, but it was probably a cigarette.

'Palmcrona dies,' Pollock says slowly. 'He leaves his entire fortune to his son, and three days later his son is dead.'

'So the fortune passes to his mother?' Joona says.

'Yes.'

They fall silent and hear slow, shuffling steps in the corridor before Tommy Kofoed appears in Joona's room.

'I've opened Palmcrona's safe,' Kofoed says triumphantly. 'There was nothing in there apart from this.'

He holds up a beautifully bound leather book.

'What's that?' Pollock asks.

'Life story,' Kofoed says. 'Fairly common with people of his class.'

'A diary, you mean?'

Kofoed shrugs.

'More an unassuming sort of memoir, not intended for publication. Supposed to add to the accumulated shared history of the family. Handwritten . . . It starts with a family tree, his father's career and then just a tedious account of his own schooling, exams, military service and professional career . . . He makes a number of unsuccessful investments and his personal finances get rapidly worse, and he sells land and property. It's all described very drily . . .'

'What about his son?'

'His relationship with Siv Bergkvist is mentioned only briefly, as a mistake,' Tommy Kofoed replies, and takes a deep breath. 'But before too long he starts to mention Stefan by name, and his entries for the past eight years are about nothing but his son. He follows the boy's life from a distance, knows what school Stefan goes to, what his interests are, what friends he socialises with. He mentions a number of times that his inheritance is going to be restored. It sounds like he was saving all his money for his son. In the end he simply writes that he's thinking of paying his son a visit when he turns eighteen. He writes that he hopes his son will forgive him and that they will be able to get to know each other after all these years. And now all of a sudden they're both dead.'

'What a nightmare,' Pollock mutters.

'What did you say?' Joona asks, looking up.

'I was just thinking that this is like a nightmare,' Pollock says. 'He does all he can for his son's future, and then it turns out that the son only outlives his father by three days, without ever finding out who his father was.'

60

A little more time

Beverly is already lying in his bed when Axel walks into the bedroom. He only slept two hours last night, and feels dizzy with tiredness.

'How long does it take for Evert to drive here?' she asks in a clear voice.

'Your dad, you mean? Six hours, maybe.'

She gets up from the bed and starts to walk towards the door.

'What are you doing?' Axel asks.

She turns round.

'I thought he might be sitting in the car waiting for me.'

'You know he's not coming to Stockholm,' Axel says.

'I'll just take a look out of the window, just in case.'

'We can call him – would you like to do that?'

'I've already tried.'

He reaches out and pats her cheek gently, and she sits back down on the bed again.

'Are you tired?' she asks.

'I feel almost ill.'

'Do you want us to sleep in the same bed?'

'Yes, please.'

'I think Dad will want to talk to me tomorrow,' she says in a low voice.

Axel nods:

'I'm sure it'll be fine tomorrow.'

Her big, shining eyes make her look younger than ever.

'Lie down, then,' she says. 'Lie down so you can get some sleep, Axel.'

He blinks at her tiredly and watches her lie down carefully on her side of the bed. Her nightdress smells of freshly laundered cotton. When he lies down behind her he wants to cry. He feels like telling her that he's thinking of getting her a psychologist, to help her get through this phase, and that it will get better, it always gets better.

He gently puts one hand on her upper arms, puts the other on her stomach, and hears her whimper slightly as he draws her to him. He presses his face into the back of her neck, breathing against her skin, holding her tight. After a while he hears her quick breathing slow down. They lie perfectly still, get warm and sweaty, but he doesn't let go of her.

The next morning Axel gets up early, he's slept for four hours, and his muscles ache. He stands at the window and looks at the dark flowers on the lilacs.

When he reaches his new workplace he still feels frozen and tired. Yesterday he had been moments away from signing his name on a contract drawn up by a dead man. He would have placed his own reputation in the hands of a hanged man, trusting his judgement and ignoring his own.

He feels a great sense of relief at his decision to wait, but can't help thinking that it had been a bit stupid to draw a stick-figure on the contract.

He knows that at some point in the next few days he's going to have to authorise the export of ammunition to Kenya. He opens the file containing the documents and starts to read about Sweden's trade with the region.

An hour later the door of Axel Riessen's office opens and Jörgen Grünlicht comes in, pulls a chair up to the desk and sits down. He opens the folder, takes out the contract, leafs through to the page requiring a signature, then looks Axel in the eye.

'Hello,' Axel says.

Jörgen Grünlicht can't help smiling seeing as the stick-figure with messy hair actually resembles Axel Riessen, and the word 'Hello!' is written in the speech bubble.

'Hello,' Jörgen says.

'It was too soon,' Axel explains.

'I appreciate your response, I didn't mean to put you under pressure, even if it is rather urgent,' Jörgen says. 'The Trade Minister was on my back again, and Silencia Defence are calling several times a day. But I do understand you, you know. You're completely new in post, and . . . you want to be thorough.'

'Yes.'

'And that's good, of course,' he goes on. 'But you know you can always leave the decision to the government if you feel unsure.'

'I don't feel unsure,' Axel replies. 'I'm just not ready, there's no more to it than that.'

'It's just that . . . from their perspective, it's taking an unreasonable amount of time.'

'I'm putting everything else to one side, and I can say that so far everything looks very good,' he replies. 'I'm not thinking of advising Silencia Defence against loading the ship, but I'm not ready.'

'I'll let all parties know that you're positively disposed towards the deal.'

'By all means, because as long as I don't find anything unusual . . .'

'You won't, I've been through all the documents myself.'

'Well, then,' Axel says gently.

'I won't disturb you any longer,' Jörgen says, and gets up from his chair. 'When do you think you'll have finished your evaluation?'

Axel glances at the material again.

'I'd say a couple of days, because I might have to request some information of my own from Kenya.'

'Of course,' Jörgen Grünlicht says with a smile, and leaves the room.

61

At ten o'clock Axel leaves the ISP to go and work at home. He takes all the documentation regarding the export licence with him. Tiredness is making him feel frozen and hungry, and he drives to the Grand Hotel and picks up brunch for two. He carries the food with him into the kitchen at home. Beverly is sitting in the middle of the kitchen table looking through a magazine, *Amelia Brides and Weddings*.

'Are you hungry?' he asks.

'I don't know if I want to wear white when I get married,' Beverly says. 'Maybe pale pink . . .'

'I like white,' he murmurs.

Axel prepares a tray, and they go upstairs together to the little red rococo suite by the large window in the sitting room. Between them is an octagonal eighteenth-century table. The tabletop displays the fondness of the age for inlaid veneer. The motif is a garden with peacocks and a woman playing a Chinese zither.

Axel lays out the family porcelain with the silver coat of arms, grey linen napkins and the heavy wine glasses. He pours Coca-Cola in Beverly's glass, and mineral water with a slice of lime in his.

Beverly's neck is narrow, her chin neat and beautiful. Because her hair is so short, the whole of the gentle curve of the back of her skull is visible. She drains her glass and stretches her upper body happily. A lovely, childish gesture. He thinks to himself that she'll still do the same thing as an adult, possibly even when she's old.

'Tell me about music again,' she says.

'Where were we?' Axel asks, pointing the remote at the stereo.

Alexander Malter's superlatively sensitive interpretation of Arvo Pärt's *Alina* starts to play from the speakers. Axel looks down into his glass, where bubbles in the mineral water are popping, and wishes intensely that he could drink again, he wishes he had champagne to go with the asparagus, and then some Propovan and Stesolid before he goes to bed.

Axel pours Beverly some more Coca-Cola. She looks up and thanks him silently. He looks straight into her big, dark eyes and doesn't notice her glass overflowing until the drink is spreading across the table. The pattern turns dark, as if the sun had passed behind a cloud, a wet film making the park and peacocks glisten.

He stands up and sees Beverly's reflection in the glass of the window, sees the line of her chin and suddenly realises how much she resembles Greta.

Odd that he's never noticed before.

Axel feels like turning and running away, out of the house, but he forces himself to fetch a cloth as his heartbeat calms down again.

They're not identical, by any means, but Beverly resembles Greta in a number of ways.

He stops and rubs his mouth with a trembling hand.

He thinks about Greta every day, and tries not to think about her every day.

The week of the final of the music competition haunts him.

It was thirty-four years ago, but everything in his life went dark, he was so young, only seventeen, but so much was already gone forever.

62

Sweet sleep

The Johan Fredrik Berwald Competition was without doubt the most prestigious contest for young violinists in northern Europe. It had helped several world-famous virtuosi come to prominence, putting them directly in the glare of the spotlight. There were just three soloists left in the final. During the previous six rounds fewer and fewer musicians had performed in front of a closed jury, but the final would be taking place the next day in front of a large audience in Stockholm Concert Hall in conjunction with a live television broadcast of a concert conducted by Herbert Blomstedt.

In musical circles it was sensational that two of the finalists, Axel Riessen and Greta Stiernlood, were students at the Royal College of Music in Stockholm. The third finalist was Shiro Sasaki from Japan.

For Alice Riessen, a professional musician who had never quite broken through, her son Axel's success was a great triumph, particularly as she had received a number of warnings from the school principal that Axel had been missing lectures, and was unfocused and careless.

After getting through to the third round, Axel and Greta were excused from classes so that they could devote all their time to the next stage. The contest had given them an opportunity to get to know each other, they took pleasure in each other's success, and before the final they started meeting in Axel's home to help support one another.

The last part of the contest involved each violinist playing a piece they had chosen themselves together with their tutor.

Axel and his younger brother Robert shared the seven rooms at the top of the large house in Lärkstaden. Axel spent practically no time practising his chosen piece, but he loved playing, finding his way through new pieces, trying sounds he'd never heard before, and sometimes he would sit up long into the night playing his violin and exploring its essence until the tips of his fingers stung.

There was only one day left. Tomorrow Axel and Greta would be competing in the final in the Concert Hall. Axel was sitting looking at the covers of the albums spread across the floor in front of his gramophone. There were three records by David Bowie: *Space Oddity*, *Aladdin Sane* and *Hunky Dory*.

His mum knocked on the door and came in with a bottle of Coca-Cola and two glasses with ice cubes and slices of lemon. Axel thanked her, rather surprised, took the tray and put it down on the coffee table.

'I thought the two of you were practising,' Alice said, looking round.

'Greta had to go home to eat.'

'You can carry on in the meantime, though, surely?'

'I'm waiting for her.'

'You know it's the final tomorrow,' Alice said, sitting down next to her son. 'I practise at least eight hours a day, and sometimes I used to work ten hours a day.'

'I'm not even awake ten hours a day,' Axel joked.

'Axel, you've got a gift.'

'How do you know that?'

'I just know. But that's not enough, that's not enough for anyone,' she said.

'Mum, I practise like an idiot,' he lied.

'Play for me,' she asked.

'No,' he said abruptly.

'I appreciate that you don't want to have your mother as a tutor, but you could let me help, now that it's important,' Alice went on patiently. 'The last time I heard you was two years ago, at a Christmas concert, and no one could work out what you were playing . . .'

'Bowie's "Cracked Actor".'

'It was immature of you . . . but quite impressive, for a fifteen-year-old,' she admitted, reaching out her hand to pat him. 'But tomorrow . . .'

Axel shrank away from his mother's hand.

'Stop nagging.'

'Can I at least know what piece you've chosen to play?'

'Classical,' he replied with a wide smile.

'Thank God for that.'

He shrugged his shoulders and wouldn't meet her gaze. When the doorbell rang he rushed out of the room and down the stairs.

Dusk had started to fall, but the snow was creating an indirect light, a darkness that never properly grew thicker, outside the house. Greta was standing on the steps in her beret and duffle-coat. Her striped scarf was wound round her neck. Her cheeks were glowing with cold, and the hair draped across her shoulders was covered in snowflakes. She put her violin on the dresser in the hall, carefully hung up her outdoor clothes, unlaced her black boots and took out her low-heeled indoor shoes from her bag.

Alice Riessen came downstairs and said hello. She was very excited, her cheeks were flushed with happiness.

'It's good that you're helping each other practise,' she said. 'You must be stern with Axel, otherwise he won't bother.'

'I've noticed,' Greta laughed.

Greta Stiernlood was the daughter of an industrialist who owned a lot of shares in Saab Scania and Enskilda Banken, among others. Greta had grown up alone with her father – her parents divorced when she was very young, and she had never seen her mother since then. But early on – possibly before she was even born – her father decided that she was going be a violinist.

When they got up to Axel's music room Greta went over to the grand piano. Her glossy, curly hair was spread across her shoulders. She was wearing a white blouse and a chequered skirt, a dark-blue pullover and stripy tights.

She took her violin, attached the chin-rest, brushed away some resin that had caught on the strings with a cotton cloth, adjusted her bow and put her score on the stand. She quickly checked that her violin was still in tune after being out in the cold and altered humidity.

Then she began to practise. She played the way she always did, with her eyes half closed and focused in on herself. Her long eyelashes cast trembling shadows across her flushed cheeks. Axel knew the piece very well: the first part of Beethoven's String Quartet No. 15. A serious, searching theme.

He listened, smiled and thought that Greta had a feeling for music; there was an honesty in her interpretations that filled him with respect.

'Lovely,' he said when she had finished.

She changed her score and blew on her sore fingers.

'I can't make my mind up . . . You know, Dad's found out what I ought to be playing, he says I should play Tartini, the violin sonata in G-minor.'

She fell silent, looked at the notes, scanning them with her eyes, counting the sixteenths and memorising complex legatos.

'But I'm not sure, I . . .'

'Can I hear it?' Axel asked.

'It sounds terrible,' she said, and blushed.

She played the last piece with a tense face, it was beautiful and tragic, but towards the end she lost her tempo when the violin's top notes were supposed to reach upward like questing flames.

'Damn,' she whispered, and rested the violin under her arm. 'I was going too slowly, I've been working like a Trojan, but I need to get right into the sixteenths . . .'

'But I liked the vibrato, as if you were curving a big mirror up towards . . .'

'I played it wrong,' she interrupted, and blushed even more. 'Sorry, I know you're trying to be kind, but I have to get this right. It's ridiculous, sitting here the night before, unable to make my mind up if I ought to play the easy piece or take a chance on the much harder one.'

'But you know both of them so . . .'

'No, I don't, it would be a risk,' she said. 'But give me two or three hours and I might dare to take a chance on the Tartini tomorrow.'

'You can't do that just because your dad thinks . . .'

'But he's right.'

'No, he's not,' Axel said, and slowly rolled a joint.

'I know the easy piece,' she went on. 'But that might not be enough. It depends what you and the Japanese guy choose.'

'You can't think like that.'

'How am I supposed to think, then? I haven't seen you practise once. What are you going to play – have you even decided?'

'Ravel,' he replied.

'Ravel? Without practising?'

She laughed.

'Seriously?' she asked.

'Ravel's *Tzigane*.'

'Axel, sorry, but that's an insane choice, you know that, it's too complicated, too fast, too much of a challenge, and . . .'

'I want to play like Perlman, but without the haste . . . because it doesn't actually go fast.'

'Axel, it's ridiculously fast,' she smiled.

'Yes, for the hare being chased . . . but for the wolf it goes too slowly.'

She gave him a weary look.

'Where did you read that?'

'Paganini's supposed to have said it.'

'Okay, so I've only got the Japanese guy to worry about,' she said, putting the violin to her shoulder. 'You haven't been practising, Axel, you can't play Ravel's *Tzigane*.'

'It's not as hard as everyone says,' he replied, lighting the joint.

'No,' she smiled, and started to play again.

She stopped a short while later and looked at him sternly.

'Are you going to play Ravel?'

'Yes.'

She turned serious.

'Have you been lying to me? Have you spent four years practising this piece, or what?'

'I've only just decided – when you asked.'

'How can you be so stupid?' she laughed.

'I don't care if I come last,' he said, and lay back on the sofa.

'I care,' she said simply.

'I know, but there'll be other chances.'

'Not for me.'

She started to play the difficult piece by Tartini again. It went better this time, but she still broke off, played the complicated section again, and then one more time.

Axel clapped his hands, put David Bowie's *The Rise and Fall of Ziggy Stardust and the Spiders from Mars* on the gramophone and lifted the needle onto the record. He lay back, closed his eyes and sang along.

Ziggy really sang, screwed up eyes and screwed down hairdo. Like some cat from Japan, he could lick 'em by smiling. He could leave 'em to hang.

Greta hesitated, put her violin down, went over to him and took the joint from his hand. She took a few puffs, coughed, and handed it back.

'How can anyone be as stupid as you are?' she asked, suddenly stroking his lips.

She leaned over and tried to kiss him, but slipped and ended up kissing him on the cheek, whispered an apology, and kissed him again. They carried on kissing, tentatively, searchingly. He pulled her sweater off and her hair crackled with static electricity. He got a small shock when he touched her cheek and quickly snatched his hand back. They smiled nervously at each other, and kissed again. He unbuttoned her neatly ironed white blouse and felt her small breasts through her simple bra. Her long, curling hair smelled of snow and winter, but her body was as warm as freshly baked bread.

They went into the bedroom and sank onto his bed. With trembling hands she unfastened her lined wrap-skirt, then held onto her underpants as he pulled her thick, stripy tights off.

'What is it?' he whispered. 'Do you want to stop?'

'I don't know – do you want to stop?'

'No,' he smiled.

'I'm just a bit nervous,' she said honestly.

'But you're older than me.'

'Quite – you're only seventeen, it's almost a bit improper,' she smiled.

Axel's heart beat hard as he pulled her underpants down. She lay perfectly still as he kissed her stomach, her small breasts, her neck, chin, lips. She cautiously parted her legs and he lay down on top of her and felt her slowly pressing her thighs against his hips. Her cheeks flushed bright red when he slid inside her. She pulled him to her, caressed his neck and back, and sighed quietly every time he sank into her.

When they slowed and stopped, gasping for breath, a thick layer of warm sweat had formed between their naked bodies. They lay intertwined on his bed with their eyes closed, and soon fell asleep.

63

The Johan Fredrik Berwald Contest

It was already light outside when Axel woke up on the morning of the day when he lost everything. He and Greta hadn't closed the curtains, they had just fallen asleep together on the bed, and slept the whole night through in each other's arms, exhausted and happy.

Axel got out of bed and looked at Greta, who was sleeping peacefully with the thick duvet wrapped around her. He walked to the door, stopped in front of the mirror and looked at his naked, seventeen-year-old body for a while before he carried on into the music room. He carefully closed the door to the bedroom, went over to the piano and took the violin from its case. He put it to his shoulder, went and stood by the window and looked out at the winter morning, at the snow blowing down from the rooftops, swept into long veils, and then he started to play Ravel's *Tzigane* from memory.

The piece began with a mournful Roma melody, slow and measured, but then the tempo increased. The melody conjured up increasingly rapid echoes of itself, as sparkling, fleeting memories of a summer's night.

It went incredibly fast.

He played because he was happy, he didn't think, just let his fingers dance with the bubbling, trickling stream.

Axel started to smile to himself when he remembered the painting his grandfather had in his drawing room. He claimed it was Ernst Josephson's most radiant version of his 'Water Sprite'. As a child Axel had been very fond of the stories about the magical creature who lured people to drown by playing his fiddle so beautifully.

Axel thought he resembled the water sprite at that moment, the naked youth sitting in the water playing his violin. The big difference between Axel and Josephson's water sprite was that Axel was happy.

His bow moved over the strings, changing notes with dizzying speed. He didn't care that some of the horsehair came loose and was hanging from the frog.

This is how Ravel should be played, he thought. He should be played as happy music, not exotic. Ravel is a happy composer, a young composer.

He let the echo of the last notes resonate through the violin, swirling like the snow on the roofs outside. He lowered the bow and was about to take a bow to the wintery view when he detected movement behind him.

He turned round and saw Greta standing in the doorway. She was holding the duvet around her and was looking at him with strangely dark eyes.

He grew worried when he saw the serious expression on her face.

'What is it?'

She didn't answer, just swallowed hard. Two large tears trickled down her cheeks.

'Greta, what is it?' he repeated.

'You said you hadn't practised,' she said in a monotone.

'No, I . . . I,' he stammered. 'I've told you before, I find it easy to learn new pieces.'

'Congratulations.'

'It's not like you think.'

She shook her head.

'I don't understand how I could be so stupid,' she said.

He put the violin and bow down, but she went back into the bedroom and closed the door behind her. He pulled on a pair of jeans that were hanging over the back of a chair, went over to the door and knocked.

'Greta? Can I come in?'

She didn't answer. He felt a big, dark lump of anxiety growing inside him. After a little while she came out, fully dressed. Without looking at him, she walked over to the piano, packed her violin away and left him alone.

The Concert House was packed. Greta was the first competitor to perform. She hadn't looked at him, hadn't said hello when she arrived. She was wearing a dark-blue velvet dress and a simple necklace with a heart on it.

Axel sat in his dressing room waiting with his eyes half-closed. It was completely quiet. Only a faint hum could be heard behind a dusty ventilation grille. His younger brother Robert came into the room.

'Aren't you going to sit with Mum?' Axel asked.

'I'm too nervous . . . I can't watch when you play, I'll sit here and wait instead.'

'Has Greta started to play?'

'Yes, it sounds good.'

'What piece did she choose? Was it Tartini's violin sonata or . . .'

'No, something by Beethoven.'

'Good,' Axel muttered.

They sat there in silence, saying nothing more. After a while there was a knock at the door. Axel stood up and opened it, and a woman told him it would be his turn very soon.

'Good luck,' Robert said.

'Thanks,' Axel replied, then picked up his violin and bow and walked through the corridor with the woman.

Loud applause could be heard from the stage, and Axel caught a glimpse of Greta and her father as they hurried into her dressing room.

Axel walked along the passageway, then had to wait behind a screen next to the stage, while the compere introduced him. After he heard his name, he walked straight out into the blinding spotlight, and smiled at the audience. A buzz ran through the whole hall when he said he was going to play Maurice Ravel's *Tzigane*.

He put the violin to his shoulder and raised the bow. He began to play the melancholic opening, and then increased the tempo towards the seemingly impossible. The audience held its breath. He could hear himself that it sounded astonishingly good, but this time the melody wasn't dancing like water in a stream. He wasn't playing happily, but like the water sprite in the painting. He was playing with a hot, feverish sorrow. When he was three minutes into the piece and the notes were falling like raindrops, he intentionally started to skip the odd note, slowed his pace, made a couple of mistakes, and then stopped altogether.

The Concert Hall was silent.

'I'm very sorry,' he whispered, and stepped down from the stage.

The audience clapped politely. His mother stood up from her seat and walked after him, stopping him in the aisle.

'Come here, my boy,' she said, putting her hands on his shoulders.

She stroked his cheek and her voice was warm and noticeably affected when she said:

'That was incredible, the best interpretation I've ever heard.'

'Sorry, Mum.'

'No,' she said, then turned away from Axel and walked out of the Concert Hall.

Axel went to his dressing room to get his clothes, but was stopped by the great conductor, Herbert Blomstedt.

'That sounded very good indeed until you pretended to get it wrong,' he said in a subdued voice.

The house was echoingly silent when Axel got home. It was already late in the evening. He went up to his attic rooms, through the music room and into the bedroom, and closed the door. Inside his head he could still hear the music. He could hear himself omitting notes, then unexpectedly slowing the tempo and falling silent.

He fell silent over and over again.

Axel lay down on his bed and fell asleep beside his violin case.

The next morning he woke up to hear a phone ringing somewhere in the house.

Someone was walking across the floor in the dining room, making the floor creak.

After a while he heard footsteps on the stairs. Without knocking, his mother walked straight into his bedroom.

'Sit up,' Alice said sternly.

He got worried when he looked at her. She had been crying, and her cheeks were still wet.

'Mum, I don't understand . . .'

'Be quiet,' she interrupted in a low voice. 'I've had a call from the school principal, and he . . .'

'He hates me because . . .'

'Be quiet!' Alice screamed.

Silence fell, and she put a trembling hand to her mouth and held it there as tears ran down her face.

'It's about Greta,' she eventually said. 'She's committed suicide.'

Axel looked at her and tried to comprehend what she was saying.

'No, because I . . .'

'She was ashamed,' Alice interrupted. 'She should have been practising, you promised, and I should have known, I did know . . . She shouldn't have been here, she . . . I'm not saying it's your fault, Axel, it isn't. She let herself down when it really mattered, and she couldn't bear . . .'

'Mum, I . . .'

'Quiet!' she snapped again. 'It's over.'

Alice left the room, and Axel got up from the bed in a roaring fog, stumbled, opened the violin case, took out the beautiful instrument and smashed it on the floor as hard as he could. The neck broke and the body flapped about on the loose strings, then he stamped on it, scattering splinters of wood around the room.

'Axel! What are you doing?'

His younger brother Robert rushed in and tried to stop him, but Axel pushed him away. Robert hit his back on the large wardrobe, but walked over to Axel again.

'Axel, you got some notes wrong, but what does that matter?' Robert said tentatively. 'I met Greta, she'd got some notes wrong too, everyone . . .'

'Shut up!' Axel shouted. 'You're never to mention her name to me again.'

Robert looked at him, then turned and left the room. Axel went on stamping on the remains of the instrument until it was impossible to tell that it had once been a violin.

Shiro Sasaki from Japan won the Johan Fredrik Berwald Competition. Greta had chosen the easy piece by Beethoven, but had still made mistakes. When she got home she took an overdose of sleeping pills and locked herself in her room. She wasn't found until the next morning when she failed to come down to breakfast.

Axel's memories sink like an underwater city, down into the mud and weeds, away from active thought. He glances at Beverly, who is looking at him with Greta's big eyes. He looks at the cloth in his hand and the liquid on the table, the shimmering veneer and the woman playing the Chinese zither.

The light from outside falls across the back of Beverly's head when she turns and looks at the violins hanging on the wall.

'I wish I could play the violin,' she says.

'We could do a course together,' he smiles.

'I'd like that,' she replies seriously.

He puts the cloth down on the table, feeling an immense tiredness roaring inside him. The piano music echoes through the room. It's being played without dampers, and the notes blur dreamily into each other.

'Poor Axel, you want to sleep,' she says.

'I have to work,' he mutters, almost to himself.

'Tonight, then,' she replies, and stands up.

64

The lift down

Detective Superintendent Joona Linna is in his office at the National Crime Unit. He's sitting at his desk reading Carl Palmcrona's account of his life. In one note from five years ago Palmcrona describes how he travelled to Västerås to attend the festivities to mark the end of his son's school year. He had stood at a distance when everyone gathered in the schoolyard under umbrellas in the rain and sang the traditional end-of-year hymns. Palmcrona described his son's white jeans and white denim jacket, his long blond hair, and said that his son had 'something about his nose and eyes that made me start to cry'. He had driven back to Stockholm, thinking that his son was worth everything he had done thus far and would go on to do for him.

The phone rings and Joona answers at once. It's Petter Näslund, who's sitting in the mobile command unit out on Dalarö.

'I've just been in contact with the navy's helicopter unit,' he says excitedly. 'They're flying back across Erstaviken right now, and they've got Penelope Fernandez with them.'

'She's alive?' Joona asks, feeling a surge of relief.

'She was swimming straight out to sea when they found her,' Petter explains.

'How is she? Is she okay?'

'Sounds like it – they're on their way to Södermalm Hospital.'

'That's too dangerous,' Joona says abruptly. 'Fly her here to Police Headquarters instead – we can bring in a team of medics from the Karolinska.'

He hears Petter tell someone to contact the helicopter.

'What do you know about the others?' Joona asks.

'It's complete chaos, Joona. We've lost people. This is crazy.'

'Björn Almskog?' Joona asks.

'He hasn't been found yet, but . . . it's impossible to get any information, we don't know anything.'

'What about the perpetrator? Has he vanished?'

'We'll have him soon. It's a small island. We've got guys from the Response Unit on the ground and in the air, and boats from the coastguard and marine police are on their way.'

'Good,' Joona says.

'You don't think we're going to get him?'

'If you didn't get him at once he's probably already gone.'

'Is that my fault?'

'Petter,' Joona says calmly and gently, 'if you hadn't acted as quickly as you did, Penelope Fernandez would be dead . . . and without her we wouldn't have a thing – no connection to the photograph, no witness.'

An hour later two doctors from the Karolinska Hospital examine Penelope Fernandez in a protected room directly below the headquarters of the National Police Committee. They tend to her wounds and give her a tranquilliser, as well as nutritional supplements and hydration.

Petter Näslund informs the head of the National Crime Unit, Carlos Eliasson, that the remains of their colleagues Lennart Johansson and Göran Sjödin have been identified. Ossian Wallenberg has been found dead outside his house and divers are on their way to the scene where the rescue helicopter crashed. Petter says that they're assuming that all three crew on board are dead.

The police haven't managed to catch the perpetrator, but Penelope Fernandez is alive.

The flags in front of Police Headquarters are lowered to

half-mast, and Regional Police Chief Margareta Widding and National Police Chief Carlos Eliasson hold a subdued press conference in the press room on the ground floor.

Detective Superintendent Joona Linna doesn't take part in the meeting with reporters. Instead he and Saga Bauer take the lift down to the lowest floor to see Penelope Fernandez, in the hope of getting some answers to their questions, and finding out the reasons behind everything that has happened.

65

What these eyes have seen

Five floors below the most modern part of Police Headquarters is a section containing two apartments, eight guestrooms and two dormitories. It was set up to provide secure accommodation for senior police officers in times of crisis and during emergencies. For the past ten years the guestrooms have also been used to provide protection for witnesses who are believed to be under an exceptional level of threat.

Penelope Fernandez is lying on a hospital bed, and feels cool liquid enter her arm as the speed of the drip is adjusted.

'We're just rehydrating you and giving you nutritional supplements,' Dr Daniella Richards says.

In a gentle voice she explains what she's doing as she tapes the cannula to the inside of her elbow.

Penelope's wounds have been cleaned and dressed, her injured left foot stitched and bandaged, the scratches on her back cleaned and taped, and the deep cut on her hip sewn together with eight stitches.

'I'd like to give you some morphine for the pain.'

'My mum,' Penelope whispers, moistening her lips. 'I want to talk to my mum.'

'I can understand that,' Daniella replies. 'I'll pass that on.'

Hot tears trickle down Penelope's cheeks, into her hair and

ears. She hears the doctor ask the nurse to prepare an injection of 0.5 millilitres of morphine and scopolamine.

The room looks like an ordinary hospital room, but perhaps a little cosier. There's a simple vase of flowers on the bedside table, and there are bright pictures on the yellow walls. A pale birchwood bookcase is full of previously read books, so people have clearly had time to read in here. The room has no windows, but there's a light behind a curtain-like piece of fabric to help alleviate the feeling of being in an underground bunker.

Daniella Richards explains gently to Penelope that they're going to leave her alone now, but that she can press the illuminated alarm button if she wants help with anything.

'There'll be someone here the whole time if you have any questions, or would just like a bit of company,' she says.

Penelope Fernandez is left alone in the bright room. She closes her eyes as the calm warmth of the morphine spreads through her body, pulling her towards peaceful sleep.

She hears a crunch as a woman in a black niqab stamps on two small, sun-baked clay figurines. A girl and her little brother are reduced to crumbs and dust beneath her sandal. The veiled woman is carrying a heavy pack of grain on her back, and doesn't even notice what she's done. Two boys whistle and laugh, crying that the slave children are dead, that there are only a few infants left now, and that all the Furs will die.

Penelope forces the memories from Kubbum out of her head, but before she falls asleep she experiences a short moment when tons of stone, earth, clay and concrete are lying on top of her. It's as if she's falling to the centre of the Earth, falling and falling and falling.

Penelope Fernandez wakes up, but hasn't got the strength to open her eyes: the morphine is still making her body heavy. She remembers that she's lying in a hospital bed in a secure room deep beneath Police Headquarters. She doesn't have to run any more. The relief is followed by a great wave of pain and grief. She doesn't know how long she's been asleep, and feels that she could easily drift off again, but opens her eyes anyway.

She opens her eyes, but the underground room is completely black.

She blinks, but can't see anything. Not even the alarm button beside the bed is lit up. There must be a power cut. She's about to cry out, but forces herself to keep quiet when the door to the corridor suddenly clicks. She stares out into the darkness, hears her own heartbeat pounding. Her body is tingling, every muscle is tense. Someone is touching her hair. Almost imperceptibly. She lies completely still and feels someone standing beside the bed stroking her hair, weaving their fingers slowly into her locks. She is about to start praying when the person beside her takes a hard grasp of her hair and pulls her out of bed. She screams and he throws her against the wall, shattering the framed picture and toppling the drip-stand. She collapses on the floor, surrounded by broken glass. He's still holding her hair, and drags her back, rolls her over and smashes her face against the locked wheel of the bed, then he pulls out a black-bladed dagger.

Penelope wakes up when she falls to the floor, the door opens and the nurse rushes in. All the lights are on, and Penelope realises that she's been having a nightmare. The nurse helps her back onto the bed, and speaks softly to her, then fixes guards to both sides of the bed to stop her falling again.

The sweat on her body goes cold after a while. She can't summon up the energy to move, and goosebumps rise up on her arms. She just lies there on her back with the alarm button in her hand, and is staring up at the ceiling when there's a knock on the door. A young woman with colourful ribbons woven into her mid-length blonde hair comes in and looks at her with gentle seriousness in her eyes. Behind her stands a tall man with untidy blond hair and a friendly, symmetrical face.

'My name is Saga Bauer,' the woman says. 'I'm from the Security Police. This is my colleague Joona Linna, from the National Crime Unit.'

Penelope looks at them blankly, then lowers her gaze and looks at her bandaged arms, at all the scratches and bruises, and the cannula in the crook of her arm.

'We're very sorry for everything you've been through in the past few days,' the woman says. 'And we understand that you probably just want to be left alone, but I'm afraid we're going to have to talk to you a fair bit over the next few days, and we have to start with the first questions now.'

Saga Bauer pulls out the chair from the little desk and sits down beside the bed.

'He's still hunting me – isn't he?' Penelope asks after a short pause.

'You're safe here,' Saga replies.

'Tell me he's dead.'

'Penelope, we need . . .'

'You couldn't stop him,' she says weakly.

'We're going to get him, I promise,' Saga Bauer says. 'But you have to help us.'

Penelope sighs deeply, then closes her eyes.

'This is going to feel rough, but we need answers to some questions,' Saga goes on. 'Do you know why all of this has happened?'

'Ask Björn,' she mutters. 'He might know.'

'What did you say?' Saga asks.

'I said you should ask Björn,' Penelope whispers, and slowly opens her eyes. 'Ask Björn, maybe he knows.'

She must have brought a load of spiders and insects with her from the forest, they're crawling over Penelope's skin and she scratches her forehead, but Saga calmly stops her hands.

'You've been chased by someone,' Saga says. 'I can't imagine how terrible it must have been, but we need to know if you recognised the man pursuing you. Have you ever seen him before?'

Penelope shakes her head almost imperceptibly.

'We didn't think so,' Saga says. 'But can you give us a description, a tattoo, maybe, any unusual features?'

'No,' Penelope whispers.

'Perhaps you could help to put together a Photofit picture, it doesn't take much for us to be able to put out an alert for him via Interpol.'

The man from the National Crime Unit comes closer, and his unusually pale grey eyes are like stones polished by a stream.

'It looked like you were shaking your head a moment ago,' he says calmly. 'When Saga asked if you'd met your pursuer before – is that right?'

Penelope nods.

'So you must have seen him,' Joona goes on amiably. 'Because otherwise you wouldn't know that you hadn't seen him before.'

Penelope stares into space and remembers how the man had always moved as if he had all the time in the world, yet everything still happened surprisingly quickly. In her mind's eye she sees him kneel down and take aim as she was hanging from the helicopter. She sees him raise the gun and shoot. No haste, no nervousness. Then she sees his face again, lit up by the flash of lightning, when they looked right at each other.

'We understand that you're frightened,' Joona goes on. 'But we . . .'

He falls silent when a nurse comes into the room and says that they haven't been able to get hold of Penelope's mother yet.

'She isn't at home, and she's not answering her . . .'

Penelope lets out a moan and turns away, hiding her face in the pillow. The nurse puts a comforting hand on her shoulder.

'I don't want to,' Penelope sobs. 'I don't want to . . .'

Another nurse hurries in and explains that she needs to add a dose of tranquillising medication to the drip.

'I'm going to have to ask you to leave,' the nurse says quickly to Saga and Joona.

'We'll come back later,' Joona says. 'I think I know where your mother is. I'll sort it out.'

Penelope has stopped crying, but is still breathing fast. She hears the nurse prepare the medication and thinks that the room reminds her of a prison cell. Her mum is never going to want to come here. She clenches her teeth and tries to hold back her tears for a while.

There are moments when Penelope thinks she can remember her earliest years. The smell of steaming, dirty bodies can send her right back to the cell she was born in, and the light of a torch sweeping across the prisoners' faces, and her mother passing her to someone else who immediately starts singing gently in her ear as her mum is taken away by the guards.

66

Without Penelope

Claudia Fernandez gets off the bus at the Dalarö Strand Hotel. As she walks along by the harbour she can hear the sound of helicopters and sirens vanish into the distance. The search can't be over. They have to keep on looking. A few police boats are moving about some distance from the shore. She looks around. There's no ferry in the harbour, no cars either.

'Penelope!' she shouts out. 'Penelope!'

She realises how she must look, how oddly she's behaving, but without Penelope there's nothing left.

She starts to walk along the water's edge. The grass is brown and dry, and there's rubbish everywhere. Seagulls are crying high above. She starts to run, but hasn't got the energy and starts walking again. Deserted Swiss-style villas are clustered on the hillside. She stops when she reaches a sign with the word 'Private' written on it in white paint. She carries on past the sign, out onto a concrete jetty, then looks back at the big rocks. There's no one here, she thinks, and turns back towards the harbour again. A man is walking along the road, waving to her, a dark figure with his jacket flapping behind him. She squints against the sunlight. The man shouts something. Claudia looks at him in confusion. He starts to walk faster, striding towards her, but now she can see his friendly face.

'Claudia Fernandez?' he calls.

'That's me,' she says, waiting for him.

'My name is John Bengtsson,' he says when he reaches her. 'Joona Linna sent me. He said you'd probably come out here.'

'Why?' she asks in a weak voice.

'Your daughter's alive.'

Claudia looks at the man, who repeats what he just said.

'Penelope's alive,' he says, and smiles at her.

67

Where the money goes

The atmosphere in Police Headquarters is extremely turbulent, almost fevered in its agitation. People are comparing what's happening with the police murders in Malexander in 1999, and the case of Josef Ek the year before last. The papers are writing about the drama in the archipelago, calling the perpetrator 'the police butcher'; the journalists are speculating wildly and putting pressure on their sources in the force for information.

Joona Linna and Saga Bauer are due to present a summary of the current state of the investigation to the head of National Crime, Carlos Eliasson, the head of the Security Police, Verner Zandén, Detective Superintendent Petter Näslund, head of operations Benny Rubin, as well as Nathan Pollock and Tommy Kofoed from the National Homicide Commission.

They're walking along the corridor, discussing the chances of Penelope Fernandez being able to help them make progress.

'I think she'll talk soon,' Joona says.

'That's far from certain, she could just as easily clam up altogether,' Saga replies.

Anja Larsson has stepped out into the corridor from her office, and is looking at Joona and Saga with an unhappy look on her face. When Joona sees her he smiles and waves, but doesn't have time to see her form a heart with her thumbs and forefingers before he goes into the meeting room.

They close the door, sit down and say hello to the men already sitting round the table.

'I want to start by saying that all suspicions against left-wing extremists have been dropped,' Saga says.

Verner whispers something to Nathan Pollock.

'Haven't they?' Saga says, raising her voice.

Verner looks up and nods.

'Yes, that's correct,' he says, and clears his throat.

'Take it from the start,' Carlos says to Saga.

'Okay . . . Penelope Fernandez is a peace campaigner, the chair of the Swedish Peace and Arbitration Society,' Saga goes on. 'She's in a long-term relationship with Björn Almskog, who's a bartender at the Debaser club at Medborgarplatsen. She lives at Sankt Paulsgatan 3, and he lives at Pontonjärgatan 47. Penelope Fernandez was in possession of a photograph that was taped to the glass door between her living room and hall.'

From her computer Saga Bauer projects a copy of the photograph onto the screen that covers one wall of the room.

'This picture was taken in Frankfurt in the spring of 2008,' she explains.

'We recognise Palmcrona,' Carlos says.

'Exactly,' Saga says, and then points out the other people in the box. 'This is Pontus Salman, managing director of arms manufacturer Silencia Defence. And this is none other than Raphael Guidi. He's a well-known arms dealer, has been for a long time . . . known as "the Archangel" in the trade, and does most of his business in Africa and the Middle East.'

'And the woman who's been allowed to join them for coffee?' Benny Rubin asks.

'Her name is Agathe al-Haji,' Saga says without smiling. 'She's a military advisor to the Sudanese government, and closely connected to the president, Omar al-Bashir.'

Benny slams his hand down hard on the table, and bares his teeth when Pollock shoots him a disapproving look.

'Is this ordinary behaviour?' Carlos asks. 'For them to meet like that?'

'Yes, I'd say so,' Saga replies. 'The meeting in this picture related to a large shipment of ammunition produced under licence to the Sudanese army. The deal was deemed to be politically acceptable, and would doubtless have gone through if the International Criminal Court in the Hague hadn't issued a warrant for the arrest of President al-Bashir.'

'That was in 2009, wasn't it?' Pollock asks.

'Passed me by,' Carlos says.

'It didn't attract much attention here,' Saga says. 'But the warrant was issued because the president was suspected of direct involvement in torture, rape and genocide in Darfur.'

'So no deal?' Carlos concludes.

'No deal,' she replies.

'And the photograph? What's so special about it? Nothing?' Verner asks.

'Penelope Fernandez didn't seem to think it was dangerous, seeing as she had it taped to her door,' Saga says.

'But at the same time it wasn't unimportant, seeing as she had it on display,' Carlos points out.

'We really don't know – maybe it was just a reminder of the way the world works,' Saga speculates. 'That there are a few people at the bottom fighting for peace, while the rich and powerful toast each other with champagne at the top.'

'We're hoping to be able to question Penelope Fernandez soon, but we're fairly sure that Björn Almskog has been going behind her back,' Joona goes on. 'He may know more about the photograph than Penelope, unless he was just trying his luck, because on the second of June Björn went to an internet café and sent an email from an anonymous account trying to black-mail Carl Palmcrona. The email sparked a brief correspondence: Björn wrote that he knew the photograph would cause problems for Palmcrona, and that he was prepared to sell it for a million kronor.'

'Classic extortion,' Pollock mutters.

'Björn used the word "troubling" to describe the photograph,' Saga goes on, 'which makes us think he didn't understand how severely Palmcrona was going to react.'

'Björn thought he was in control of the situation,' Joona says. 'So he was taken aback when Palmcrona replied with a serious warning. Palmcrona wrote that Björn didn't know what he was getting involved in, and begged him to send the photograph before it was too late.'

Joona drinks some water.

'What's the tone of the emails?' Nathan Pollock asks quickly. 'Aggressive?'

Joona shakes his head, and hands out printouts of the emails.

'I don't read them as aggressive, just laden with gravity.'

Tommy Kofoed reads the exchange, then nods, rubs his pock-marked cheeks and writes something down.

'Then what happened?'

'Before Palmcrona's housekeeper went home on Wednesday, she helped him hang a noose from the ceiling.'

Petter lets out a laugh:

'Why?'

'Because he couldn't do it himself after an operation on his back,' Saga says.

'Oh. Okay,' Carlos says with a slight smile.

'The following day, at lunchtime . . . after that day's post had been delivered, we assume,' Joona went on, 'Palmcrona called a number in Bordeaux and . . .'

'It hasn't been possible to trace the number any more accurately than that,' Saga points out.

'The number may have belonged to an exchange, and the call was forwarded to a different country, another continent, or even back to Sweden,' Joona says. 'Either way, it was a very short call, forty-three seconds. Maybe he just left a message. We believe he was calling about the photograph and what the blackmail email said, and to say that he was expecting help.'

'Because after that, just a few minutes later, Palmcrona's housekeeper called Taxi Stockholm and pre-booked a taxi to Arlanda Airport in Palmcrona's name at two o'clock. Exactly one hour and fifteen minutes after that brief call, Palmcrona's phone rang. He had already put his coat on, but he still answered. The call was from Bordeaux, the same number that he called. This second call lasted two minutes. Then Palmcrona sent a final email to his blackmailer, with the following message: *It's too late now, you and I are both going to die.* He sent his house-keeper home, paid the taxi-driver for the lost fare, then went back upstairs. Without taking his coat off, Carl Palmcrona went into the drawing room, stood his briefcase on end, climbed on top of it and hanged himself.'

There's silence round the table.

'But that isn't the end of the story,' Joona says slowly, 'because Palmcrona's telephone conversations set things in motion . . . An international fixer was deployed. A professional hitman was sent to get rid of all the evidence and take care of the photograph.'

'How often . . . in Sweden, I mean, do we actually come across a professional hitman?' Carlos asks in a sceptical voice. 'There must be a hell of a lot of money at stake to warrant this sort of action.'

Joona looks at him blankly.

'Yes.'

'We believe that Palmcrona read the contents of the blackmail email out over the phone, including the bank account number Björn gave him,' Saga says.

'It's not hard to trace someone if you've got their bank account number,' Verner mutters.

'At approximately the same time that Palmcrona hanged himself, Björn Almskog was in the Dreambow internet café,' Joona goes on. 'He signed into his anonymous email account and saw that he'd received two messages from Carl Palmcrona.'

'Obviously he was hoping that Palmcrona had agreed to pay a million kronor for the photograph,' Saga says.

'Instead he found Palmcrona's warning, and then the short message telling him it was already too late, and they were both going to die.'

'And they're dead,' Pollock says.

'You can imagine how frightened Björn must been,' Saga says. 'He wasn't exactly an accomplished blackmailer, he just took a chance when he spotted it.'

'What did he do?'

Petter is looking at them with his mouth wide open. Carlos pours him some water.

'Björn changed his mind and decided to send Palmcrona the photograph, to put an end to it all.'

'But Palmcrona was already dead by the time Björn wrote to him explaining that he was backing down, and was going to send him the photograph,' Joona says.

'The problem was that the photograph was taped to the door in Penelope's flat,' Saga says. 'And she didn't know anything about the attempted blackmail.'

'He needed to get hold of the photograph without having to explain about the extortion,' Tommy Kofoed says with a nod.

'We don't know how he was planning to explain to Penelope that the photograph had gone missing,' Saga says with a smile. 'He probably acted in panic, wanted to draw a line under everything, and hoped it would all blow over while they were out on his boat in the archipelago.'

Joona stands up and goes over to the window and looks out. A woman is carrying a child in her arms and pushing a buggy laden with bags of groceries along the pavement in front of her.

'Early the following morning Penelope went off in a taxi to appear in a discussion on television,' Saga goes on. 'As soon as she left, Björn went into her flat, grabbed the photograph, took the underground to the Central Station, where he bought stamps and an envelope and sent the photograph to Palmcrona. Then he ran to the internet café and sent Palmcrona a final email telling him that the photograph was on its way. Björn went home to his flat, collected his and Penelope's bags and went off to his boat, which was moored at the marina at Långholmen. When Penelope left the television studio, she took the underground from Karlaplan and got off at Hornstull, and walked the last bit of the way to Långholmen.'

'By that point the fixer had already searched Björn's flat and started the fire that destroyed that entire floor of the building.'

'But I've read the report . . . The fire investigators concluded that the cause was an electric iron that had been left on in the neighbouring flat,' Petter says.

'And that's probably correct,' Joona says.

'Just like a gas explosion would have been the cause of the fire in Penelope's flat,' Saga says.

'The fixer's aim was presumably to get rid of any evidence,'

Joona goes on. 'When he didn't find the photograph in Björn's flat he set fire to it, then followed Björn to his boat.'

'To look for the photograph,' Saga adds. 'And to murder Björn and Penelope and make it look like a boating accident.'

'What the fixer didn't know was that their plans changed at the last minute and that Penelope's sister had gone with them on the boat.'

Joona falls silent and thinks about the dead woman lying in the mortuary. Her young, vulnerable face. The red mark across her chest.

'My guess is that the youngsters dropped anchor at some island in Jungfrufjärden, off Dalarö,' Joona goes on. 'And before the fixer arrived, Penelope went ashore for whatever reason. When the fixer got onto the boat he found Viola. Believing her to be Penelope, he drowned her in a wash-tub and then put her on the bed in the front cabin. While he waited for Björn he probably looked for the photograph, and when he didn't find it he prepared an explosion on the boat. You've got Erixon's report in front of you. We don't quite know what happened, but somehow Penelope and Björn managed to get away from the fixer.'

'And the boat with Viola Fernandez's body on board was abandoned.'

'We don't know how they got there, but on Monday they were on Kymmendö.'

The corners of Benny's mouth twitch.

'In Ossian Wallenberg's house? He used to be bloody good, but he was obviously too much for this dull country.'

Carlos clears his throat as he pours more coffee.

'When the fixer realised he'd lost them, he went to Penelope's flat to look for the photograph,' Joona goes on, without acknowledging Benny's comment. 'Erixon and I showed up and interrupted him. It wasn't until then, when I was actually confronted with him, that I understood that we're dealing with a top-class international fixer.'

'He can probably get into our systems, listen to our communications and so on,' Saga says.

'Was that how he managed to find Björn and Penelope out on Kymmendö?' Petter asks.

'We don't know,' Joona replies.

'But he acts fast,' Saga says. 'He probably returned to Dalarö to look for Penelope right after the confrontation with Joona and Erixon in the flat.'

'So he was already there when I spoke to the marine police,' Petter says, leaning forward on the table and adjusting the sheet of paper with the agenda of the meeting on it.

'What happened?' Carlos asks.

'We've only just started work on the reconstruction,' Petter says. 'But somehow he managed to hijack the police speedboat, killed Lennart Johansson and Göran Sjödin, went out to Kymmendö, murdered Björn Almskog and Ossian Wallenberg, blew up the police boat, set off after Penelope and shot down the rescue helicopter.'

'And vanished,' Carlos sighs.

'But because of Petter Näslund's skilful leadership we were able to rescue Penelope Fernandez,' Joona says, and sees Pollock turn to look at Petter with interest.

'The exact sequence of events obviously needs to be investigated,' Petter says with a sternness that does nothing to hide his delight at the praise.

'That's going to take a hell of a long time,' Kofoed smiles mirthlessly.

'What about the photograph, then?' Petter sighs.

'Seven people have died because of it,' Joona says seriously. 'And more will probably follow if we can't . . .'

Joona falls silent and looks out of the window.

'The photograph could be a lock – a lock that requires a key,' he says.

'What sort of key?' Petter asks.

'The photographer,' Saga says.

'Penelope Fernandez, is she the photographer?' Pollock wonders.

'That would explain why she was being hunted,' Carlos declares, rather too loudly.

'It would,' Saga says hesitantly.

'But?' Carlos says.

'What's the evidence to suggest otherwise?' Benny asks.

'That Joona doesn't think Penelope is the photographer,' Saga says.

'Oh, for God's sake!' Petter exclaims.

Carlos clamps his mouth shut, stares at the table and has the sense to stay silent.

'Penelope is understandably in a state of shock, so we don't yet know what her role in all this is,' Saga says.

Nathan Pollock clears his throat and hands round copies of Carl Palmcrona's will.

'Palmcrona had an account with a bank in Jersey,' he tells them.

'The tax-free paradise,' Petter Näslund nods, removing the chewing tobacco from under his lip. He wipes his thumb on the table without noticing the exasperated look on Carlos's face.

'Is it possible to find out how much he had in the account?' Verner asks.

'There's no way of getting access to his transactions,' Joona says. 'But according to his will, it should be around nine million euros.'

'His personal finances weren't great, so it's impossible to understand how he could have earned money like that legally,' Pollock says.

'We've been in touch with Transparency International – they're a global organisation fighting corruption, but they've got nothing on Carl Palmcrona, or anyone else at the ISP. Not even a hint of anything.'

'Palmcrona's assets were bequeathed to a sixteen-year-old boy by the name of Stefan Bergkvist, who, it turns out, was Palmcrona's son. A son he never met . . . but the boy died in a fire in Västerås just three days after Palmcrona committed suicide.'

'The boy never found out who his real father was,' Saga adds.

'According to the preliminary police report it was an accident,' Carlos says.

'Yes, but does anyone seriously believe that the fire that killed Carl Palmcrona's son three days after his suicide is a coincidence?' Joona asks.

'How could it be?' Carlos says.

'This is completely sick,' Petter says, with red cheeks. 'Why would anyone murder the son he'd never even met?'

'What the hell is this all about?' Verner asks.

'Palmcrona keeps cropping up,' Joona says, tapping his finger on the man smiling in the photograph. 'He's in the photograph, he's the subject of a blackmail attempt, he's found hanged, his son dies, and he's got nine million euros in an offshore bank account.'

'The money's interesting,' Saga says.

'We've taken a close look at his life,' Pollock says. 'He had no other family, no hobbies, didn't deal in stocks or shares, or . . .'

'If this money really is in that account, then it must somehow be connected to his position as director general of the ISP,' Joona says.

'He could have engaged in insider trading via fake accounts or intermediaries,' Verner says.

'Or he could have been taking bribes after all,' Saga says.

'Follow the money,' Pollock whispers.

'We need to talk to Palmcrona's successor, Axel Riessen,' Joona says, getting to his feet. 'If there's anything odd about the decisions Palmcrona took, he ought to have found out about it by now.'

68

From a distance, over by the Royal Institute of Technology, Joona can hear the sound of trumpets, whistles and drums. A procession is heading along Odengatan. It looks like about seventy young people carrying anti-fascist symbols and carrying banners protesting against the Security Police's treatment of the members of the Brigade. Joona sees one colourful flag with the rainbow symbol and a hammer and sickle fluttering in the breeze, and hears them chanting:

'The Security Police stink of fascism, the state is sponsoring terrorism!'

The angry sounds on Odengatan disappear as Joona Linna and Saga Bauer walk up Bragevägen, which curves up towards Engelbrekt Church. They've contacted the ISP and have been told that the director general is working from home this morning.

On the left side of the street is the attractive townhouse where the Riessen brothers live in two separate apartments. The façade is very striking, with dark, handmade bricks, leaded windows, elegant woodwork and tarnished copper around the bay windows and chimneys.

They walk up to the single, highly polished wooden door bearing a brass sign with Axel Riessen's name on it. Saga presses the doorbell with her finger. After a while the heavy door is opened by a tall, suntanned man with a friendly face.

Saga introduces herself as a superintendent with the Security Police, and explains why they're there. Axel Riessen looks at her ID carefully, then looks up.

'I'm not sure I'm going to be of any great use to you, but . . .'

'It'll still be a pleasure to have a chat,' Joona Linna says.

Axel looks at him in surprise, but smiles appreciatively at the joke as he shows them into the tall, bright hall. He's wearing dark-blue suit trousers, a pale blue shirt unbuttoned at the neck, and a pair of slippers on his feet. He takes two more pairs of slippers from a low, polished cabinet and offers them to Saga and Joona.

'I suggest that we go and sit in the orangery, it tends to be a bit cooler there.'

They follow Axel through the large apartment, past the wide mahogany staircase with its dark panelling, and two large reception rooms.

The orangery is a glazed conservatory facing the garden, where the tall hedge is casting green shadows, forming a fluid wall of leaves. Pots of herbs and scentless orchids are arranged neatly on copper tabletops and tiled surfaces.

'Please, sit down,' Axel says, gesturing towards the chairs. 'I was just thinking of having some tea and crumpets, and it would be a pleasure if you'd join me.'

'I haven't eaten crumpets since I went on a language trip to Edinburgh,' Saga smiles.

'Well, then,' Axel says happily, and leaves the room.

He comes back a few minutes later with a metal tray. He puts the teapot, sugar-bowl and a small saucer of lemon slices in the middle of the table. The warm cakes are wrapped in a linen napkin beside a butter-dish. Axel carefully lays the table for the three of them, setting out cups and saucers, plates and napkins before he pours the tea.

Through the doors and walls they can hear faint violin music.

'So tell me, how can I help you?' Axel asks.

Saga gently puts her cup down, clears her throat, then says in a clear voice:

'We need to ask a few questions about the ISP, and we're hoping you can help us.'

'Of course, but I should probably just make a quick call to make sure that it's okay,' he explains amiably, and takes out his mobile phone.

'By all means,' Saga says.

'I'm so sorry, I've forgotten your name . . .'

'Saga Bauer.'

'Could I possibly see your ID again?'

She hands it over, and he stands up and leaves the room. They hear him talking briefly, then he comes back in, thanks her and returns her ID.

'Last year the ISP authorised export licences for South Africa, Namibia, Tanzania, Algeria and Tunisia,' Saga says, as if the pause hadn't happened. 'Ammunition for heavy machine-guns, portable anti-tank guns, grenade launchers . . .'

'And the JAS Gripen, of course,' Axel adds. 'Sweden has long-standing relationships with a number of those countries.'

'But never with Sudan?'

He looks her in the eye and a trace of a smile crosses his face.

'I can't imagine so.'

'I meant before the warrant for President al-Bashir's arrest was issued,' she explains.

'I realised that,' he replies, amused. 'Otherwise it would be completely unthinkable, what we would call an insurmountable obstacle, where there's simply nothing to discuss.'

'Presumably you've had a chance to look through a fair number of the decisions taken by Palmcrona?' Saga says.

'Of course,' Axel replies.

'Have you noticed anything unusual?'

'What do you mean by unusual?'

'Decisions that seem strange,' Saga says, sipping her tea.

'Are there grounds to believe that there would be?' he asks.

'That's what we're asking you,' she smiles.

'In that case, my answer is no.'

'How far back have you looked?'

Joona listens to Saga's introductory questions about classification, advance notification and export licences as he watches Axel Riessen's calm, attentive face. Suddenly he hears the violin music again. It's coming from outside, from the open window facing the garden. The high, mournful notes of a mazurka. Then the violin stops, starts from the beginning again, stops once more, and then begins again.

Joona listens to the music, thinking about the photograph of four people in a private box at the concert hall. He absent-mindedly touches the bag containing a copy of the picture.

He thinks about Palmcrona, hanging from the ceiling with a washing-line tied round his neck, and his will, and his son's death.

Joona sees Saga nod at something Axel says. A hint of green crosses Riessen's face, a reflection from the copper tray on the table.

Palmcrona realised instantly how serious it was, Joona reasons. All Björn Almskog had to do in his email was say that Palmcrona had been photographed in the company of arms dealer Raphael Guidi. Carl Palmcrona didn't doubt the veracity of the photograph for a moment.

Perhaps he was already aware of its existence.

Unless the blackmailer's knowledge that the meeting in the concert-hall box was itself proof that the picture was real – if not, he wouldn't have known about it.

Axel pours more tea for Saga. She brushes a crumb from the corner of her mouth.

This doesn't make sense, Joona thinks.

Pontus Salman had been able to date the meeting. He didn't seem to find the picture's existence awkward.

So why was it so problematic in Palmcrona's eyes?

He hears Axel and Saga discuss the way political and security conditions change whenever embargoes are imposed on countries, or removed.

Joona murmurs slightly so that they think he's following the conversation, but carries on thinking about the photograph.

The table in the box had been set for four people, and four people were visible on the photograph. That meant that the fifth person, the person holding the camera, wasn't one of the guests, wasn't going to be offered a place at the table, wasn't going to be offered a glass of champagne.

The fifth person could still hold the answer to the whole mystery.

We have to get Penelope Fernandez to talk, and soon, Joona thinks. Because even if she isn't the photographer, she could very well be the key that unlocks the riddle.

He returns in his mind to the people in the photograph: Carl Palmcrona, Raphael Guidi, Agathe al-Haji, and Pontus Salman.

Joona thinks about their meeting with Pontus Salman, where he identified himself on the picture. According to him, the only remarkable thing about it was that Carl Palmcrona hadn't declined the offer of champagne, seeing as there was nothing to celebrate, and because this was a first meeting.

But what if there was something to celebrate?

Joona's pulse quickens.

What if all four of them raised their glasses a moment later and drank a toast?

Pontus Salman had identified himself and told them the reason for the meeting, its location and when it took place.

When it took place, Joona muses. The photograph could have been taken on a different occasion.

We only have Pontus Salman's word that the meeting took place in Frankfurt in the spring of 2008.

We need Penelope Fernandez's help.

Joona looks at his hands, resting on his bag. He's thinking that it ought to be possible to identify the four musicians in the background of the photograph, because their faces are visible. Someone must be able to recognise them.

And if we can identify the musicians, it might be possible to confirm the date of the meeting. Four people playing – a string quartet.

Perhaps the four of them only played together on that one occasion. That would fix the date beyond all doubt.

Of course, he tells himself. They should have done this already. He considers leaving Saga to talk to Axel Riessen and going back to Police Headquarters, to talk to Petter Näslund and ask if it's occurred to them that this group of musicians might be able to give a precise date for the photograph.

He looks at Saga, sees her smile at Axel Riessen and then ask him about the consolidation of the US defence industry. She mentions two of the new mammoth corporations, Raytheon and Lockheed Martin.

Once again he can hear music through the open window. A faster piece this time. It falls silent, then it sounds as if two strings are being checked against each other.

'Who's that playing?' Joona asks, sitting up.

'My brother, Robert,' Axel replies in a rather surprised voice.

'I see – is he a violinist?'

'The pride of the family . . . But first and foremost he makes violins, he has his studio here, at the back of the house.'

'Do you think I could ask him about something?'

69

The string quartet

Joona follows Axel along the marble path. There's a strong scent from the lilacs. They walk to the studio and knock on the door. The violin stops and the door is opened by a middle-aged man with thinning hair, a handsome, intelligent face and a body that had once been skinny but had gradually filled out over the years.

'The police want to talk to you,' Axel says seriously. 'You're suspected of disorderly conduct.'

'I confess,' Robert says.

'Great,' Joona says.

'Was there anything else?'

'We've actually got quite a few cases that haven't been solved,' Joona says.

'I'm sure I'm guilty.'

'Thanks very much,' Joona says, and shakes Robert's hand. 'Joona Linna, National Crime.'

'How can I help?' Robert asks with a smile.

'We're looking into a sudden death, the former director general of the ISP, which is why I've been talking to your brother.'

'I don't know anything about Palmcrona apart from what's been printed in the papers.'

'Can I come in for a few minutes?'

'Of course.'

'I'll get back to your colleague,' Axel says, and shuts the door behind Joona.

The studio ceiling is low and sloping, like an attic roof. The studio looks like it was made from an existing cellar: a beautiful, polished wooden staircase leads down into the workshop. The air is full of strong smells: fresh-sawn wood, resin, and turpentine. There are violin parts everywhere, specially selected wood, carved scrolls, special tools, planes the size of corkscrews, curved knives.

'I heard you playing through the window,' Joona says.

Robert nods and gestures towards a beautiful violin.

'It needed to be adjusted slightly.'

'You made it yourself?' Joona asks.

'Yes.'

'It looks astonishing.'

'Thanks.'

Robert picks the violin up and hands it to Joona. The polished instrument is almost weightless. Joona turns the instrument over, then smells it.

'The varnish is the secret,' Robert says, taking the violin and putting it in a case lined with wine-red padding.

Joona opens his bag, takes out the plastic sleeve and hands over the photograph that Björn Almskog sent to Carl Palmcrona.

'Palmcrona,' Robert says.

'Yes. But do you recognise any of the people in the background, the musicians?'

Robert looks at the picture again, then nods.

'That's Martin Beaver,' he says, pointing. 'Kikuei Ikeda . . . Isomura, and Clive Greensmith on the cello.'

'They're famous musicians?'

Robert can't help smiling at the question.

'They're practically legendary . . . the Tokyo String Quartet.'

'The Tokyo String Quartet – the same four people every time?'

'Yes.'

'Always?'

'For a very long time – things have been going very well for them.'

'Can you see anything unusual about this photograph?'

Robert looks at it intently.

'No,' he says after a while.

'They don't just play in Tokyo, then?' Joona asks.

'No, they play all round the world, but their instruments are owned by a Japanese trust.'

'Is that common?'

'Yes, when we're talking about really special instruments,' Robert replies seriously. 'And these ones, the ones in this picture, are undoubtedly among the finest in the world.'

'I see.'

'The Paganini Quartet,' Robert says.

'The Paganini Quartet,' Joona repeats, looking at the musicians again.

The dark wood is shimmering, the musicians' black outfits reflected in the varnish.

'They were made by Stradivarius,' Robert says. 'The oldest of them is Desaint, a violin dating back to 1680 . . . Kikuei Ikeda is playing that one. Martin Beaver is playing the violin that Count Cozio di Salabue gave Paganini.'

Robert falls silent and gives Joona a questioning glance, but Joona nods to indicate that he'd like him to go on.

'All four instruments were owned by Nicolò Paganini. I don't know how much you know about Paganini, but he was a virtuoso, both as a violinist and a composer . . . He wrote pieces that were regarded as ridiculous because they were impossible to play, until Paganini himself picked up the violin. After his death it's supposed to have taken a hundred years before anyone could play his pieces again . . . and some of his techniques are still regarded as impossible . . . Yes, there are plenty of stories about Paganini and his violin duels.'

They fall silent. Joona looks at the photograph again, at the four men sitting on the stage in the background. He looks at their instruments.

'So the Tokyo String Quartet often play together using these instruments?'

'Yes, they probably perform eight or nine concerts a month.'

'When would you estimate that this photograph was taken?'

'It can't be more than ten years old, if you look at Martin Beaver, who I've met a couple of times.'

'Would it be possible to identify the date if we could specify the location?'

'That's the Alte Oper in Frankfurt.'

'You're sure?'

'I know they play there every year,' Robert says. 'Sometimes several times a year.'

'*Perkele*,' Joona swears.

There has to be some way of identifying when the photograph was taken, either to confirm or disprove Pontus Salman's version of events.

Joona opens the plastic sleeve in order to put the photograph away, thinking that Penelope is probably the only person who can cast any light on the circumstances.

He looks at the picture again, at one of the violinists, the movement of the bow, the right elbow, and then he looks up at Robert with his pale grey eyes.

'Do they always play the same pieces when they tour?' Joona asks.

'The same pieces? No, goodness . . . they've been through all of Beethoven's quartets, and that alone means there's lots of variety. But of course they also play plenty of other pieces, sometimes Schubert and Bartók. And Brahms, of course. It's a long list . . . Debussy, Dvořák, Haydn, lots of Mozart and Ravel, et cetera, et cetera.'

Joona is staring ahead of him, then stands up, walks a few paces, stops, and looks back at Robert.

'I've had an idea,' Joona says with sudden intensity. 'From this picture, just by looking at the musicians' hands, would it be possible . . . would it be possible to identify what piece they're playing just by looking at the picture?'

Robert opens and closes his mouth, shakes his head, but still looks at the photograph again with a smile. In the spotlights on the stage of the Alte Oper, the Tokyo String Quartet are performing: Clive Greensmith's thin face, looking oddly vulnerable, his high forehead shining. And Kikuei Ikeda is playing a high note, with the little finger of his left hand on the fingerboard.

'I'm sorry, it's impossible, they could be playing . . . well, I was going to say any notes, but . . .'

'But with a magnifying glass . . . you can actually see their fingers on the strings, the necks of the instruments . . .'

'Of course, theoretically . . .'

He sighs and shakes his head.

'Do you know anyone who might be able to help me?' Joona goes on, with a hard edge of stubbornness in his voice. 'Some musician or teacher at the College of Music, someone who might be able to analyse this photograph for us?'

'I wish I . . .'

'It's not going to be possible, is it?' Joona asks.

'In all seriousness, no,' Robert replies, shrugging his shoulders. 'If not even Axel could do it, then I doubt it can be done.'

'Axel? Your brother?'

'Hasn't he looked at the photograph?' Robert asks.

'No,' Joona replies.

'But you've been speaking to him.'

'Not about music – you're the musician, after all,' Joona smiles.

'Talk to him anyway,' Robert says by way of conclusion.

'Why would . . .'

Joona stops when there's a knock on the door of the studio. A moment later Saga Bauer comes in. The sunlight shines through her blonde hair.

'Is Axel here?' she asks.

'No,' Joona replies.

'More detectives?' Robert asks with a smile.

'Security Police,' Saga says curtly.

The silence that follows is slightly too long. Robert doesn't seem to be able to take his eyes off her.

'I didn't know the Security Police had a department for elves,' he says with a broad smile after a while, then tries to be serious:

'Sorry, I don't mean to be rude, but you really do look like an elf or a princess in one of Bauer's paintings.'

'Appearances can be deceptive,' she says drily.

'Robert Riessen,' he says, introducing himself and holding his hand out.

'Saga,' she says.

70

A feeling

Joona Linna and Saga Bauer leave the Riessen family residence and get in the car. Saga's phone buzzes, and she looks at the message and smiles to herself.

'I'm having lunch at home,' Saga says, and blushes quickly.

'What time is it?'

'Half eleven,' she says. 'Are you going to carry on working?'

'No, I'm going to a lunchtime concert at Södra Teatern with a friend.'

'Could you drop me off on Södermalm, then? I live on Bastugatan.'

'I can drive you home if you like,' he says.

When Joona went down to Robert Riessen's studio, Saga stayed to talk to Axel. He had just started to describe his career at the United Nations when his phone rang. Axel looked at the screen, excused himself and left the room. Saga sat and waited, but when fifteen minutes had passed she got up and started to look for him. When she couldn't find him she went down to Robert's studio. Then Robert and Joona helped look for Axel, before concluding that he had left the house.

'What did you want with Axel Riessen's brother?'

'Just a feeling,' Joona says.

'Hurray,' Saga mutters. 'A feeling.'

'You know . . . when we showed the photograph to Pontus

Salman,' Joona goes on. 'He identified himself, talked openly about the meeting in Frankfurt, about the potential deal with the Sudanese government, then said all negotiations had stopped when the ICC in the Hague issued that arrest warrant for . . .'

He breaks off when his phone rings, and he digs it out and answers without taking his eyes off the traffic.

'That was quick.'

'The timing fits,' Anja Larsson says. 'The Tokyo String Quartet played at the Alte Oper and Pontus Salman was in Frankfurt.'

'I see,' Joona says.

Saga looks at him, sees him listen to what he's being told, then nod and say thank you before ending the call.

'So Pontus Salman was telling the truth?' Saga says.

'I don't know.'

'But the timings have been confirmed?'

'Only that Pontus Salman travelled to Frankfurt and that the Tokyo String Quartet were performing at the Alte Oper . . . but Pontus has been to Frankfurt plenty of times, and the Tokyo Strong Quartet play at the Alte Oper at least once a year.'

'Are you trying to say that you think he lied about the timing, even though you've just had it confirmed?'

'No, but . . . I don't know, like I said, it's just a feeling,' Joona says. 'He has a pretty good reason to lie if he and Carl Palmcrona were negotiating with Agathe al-Haji after the arrest warrant was issued.'

'That would be a criminal offence. Christ, that would look like they were exporting arms directly to the militia in Darfur, which would be a breach of international law, and that . . .'

'We believed Pontus Salman because he identified himself,' Joona replies. 'But the fact that he told the truth about one thing doesn't mean he was telling the truth about everything.'

'Is that your feeling?'

'No, there was something about Salman's voice . . . when he said that the only remarkable thing about the picture was that Carl Palmcrona hadn't turned down the offer of champagne.'

'Seeing as there was nothing to celebrate,' Saga says.

'Yes, that was how he put it, but my instinct tells me that, on the contrary, there *was* something to celebrate, and that they were drinking a toast because they'd come to an agreement.'

'All the facts contradict what you're suggesting.'

'But think about the photograph,' Joona says stubbornly. 'There's an atmosphere in that box . . . their faces, they're happy, as if a contract's been signed.'

'Even if that's true, we can't confirm the date of the picture without Penelope Fernandez.'

'What are her doctors saying?' Joona asks.

'That we'll be able to talk to her soon, but that she's still far too mentally exhausted.'

'We have no idea how much she knows,' Joona says.

'No, but what the hell else have we got to go on?'

'The photograph,' Joona replies quickly. 'Because the four musicians are clearly visible in the background, and it might be possible to tell what piece they're playing from the position of their hands, and identify the date that way.'

'Joona,' she sighs.

'Yep,' he smiles.

'That's completely bloody mad – as I hope you realise.'

'Robert said that it ought to be possible, theoretically.'

'We'll have to wait until Penelope's feeling better.'

'I'll call,' Joona says, and takes out his phone, dials the National Police Unit and asks to be put through to room U12.

Saga looks at his calm face.

'My name is Joona Linna, I'm . . .'

He falls silent and a wide smile spread across his face.

'Of course I remember you, and your red coat,' he says, then listens. 'Yes, but . . . I thought you might suggest hypnosis?'

Saga can hear the doctor laughing at his joke.

'No,' he says. 'But seriously – we really, really need to talk to her.'

His face grows solemn.

'I see, but . . . it would be best if you could persuade her that . . . Okay, we'll figure it out . . . Bye.'

He ends the call and turns into Bellmansgatan.

'That was Daniella Richards,' Joona tells Saga.

'What does she say?'

'She thinks we'll be able to talk to Penelope in a couple of days, but that she needs somewhere else to live first – she's refusing to stay in that underground room, and says . . .'

'There's nowhere safer.'

'Not if she refuses to stay,' Joona says.

'We'll have to explain how dangerous the situation is.'

'She already knows that better than us,' he says.

71

Seven million choices

Disa and Joona are sitting opposite each other at a table in the dining room at Mosebacke. Sunlight filters through the huge windows looking out across Gamla stan, Skeppsholmen and the sparkling water. They've eaten pan-fried herring with mashed potato and lingonberry sauce, and are just pouring the last of their low-strength beer. Ronald Brautigam is sitting at a black grand piano on the little stage, and Isabelle van Keulen's right elbow is raised as she follows through with her bow.

The music stops, the last violin note quivers in the air, outlasting the piano and ending on a high, tremulous tone.

Joona and Disa leave the restaurant after the concert and emerge onto Mosebacke torg, where they stop to look at each other.

'What was that about Paganini?' she says, adjusting his shirt-collar. 'You were talking about Paganini?'

He gently catches her hand.

'I just wanted to see you . . .'

'So that I can tell you off for not taking your medication?'

'No,' he says seriously.

'Are you taking it, then?'

'I will do soon,' he replies with a hint of impatience in his voice.

She says nothing, just lets her pale green eyes meet his gaze for a moment. Then she takes a deep breath and suggests they start walking.

'That was a great concert, anyway,' Disa says. 'The music somehow matches the light outside, so soft. I always thought Paganini was . . . you know, too balanced, too fast . . . I actually heard Yngwie Malmsteen play *Caprice* No. 5 at Gröna Lund once.'

'When you were going out with Benjamin Gantenbein.'

'We've become friends on Facebook after all these years.'

They walk hand in hand across Slussen, down towards Skeppsbron.

'It ought to be possible to tell what notes someone is playing on a violin just from their fingers, don't you think?'

'Without hearing anything, you mean?'

'From a photograph.'

'More or less, I'd imagine . . . it probably depends how well you know the instrument,' she says.

'But how exact could it be?'

'I can ask Kaj if it's important,' she says.

'Kaj?'

'Kaj Samuelsson, from the musicology department at the university. He taught me to drive, but I really know him through Dad.'

'Can you give him a call now?'

'Okay,' Disa says, raising one eyebrow slightly. 'You want me to call him right now?'

'Yes,' Joona replies.

She lets go of his hand, takes out her phone, looks through her contacts and calls the professor.

'Hello, it's Disa,' she says with a smile. 'Am I calling in the middle of lunch?'

Joona hears a cheerful male voice through the phone. After chatting for a while, Disa asks:

'I've actually got a friend with me who wants me to ask you a question.'

She laughs at something he says, then asks straight out:

'Is it possible to tell what notes a violinist is playing . . . No, not . . . I mean, from their fingers.'

Joona looks at Disa as she listens with a furrowed brow. They can hear the sound of a marching band from somewhere among the alleyways of Gamla stan.

'Okay,' Disa says after a while. 'You know what, Kaj? Maybe it would be best if you speak to him yourself.'

She hands the phone to Joona without a word.

'Joona Linna.'

'Who Disa talks so much about,' Kaj Samuelsson says breezily.

'A violin only has four strings,' Joona says. 'So it really shouldn't be possible to play so many different notes . . .'

'What do you mean by play?' the professor wonders.

'The lowest note has to be an open G-string,' Joona says calmly. 'And somewhere there must be a highest note . . .'

'Nice idea,' the professor interrupts. 'The French scientist Mersenne published *Harmonie Universelle* in 1636, in which he claimed that the best violinists can play up to an octave above every open string. That means the range stretches from G below middle C to E3 . . . which gives a total of thirty-four notes on the chromatic scale.'

'Thirty-four notes,' Joona repeats.

'But if we move forward to more modern musicians,' Samuelsson goes on brightly, 'the range has been expanded with the new fingerboard . . . so we can count on reaching A3, giving a chromatic scale of thirty-nine notes.'

'Go on,' Joona says, as Disa stops in front of a gallery with some odd, blurred paintings in the window.

'By the time Richard Strauss revised Berlioz's treatise on instrumentation in 1904, G4 was identified as the highest possible note for a professional violinist, giving forty-nine notes.'

Kaj Samuelsson chuckles to himself in response to Joona's wary silence.

'The upper limit has by no means been reached,' the professor explains. 'And then there are all the harmonics and quarter tones.'

They pass a recently built Viking longboat by Slottskajen and slowly head towards Kungsträdgården.

'How about a cello?' Joona asks impatiently.

'Fifty-eight,' he replies.

Disa looks at him restlessly, and points at an outdoor café.

'What I'm really wondering is if you could take a look at a photograph of four musicians – two violinists, a viola player and a cellist,' Joona says. 'From a sharp photograph, would it be possible to tell, just by looking at the musicians' fingers, the strings and necks of the instruments, what piece they were playing?'

Joona hears Kaj Samuelsson muttering to himself.

'There'd be an awful lot of alternatives, thousands . . .'

Disa shrugs her shoulders and walks off without looking at him.

'Seven million combinations,' Kaj Samuelsson says after a pause.

'Seven million,' Joona repeats.

They fall silent again.

'But on my photograph,' Joona goes on in a voice full of obstinacy, 'you can clearly see the fingers and strings, so it would be easy enough to rule out an awful lot of possibilities.'

'I'd be happy to look at the photograph,' the professor says. 'But I won't be able to guess the notes, that's simply not possible, and . . .'

'But . . .'

'And just imagine, Joona Linna,' he goes on cheerily, 'imagine that you actually managed to identify the notes, more or less . . . how would you work out where that combination of notes appeared in all the thousands of string quartets . . . Beethoven, Schubert, Mozart . . .'

'I get it. It's impossible,' Joona says.

'Seriously, yes,' Kaj replies.

Joona thanks him for his time, then goes and sits down beside Disa, who is waiting on a wall next to a fountain. She leans her cheek against his shoulder. Just as he puts his arm round her he remembers what Robert Riessen said about his brother: *If not even Axel could do it, then I doubt it can be done.*

72

The riddle

As Joona Linna strides quickly along the pavement up Bragevägen he can hear children's laughter and cries from the German School.

He rings on Axel's door, and hears the melodic bell ring inside the house. After waiting a while he decides to go round the house. Suddenly he hears a jarringly shrill note from a string instrument. Someone is standing in the shadows under a tree. Joona stops at a distance. On the marble terrace there's a girl holding a violin. She looks like she's about fifteen years old. Her hair is extremely short, and she's been drawing on her arms. Beside her stands Axel Riessen, nodding and listening intently as she draws the bow across the strings. It looks like she's holding the instrument for the first time. Maybe she's Axel's daughter, or even granddaughter, because he's looking at her with an affectionate, curious gaze.

The bow glances across the strings, making a shrieking, grating sound.

'It's probably badly out of tune,' she suggests as an explanation for the terrible noise.

She smiles and carefully hands the instrument back.

'Playing the violin is all about listening,' Axel says warmly. 'You listen, hear the music inside you, then just convey that in reality.'

He puts the violin to his shoulder and plays the introduction to 'La seguidilla' from Bizet's opera, *Carmen*, then stops to show her the violin.

'Now I'm going to retune the strings, a bit randomly, like this,' he says, turning the pegs in different directions.

'But why . . .'

'Now the violin is completely out of tune,' he goes on. 'And if I'd merely learned the piece mechanically, with the precise finger positions, the same as I played it just now, it would sound like this.'

He plays 'La seguidilla' again, and it sounds terrible, almost unrecognisable.

'Beautiful,' she jokes.

'But if you listen to the strings instead,' he says, plucking the E-string. 'Do you hear? It's far too low, but that doesn't matter, you just have to compensate by marking the note higher up on the neck.'

Joona watches Axel Riessen put the violin to his shoulder and play the piece again on a violin that's completely out of tune, with very odd finger placings, but exactly the right notes. 'La seguidilla' suddenly sounds perfect again.

'You're a magician,' the girl laughs, and claps her hands.

'Hello,' Joona says, walking over and shaking Axel by the hand, then the girl.

He looks at Axel, who's still holding the untuned violin.

'Impressive.'

Axel looks down at the violin and shakes his head:

'I haven't actually played for thirty-four years,' he says in an odd tone of voice.

'Do you believe that?' Joona asks the girl.

She nods, then answers enigmatically:

'Don't you see the glow?'

'Beverly,' Axel says quietly.

She looks at him with a smile, then walks off under the trees.

Joona nods to Axel:

'I need to talk to you.'

'I'm sorry I just vanished like that,' Axel says, as he starts to tune the violin again. 'But I was called away urgently.'

'No problem – I've come back.'

Joona looks at Axel as he watches the girl pick the flowers of some weeds growing in the shady lawn.

'Is there a vase indoors?' she asks.

'In the kitchen,' he replies.

She carries the little bunch of dandelion seed-heads in through the door.

'Her favourite flowers,' Axel says, then listens to the G-string, fine-tunes the peg, and puts the violin down on the mosaic tabletop.

'I'd like you to take a look at this,' Joona says, taking the photograph out of its plastic sleeve.

They sit down at the table. Axel takes a pair of reading glasses from his breast pocket and looks at the picture carefully.

'When was this taken?' he asks quickly.

'We don't know, but possibly the spring of 2008,' Joona replies.

'Yes,' Axel says, looking instantly more relaxed.

'Do you recognise these people?' Joona asks calmly.

'Of course,' Axel says. 'Palmcrona, Pontus Salman, Raphael Guidi and . . . Agathe al-Haji.'

'But I'm actually here because I'd like you to look at the musicians in the background.'

Axel gives Joona a curious glance, then looks down at the photograph again.

'The Tokyo String Quartet . . . they're good,' he says coolly.

'Yes, but I was wondering . . . I've been trying to work out if it's possible for a knowledgeable person to identify, from the picture alone, what piece the string quartet are playing?'

'Interesting question.'

'Would it be possible to make a qualified guess, even? Kaj Samuelsson doesn't seem to think so, and when your brother Robert looked at the picture, he said it was completely impossible.'

Joona leans forward, and his eyes look soft and warm in the leafy shade.

'Your brother was certain that no one could do it – if you couldn't.'

A smile plays at the corners of Axel's mouth.

'He said that, did he?'

'Yes,' Joona says. 'But I wasn't sure what he meant . . .'

'Nor me,' Axel says.

'I'd still like you to take a look at the photograph with a magnifying glass.'

'You're thinking that knowing what piece was being played could help you to confirm when the photograph was taken?' Axel asks with new seriousness.

Joona nods, takes a magnifying glass from his bag and hands it to Axel.

'You should be able to see their fingers now,' Joona says.

He sits in silence as Axel studies the photograph, thinking once again that if the picture was taken before the warrant was issued for the Sudanese president, Omar al-Bashir, in March 2009, then his gut-feeling has led him in the wrong direction. But if it was taken after that, he'll be proved right, because it would then be a record of criminal activity.

'I can certainly see their fingers,' Axel says slowly.

'Can you hazard a guess as to what notes they're playing?' Joona asks in a subdued voice.

Axel sighs, hands the photograph and magnifying glass back to Joona, then suddenly sings four notes. Fairly quietly, but perfectly clear notes. He thinks for a while, then picks up the violin from the mosaic table and plays two higher, trembling notes.

Joona Linna has got to his feet.

'Are you kidding?'

Axel Riessen looks him in the eye.

'Martin Beaver is playing a C3, Kikuei is playing a C2. Kazuhide Isomura isn't playing, and Clive is playing a four-note pizzicato. That was what I was singing: major E, major A, A3, and C4 sharp.'

Joona writes that down, then asks:

'How precise a guess is that?'

'It's not a guess,' Axel replies.

'Do you think this combination of notes is found in many pieces? I mean . . . from these notes alone, would it be possible to identify which piece the Tokyo String Quartet might have been performing in this picture?'

'These notes only occur in one piece,' Axel replies.

'How do you know that?'

Axel looks up at the window. The big, trembling leaves are reflected in the glass.

'Please, go on,' Joona says.

'I'm sure I haven't heard all the music they've ever played . . .'

Axel shrugs his shoulders apologetically.

'But you still think these notes are only found in one particular piece?' Joona says.

'This combination of notes is only found in one place, as far as I'm aware,' Axel goes on. 'In bar 156 of the first movement of Béla Bartók's second string quartet.'

He picks up the violin again and puts it to his shoulder.

'*Tranquillo* . . . the music becomes wonderfully peaceful, like a lullaby. Listen to the first part,' he says, and starts to play.

His fingers move tenderly, the notes tremble, swaying gently, light and perfectly soft. After just four bars he stops.

'The two violins shadow each other, the same notes, but different octaves,' he explains. 'It's almost too beautiful, but against the cello's major A the violins provide a degree of dissonance . . . even if that isn't quite how they sound because they're almost transitional notes that . . .'

He breaks off, falls silent and puts the violin down.

Joona looks at him.

'You're quite certain the musicians are playing Bartók's second string quartet in this photograph?' he asks quietly.

'Yes.'

Joona takes a few steps across the terrace, stops beside the blossoming lilac bushes and tells himself that he has probably just heard all he needs to confirm the date of the meeting.

He smiles to himself, hides his smile with his hand, then turns round and takes a red apple from the fruit-bowl on the mosaic table and meets Axel's wondering gaze.

'You're sure?' he asks again. 'Properly sure?'

Axel nods, and Joona hands him the apple, excuses himself, pulls his phone from his pocket and calls Anja.

'Anja, this is urgent . . .'

'We were supposed to have a sauna together at the weekend,' Anja interrupts.

'I need help.'

'I know,' Anja giggles.

Joona tries to conceal the stress in his voice.

'Can you check the Tokyo String Quartet's repertoire for the past ten years?'

'I've already checked their repertoire.'

'Can you see what they've played at the Alte Oper in Frankfurt during that time?'

'Yes, they've played there every year, sometimes more than once.'

'Have they ever played Béla Bartók's second string quartet?'

She checks, then replies:

'Yes, once. Opus 17.'

'Opus 17,' Joona repeats, looking at Axel, who nods in response.

'What?' Anja asks.

'When was it?' Joona asks in a serious voice. 'When did they play Bartók's second string quartet?'

'Thirteenth of November, 2009.'

'You're sure?' Joona asks.

The people in the photograph met eight months after the warrant was issued for the arrest of the Sudanese president, he thinks. Pontus Salman lied to us about the date. They met in November 2009. That's why all this has happened. People are dead, and more may end up dying yet.

Joona reaches out his hand and touches the clusters of violet-coloured lilac blossom, while simultaneously smelling a barbecue in a neighbouring garden, and thinks that he needs to get hold of Saga Bauer to tell her about the breakthrough.

'Was that everything?' Anja says over the phone.

'Yes.'

'And what do we say?'

'Yes, sorry . . . *Kiitokseksi saat pusun,*' Joona says in Finnish. 'You can have a kiss as thanks.' He ends the call.

Pontus Salman lied to us, he thinks once more. There was a complete arms embargo in place when he met Palmcrona, Raphael and Agathe al-Haji. Any deals of that sort were forbidden, there were no exceptions or loopholes.

338

But Agathe al-Haji wanted to buy ammunition, and the others wanted to earn money. And didn't care about human rights or international law.

Pontus Salman lied about the date, clinically and coolly. He assumed that a few unexpected truths in what he said would conceal the lie. By admitting unreservedly that it was him in the picture, he thought we'd take his word for it and accept the lie about the date.

In his mind's eye Joona can see Salman's impassive face as he spoke, pale and grey, and lined with deep wrinkles. Then his feigned frankness when he identified himself and told them the date of the meeting.

Arms smuggling, a voice in his head whispers. Arms smuggling is what this is all about, the photograph, the attempted blackmail, all the deaths.

He remembers how Saga Bauer stood up after Salman's testimony, and how she left a full set of fingerprints on the table as a silent memento.

In March 2009 the International Criminal Court in the Hague issued a warrant for the arrest of the Sudanese president, Omar al-Bashir, for direct involvement in the attempted genocide of three tribes in Darfur. And since then, all deliveries of ammunition from the rest of the world have been banned. The Sudanese army still has its weapons, machine-guns and assault rifles, but very little ammunition. And the first people who will notice the strangled supply-line are of course the militia in Darfur. But Carl Palmcrona, Pontus Salman, Raphael Guidi and Agathe al-Haji considered themselves above international law. They met in November 2009, even though the president's involvement in genocide was made public eight months earlier.

'What did you find out?' Axel asks, getting to his feet.

'What?' Joona asks.

'Were you able to fix the date?'

'Yes,' Joona replies curtly.

Axel tries to look him in the eye.

'What's wrong?' he asks.

'I have to go,' Joona mutters.

'Did they meet after the warrant for al-Bashir's arrest was issued? They can't have done. I have to know if that's the case!'

Joona glances up and looks him in the eye. His eyes are perfectly calm, radiant.

73

Saga Bauer is lying on her front on the shabby, pale-coloured rug. She has her eyes closed while Stefan slowly kisses her back. Her fair hair is spread out like a shimmering sky across the floor. Stefan's warm face moves across her skin.

Keep going, she thinks.

The gentle touch of his lips tickles her between her shoulder-blades. She forces herself to lie still, and shivers with pleasure.

The stereo is playing Carl Unander-Scharin's erotic duet for cello and mezzo-soprano. The two melodies cross rhythmically and repetitively, like the slow sparkle of a dark stream.

Saga lies perfectly still, and feels her body getting aroused. She is breathing through half-open lips, and moistens them with her tongue.

His hands slide over her waist, around her hips, and lift her backside as lightly as a feather.

No other man she has ever met has moved so gently, Saga thinks, and smiles to herself.

He looks at her and she parts her thighs. She is starting to glow inside, a core of slippery, throbbing heat.

She hears herself moan as she feels his tongue.

Very gently, he turns her body over. The rug has left stripy marks across her stomach.

'Keep going,' she whispers.

'Or you'll shoot me,' he says.

She nods and smiles, her face open and happy. Stefan's black hair has fallen across his face, and his thin ponytail is hanging across his chest.

'Come here,' Saga says.

She pulls his face down towards hers and kisses him, meeting his warm, wet tongue.

He quickly pushes his trousers down and lies naked on top of her. She lets out a protracted moan, then breathes quickly when they stop for a moment, enjoying their dizzying closeness. Stefan thrusts very gently, his narrow hips moving slowly. Saga runs her fingers over his shoulder-blades, back, buttocks.

Then her phone rings. Typical, she thinks. The sound of ZZ Top's 'Blue Jean Blues' comes from the pile of clothes on the sofa, beneath her white vest, underpants and inside-out jeans.

'Let it ring,' she whispers.

'It's your work phone,' he says.

'I don't care, it's not important,' she murmurs, trying to hold onto him.

But he pulls out of her, kneels up and feels in her trouser pockets for her phone. He can't find it, and the muffled ringtone carries on. In the end he turns her jeans upside-down and shakes her phone onto the floor. It's stopped ringing. A little buzzing sound announces that she's got a new voicemail.

Twenty minutes later Saga Bauer is half-running through the corridor of the National Crime Unit. Her hair is still damp from the hasty shower, and she can feel the lingering tingle of unsatisfied lust in her body. Her underpants and jeans feel uncomfortable.

She glimpses Anja Larsson's quizzical round face above her computer as she hurries towards Joona's room. He's standing in the middle of the floor with the photograph in his hand, waiting for her. When she meets his sharp, icy grey gaze a shiver of unease runs down her spine.

'Close the door,' he says.

She does so, then turns to face him and waits. She's breathing fast and quietly.

'Axel Riessen remembers all the music he's ever heard, every note from every instrument in an orchestra . . .'

'I don't understand what you're trying to say.'

'He could see what piece the string quartet were playing in the photograph. Béla Bartók's second string quartet.'

'Okay, you were right,' she says quickly. 'It was possible to identify the piece, but we . . .'

'The photograph was taken on the thirteenth of November 2009,' Joona interrupts with unusual sharpness in his voice.

'So those bastards were selling arms to Sudan after the warrant for al-Bashir's arrest was issued,' she says coldly.

'Yes.'

'They knew that the ammunition was going to be pumped into Darfur,' she whispers.

Joona nods, and his jaw muscles move beneath his skin.

'Carl Palmcrona shouldn't have been in that box,' he says. 'Pontus Salman shouldn't have been there, none of them should have been . . .'

'But now we've got them on a photograph,' she says with restrained excitement. 'Raphael Guidi stitching together a huge deal with Sudan.'

'Yes,' Joona replies, looking into Saga's summer-blue eyes.

'The really big fish are always the meanest,' Saga states. 'That's nothing new, most people know that . . . but the big ones always get away.'

They stand in silence, examining the photograph again, looking at the four people in the box at the Alte Oper, the champagne, their faces, the musicians playing Paganini's old instruments.

'Okay, now we've solved the first mystery,' Saga says, and takes a deep breath. 'We know the photograph is directly linked to Sudan's attempts to buy arms when there's an embargo.'

'Palmcrona was there, so that money in his bank account is probably bribes,' Joona says hesitantly. 'But at the same time . . . Palmcrona never authorised any arms exports to Sudan after the business with the president, that would have been unthinkable, he'd never have . . .'

He breaks off when his phone suddenly rings in his jacket

pocket. Joona answers, listens for a moment in silence, then ends the call. He looks at Saga.

'That was Axel Riessen,' Joona tells her. 'He says he's figured out what the photograph is about.'

74

A perfect plan

A solitary boy made of iron, only fifteen centimetres tall, sits with his arms round his knees in the back yard of the Finnish Church in Gamla stan. Three metres away Axel Riessen is leaning against the ochre-coloured wall, eating noodles from a carton. He has a mouthful of food and waves his chopsticks when he sees Joona and Saga come through the gate.

'So, what have you figured out?' Joona asks.

Axel nods, puts the carton down on the windowsill, wipes his mouth with a paper napkin and then shakes hands with Saga and Joona.

'You said you'd figured out what the photograph was about,' Joona repeats.

Axel lowers his gaze, breathes out hard, then looks up again.

'Kenya,' he says. 'The four people in the concert-hall box are drinking a toast with champagne because they've reached agreement about a large shipment of ammunition to Kenya.'

He falls silent for a moment.

'Go on,' Joona says.

'Kenya's buying 1.25 million rounds of 5.56 x 45 mm ammunition manufactured under licence.'

'For assault rifles,' Saga says.

'The shipment goes to Kenya,' Axel goes on heavily. 'But the ammunition isn't for Kenya. It's going on to Sudan, to the militia in Darfur. I suddenly worked it all out. It's obvious that the ammunition is going to Sudan, because the buyer is represented by Agathe al-Haji.'

'Where does Kenya fit into this?' Joona asks.

'The four people in that box at the concert hall met after al-Bashir's arrest warrant was issued, didn't they? Bartók's second string quartet was only played once. It's forbidden to export arms to Sudan, but not to Kenya: there are still no problems with the neighbouring country to the south.'

'How can you be so sure of this?' Saga says.

'Carl Palmcrona left this contract for me to deal with by committing suicide. It was the last thing he was working on, but he didn't complete it. I've promised to sign off on the export licence today,' Axel replies bitterly.

'It's the same ammunition, the same deal. After the warrant was issued for the president's arrest, they just crossed out Sudan and wrote Kenya instead,' Saga says.

'It's rock solid,' Axel says.

'Or was, until someone took a photograph of the meeting,' Joona points out.

'The evaluation had been concluded by the time Palmcrona killed himself. Everyone probably thought he'd already signed the export licence,' Axel says.

'They probably got pretty freaked out when they realised he hadn't,' Joona smiles.

'The whole deal was left hanging in the air,' Saga says.

'I was recruited very quickly,' Axel tells them. 'They quite literally put the pen in my hand to get me to sign the contract.'

'But?'

'I wanted to conduct my own evaluation.'

'And you have.'

'Yes.'

And it looked okay?' Saga asks.

'Yes . . . and I promised to sign, and I would have done so if I hadn't seen that photograph and made the connection to Kenya.'

They all stand in silence, looking at the little iron statue, Stockholm's smallest public work of art. Joona leans forward and pats the boy's shiny head. The metal seems to radiate body-heat after a day in the sun.

'They're busy loading the ship in Gothenburg harbour,' Axel says in a low voice.

'So I understand,' Saga says. 'But without an export licence, then . . .'

'That ammunition isn't going to be leaving Sweden,' Axel declares.

'You said they're expecting you to sign the export licence today,' Joona says. 'How can you delay the process? It's vitally important to our investigation that they don't realise anything is wrong.'

'They won't just sit back and wait.'

'Say you're not quite finished,' Joona says.

'Yes, but that could be tricky. The deal is already delayed because of me, but I can try,' Axel says.

'This isn't just to do with our investigation, but also your security, Axel,' he explains.

Axel smiles and asks with a degree of scepticism in his voice:

'You think they'd threaten me?'

Joona smiles back.

'As long as they're expecting a positive result, there's no danger at all,' he replies. 'But if you say no, people are going to lose huge amounts of money. I can't even imagine how big the bribes must have been to get all the necessary people in Kenya to avert their eyes.'

'I'm not going to be able to delay signing the licence indefinitely. Pontus Salman has been trying to get hold of me all day. These people know the business, they can't be fooled,' Axel says, just as his phone starts to ring.

He looks at the screen and stiffens.

'I think it's Pontus Salman again . . .'

'Take the call,' Joona says.

'Okay,' Axel says, and answers.

'I've tried to call you several times,' Salman says in his drawling voice. 'You know . . . we've finished loading the ship, it costs money to have it lying in port, the shipping company have been trying to get hold of you, they don't seem to have received the export licence.'

'I'm sorry,' Axel says, glancing at Joona and Saga. 'I'm afraid I haven't had time to go through the last few . . .'

'I've already spoken to the Cabinet Office, you were supposed to be signing it today.'

Axel hesitates as his thoughts head off in several different directions. He wishes he could just hang up, but clears his throat instead, apologises, then goes on.

'Another matter has got in the way.'

Axel can hear the fake tone in his voice, he took a little too long to answer. He had been on the point of telling the truth, that there isn't going to be any export licence seeing as they're planning to smuggle the ammunition to Darfur.

'The impression I got was that the matter was going to be dealt with by today at the latest,' Salman says, unable to conceal his irritation.

'You took a gamble,' Axel says.

'What do you mean?'

'Without an export licence, there can't be any . . .'

'But we've already . . . Sorry.'

'You were given authorisation to manufacture the ammunition, you've had a positive advance notification, and I've given positive signals, but that's all for the time being.'

'There's a lot at stake here,' Salman says, more amenably. 'Can I pass on any message to the shipping company? Could you give me an idea of how long you think it's going to take? They need to know how long they're going to be in harbour, it's all about the logistics.'

'I'm still positively inclined to the export, but I'm going to look through everything one last time, and then you'll be notified,' Axel says.

75

Saga Bauer has been skipping rope for fifty minutes in the police gym when an anxious colleague walks over and asks how she's feeling. Her face is sweaty and impassive, but her feet are still dancing, apparently unconcerned by the quickly passing rope.

'You're too hard on yourself,' he says.

'No,' she replies, and carries on skipping with her jaw firmly clenched.

Twenty-five minutes later Joona Linna comes down into the gym, walks over to her and sits down on the sloping bench in front of some weights.

'Fucking hell,' she says, without interrupting her skipping. 'They're going to pump ammunition into Darfur, and there isn't a damn thing we can do about it.'

'At least we know what this is all about now,' Joona says calmly. 'We know they're using Kenya as a conduit to . . .'

'But what the hell are we going to do?' she asks as she jumps. 'Bring in that bastard, Pontus Salman? Contact Europol about Raphael Guidi?'

'We still can't prove anything.'

'This is big, bigger than anyone would have liked. Even we don't want it to be this big,' she reasons as the rope whines past her face and ticks against the floor. 'Carl Palmcrona was caught up in it, and Pontus Salman from Sweden . . . Raphael Guidi, he's a huge figure . . . but also someone in the Kenyan government, otherwise it wouldn't work . . . and maybe someone in the Swedish government . . .'

'We won't be able to get all of them,' Joona concludes.

'The smartest option would probably be to drop the case,' she says.

'Let's do that, then.'

She laughs at the joke, then goes on skipping with her lips pursed.

'Palmcrona was probably taking bribes for years,' Joona says thoughtfully. 'But then he received Björn Almskog's email, and he got scared that the party was over . . . so he called someone, probably Raphael . . . But during the course of that conversation he realised that he was replaceable . . . and that because of the photograph, he was regarded as a problem. He had become a problem to the people who had invested in the deal. They weren't prepared to lose their money and risk their livelihoods for him.'

'So he killed himself,' Saga says, skipping faster.

'Which meant he was out of the way. Leaving just the photograph and the blackmailer.'

'So they employed a professional fixer,' she says breathlessly.

Joona nods as she starts to pick her knees up high when she jumps.

'If Viola hadn't been on that boat, he would have murdered Björn and Penelope and then sunk the boat,' he says.

Saga speeds up even more, before finally stopping.

'And we . . . we would have written it off as an accident,' she pants. 'He would have taken the photograph, wiped all the computers and left the country without a trace, completely invisible.'

'My impression of him is that he isn't really worried about being seen, he's just being practical,' Joona says. 'It's easier to solve his problems if the police aren't involved, but it's the problems he's mostly concerned about . . . because otherwise he wouldn't have tried to burn both flats. That sort of thing attracts a lot of attention, but he wanted to be thorough, and he prioritises thoroughness above everything else.'

Saga is leaning on her thighs as sweat drips from her face.

'Obviously we would have connected the fires with the sinking of the boat sooner or later,' she says, straightening up.

'But by then it would already have been too late,' he replies. 'The fixer's task is to get rid of all the evidence and all the witnesses.'

'But now we've got both the photograph and Penelope,' she says with a smile. 'The fixer hasn't fixed the problem.'

'Not yet . . .'

She throws a few tentative punches at the bag hanging from the ceiling, then looks at Joona thoughtfully.

'While I was training I had to watch a recording from a bank robbery where you neutralised a man using just a faulty pistol.'

'I was lucky,' he replies.

'Yes.'

He laughs and she comes closer, does a bit of footwork, circles round him, then stops. She holds out her arms and hands and meets his gaze. She beckons him towards her with her fingers. She wants him to try to land a blow on her. He smiles and understands the reference to Bruce Lee: the beckoning hand. He shakes his head, but doesn't take his eyes off her.

'I've seen how you move,' he says.

'So you know,' she says curtly.

'You're quick, and you might land the first blow, but after that . . .'

'I'd be gone,' she concludes.

'Nice idea, but . . .'

She repeats the gesture, luring him to her, slightly more impatiently.

'But,' he goes on, amused, 'you'll probably come in far too hard.'

'No,' she replies.

'Try it and see,' Joona says calmly.

She beckons him to her, but he ignores the invitation and turns his back on her, and starts walking towards the door. She moves quickly after Joona and aims a right hook at him. He simply bends his neck so that the blow passes over his head. And, in a continuation of the same movement, he spins round, draws his pistol and knocks her to the floor at the same time by kicking out at her knee.

'I have to say one thing,' Saga says quickly.

'That I was right, you mean?'

'Don't get any ideas,' she says with a flash of anger, then gets up.

'If you go in too hard against . . .'

'I didn't go in hard,' she interrupts. 'I slowed down because I realised something important that . . .'

'Of course you did,' he laughs.

'I don't care what you think,' she goes on. 'But I realised that we have to use Penelope as bait.'

'What are you talking about?'

'I started to think about the fact that she's moving to a safe-house, and just as I was going to hit you I had an idea. I pulled my punch because I didn't want to knock you out if we were going to talk.'

'So talk,' he says amiably.

'I realised that Penelope is going to act as bait for the fixer whether we like it or not. She's going to draw him to her.'

Joona is no longer smiling, and nods thoughtfully.

'Go on.'

'We don't know if the fixer is listening to our radio communications, if he can hear everything being said over the RAKEL system . . . but it seems pretty likely, seeing as he managed to find Penelope out on Kymmendö,' Saga says.

'I agree.'

'So he'll find her again somehow, that's what I think. And he doesn't care about the fact that she's got police protection. Obviously we'll do all we can to keep her location secret, but I mean, we can't keep her safe without the use of radio communication.'

'He's going to find her,' Joona agrees.

'I was thinking . . . Penelope is going to act as bait whatever happens. The only question is whether we're going to be ready for him or not. Obviously she'll get full protection, just as planned, but if we get Surveillance to monitor the location at the same time, we might be able to catch the fixer.'

'That's right . . . you're absolutely right,' Joona says.

76

The secure apartment

Carlos, Saga and Joona are walking quickly along the corridor leading to Security Police Headquarters. Verner Zandén is already waiting on a soft sofa when they arrive. Without wasting any time on pleasantries, he starts talking the moment they close the door behind them.

'Klara Olofsdotter at the International Prosecution Authority has been brought in . . . This is a major operation for National Crime and the Security Police, but who the hell are we trying to catch?'

'We know very little about him,' Saga replies. 'We don't even know if he's working alone. We could be dealing with professionals from Belgium or Brazil, or leftovers from the KGB or anywhere else in the former Eastern Bloc.'

'It isn't actually that difficult to listen to our radio communications,' Carlos says.

'Obviously the fixer knows that Penelope is under guard, and that it's going to be difficult to get to her,' Joona says. 'But doors have to be opened sometimes, bodyguards change shifts, she has to have food, see her mother, a psychologist, Niklas Dent from the GMP, and . . .'

He breaks off when his phone rings, and he glances quickly at the screen, then rejects the call.

'Our priority is obviously to protect Penelope,' Saga says. 'But at the same time as doing that, we also have a chance to get hold of the man who killed several of our colleagues.'

'Presumably I don't have to remind anyone about how dangerous he is,' Joona says, 'None of us is ever going to meet anyone else this dangerous.'

The secure apartment is at Storgatan 1, with windows facing Sibyllegatan and a view of Östermalmstorg. There are no apartments opposite the windows: the closest building is more than a hundred metres away.

Saga Bauer holds the steel door open as Dr Daniella Richards carefully leads Penelope Fernandez from the lead-grey police van. They are surrounded by heavily armed security officers.

'This is the most secure residence above ground-level in the whole of Stockholm,' Saga says.

Penelope shows no reaction. She merely follows Daniella Richards to the lift. There are security cameras everywhere in the lobby and stairwell.

'We've installed motion detectors, an extremely advanced alarm system and two encrypted direct lines to the Communications Centre,' Saga explains as the lift carries them upwards.

On the third floor Penelope is led through a heavy security door to an airlock where a uniformed guard is sitting. She opens a further security door and lets them into the apartment.

'The flat has been designed to the highest standards of fire safety, and has its own electricity supply and ventilation system,' Saga says.

'You're safe here,' Daniella Richards says.

Penelope raises her eyes and looks blankly at the doctor.

'Thanks,' she says in a whisper a few seconds later.

'I can stay, if you like?'

Penelope slowly shakes her head, and Daniella leaves the flat with Saga.

Penelope locks the door, then goes and stands by one of the bulletproof windows looking out over Östermalmstorg. Some sort of foil on the glass makes the windows impossible to see through from the outside. She looks out and thinks that some of the people moving about in the square are probably plain-clothed police officers.

She touches the window tentatively. She can't hear any sound from outside.

Suddenly the doorbell rings.

Penelope starts, and her heart begins to beat hard and fast.

She goes over to the monitor and presses the button for the entry-phone. The female police officer in the airlock is looking up at the camera, and explains that her mother has come to see her.

'Penny? Penny!' her mother asks anxiously behind the officer.

Penelope turns the lock and hears the heavy mechanism click, then she opens the heavy steel door.

'Mum,' she says, with a feeling that her voice can't possibly penetrate the silence hanging over the apartment.

She lets her mother in, closes and locks the door again, then just stands there by the door, purses her lips and feels herself start to shake, but forces all emotion away from her face.

She glances quickly at her mother, not daring to look her in the eye. She knows her mother is going to blame her for not protecting her sister.

Claudia takes a few cautious steps across the hall, and looks round warily.

'Are they taking care of you now, Penny?' she asks.

'I'll be fine here.'

'They have to protect you.'

'They are, I'm safe here.'

'That's the only thing that matters,' Claudia says, almost inaudibly.

Penelope tries to swallow her tears. Her neck is aching and straining.

'There's so much I have to sort out,' her mum goes on, turning her face away. 'I . . . I can't, I just can't comprehend that I'm having to arrange Viola's funeral.'

Penelope nods slowly. Suddenly her mother reaches out her hand and gently touches her cheek. Penelope starts involuntarily, and Claudia quickly pulls her hand away.

'They say this will all be over soon,' Penelope says. 'The police are going to catch the man . . . the man who . . . killed Viola and Björn.'

Claudia nods, then turns towards her daughter again. Her face is naked and unprotected, and to her surprise Penelope sees that her mum is smiling.

'Just think, you're alive,' Claudia says. 'I've got you, that's the only thing that matters, the only . . .'

'Mum . . .'

'My little girl.'

Claudia reaches out her hand again, and this time Penelope doesn't pull away.

77

In the bay window of a flat on the third floor of Nybrogatan 4A sits Jenny Göransson, operational commander, waiting. Hours pass, but no one has anything to report. Everything is quiet. She looks down at the square, up at the rooftop above Penelope's apartment, over towards the roof of Sibyllegatan 27, where some pigeons take off and fly away.

Sonny Jansson is stationed there. He probably moved and frightened the birds off.

Jenny contacts him and he confirms that he changed position to be able to see into another flat.

'I thought I could see a fight, but they're just playing with a Wii, waving their arms about in front of a television.'

'Resume your previous position,' Jenny says drily.

She picks up her binoculars and scans the darker area between the kiosk and the elm tree, which she has identified as a possibly insecure location.

Blomberg, who is wearing a brown tracksuit and running up Sibyllegatan, contacts her.

'I can see something in the churchyard,' he says in a tense voice.

'What can you see?'

'Someone's moving under the trees, maybe ten metres from the railings facing Storgatan.'

357

'Check it out, Blomberg, but be careful,' she says.

He runs past the equestrian steps at the end of the Army Museum, then slowly makes his way into the churchyard. The summer night is warm and green. He walks silently along the grass beside the path, thinking that he should probably stop and pretend to do some stretches, but carries on instead. The leaves are rustling gently. The light sky is shadowed by the branches and the ground between the graves is dark. Suddenly he sees a face, close to the ground. It's a woman in her twenties. Her red hair is cropped short, and her khaki rucksack is lying next to her head. She's smiling happily as another woman pulls her top up and starts kissing her breasts.

Blomberg moves back cautiously before he reports back to Jenny Göransson.

'False alarm, just a couple making out.'

Three hours have passed. Blomberg shivers, it's starting to get cold, there's dew on the ground. He jogs round a corner and comes face to face with a haggard-looking middle-aged woman. She appears to be very drunk, and is swaying noticeably as she holds two poodles on leashes. The dogs are sniffing about, eager to carry on, but she yanks them back angrily.

A woman in an air-hostess's uniform is walking past the edge of the churchyard, the wheel of her navy-blue cabin-bag rattling on the pavement. She glances neutrally at Blomberg and he pretends not to have noticed her, even though they've been colleagues for over seven years.

Maria Ristonen walks on with her cabin-bag, heading towards the entrance to the underground station to check out the person who's standing hidden in the doorway alongside. She keeps walking, the click of her heels echoing off the walls. The cabin-bag catches on the kerb and she has to stop and sort it out, simultaneously glancing at the individual. It's a man, fairly well-dressed, with a peculiar expression on his face. He seems to be looking for something, and glances at her anxiously. Maria Ristonen's heart skips a beat, and turns away as she hears operational commander Jenny Göransson in her earpiece:

'Blomberg has eyes on him too, he's on his way,' Jenny says. 'Wait for Blomberg, Maria. Wait for Blomberg.'

Maria adjusts her case, but can't delay any longer, she's going to have to carry on. She tries to walk more slowly as she approaches the man with the anxious expression. She has to pass him and carry on with her back to him. The man retreats further into the doorway when she approaches. He's holding one hand inside his clothes. Maria Ristonen feels adrenalin pumping through her veins as the man suddenly takes a step towards her and holds up something he had been hiding inside his coat. Behind his shoulder Maria sees that Blomberg has drawn his pistol to shoot, but stops when Jenny calls through his earpiece that it's a false alarm, that the man is unarmed, that it's just a can of beer.

'Cunt,' the man snarls, and sprays beer at her.

'Dear God,' Jenny sighs through the earpiece. 'Just keep heading for the underground station, Maria.'

The night passes without incident, the last nightclubs close and then there are only a few dog-walkers and can-collectors out on the streets, then people delivering newspapers, followed by different dog-walkers and joggers. Jenny Göransson starts to long for eight o'clock, when she's going to be relieved. She looks across at Hedvig Eleonora Church, then at Penelope Fernandez's opaque windows, before glancing down at Storgatan and the building containing the parsonage where film director Ingmar Bergman grew up. She puts a piece of nicotine gum in her mouth and studies the square, park benches, trees, the sculptures of the reclining woman with her legs apart and the man with a side of meat on his shoulder.

Suddenly Jenny Göransson detects movement in the doorway covered by the tall steel gate that leads to Östermalm market-hall. It's dark, but the weak reflection in the glass is impeded by rapid movement. Jenny Göransson calls Carl Schwirt. He's sitting with two bin-bags full of empty drinks cans on a bench between the trees.

'No, I can't see a thing,' he replies.

'Stay where you are.'

Maybe, she thinks, she should get Blomberg to leave his position by the church and jog down towards Humlegården to check out the doorway.

Jenny looks again: there seems to be someone sitting on their knees behind the black gate. An unlicensed taxi has driven the wrong way and is turning round on Nybrogatan. Jenny quickly picks up her binoculars and waits as the car's headlamps slide across the red-brick walls of the market-hall. The light passes the doorway, but she can't see anything now. The car stops, then reverses.

'Idiot,' she mutters as the driver ends up with one wheel on the pavement.

But suddenly the headlights are shining into a shop window a short distance away, and the reflection is lighting up the doorway.

There's someone behind the tall gate.

It only takes Jenny a second to put together her fragmentary impressions: a man adjusting the sights on a weapon.

She puts the binoculars down and calls National Communication Centre over the radio:

'Live situation, I can see a weapon,' she says, almost shouting. 'A military weapon with sniper sights, a man in the doorway of the market-hall . . . I repeat, a sniper at ground-level at the corner of the block, at the crossing of Nybrogatan and Humlegårdsgatan!'

The man in the doorway is behind the gate. He has been watching the empty square for a while, waiting for a man collecting empty tins to get up from a bench and walk off, but decided to ignore him when it looked like he was going to be spending the rest of the night there. Under cover of darkness he unfolds the tubular butt with padded shoulder-rest of a Modular Sniper Rifle, a sand-coloured semi-automatic rifle for distances of up to two kilometres, with precision ammunition. Without any urgency or nervousness he attaches a titanium flare-guard to the barrel, then inserts the magazine and folds down the front support.

He had gone into the market-hall just before closing time, where he hid in a storeroom and waited for the cleaners to finish and the security company to do their rounds. As soon as the premises were silent and dark he went out into the market-hall.

From the inside he disconnected the alarm on the main doors in the corner, then went out into the archway, which was protected from the street by a sturdy iron gate.

Behind the gate the deeply recessed doorway is like a small room. He is protected on all sides, but has a completely open view to the front. He can't be seen at all when he's still. If anyone did walk up to the gate, all he has to do is turn away, into the darkness.

He aims the rifle at the building where Penelope Fernandez is staying, and checks off the rooms through the electro-optic sniper sight. He is slow and systematic. He's been waiting a long time, morning is approaching, and soon he will be obliged to abandon his position and wait for the following night. Because he knows that at some point she will look out at the square in the belief that the laminated glass will protect her.

He adjusts the sights, is caught by the light from a car, turns away for a while, then goes back to studying the apartment at Storgatan 1. Almost at once he discovers a source of heat behind a dark window. The signal is weak and grainy, obscured by distance and the reinforced glass. Worse than he had expected. He tries to identify the outer edges of the hazy thermal image, then finds its centre. A pale pink shadow moves in the speckled purple, then thins out before solidifying again.

Suddenly something is happening in the square straight ahead of him: two plain-clothed police officers are running towards him with their pistols drawn, held close to their bodies.

78

The market-hall

Penelope wakes up early and can't get back to sleep. She lies in bed for a long time, but eventually gets up and puts some water on to make tea. She thinks about the police, and the fact that they will only be able to maintain this level of security for a few days. It won't be financially justifiable for any longer than that. If the perpetrator hadn't murdered police officers they wouldn't have been here at all, there wouldn't have been the resources.

She takes the boiling water off the stove, fills the teapot and adds two lemon teabags. She takes the pot and a cup into the dimly lit living room, puts them down in the window recess, lights the lamp with the green shade that's hanging in the window, and looks down into the deserted square.

Suddenly she sees two people running across the paving stones, then they fall and remain lying down. It looks odd. Quickly she turns the lamp out. It starts to sway, and scrapes against the glass. She moves off to the side of the window, then glances out again. A SWAT team is running along Nybrogatan, and then she sees something flicker in a doorway over by the market-hall, and a fraction of a second later there's a sound, as if someone had thrown a wet rag at the window. A bullet goes straight through the laminated glass and into the wall behind her. She throws herself on the floor and crawls away. Splinters of glass from the hot lamp in the window are lying on the floor, but she doesn't even notice when she cuts her palms.

Stewe Billgren has just transferred from a quiet posting to the operational section of the Special Operations Unit of the National Crime Police. Now he's sitting in the passenger seat beside his immediate superior, Mira Carlsson, in surveillance vehicle Alpha, a civilian car that's slowly driving up Humlegårdsgatan. Stewe Billgren has never been in a live situation before, but has often wondered how he would handle it. The thought of it has started to worry him, particularly since his partner came out of the bathroom last week with a big grin on her face and showed him the pregnancy test.

Stewe Billgren feels tired after the previous day's football match. He can feel the aches developing in his calves and thighs.

Dull thuds can be heard outside and Mira just has time to look out through the windscreen and wonder:

'What the hell . . .?'

She hears a voice shouting over the radio that two officers have been hit in the middle of Östermalmstorg, that Group 5 need to go in from Humlegårdsgatan.

'We've got him,' the Security Police's operations coordinator says in a raised voice. 'There are only four entrances to the market-hall, and . . .'

'Are you sure of that??' Jenny Göransson cuts in.

'One door on Nybrogatan, one on the corner and two on Humlegårdsgatan.'

'Move more people in, more people!' Brolin calls to someone.

'We're trying to get hold of the map of the market-hall.'

'Move Groups 1 and 2 to the main door,' someone else shouts. 'Group 2 go in, Group 1 secure the door.'

'Go, go, go!'

'Group 3, move to the side entrances and provide backup to Group 4,' Jenny says in a focused voice. 'Group 5 have already got orders to go into the market-hall, we'll have to use surveillance vehicle Alpha, they're there, they're already in the vicinity.'

Head of Deployment, Ragnar Brolin from Operational

Command, contacts vehicle Alpha. Stewe Billgren glances nervously at Mira Carlsson, then takes the call. Brolin sounds stressed as he tells them to drive up Majorsgatan and await further orders. He explains quickly that the operational area has been expanded and that they're probably going to have to provide backup for Group 5.

He repeats several times that the situation is live, and that the suspected perpetrator is inside the market-hall.

'Shit,' Stewe whispers. 'I shouldn't be here, I'm so damn stupid . . .'

'Calm down,' Mira says.

'It's just that my girlfriend's pregnant, I only found out last week, I'm going to be a dad.'

'Congratulations.'

He's breathing fast, and bites his thumbnail as he stares in front of him. Through the windscreen Mira watches three heavily armed police officers rush down Humlegårdsgatan from Östermalmstorg.

They stop in front of the first side entrance to the market-hall and break open the gate. Two of them take the safety catches off their laser-sighted semi-automatics and go inside. The third moves on to the second side entrance and breaks the lock.

Stewe Billgren stops biting his thumbnail and turns white when Brolin calls their car again.

'Surveillance vehicle Alpha, come in!'

'Answer,' Mira tells Stewe.

'Alpha, vehicle Alpha!' the head of deployment says impatiently. 'Go on!'

'Vehicle Alpha here,' Stewe answers reluctantly.

'We haven't got time to move people,' Brolin says, almost shouting. 'We're going in at once, you have to provide backup for Group 5. I repeat, we're going in, you're providing backup for Group 5. Is that understood?'

'Yes,' Stewe replies, and feels his heart start to thud hard.

'Check your weapon,' Mira says in a tense voice.

As if in a slow dream, he takes out his service pistol, releases the magazine and checks the ammunition.

'Why are . . .'

'We're going in,' Mira says.

Stewe shakes his head and mumbles:

'He's killing police officers like flies . . .'

'Now!' she says harshly.

'I'm going to be a dad, so maybe . . . maybe I should . . .'

'I'm going in,' Mira snaps. 'Get behind the car, watch the door, maintain constant radio contact, and be prepared for him to make a run for it.'

Mira Carlsson takes the safety catch off her Glock and leaves the car without looking at her colleague. She runs over to the nearest door, with its broken-open doors swinging loose, glances quickly inside, then pulls her head back. Her colleague from Group 5 is standing on the top step waiting for her. Mira takes a deep breath, feels the fear coursing through her body, then goes in through the narrow doorway. It's dark, and a vague smell of garbage hits her from the storage area below the market-hall. Her colleague looks her in the eye, gestures to her to follow him and secure the line of fire from the right. He waits a few seconds, then signals the count-down: three, two, one. His face is tense and focused as he turns back to the market-hall, runs in through the door and takes cover behind the counter immediately in front of them.

Mira goes in and checks the aisle to her right for movement. Her colleague is crouched behind the counter of a stall containing cheeses the size of car-tyres. He's breathing hard, and is in radio contact with the operational leadership team. A glowing red dot from his laser-sights is quivering on the floor in front of his feet. Mira goes in behind the counter to the right and tries to see if there's anything further down the aisle. Greyish light is coming in through the skylights twenty metres above. She raises her Glock again and sees a shiny expanse of stainless steel above the sights. There's a large, tenderised beef fillet in a glass cabinet. Something is moving among the reflections. She can make out a thin figure with speckled wings. An angel of death, she thinks, just as the dark walls of the market-hall light up with the flare from a silenced automatic rifle.

Stewe Billgren is crouching behind the unmarked police car with reinforced doors and windows. He's drawn his Sig Sauer and is resting it on the bonnet of the car as his eyes dart between the two side entrances to the market-hall. The sound of sirens is approaching from several directions. Police officers in heavy equipment are gathering in the square in front of the main entrance. Suddenly there's the sound of rattling pistol shots through the walls. Stewe starts, and prays to God that nothing happens to him, before contemplating running away and giving up being a police officer.

79

Joona Linna wakes up in his flat on Wallingatan. He opens his eyes and looks out at the early summer sky. He never draws the curtains, much prefers natural light.

It's early morning.

Just as he rolls over in bed to go back to sleep his phone rings.

He realises what the call is about before he sits up and answers. He picks up the phone, listens to the garbled account of the operation, then opens his gun-cabinet and takes out his pistol, a silver-coloured Smith & Wesson. The suspected perpetrator is inside Östermalm market-hall, and the police have just stormed the building without any firm strategy at all.

Only six minutes have passed since the alarm was sounded and the perpetrator disappeared into the market-hall. The operations leadership team is now trying to coordinate their actions, cordon off an expanded area and move their teams without compromising Penelope Fernandez's security.

A SWAT team makes its way in through the entrance on Nybrogatan. Inside the door they turn immediately left, past the chocolate shop and in amongst the tables of the fish restaurant, with its upturned chairs and chiller counters full of lobsters and turbot on crushed ice. The quick footsteps of the police officers echo off the floor as they hurry forward at a crouch, taking cover behind the pillars. While they wait for fresh orders they can hear someone moaning up ahead in the darkness: a colleague is lying injured in their own blood behind the charcuterie counter.

The summer sky has started to appear behind the grimy glass skylights. Mira's heart is beating very fast. Two heavy shots went off a few moments ago, followed by four pistol shots, then two more heavy shots. One police officer is silent, the other is wounded, screaming that he's been hit in the stomach and needs help.

'Can't anyone hear me?' he moans.

Mira looks at the reflection in the pane of glass, at the figure moving behind a display of hanging pheasants and smoked reindeer meat. She gestures to her colleague that there's someone off to one side ahead of them. He calls the management team and asks quietly if they're aware of any police officers in the central aisle. Mira wipes the sweat from her hand, then grips her pistol again as she follows the peculiar movements with her eyes. She moves slowly forward, crouching down, her side pressed against a vegetable counter. A smell of parsley and earthy potatoes hits her. The Glock is shaking in her hand and she lowers it, takes a deep breath, and creeps towards the corner. Her colleague gestures to her. He is coordinating a move with three other colleagues who have come in from Nybrogatan. He moves towards the perpetrator along the game counter. Suddenly a high-velocity weapon fires towards the restaurant. Mira hears the wet, sucking sound as the bullet goes through one of her older colleague's protective vests, through the plates of boron carbide and into soft flesh. The empty case from the high-velocity weapon clatters as it hits the stone floor, very close to her.

The fixer sees his first shot enter the policeman's chest and exit between his shoulder-blades. He's already dead before his knees start to buckle. The fixer doesn't look at him as he collapses sideways, taking down one of the tables as he falls. A little cruet set hits the floor, and the salt and pepper pots roll beneath a chair.

The fixer doesn't stop, he moves quickly deeper into the market-hall, taking care to limit possible lines of fire He realises that there's another police officer hiding behind a brick wall by the side of the fish counter. A third is approaching with the light on his weapon switched on, in the aisle with the dangling hares and venison. The fixer turns and fires two quick shots before carrying on towards the kitchen of the fish restaurant.

Mira hears two more shots and sees her young colleague's body jerk as blood flies out through the exit holes in his back. His semi-automatic hits the floor. He stumbles backwards and collapses, hitting the ground so hard that his helmet comes off and rolls away. The light from his weapon is pointing straight at Mira. She moves away and curls up on the floor beside the vegetable counter. Suddenly the market-hall is stormed by twenty-four police officers, six through each entrance. She tries to report back, but can't contact anyone. The next moment she sees the perpetrator, just ten metres away. He's moving with peculiar speed and gentle precision. He's on his way into the kitchen of the fish restaurant as Mira raises her Glock, aims, and fires three shots at him.

The fixer is hit by a bullet in his upper left arm just as he's going through the swing door into the dark kitchen. He carries on past the clean hotplate, pulling down some pans as he walks quickly towards a narrow metal door. He can feel warm blood running over the back of his hand. The bullet from the pistol has caused damage. Hollow-tipped ammunition, and he realises that the back of his arm is seriously injured, but that his artery is intact.

Without stopping to examine the wound he opens the door to a goods lift, walks through to the other side, opens the other lift door, emerges into a narrow passageway and kicks a grey metal door open. He keeps going, out into the morning light and across a tarmacked inner courtyard containing eight parked cars. The high wall of the market-hall is yellow and perfectly smooth, like the back of a piece of scenery. He folds the butt of his rifle away, runs over to an older red Volvo without an immobiliser and kicks in the rear side window, then reaches in and opens the front door. He can hear automatic fire inside the market-hall. He gets in the car and pulls off the moulding around the ignition switch, breaks the steering lock, pulls off the back of the ignition and starts the car with his knife.

80

The pressure wave

Stewe Billgren has just watched twelve heavily armed police officers run into the market-hall, six through each of the side doors. He has been standing with his pistol aimed at the nearest door since Mira went in with their colleague from Group 5 less than ten minutes ago. Now she has got backup. He straightens up, relieved, and gets in the driver's seat. Blue lights are flashing on the walls down near Sturegatan. Stewe looks at the police radio, and the blue glare of the RAKEL unit attached to the top of the ordinary radio, S70M. Suddenly he sees unexpected movement in the rear-view mirror. The front of a red Volvo is edging out of an archway beneath the building next to the market-hall. It pulls out slowly across the pavement and turns right into Humlegårdsgatan. The car approaches him from behind, passes and turns into Majorsgatan in front of him. The pale sky is reflected off the windows and he can't get a clear view of the person behind the wheel. He looks up towards the square again and sees the head of the operation talking on her radio. Stewe wonders about going up to her and asking about Mira when a number of observations slot together inside his head. It happens entirely out of the blue. The man driving the red Volvo let go of the steering wheel to change gear. He didn't use his left arm. His black jacket looked shiny. It was wet, Stewe thinks, as his heart starts to beat faster. His left arm was wet,

371

and the sky wasn't reflected in the rear side window. The pale night sky that meant he couldn't see the driver's face clearly wasn't reflected because there wasn't a window. The back seat sparkled with fragments of glass. The window was broken and the driver's arm was bloody.

Stewe Billgren reacts quickly and correctly. He calls the head of the operation just as the red Volvo starts to drive up Majorsgatan. When he doesn't get any response he decides to follow the suspicious vehicle. It isn't really a considered decision, he just reacts, no longer thinking about his own safety. He starts the unmarked car and puts it in gear. As he turns into Majorsgatan the red Volvo accelerates away from him. The driver has realised he's been spotted. The tyres shriek as they spin before they get purchase. The two cars gain speed rapidly, heading up the narrow street, past the neo-Gothic Holy Trinity Church and up towards the T-junction at the end of the street.

Stewe changes up to fourth gear, thinking that he needs to pull alongside the car and force the driver to stop. The building on the other side of the T-junction is approaching with dizzying speed. The Volvo turns right into Linnégatan, but the corner is so sharp that the car is forced up onto the pavement beneath a red canopy. The car crashes into some bistro tables outside a café with immense force. Splintered wood and metal fly through the air. The left wing of the car is hanging off, scraping along the tarmac. Stewe follows, accelerating up the narrow street, reaches the junction, brakes and corners, slides, and gains a few seconds as he does so. He changes gear again, catching the Volvo from behind. The two cars drive down Linnégatan at great speed. The front wing of the Volvo breaks off and flies up into Stewe's windscreen with a crash. He loses speed momentarily, but accelerates hard again. A taxi in a side-street sounds its horn at them. They both pull into the wrong lane to overtake two slower cars. Stewe just has time to notice the badly positioned roadblocks around Östermalmstorg. Curious onlookers have already begun to gather. The street gets wider near the History Museum, and Stewe tries to contact operational command again on the radio.

'Surveillance vehicle Alpha,' he shouts.

'Receiving you,' a voice replies.

'I'm following him in the car down Linnégatan, heading towards Djurgården,' Stewe shouts into the radio. 'He's driving a red Volvo which . . .'

Stewe drops the radio handset and it falls into the foot-well in front of the passenger seat as his car hits a wooden barrier in front of a pile of sand. The front right wheel lifts from the ground and the car veers left, skirting round the hole in the road. He slams the clutch down and steers into the slide, and crosses into the other lane before regaining control of the car and hitting the accelerator again.

He chases the Volvo towards Narvavägen's dual carriageways and central tree-lined avenue. A bus is forced to brake hard by the Volvo and slides out across the junction, its back end crashing into a lamppost. Another driver swerves to miss the bus and drives straight through a bus-shelter. The glass sides shatter across the grass and pavement. A woman throws herself out of the way just in time and lands on the ground. The bus-driver is still trying to brake, the tyres lurch up onto the kerb and the roof of the bus tears a large branch from a tree.

Stewe follows the Volvo towards the Berwald Hall, pulls up alongside it and sees the driver aim a pistol at him. He brakes just as the shot goes off and passes through the side window, only just in front of his face. The car fills with swirling splinters of glass. The Volvo hits a stationary bicycle advertising Linda's Café. There's a crash as the bicycle hits the bonnet of the car, then flies over the roof before hitting the ground in front of Stewe's car. The tyres and suspension clatter loudly over the bicycle frame.

They take the sharp turn towards Strandvägen very fast, straight across the central reservation between trees. Stewe accelerates out of the curve. His tyres spin on the tarmac. They race on through the early morning traffic, hearing the shriek of brakes and a dull thud as two cars collide, then turn left at Berwald Hall, across the grass and onto Dag Hammarskjölds väg.

Stewe draws his pistol and puts it down among the broken glass on the passenger seat. His plan is to catch up with the

Volvo on Djurgårdsbrunnsvägen and try to incapacitate the driver from behind. Their speed is approaching 130 kilometres an hour as they pass the US Embassy behind its tall, military grey fence. Suddenly the Volvo leaves the road with a shriek of tyres, turning sharp left just after the Norwegian Embassy, up over the pavement and onto the footpath between the trees. Stewe reacts a little too late and is forced to make a wider curve, in front of a bus, across the pavement and through some low bushes. His tyres thud against the kerb as he goes past the Italian Cultural Institute. He crosses the pavement and swerves left onto Gärdesgatan, and sees the Volvo immediately.

It's standing in the middle of the intersection, approximately a hundred metres away, at the junction with Skarpögatan.

Stewe can see the driver inside the car through the rear window. He picks his pistol up from the seat, takes the safety catch off and drives slowly closer. The blue lights from a number of police cars on Valhallavägen are visible beyond the studios of Swedish Television. The black-clad man gets out of the red Volvo and starts to run down the road towards the German and Japanese Embassies. Stewe accelerates just as the Volvo explodes in a ball of flame and smoke. He feels the pressure wave on his face as the blast knocks out his hearing. The world is miraculously silent as he drives onto the pavement, into the billowing black smoke and across the burning debris. He can't see the driver anywhere. There's nowhere he could have gone. He speeds up and drives past the tall fences, stops when he reaches the end of the road, gets out of the car and starts to run back up it with his pistol in his hand.

The man has vanished. The world is still quiet, but now there's a strange rushing sound, as if a gale is blowing. Stewe has a good view of the road and the embassies behind their grey fences. The man couldn't have got any further in such a short space of time. He must have made his way into one of the embassy compounds, either through one of the gates with coded locks, or over a fence.

People have started to come out to see what caused the explosion. Stewe looks round, takes a few steps, turns and scans his surroundings. Suddenly he sees the man, inside the compound of the German Embassy, beside the main building. He's walking in a perfectly ordinary way, and simply opens the door of the main entrance and walks in.

Stewe Billgren lowers his pistol and tries to calm down and breathe more slowly. A loud ringing sound is filling his head now. He knows that the diplomatic missions enjoy territorial privileges, which prevents him from going after the man without express permission. He has to stop, there's nothing he can do: the authority of the Swedish police force stops at the gate to the embassy compound.

81

A uniformed police officer is standing ten metres in front of the roadblock on Sturegatan along the side of Humlegården as Joona Linna drives up at speed. The officer tries to direct him to turn back and take a different route, but Joona keeps driving, then pulls over to the kerb and gets out of the car. He flashes his ID, dodges under the plastic tape marking the cordon, and starts to run up Humlegårdsgatan towards the market-hall.

It's only eighteen minutes since he received the call, but the shooting is already over and ambulances are starting to arrive at the scene.

The head of the operation, Jenny Göransson, is just receiving a report about the outcome of the car chase through the diplomatic quarter. The perpetrator is believed to have entered the precinct of the German Embassy. Saga Bauer is standing outside the market-hall talking to a police officer who has a blanket round her shoulders. Saga catches Joona's eye and beckons him over. He walks over to the two women and nods at Saga.

'I thought I'd be the first here,' he says.

'You're too slow, Joona.'

'Clearly,' he says with a smile.

The woman with the blanket round her shoulders looks up and Joona and says hello.

'This is Mira Carlsson from Surveillance,' Saga says. 'She was one of the first to go into the market-hall, and she thinks she hit the perpetrator with a shot from her pistol.'

'But you didn't see his face?' Joona asks.

'No,' Mira replies.

Joona looks at the entrance to the market-hall, then turns to Saga.

'They said all surrounding buildings were going to be secure,' he mutters.

'The strategists must have thought the distance was too great to . . .'

'They were wrong,' Joona says, cutting her off.

'Yes,' Saga says, gesturing towards the market. 'He was behind this gate, and fired one shot through her window.'

'So I heard – she was lucky,' he says in a low voice.

The area around the main entrance to Östermalm market-hall is cordoned off, and small numbered signs indicate the first findings of the forensic search: a shoeprint and an empty cartridge from fully jacketed American precision ammunition. Further in, through the open doors, Joona can see some toma-toes that have rolled onto the floor, and the curved magazine from a Swedish AK 5 assault rifle.

'Stewe Billgren,' Saga says, 'Mira's colleague at Surveillance . . . he's the officer who followed the suspect to the diplomatic quarter and says he saw him go through the main entrance of the German Embassy.'

'Could he have been mistaken?'

'It's possible . . . We've contacted the Embassy, and they claim that . . .' She consults her notebook. 'They claim that there has been no unusual activity in the area.'

'Have you spoken to Billgren?'

'Yes.'

Saga gives Joona a serious look.

'There was an explosion, he can hardly hear anything, but he's sure of what he saw: he clearly saw the perpetrator go inside the Embassy.'

'He could have snuck out through the back.'

'We've got people surrounding the entire property now, and

we've got a helicopter in the air. We're waiting for permission to enter the precinct.'

Joona glances irritably at the market-stalls.

'That could take time.'

He takes out his phone and says, almost to himself:

'I'll call Klara Olofsdotter.'

Klara Olofsdotter is a senior prosecutor at the International Prosecution Authority. She answers on the second ring.

'I know it's you, Joona Linna,' she says without saying hello. 'And I know what you're calling about.'

'Then presumably you also know that we need to get in,' Joona says.

A trace of his incorrigible stubbornness creeps into his voice as he says this.

'It's not that easy. This is fucking sensitive stuff, if you'll pardon the expression. I've spoken to the Ambassador's secretary by phone,' Klara Olofsdotter says. 'And she claims that everything is as it should be at the Embassy.'

'We believe he's in there,' Joona says obstinately.

'But how could he have got into the Embassy?'

'He could be a German citizen, claiming to need consular assistance. They'd just opened for the day. He could be a Swedish employee with a passcard, or some sort of diplomatic status, possibly immunity. Or he could be being protected by someone, we don't know yet. Maybe he's a close relative of the Defence Attaché, or Joachim Rücker.'

'But we don't even know what he looks like,' she says. 'There are no witnesses, so how can we go into the Embassy without knowing what . . .?'

'I can get a witness,' Joona interrupts.

The line goes quiet for a few moments. Joona can hear Klara Olofsdotter breathing.

'Then I'll see to it that you get in.'

82

Joona Linna and Saga Bauer are standing in the secure apartment overlooking Östermalmstorg. None of the lights are on. The morning sky shines outside the windows. Penelope Fernandez is sitting on the floor, with her back against the innermost wall, pointing at the window.

'Yes, that's where the bullet came in,' Saga confirms quietly.

'The lamp saved my life,' Penelope mumbles, then lowers her hand.

They look at the remains of the lamp in the window, the dangling lead and broken plastic base.

'I turned it off to see better, so I could get a better view of what was happening out in the square,' Penelope says. 'The lamp started to sway, and he thought it was me, didn't he? He thought it was me moving, that the heat was from my body.'

Joona turns to Saga.

'Did he have an electro-optical sight?'

Saga nods and says:

'Yes, according to Jenny Göransson.'

'What?' Penelope asks.

'You're right – the lamp saved your life,' Joona replies.

'Oh, God,' she moans.

Joona looks at her calmly and his grey eyes shimmer.

'Penelope,' he says seriously. 'You've seen his face, haven't you? Not this time, but before. You told us you didn't, though. I understand that you're frightened, but . . . I want you to nod your head if you think you can describe him.'

She wipes her cheeks quickly and then looks up at the tall detective and shakes her head.

'Can you tell us anything about him?' Saga asks gently.

Penelope thinks about the detective superintendent's voice, his soft Finnish accent, and wonders how he can know that she saw the killer's face. She did see him, but doesn't know if she could describe him. It happened so quickly. She only caught a glimpse of him, with the rain in his face, moments after he had killed Björn and Ossian.

She wishes she could suppress every memory of it.

But his weary, almost troubled face keeps lighting up in the white flash of the lightning.

Saga Bauer goes over to Joona, who is standing at the window with the bullet-hole in it, reading a long text message on his phone.

'Klara Olofsdotter has spoken to the Chief Legal Officer, who's spoken to the Ambassador,' Joona says. 'An hour from now, three people will have access to the Embassy for forty-five minutes.'

'We should head out there now,' Saga says.

'There's no rush,' Joona says, his gaze lingering on the square.

Journalists are jostling outside the police cordon around the market-hall.

'Did you tell the prosecutor that we need armed backup?' Saga asks.

'We'll have to discuss that with the German security guards.'

'Who's going in? How do we decide?'

Joona turns to her.

'I'm thinking . . . the officer who followed the fixer . . .'

'Stewe Billgren,' she says.

'Yes, Stewe Billgren,' Joona says. 'Would he be able to identify him?'

'He didn't see his face, no one has seen his face,' Saga replies, then goes and sits on the floor next to Penelope.

She sits beside her for a while, leaning against the wall just like she is, breathing slowly, before she asks her first question.

'What does he want with you? The man who's after you – do you know why all this is happening?'

'No,' Penelope says carefully.

'He wants a photograph that you had stuck to the glass door in your flat,' Joona says with his back to her.

She lowers her head and nods weakly.

'Do you know why he wants the photograph?' Saga asks.

'No,' she replies, and starts crying.

Saga waits a few moments, then says:

'Björn tried to blackmail Carl Palmcrona for money, and . . .'

'I didn't know anything,' Penelope interrupts with hard-won calmness in her voice. 'I wasn't part of it.'

'We realise that,' Joona says.

Saga gently puts her hand on Penelope's.

'Were you the photographer?' she asks.

'Me? No, I . . . the picture was just sent to the Swedish Peace and . . . I'm the chairperson, so . . .'

She falls silent.

'Was it sent through the post?' Joona asks.

'Yes.'

'Who from?'

'I don't know,' she replies quickly.

'There was no letter with it?' he asks.

'No, I don't think so. I mean, not that I saw.'

'Just an envelope containing a picture?'

She nods.

'Have you still got the envelope?'

'No.'

'What did it say on it?'

'Just my name and "Swedish Peace and Arbitration Society" . . . just the name, not our post office box number, 2088.'

'Penelope Fernandez,' Saga says, 'Swedish Peace and Arbitration Society.'

'You opened the envelope and took out the photograph,' Joona says. 'What did you see at that moment? What did the photograph mean to you?'

'What it meant?'

'What did you see when you looked at it? Did you recognise the people on it?'

'Yes . . . three of them, but . . .'

She falls silent.

'Tell us what you thought when you looked at the picture.'

'That someone must have seen me on television,' she says, then collects herself for a moment before going on. 'I thought that it was so damn typical . . . Palmcrona is supposed to be neutral, that's the whole point . . . and there he was at the opera, drinking champagne with the boss of Silencia Defence and an arms dealer active in Africa and the Middle East . . . It's actually a scandal.'

'What were you thinking of doing with the picture?'

'Nothing,' she replies. 'There was nothing we could do with it, that's just the way things are, but at the same time . . . I remember thinking that . . . at least now I knew where I had Palmcrona.'

'Yes.'

'It reminded me of those idiots at the Migration Office, whenever it was, drinking champagne because they'd managed to expel a family. They were celebrating after turning down a desperate family's application for asylum in Sweden, a family with a sick child . . .'

Penelope tails off again.

'Do you know who the fourth person in the picture is? The woman?'

Penelope shakes her head.

'Agathe al-Haji,' Saga says.

'Is that Agathe al-Haji?'

'Yes.'

'But why was . . .?'

Penelope breaks off and stares at Saga with her big brown eyes.

'Do you know when the photograph was taken?' Saga asks.

'No, but the warrant for al-Bashir's arrest was issued in March 2009, and . . .'

Penelope breaks off abruptly again, and her face turns bright red.

'What is it?' Saga asks, almost in a whisper.

'The photograph was taken after that,' Penelope says in a shaky voice. 'Wasn't it? The photograph was taken after the president's arrest warrant was issued.'

'What makes you say that?' Saga asks.

'That's right, isn't it?' Penelope says again.

'Yes,' Joona replies.

All the colour drains from her cheeks.

'The deal with Kenya,' Penelope says, her mouth trembling. 'That's what's going on in the picture, that's what this is all about, the Kenyan contract, that's what Palmcrona's doing, authorising the sale of ammunition to Kenya. I knew there was something dodgy about that, I just knew it.'

'Go on,' Joona says.

'Kenya has long-standing contracts in place with Britain, of course. It's Sudan that wants the weapons. The shipment is only going to be delivered via Kenya, for onward transportation to Sudan and Darfur.'

'Yes,' Saga says. 'We believe that's the plan.'

'But that's illegal, it's worse than illegal . . . it's treachery, it's a breach of international law, it's a crime against humanity . . .'

She falls silent again.

'That's why all this has been happening,' she eventually says, very quietly. 'Not because Björn was trying to blackmail Palmcrona.'

'His attempted blackmail only meant that these people realised that there was a photograph that could expose them.'

'I just thought the photograph was embarrassing,' Penelope says. 'Embarrassing, but no more than that.'

'From their perspective, it all started when Palmcrona phoned to let them know about the attempted blackmail,' Saga explains. 'They didn't know that the photograph existed until then. Palmcrona's message alarmed them. They couldn't be sure how much or how little the picture exposed. But they realised of course that it wasn't good. We don't know exactly what they were thinking. Maybe they thought that it was either you or Björn who photographed them in that box in the concert hall.'

'Although . . .'

'They couldn't be sure how much you knew. But they weren't prepared to take any risks.'

'I get it,' Penelope says. 'And the same thing still applies, doesn't it?'

'Yes.'

Penelope nods to herself.

'In their eyes, I could be the only witness to the deal,' she says.

'They've staked an awful lot of money on this contract with Kenya.'

'It's not on,' she whispers.

'Sorry, what do you mean?'

Penelope raises her head, looks Saga in the eye and says:

'They can't be allowed to pump ammunition into Darfur,' she says. 'It's not on. I've been there twice . . .'

'They don't care, it's just about money,' Saga says.

'No, it's about . . . it's about so much more,' Penelope says, and turns to look at the wall. 'It's about . . .'

She falls silent and remembers the crunching sound as a clay figure was crushed beneath a goat's hooves. A tiny woman made of sun-dried clay, crushed to dust. A child laughed and shouted that it was Nufi's ugly mother. *All Furs must die, they must all be wiped out*, the other children shouted, grinning as they did so.

'What are you trying to say?' Saga ask.

Penelope looks at her, gazes at her for a few moments, but doesn't reply. She sinks back into memories of her month in Kenya and south-western Sudan.

After a long, hot drive she had arrived at the camp in Kubbum, south-west of Nyala in Janub Darfur in west Sudan. She spent her first day struggling alongside Jane and the man called Grey to help the victims of the Janjaweed's raids.

That night Penelope woke up when three teenage boys belonging to the militia started screaming in Arabic that they were going to kill the slaves. They walked down the middle of the road, and one of them had a revolver in his hand. Penelope stood at the window watching them as they suddenly walked over and shot an old man cooking sweet potatoes.

The boys walked out into the road again and looked round, then pointed and came over to the barracks where Penelope and Jane lived. Penelope held her breath as she heard them stomp about on the veranda, talking excitedly to each other.

Suddenly they kicked in the door of the barracks and marched into the corridor. Penelope lay motionless beneath her bed, reciting the Lord's Prayer to herself. They overturned furniture and kicked it to pieces. Then she heard the boys out in the road again. One of them was laughing and shouting that the slaves would die. Penelope crept out and went over to the window again. The boys had taken Jane, they dragged her by her hair and threw her down in the middle of the road. The door to the other barrack flew open and Grey came out with a machete in his hand. The skinny boy walked towards him. Grey was a good head taller than the boy, and very broad-shouldered.

'What do you want?' Grey asked.

His face was sombre and wet with sweat.

The skinny boy didn't answer him, he just raised the revolver and shot him in the stomach. The blast echoed between the buildings. Grey stumbled backwards and fell, tried to get back up, then just lay there clutching one hand to his stomach.

'One dead Fur,' one of the other boys holding Jane shouted.

The other boy forced her legs apart. She struggled and spoke to them constantly in a hard, calm voice. Grey shouted something to the boys. The skinny boy with the revolver walked over to him again, screamed at him, pressed the barrel of the revolver to his forehead and pulled the trigger. It clicked, and he tried again and again, but the revolver was empty, and clicked uselessly six times. The atmosphere out on the road changed, then the doors of other barracks opened and African women emerged. The teenagers let go of Jane and started to run. Penelope saw five women chase after them. She grabbed the blanket from her bed, unlocked the door, rushed through the corridor and out into the road. She ran over to Jane and put the blanket round her, and helped her to her feet.

'Get back inside,' Jane said. 'They could come back with more ammunition, you mustn't be out here . . .'

Jane spent the rest of that night and most of the following

morning at the operating table. She didn't go back to bed in the barrack until ten o'clock in the morning, when she was sure she'd done enough to save Grey's life. When evening came she was back at work as usual, and the following day the routine in the hospital tent was back to normal. The young boys helped her, but were more wary, and sometimes pretended not to hear what she said when they thought she was being too demanding.

'No,' Penelope whispered.

'What are you trying to say?' Saga repeats.

Penelope thinks to herself that they mustn't be allowed to export ammunition to Sudan.

'They mustn't,' she says, then tails off.

'You were better protected in the underground room,' Saga says.

'Protected? No one can protect me,' Penelope replies.

'We know where he is, he's in the German Embassy, and we've surrounded the building . . .'

'But you haven't got him,' Penelope interrupts in a raised voice.

'We believe he's injured, he was shot, and we're going to go in and . . .'

'I want to come,' Penelope says.

'Why would . . .'

'Because I've seen his face,' she replies.

Both Joona and Saga start at this. Penelope looks at Joona.

'You were right,' she says. 'I did see him.'

'We haven't got long, but there's time to put together a Photofit picture,' Saga says anxiously.

'There's no point,' Joona says. 'We can't take a person into custody from another country's embassy on the basis of their resemblance to a Photofit picture.'

'What if he's identified by a witness?' Penelope says, standing up and looking him calmly in the eye.

83

The perpetrator

Penelope is standing between Saga Bauer and Joona Linna behind an armoured police van on Skarpögatan in front of the Japanese Embassy. They're only fifty metres from the entrance to the German Embassy. She can feel the weight of the bullet-proof vest over her shoulders and pressing across her chest.

In five minutes three people will gain access to the embassy compound for forty-five minutes to try to identify and arrest the suspected perpetrator.

Penelope silently consents to Joona placing an extra pistol in a holster behind her back. He adjusts the angle several times so that he can easily grab a reserve weapon from her.

'She doesn't want that,' Saga says.

'It's okay,' Penelope says.

'We don't know what we're going to find in there,' Joona says. 'I hope it's all going to pass off calmly, but if it doesn't, this weapon could make all the difference.'

The entire area is crawling with Swedish police officers, people from the Security Police, SWAT teams and paramedics.

Joona Linna looks at the remains of the burned-out Volvo. There's hardly anything left but the chassis. Pieces of the vehicle lie scattered across the junction. Erixon has already found a detonator and traces of nitroamines.

'Probably hexogen,' he says, pushing his glasses up his nose.

'Plastic explosives,' Joona says, looking at his watch.

An Alsatian moves restlessly about in front of a police officer, then lies down on the tarmac panting with its tongue out.

Saga, Joona and Penelope are escorted by a rapid response team to the fence, where four German military police officers are waiting, their faces impassive.

'Don't worry,' Saga says gently to Penelope. 'You're just going to identify the perpetrator, and once you've done that we'll escort you out. The Embassy's security personnel will wait until you're safe before they remove him.'

A heavily built military police officer with a freckled face opens the gate, lets them into the loading area, welcomes them in a friendly voice and introduces himself as Karl Mann, head of security.

They walk with him to the main entrance.

The morning air is still cool.

'We're dealing with an extremely dangerous individual,' Joona says.

'So we understand, we've been briefed,' Karl Mann says. 'But I've been here all morning and there are only diplomatic staff and German citizens here.'

'Can you get hold of a list?' Saga asks.

'I can tell you that we're looking at footage from our security cameras,' Karl Mann says. 'Because I have a feeling your colleague must be mistaken. I think the perpetrator went past the gates, but instead of going inside, just went round the Embassy and across the grass towards the television studios.'

'That's possible,' Joona says calmly.

'How many people are in the Embassy?' Saga asks.

'The consular section is open and right now four cases are being dealt with.'

'Four people?'

'Yes.'

'And how many staff?' Saga asks.

'Fifteen.'

'And how many security personnel?'

'There are five of us right now,' he replies.

'No one else?'

'No.'

'No workmen or . . .'

'No.'

'So, twenty-five people in total,' Saga says.

'Do you want to start by taking a look round for yourselves?' Karl Mann says mildly.

'We'd like you with us, if possible,' Saga says.

'How many?' Karl Mann asks.

'As many as possible, and as heavily armed as possible,' Joona replies.

'You really must think he's dangerous,' he smiles. 'I can let you have another two men.'

'We don't know what's likely to happen if . . .'

'You believe he's been shot in the shoulder,' Karl Mann interjects. 'I can't say that I feel particularly scared.'

'Perhaps he never came in, perhaps he's already left the Embassy,' Joona says quietly. 'But if he is here, we need to be prepared for casualties.'

In silence Joona, Saga and Penelope walk through the corridor on the ground floor in the company of three military police officers armed with assault rifles and shock grenades. The Embassy building has been undergoing renovations for several years while the staff moved to premises on Artillerigatan. Despite the fact that work hasn't yet been completed, they moved back in during the spring. There's a smell of paint and freshly cut wood, and some of the floors are still covered by protective paper.

'First we'd like to see the visitors, anyone who isn't a member of staff,' Joona says.

'Yes, I anticipated that,' Karl Mann says.

Feeling oddly calm inside, Penelope walks between Saga Bauer and Joona Linna. For some reason she can't imagine she's going to encounter the killer here at the Embassy. It feels far too ordinary and calm a location.

Then she suddenly notices Joona become more alert: his pattern of movement beside her changes, and she sees him glance at the doors and ventilation grilles.

An alarm starts to sound through the walls and the group

389

stop walking. Karl Mann takes out his radio and exchanges a few words of German with a colleague.

'The alarm on one of the doors is playing up,' he explains in Swedish. 'The door is locked, but the alarm is acting as if the door has been open for thirty seconds.'

They carry on along the corridor and Penelope Fernandez becomes more aware of the pistol rubbing against her back with each step she takes.

'Martin Schenkel, our Business Attaché, is in the office straight ahead,' Karl Mann says. 'He's got a visitor at the moment, Roland Lindkvist.'

'We'd like to meet them,' Joona says.

'He's asked not to be disturbed before lunch.'

Joona doesn't answer.

Saga takes hold of Penelope's upper arm and they stop while the others walk on towards the closed door.

'Wait a moment,' the military police officer says to Joona, then knocks.

A voice answers, he opens the door, goes inside and closes it behind him.

Joona looks over towards a room with no door. The doorway is covered with industrial grey polythene. He can make out a stack of plasterboard inside the room. The plastic bulges outwards like a sail, making a faint rustling sound. He's just taken a step towards the plastic when there's a noise behind the closed door of the Business Attaché's office, voices, followed by a heavy thud. Penelope moves backwards, she just wants to get away.

'We'll wait here,' Saga says, drawing her pistol.

Penelope thinks back to how this Embassy was occupied in the spring of 1975 by a group calling themselves Kommando Holger Meins. They held twelve people hostage. She remembers that their main demand was that Andreas Baader, Ulrike Meinhof, Gudrun Ensslin and another twenty-three members of the Red Army Faction should be released from prison in West Germany. These were the corridors where they ran, shouting at each other, this was where they dragged Ambassador Dietrich Stoecker by his hair and pushed Heinz Hillegaart's bloodstained body down the stairs. She can't recall what negotiations are supposed to have taken place, but after German Chancellor Helmut Schmidt told the Swedish Prime Minister Olof Palme that they weren't going to give in to the demands, two of the hostages were shot. Karl-Heinz Dellwo screamed in a shrill voice that he would shoot one hostage every hour until their demands were met.

Now Penelope watches Joona Linna turn and walk back to the door to the Business Attaché's office. The two other military police officers are standing completely still. Joona draws his large, silver-coloured pistol, removes the safety catch and then knocks on the door.

A smell is spreading through the corridor, as if someone has left a pan on the stove.

Joona knocks again, listens, and hears a monotonous voice; it seems to be repeating the same phrase over and over again. He waits a few seconds, hides the pistol behind his back and presses the handle down.

Head of Security Karl Mann is standing immediately below the ceiling light with his assault rifle hanging by his hip. He looks at Joona, then turns to the other man, who is sitting in an armchair at the back of the room.

'Herr Schenkel, this is the Swedish detective superintendent,' he says.

Books and files are scattered across the floor, as if they had been swept off the desk in anger. Business Attaché Martin Schenkel is sitting in an armchair staring at a television, which is showing a live broadcast of a football match from Beijing, DFB-Elf against the Chinese national team.

'Weren't you supposed to be seeing a visitor, Roland Lindkvist?' Joona asks in a reserved tone of voice.

'He's gone,' Martin Schenkel replies without taking his eyes off the screen.

They carry on along the corridor. Karl Mann is in a worse mood now, snapping at the two military policemen. A woman in a pale grey knitted cardigan quickly crosses the brown protective paper covering the freshly polished floor in the next corridor.

'Who's that?' Joona asks.

'The Ambassador's secretary,' Karl Mann replies.

'We'd like to talk to her and . . .'

A howling alarm suddenly rings out throughout the whole building, and a pre-recorded voice announces in German that this isn't a fire drill, and that everyone should leave the building immediately and not use the lift.

84

The fire

Karl Mann talks quickly into his comms radio, then starts walking towards the stairs.

'There's a fire upstairs,' he says tersely.

'How far has it spread?' Joona asks, matching his pace.

'They don't know yet, but we're evacuating the Embassy, there are eleven people up there.'

Karl Mann takes a foam extinguisher from a red-fronted cabinet and pulls out the pin.

'I'll take Penelope out,' Saga calls.

'He's the one who started the fire,' Penelope says. 'He's going to disappear while they try to put the fire out.'

Joona heads towards the stairs with the three military policemen. Their steps echo between the bare concrete walls. They run silently up the stairs and along the corridor on the upper floor. There's a strong smell of smoke, and grey veils of smoke are creeping along beneath the ceiling.

Karl Mann opens a door and looks into an empty office. Joona opens the next door, there's no one there either. They keep moving.

'It looks like the fire's in the Schiller Room, there's a kitchen next to it,' Karl Mann says, pointing.

At the end of the corridor a steady stream of black smoke is seeping out from beneath the double doors. The smoke creeps up the walls and doors and spreads across the ceiling like murky water.

Somewhere a woman screams. There's a low rumble in the building, like thunder deep within the fabric of the Embassy. Suddenly there's an explosion behind the double doors, as if a large pane of glass has shattered in the heat.

'We need to get everyone out,' Joona says. 'It's . . .'

Karl Mann gestures to Joona to stop when he gets a call on his radio. He puts the fire extinguisher down on the floor and answers, exchanges a few words and then turns to the group.

'Okay, listen up,' he says in a firm voice. 'Security control have just seen a man dressed in black on their monitors, he's in the men's bathroom, and there's a pistol on one of the washbasins.'

'That's him,' Joona says.

Karl Mann calls the control room and lowers his voice as he asks about the man's location inside the bathroom.

'Two metres to the right of the door,' Karl Mann says. 'He's bleeding heavily from his shoulder and is sitting on the floor . . . but the window is open, it's possible that he's going to try to escape that way.'

They run across the brown paper covering the floor, past a stepladder, and come to a halt behind Karl Mann. It's noticeably warmer here and the smoke is billowing across the ceiling like a broken water pipe. The building is creaking and groaning, and it feels like the floor is shaking beneath their feet.

'What's he armed with?' Joona asks quietly.

'They could only see the pistol on the washbasin, not . . .'

'Ask if he's got a rucksack with him,' Joona says. 'Because he carries . . .'

'I'm leading this operation,' Karl Mann hisses.

He gestures towards his men, they quickly check their assault rifles, then follow him into the cloakroom. Joona feels like warning them again as he watches them go. He knows that their standard tactics won't work against the fixer. They're like flies approaching a spider. One by one they're going to get caught in his net.

Joona feels the smoke sting his eyes.

A spider spins its webs out of two different sorts of silk, he thinks. Sticky threads to catch prey, and threads to climb on without getting caught.

Joona takes the safety catch off his Smith & Wesson and cautiously follows the military police officers. They've already taken up positions outside the door to the men's toilets. One of them, his long blond hair tucked under his helmet, removes the pin from a shock grenade. He opens the door, rolls the grenade in across the tiled floor, then closes the door. There's a muffled blast and the other officer opens the door and aims his weapon into the darkness. Karl Mann gestures impatiently with his hand. Without a moment's hesitation the blond officer rushes in with his assault rifle raised and the butt against his shoulder.

A jolt of anxiety hits Joona's heart. Then he hears the blond military policeman say something in a frightened voice. It sounds almost childish in its vulnerability. A moment later there's a powerful explosion. The military policeman is thrown back out of the bathroom in a whirl of smoke and brick-dust. The door is torn from its hinges. The second officer drops his gun, falls sideways and hits one knee on the floor. The pressure wave makes Joona take a step back. The blond military policeman is lying on his back in the corridor. His mouth is open and there's blood between his teeth. He's unconscious, and a large piece of shrapnel has penetrated his thigh. Bright red blood is pumping rhythmically onto the floor. Joona rushes over and drags him further away, feeling the warmth of the gushing blood on his hands as he fashions a makeshift tourniquet from the man's belt and a torn shirt-sleeve.

One of the men is huddled in a ball. He's sobbing in a scared, shaking voice.

Two military police officers are helping a grey-haired man along the corridor, his face is sooty and he can hardly walk. A woman has wrapped her cardigan over her mouth and is hurrying along the passageway with wide, frightened eyes.

With his pistol in his hand, Karl Mann goes into the bathroom, across the shattered tiles and mirrors on the floor. He finds the fixer lying on the floor. The man is still alive. His legs are twitching and his arms are fumbling helplessly. His chin and large parts of his face have been blown off. Karl Mann looks round, sees the metal wire and concludes that the man was probably planning to lay a trap using a hand-grenade, before the shock grenade caught him by surprise and he dropped his own grenade.

'We'll evacuate everyone else,' Karl Mann whispers to himself, and leaves the bathroom.

Joona wipes the blood from his hands and calls the command centre to request an ambulance as he watches Penelope emerge from the stairwell. Saga is following her along the corridor. Penelope's eyes look black, as if she's been crying for hours. Saga is trying to calm her down and hold her back, but she pulls free.

'Where is he?' Penelope demands in an uneven voice. 'I want to see him.'

'We have to get out,' Joona calls. 'This corridor is going to be in flames any moment now.'

Penelope pushes past Joona towards the men's bathroom, and looks inside the shattered room. She sees the man on the floor, his body twitching, his face a bloody mess. She lets out a moan, stumbles backward, out into the corridor again, and reaches out to the wall for support, pulling down a framed letter from former Chancellor Willy Brandt. It slides to the floor and the glass breaks, but it remains upright against the wall.

Penelope is breathing quickly, her stomach is churning, she swallows and feels Saga try to hold onto her and lead her back towards the stairs.

'It's not him,' Penelope whimpers.

'We have to get out,' Saga says comfortingly, and leads her away.

Paramedics in protective masks are carrying the injured military policeman out. There's another explosion, like a deep exhalation of breath. Splinters of glass and wood fly through the corridor. A man stumbles and falls over, but manages to get to his feet again. Smoke is pouring through an open door. A thickset man is standing still in the corridor as blood runs from his nose, down over his shirt and tie. The military police are shouting to everyone to make their way to the emergency exit. Flames are flickering from the doorway to one of the offices. The protective paper on the floor catches light and curls up in the flames. Two people come running past, hand in hand. A woman whose summer dress is on fire is screaming, and one of the military police officers sprays her with white foam.

The smoke is making Joona cough, but he still makes his way into the men's bathroom to survey the devastation from the grenade blast. The fixer is lying completely still now, his face provisionally wrapped in compresses and a gauze bandage. Dark red blood is pulsing from the gunshot hole in his black jacket. The first-aid box is on the floor, its plasters and compresses scattered among the dust and broken tiles. The walls are soot-stained and a lot of the tiles have come off. The cubicles have been demolished, the mirrors shattered, and water is pouring across the floor from a broken pipe.

In one of the washbasins is a Heckler & Koch pistol and seven magazines. Behind the toilet in the remains of one of the cubicles is the man's empty black nylon rucksack.

He can hear cries, frightened voices and barked orders. Karl Mann appears in the men's bathroom with two paramedics.

'I want someone to watch him,' Joona says, gesturing towards the fixer as the paramedics lift the body onto a stretcher and strap him down.

'He's going to die before the ambulance reaches the hospital,' Karl Mann replies, and coughs into his hand.

'I still want you to keep him under observation for as long as he's on Embassy property.'

Karl Mann looks Joona in the eye, then quickly orders one of his men to watch the prisoner and hand him over to the Swedish police.

Thick, black smoke is billowing along the corridor, and there's a loud roaring, crackling noise. People are coughing and screaming. Everyone is rushing to get out with looks of terror on their faces. Karl Mann takes a call on his radio, squats down beneath the smoke and talks quickly.

'One person's still missing, he should be up here,' he says, and coughs again.

Joona takes a long stride over the door lying on the floor, walks over to a closed door and reaches for the handle. The lights flicker and then go out. The only light in the smoky corridor comes from the flames and sparks swirling out from a doorway.

The crackling and rumbling is getting louder, and there are small explosions as metal contorts and breaks.

Joona looks at Karl Mann and motions to him to move back. He draws his pistol and opens the door slightly, steps back, waits a few seconds, then peers into the darkness.

He can't see anything, just the black outlines of office furniture etched against the closed blinds.

'Evacuate the building!' someone shouts behind him.

Joona turns round and sees four firemen in full breathing gear hurrying along the corridor, spreading out and systematically searching the rooms.

Before Joona has time to warn them, one of the firemen shines his bright torch into the room. Two eyes glow in the darkness, and a labrador barks tiredly.

'We'll take over,' one of the men says. 'Can you get out on your own?'

'One person's missing,' Karl tells them.

'Be careful,' Joona says, and looks the young fireman in the eye.

'Come on!' Karl calls to him.

'I just want to look at something.'

Joona coughs, goes back into men's bathroom, sees the blood on the floor and walls, then hurries into the remains of one of the cubicles and snatches up the fixer's black rucksack.

85

Penelope's legs are shaking, and she's leaning against the fence with one hand, staring down at the ground. She's fighting the urge to throw up. The image of the men's bathroom is shimmering in front of her eyes. The devastated face, the teeth and all the blood.

The weight of the bulletproof vest makes her want to sit down right where she's standing. The sound of her surroundings reaches her in waves. She can hear the wailing siren of the second ambulance. Police officers are shouting at each other, talking into their radios. She sees paramedics run past with a stretcher. It's the man from the bathroom. He's lying on his back. His face is covered, but the blood has already soaked through the compresses.

Saga is walking towards Penelope with a nurse. She says she thinks that Penelope is going into a state of shock.

'It wasn't him,' Penelope sobs as they wrap a blanket round her.

'A doctor will come and take a look at you in a moment,' the nurse says. 'But I can give you something to help calm you down. Have you ever had any problems with your liver?'

When Penelope shakes her head the nurse hands her a blue pill.

'It has to be swallowed whole . . . it's half a milligram of Xanor,' she explains.

'Xanor,' Penelope repeats, looking at the pill in her hand.

'It'll help calm you down, it's not at all dangerous,' the nurse explains before hurrying away.

'I'll get you some water,' Saga says, and walks off towards one of the police vans.

Penelope's fingers feel cold. She looks at her hand, then at the little blue pill.

Joona Linna is still in the building. They're continuing to bring more people out, soot-smeared and suffering from smoke inhalation. The shocked diplomats have gathered by the fence in front of the Japanese Embassy while they wait to be taken to the Karolinska Hospital. A woman in a dark-blue skirt and cardigan sinks to the ground, weeping openly. A police officer sits down beside her, puts her arms round her shoulders and tries to reassure her. One of the diplomats keeps licking his lips, wiping his hands on a towel over and over again, as if he could never get clean again. An older man in a crumpled suit is standing stiffly talking on the phone. The Military Attaché, a middle-aged woman with dyed red hair, has dried her tears and is trying to help, even though she looks badly dazed as she holds a bag of blood substitute while the paramedics move one of the casualties. One man with bandages on his burned hands has spent a while sitting with a blanket round his shoulders, his face lowered, but now he's standing up, and drops the blanket on the ground as he starts to walk slowly up the road, staring distantly at the fence.

One military police officer is standing with one hand on a flagpole, crying.

The man with the burned hands carries on walking in the clear morning light, and turns right into Gärdesgatan.

Penelope suddenly gasps for breath. Like an injection of ice, a horrifying realisation spreads through her body. She didn't see his face, but she saw his back. The man with the injured hands. She knows it's him, her pursuer, walking toward Gärdet, ambling slowly away from the police and paramedics. She didn't need to see his face, because she's seen his back and neck before, on the boat beneath the Skurusund Bridge, back when Viola and Björn were still alive.

Penelope opens her hand and lets the blue pill fall to the ground.

With her heart pounding she starts to walk towards him, letting her blanket fall to the ground, just as he had done. She turns into Gärdesgatan and speeds up. She starts to run when she sees him slip in amongst a clump of trees straight ahead of her. He looks weak, probably because of the blood he's lost after being shot in the shoulder, and she already knows he won't be able to outrun her. Some jackdaws fly up from the treetops and flap away. Penelope heads into the trees, feeling full of power as she strides through the grass and catches sight of him fifty metres away. He stumbles and reaches out his hand to steady himself against a tree. The bandage comes loose and dangles limply from his fingers. She runs after him as he leaves the shelter of the trees and starts to limp across the large expanse of sunlit grass. Without stopping she draws the pistol that Joona Linna has strapped to her back, looks at it, removes the safety catch as she moves between the trees, then she slows down and holds the gun out with her arms straight, and aims at his legs.

'Stop,' she whispers, and squeezes the trigger.

The gun fires, the recoil jolts her arm and shoulder, and the powder scorches the back of her hand.

The bullet disappears and Penelope sees the man try to run.

You shouldn't have touched my sister, she thinks.

The man crosses a footpath, stops and clutches his shoulder, then carries on across the grass.

Penelope runs after him, emerging into the sunlight, gets closer and crosses the path that he's just passed, and raises the gun again.

'Stop!' she shouts.

The shot goes off and she sees the bullet tear into the grass ten metres in front of him. Penelope feels adrenalin pumping through her body, and she feels perfectly clear and focused. She aims at his legs and fires. She hears the shot, feels the recoil in her arm, and sees the bullet go in through the back of his knee and out through his kneecap. He screams out loud in pain and falls to the grass. He tries to keep moving, but she closes in on him, marching towards him as he uses a birch tree for support and tries to get back on his feet.

Stop, Penelope thinks, and raises the pistol again. You killed

Viola, you drowned her in a bucket and then you killed Björn.

'You murdered my little sister,' she says out loud, and fires again.

The shot hits him in his left foot and blood sprays across the grass.

When Penelope reaches him he's leaning back against the tree, his head is hanging, his chin resting on his chest. He's bleeding heavily, gasping for breath like an animal, but is otherwise completely still.

She stops in front of him, stands with her feet wide apart on the grass in the shade of the tree, and aims the pistol at him again.

'Why?' she asks in a low voice. 'Why is my sister dead? Why is . . .'

She breaks off, swallows, then kneels down so she can see his face.

'I want you to look at me when I shoot.'

The man moistens his mouth and tries to raise his head. It's too heavy, he can't do it. He's clearly on the brink of passing out through lack of blood. She takes aim at him with the pistol but stops herself again, reaches out with her other hand, lifts his chin and looks at him. She clenches her jaw hard when she sees those weary features again, the face she saw during the storm out on Kymmendö. Now she remembers the calm in those eyes, and the deep scar across his mouth. He looks just as calm now. Penelope has time to think how odd it is that he isn't at all afraid of her when he suddenly lunges at her. He moves with unexpected speed, grabs her by the hair and yanks her towards him. There's so much strength in his arm that she falls forward and hits her head against his chest. She doesn't have time to pull away before he changes his grip, grabs hold of her wrist and twists the gun from her hand. With all the strength she can muster she throws her arms out and kicks hard, and falls backwards onto the grass. When she looks up again he is already pointing the pistol at her, and fires two shots in quick succession.

86

The white trunk of the birch

It isn't until Detective Superintendent Joona Linna emerges from the stairwell in the Embassy and hurries along the ground-floor corridor that he feels the strain in his lungs and how badly his eyes are stinging. He has to get outside, has to breathe fresh air. He coughs, leans against the wall, then keeps going. He hears another explosion from up above, and a ceiling lamp comes loose and crashes to the floor in front of him. He can hear the sirens of the emergency vehicles outside. He quickly walks the last few steps towards the main entrance of the Embassy. On the paved driveway in front of the door there are six German military police officers managing the provisional security arrangements. Joona breathes clean air into his lungs, coughs, and looks round. Two fire-trucks are aiming their ladders at the Embassy. The street outside the gates is full of police officers and paramedics. Karl Mann is lying on the grass and a doctor is leaning over him listening to his lungs. Penelope Fernandez is walking slowly along the fence of the Japanese Embassy with a blanket round her shoulders.

Joona went back into the men's bathroom at the last minute to retrieve the rucksack that had been pushed in behind one of the toilets. It was a spur-of-the-moment decision: he couldn't understand why the fixer would have wanted to hide an empty rucksack when he had left his pistol and magazines fully visible in a washbasin.

He coughs again, opens the coarse nylon rucksack and looks inside it. It isn't completely empty. It contains three passports and an attack knife with fresh blood on the blade.

Who have you hurt now? Joona silently asks.

He looks at the knife again. The white blade is coated in sintered metallic powder, and the blood has started to congeal. He then looks around again, at the ambulances and people on the other side of the Embassy gates. A woman in a burned dress is lying on a stretcher, holding another woman's hand. An older man with soot stains on his forehead is talking on his phone with a completely blank look on his face.

Joona realises his mistake, drops the rucksack and the bloody knife on the ground and runs to the gate, yelling to the guard to let him through.

He rushes out of the Embassy compound, past some of his colleagues, stepping over the plastic police cordon and pushing through the journalists into the middle of the road. He stops in front of a bright yellow ambulance that's about to drive away.

'Have you taken a look at the injury to his arm?' he calls as he holds up his ID.

'What do you mean?'

'The patient who was injured in the explosion, he had an injury to his shoulder, and I . . .'

'That was hardly the priority, considering . . .'

'I need to look at that injury,' Joona says, cutting him off.

The ambulance driver is about to protest again, but something in Joona's voice stops him, and he does as he says.

Joona goes round to the back of the ambulance and opens the doors. The face of the man on the stretcher is completely covered with compresses, he has an oxygen mask over his nose and a suction tube leading to what's left of his mouth. One of the paramedics quickly cuts open the black jacket and shirt and uncovers the injury to his shoulder.

It isn't a gunshot wound. There's no doubt that it was inflicted with a knife, a deep stab-wound.

Joona gets out of the ambulance, scans the area and his eyes meet Saga's through the crowd of people and vehicles. She's holding a plastic cup of water, but as soon as she sees the look on his face she throws the cup down and runs towards him.

'He's getting away again,' he says to himself. 'We can't let him get away.'

Joona looks round, thinking about the fact when he rushed out from the Embassy just now, he saw Penelope Fernandez walking along the fence of the Japanese Embassy, with a blanket round her shoulders, then she turned into Gärdesgatan.

'Get a rifle,' Joona yells, and starts to run.

He follows the line of the fence, turns right and looks round, but he can't see Penelope or the fixer anywhere.

A woman is letting her Dalmatians run loose on the grass beyond the Italian Cultural Institute.

Joona rushes past a dazzling white building, draws his pistol and thinks that the fixer was rescued from the smoke-filled Embassy along with everyone else.

Saga shouts something behind him but he doesn't hear what, his heart is beating too fast, and there's a roaring sound inside his head.

He's quickening his pace even more, running towards a small patch of trees, when he suddenly hears a pistol shot. He stumbles into a ditch, struggles up a slope and rushes into the trees.

More pistol shots, short and sharp.

Joona pushes through the dense branches and emerges onto the sun-drenched grass. Three hundred metres away he sees Penelope beneath a birch tree, moving slowly. A man is sitting against the trunk with his head bowed. Penelope crouches down in front of him, then suddenly everything changes. She jerks forward, then falls backwards. The man is aiming a pistol straight at her. Joona starts to run, raises his pistol and takes aim, but the distance is too great. He stops, and is holding his gun with both hands when the fixer shoots Penelope in the chest with two rapid shots. Her body is thrown back and remains lying on the ground.

Joona runs. The fixer is tired, but he raises the pistol towards her again. Joona fires but misses. He runs closer and sees Penelope kicking her legs to get away. The fixer looks at Joona, then he looks back at Penelope again. He looks her in the eye and aims the pistol at her face. A shot rings out. Joona hears the powerful blast behind him. He hears a whining sound flash past his right ear and a fraction of a second later a cascade of blood shoots out behind the fixer. The blood spatters the white bark of the birch tree. The jacketed bullet has passed right through the fixer's chest and heart. Joona keeps running, still aiming his pistol in front of him. A second shot rings out and Joona sees the already dead man jerk as the bullet hits his chest just centimetres above the previous entry hole. Joona lowers his pistol, turns round and sees Saga Bauer standing at the edge of the clump of trees with a sniper rifle held to her shoulder. Her fair hair is shimmering in the sunlight filtering through the leaves, and there's a look of intense concentration on her face as she lowers the rifle.

Penelope gets to her feet and moves back, coughing hard, into the sunshine. She stares at the dead man. Joona walks over to the fixer, kicks the pistol away from his hand and feels his neck to make sure he really is dead.

Penelope unfastens the bulletproof vest and lets it fall onto the grass. Joona walks over to her. She takes a step towards him and it looks like she's going to faint. He puts his arms round her and feels how exhausted she is as she leans her cheek against his chest.

87

The dead end

The man whose face had been destroyed in the men's bathroom of the German Embassy died an hour after he reached hospital. He was identified as Dieter Gramma, the Cultural Attaché's secretary. On closer inspection chief pathologist The Needle found traces of tape on his clothes, and bruises and cuts on his wrists and neck that indicated he had been tied up at the time of the explosion. Once the preliminary crime scene investigation was complete and the recordings from the security cameras were analysed the sequence of events could be mapped fairly precisely: after he arrived at his office on the upper floor of the Embassy, Dieter Gramma opened his computer and checked his emails. He didn't reply to any but flagged three of them. Then he went to the kitchen, switched on the espresso machine and went to the men's toilets. Just as he was opening the door to one of the cubicles he realised that there was a man wearing a balaclava standing in front of the mirror by the washbasins.

The man in black was the wounded fixer whose German passport had gained him access to the Embassy when he was trying to escape from the police and buy himself some time.

The fixer quickly evaluated Dieter Gramma's build in the mirror before he casually placed a piece of tape over the lens of the security camera. Dieter Gramma presumably didn't have time to say much before the fixer pointed a gun at his chest, forced him down on his knees and taped his mouth. The fixer swapped his black jacket for Dieter Gramma's blazer, then tied him to the water pipes with his back to the camera. He drew his knife and drove the double-edged blade through the hole in his jacket, deep into Dieter Gramma's left shoulder.

Pain, fear and a rush of endorphins probably made Dieter Gramma so confused that he didn't really understand what was going on. The fixer cut a piece of steel wire with a pair of pliers, put it round Dieter Gramma's neck and twisted the ends together. Through this noose he threaded a longer piece of steel wire, took out a Shgr 2000 hand-grenade, fastened one end of the wire to the grenade, then held the detonator closed with his hand. If he let go of the detonator, the grenade would have been triggered and three seconds later would have exploded.

But the fixer taped the grenade, with its detonator pressed against Dieter Gramma's chest, then passed the wire that was already threaded through the noose around Dieter Gramma's neck around the drainage pipe beneath the washbasin and pulled it tightly in front of the door so that it acted as a tripwire.

The idea was that someone would come in and detonate the grenade, and in the midst of the ensuing chaos the police would assume that the man with the bullet-hole in his jacket and blown-off face was the person they had been searching for.

The fixer may have been slower than usual because of the amount of blood he had lost, but it still took no more than four minutes from the moment Dieter Gramma entered the bathroom to when the fixer placed his pistol and magazines in the wash-basin, disposed of the roll of tape, hid the rucksack containing the bloody knife behind one of the toilets, removed the tape from the camera lens, stepped over the tripwire and left the room.

He went along the corridor to the conference room, opened the double doors, went in and started a fire, then walked out and knocked on counsellor Davida Meyer's room, was asked in, and had just started to explain a fabricated consular problem when the fire alarm went off.

Dieter Gramma spent almost twenty-five minutes on his knees, tightly bound with a grenade pressed to his chest, before he was spotted on the security camera. He had probably tried to sound the alarm, but was terrified of dislodging the grenade. The post-mortem showed that some of the blood vessels in his neck had burst, and that he had bitten his own cheeks and tongue horribly.

The door to the men's toilets opened and a shock grenade bounced in across the tiled floor, a grenade that doesn't spread shrapnel and ball-bearings like an ordinary hand-grenade but merely causes a powerful pressure wave in an enclosed room. The shock grenade exploded and Dieter Gramma hit his head against the pipe and tiled wall, and lost consciousness. A young military policeman named Uli Schneider ran in through the door with his assault rifle raised. The bathroom was full of smoke from the first grenade, and it took the young officer a couple of seconds too long to realise what the wire he had just walked into meant.

The grenade was pulled from the tape on Dieter Gramma's chest and the detonator was triggered. The hand-grenade was prevented from falling by the noose around his neck, but slipped slightly because he had passed out, and then exploded, with horrific results.

88

The visitor

Joona Linna, Saga Bauer and Penelope Fernandez are being driven through Stockholm in an armoured police van, away from the diplomatic quarter, along Strandvägen with the glittering water to their left.

'I'd seen him,' Penelope says in a monotone. 'I knew he was never going to give up, he was just going to carry on hunting me down . . .'

She tails off and stares in front of her.

'Until he killed me,' she says.

'Yes,' Saga says.

Penelope closes her eyes, sits still and feels the gentle movement of the van. They pass the unusual memorial to Raoul Wallenberg's memory, like foaming waves or Hebrew writing blowing across the ground.

'Who was he?' Penelope asks. 'The man who was after me?'

'A professional hitman,' Joona replies. 'They're called fixers, or grob.'

'Neither Europol nor Interpol have anything on him,' Saga says.

'A professional hitman,' Penelope repeats slowly. 'So someone sent him?'

'Yes,' Saga replies. 'Someone sent him, but we're not going to be able to find any connection between him and his employer.'

'Raphael Guidi?' Penelope suggests in a low voice. 'Is it him? Or Agathe al-Haji?'

'We believe it's Raphael Guidi,' Saga says. 'Because it wouldn't really matter to Agathe al-Haji if you were to give evidence and say that she was trying to buy ammunition . . .'

'Because of course what she's doing is no secret,' Joona says.

'So Raphael Guidi sent a murderer, but . . . what does he want? Do you know? Is it all about the photograph? Is that it?'

'Raphael Guidi probably thinks you took the photograph yourself, he thinks you're a witness, that you've seen and heard things that could incriminate him.'

'Does he still think that?'

'Probably.'

'So he'll send another killer?'

'That's what we're afraid of,' Saga replies.

'How long will I have police protection? Am I going to get a new identity?'

'We'll have to discuss that, but . . .'

'I'm going to be hunted until I haven't got the strength to run any more,' Penelope says.

They pass the NK department store and see three youngsters having a sit-down protest in front of the main entrance.

'He's not going to give up,' Joona confirms in a sombre voice. 'That's why we have to expose the whole deal, because if we do that . . . then there won't be any reason to come after you.'

'We can't get at Raphael Guidi, we're very aware of that,' Saga says. 'But we can do a hell of a lot in Sweden, and he'll feel the effects of that . . .'

'Like what?'

'We can start by blocking the deal,' Saga says. 'Because that container ship can't leave Gothenburg without an export licence from Axel Riessen.'

'And why would he refuse to sign that, then?'

'He'll never sign,' Joona says. 'Because he knows as much about this as we do.'

'Good,' Penelope whispers.

'We stop the deal and then we take down Pontus Salman and everyone else who's involved,' Saga says.

They fall silent.

'I need to call my mum,' Penelope says after a while.

'You can use my phone,' Saga says.

Penelope takes it, appears to hesitate, then taps in a number and waits.

'Hi, Mum, it's me, Penny. That man who . . .'

'Penny, there's someone at the door, I have to . . .'

'Mum, wait!' Penelope says anxiously. 'Who's at the door?'

'I don't know.'

'But are you expecting anyone?'

'No, but . . .'

'You mustn't open it!' Penelope snaps.

Her mother says something and puts the phone down. Penelope hears footsteps across the floor, then the doorbell rings again. The door opens and she hears voices. Penelope doesn't know what to do. She looks at Saga and Joona who are watching her intently. The line crackles, there's an odd echo, and then she hears her mum's voice again.

'Are you still there, Penny?'

'Yes.'

'It's someone who's trying to get hold of you,' her mum says.

'Get hold of me?'

Penelope licks her lips.

'Okay, Mum. Pass the phone over.'

The line crackles again, then Penelope hears a woman say her name:

'Penelope?'

'Yes,' she replies.

'We need to meet.'

'Who am I talking to?' Penelope asks.

'I'm the person who sent you the photograph.'

'I haven't received any photograph,' Penelope replies.

'Good answer,' the woman says. 'We don't know each other, but it was actually me who sent you the picture.'

Penelope doesn't reply.

'I have to see you today, as soon as possible,' the woman says, sounding agitated. 'I sent you a photograph of four people in a private box at a concert hall. I took the picture in secret on the thirteenth of November 2009. One of the four people is my husband, Pontus Salman.'

89

The meeting

Pontus Salman's house is located on Roskullsvägen on Lidingö. It's a 1960s villa, which still exudes the spirit of the age even though it's seen slightly better days. They park on the paved driveway and get out of the car. Someone has drawn a childish, stylised penis on the large garage door.

They decide that Joona should stay in the car with Penelope while Saga goes over to the house. The door is open, but Saga still rings the doorbell, which is shaped like a lion's head. She hears a pleasant, three-note ring, but nothing happens. Saga draws her Glock, checks the magazine, removes the safety catch, rings the bell again, then enters the house.

It's a split-level house, and a large kitchen–diner opens off the hallway. Tall windows afford a stunning view of the water.

Saga walks through the kitchen, looks in the empty bedrooms, then goes back to the hall and down the stairs. She can hear music behind a door with the letters 'R&R' on a brass sign. She opens the door and the music gets louder, Verdi's *La Traviata* with Joan Sutherland.

At the end of the tiled corridor she can see the reflected blue shimmer of an illuminated swimming pool.

Saga creeps forward, trying to listen out for anything apart from the music. She thinks she can hear footsteps, bare feet on a tiled floor.

Keeping her pistol hidden by her side, she moves forward, and can now see cane furniture and palm leaves. The air is warm and humid. There's a growing smell of chlorine and jasmine. She reaches a large pool with pale blue tiles. There are large windows facing the garden and the water beyond. A slender woman in her fifties is standing at a bar-counter in a gold-coloured bathing costume, holding a glass of white wine in her hand. She puts the glass down when she catches sight of Saga, and walks towards her.

'Hello, my name is Saga Bauer.'

'What agency?'

'Security Police.'

The woman lets out a laugh as she kisses Saga's cheeks and introduces herself as Marie-Louise Salman.

'Have you got your costume with you?' she asks, returning to the bar.

Her feet leave long, thin prints on the terracotta-coloured tiles. Her body is slim and she looks like she works out. There's something artful about the way she walks, as if she wants to give Saga a chance to look at her.

Marie-Louise Salman picks up the glass, then turns and looks curiously at Saga, as if to check that she is actually watching her.

'A glass of Sancerre?' she asks in her cool, modulated voice.

'No, thanks,' Saga replies.

'I swim to keep in shape, even if I've cut back on the modelling. It's easy to succumb to narcissism in this business. Well, of course you know that. It feels like a kick in the face when no one lights your cigarette for you any more.'

Marie-Louise leans forwards and whispers theatrically:

'I'm having an affair with the youngest guy in the Chippendales. Do you know who they are? Never mind, they're all gay.'

'I'm here to talk about the photograph that you sent to . . .'

'I knew he couldn't keep his mouth shut,' she exclaims with feigned outrage.

'Who?'

'Jean-Paul Gaultier.'

'The designer?' Saga asks.

'Yes, the designer, with his stripy top, golden stubble and a vicious little mouth. He still hates me. I knew it.'

Saga smiles patiently at Marie-Louise, and offers her a dressing-gown when she sees the goosebumps on her skin.

'I like being cold . . . it makes me look better. At least that's what Depardieu told me last spring, unless it was – I can't quite remember – perhaps it was Renaud, the little sweetheart, who said that. Well, no matter!'

Suddenly they hear footsteps heading towards the pool. Marie-Louise looks nervous and glances round for an escape route.

'Hello?'

'Saga?' Joona calls.

Saga takes a step forward and sees Joona and Penelope walk into the pool area with a woman in her fifties. The woman's dark hair is cut in a neat, boyish style.

'Marie-Louise,' the woman says with an anxious smile. 'What are you doing here?'

'I thought I'd have a swim,' she replies. 'Need to cool down between my legs.'

'You know I said I wanted you to call before you come.'

'Of course, sorry, I forgot.'

'Marie-Louise is Pontus's sister, my sister-in-law,' the woman explains, then turns to Saga and introduces herself.

'Veronique Salman.'

'Saga Bauer, Security Police.'

'Let's go and sit in the library,' Veronique says, and starts to walk back along the corridor.

'Can I have a swim seeing as I'm here?' Marie-Louise calls.

'Not naked,' Veronique replies without looking back.

90

Saga, Joona and Penelope follow her through the various ground-floor rooms and into the library. It's a fairly small space with leaded windows with yellow, brown and pink glass. The books are kept in glass-fronted bookcases, and there are brown leather armchairs, an open fire and a brass samovar.

'You'll have to excuse me not offering refreshments, but I'm in a bit of a hurry, I leave an hour from now . . .'

Veronique Salman looks round nervously and runs her hands across her skirt before she goes on.

'I just . . . I just want to say what I've got to say,' she says in a subdued voice. 'I won't testify in public – if you try to force me I'll deny everything I've said, regardless of the consequences.'

She adjusts a lampshade, but her hand is shaking so much that it ends up crooked again.

'I'm travelling without Pontus, he won't be joining me,' she says, looking at the floor. Her mouth trembles and she takes a few moments to compose herself before she continues.

'Penelope,' she says, and looks her in the eye. 'I want you to know that I understand that you think Pontus is scum, but he isn't, he really isn't.'

'I've never said . . .'

'Please, just wait,' she says. 'I just want to say that I love my husband, but that I . . . I no longer know what I think about what he does. Up to now I've told myself that people have always traded in weapons. The arms trade has existed as long as human beings have been around. I don't mean that as an excuse. I spent several years working on security policy at the Foreign Ministry. And if you're involved in that sort of work, you soon realise that we're a long way from the utopian dream of a world without armed conflict. In practice every country needs to maintain defence forces, but . . . I can't help thinking that there are different nuances . . .'

She walks over to the door, opens it and looks out, then closes it again.

'Exporting arms to countries that are at war, to unstable areas, fanning the flames of conflicts by injecting more weapons – that mustn't be allowed to happen.'

'No,' Penelope whispers.

'I understand Pontus as a businessman,' Veronique Salman goes on. 'Because Silencia really did need that deal. Sudan is a large country with an unreliable supply of ammunition for its assault rifles. They use almost nothing but Fabrique Nationale, and Belgium isn't exporting any ammunition given the current state of things. People have got their eyes on them, but Sweden has never been a colonial power, we have a good reputation in the region, and so on. Pontus saw the opportunities and acted quickly once the civil war in Sudan was over. Raphael Guidi put the deal together. They were about to sign the contract. Everything was ready when the International Criminal Court in the Hague suddenly issued a warrant for the arrest of President al-Bashir for his involvement in the genocide carried out by the militia in Darfur.'

'Any shipment would be a breach of international law,' Saga says.

'Everyone knew that, but Raphael Guidi didn't cancel the deal, he just said he'd got a new interested party. It took several months, but he eventually explained that the Kenyan army wanted to continue with the suspended deal. The same amount of ammunition, the same price, and so on. I tried to talk to Pontus, I said it was obvious that the ammunition was going to end up in Sudan, but Pontus just claimed that Kenya had seen an opportunity, it was a good deal, and they needed ammunition. I don't know if he actually believed that, I don't think he could have done, but he shifted all the responsibility onto Carl Palmcrona and the ISP. If Palmcrona granted an export licence, then it was obviously all above board, he said, and . . .'

'A good way of not having to take responsibility for anything,' Penelope says.

'That was why I took the photograph, I wanted to know who was there, I just went into the box and took a picture on my mobile, I said I was trying to make a call and told Pontus I wasn't feeling well, and that I was going to take a taxi back to the hotel.'

'That was brave,' Penelope says.

'But I didn't know how dangerous it was, or I wouldn't have done it,' Veronique says. 'I was angry with Pontus, I wanted to get him to change his mind. I left the Alte Oper in the middle of the concert and looked at the picture in the taxi. The whole thing was crazy, the buyers were represented there by Agathe al-Haji. And she's a military advisor to the Sudanese president, so it was obvious that the ammunition was going to be pumped into the civil war that no one wanted to talk about.'

'Genocide,' Penelope whispers.

'When we got home I told Pontus he had to pull out of it . . . I'll never forget the look on his face when he looked at me and told me that was impossible. "I've entered into a Paganini contract," he said, and when I saw the look in his eyes I felt properly frightened. He was terrified. I didn't dare keep that picture on my phone, so I printed it out, deleted it from the memory, and from the hard disk of the computer, and then I sent it to you.'

Veronique Salman stands in front of Penelope with her arms hanging limply by her sides, a look of utter exhaustion on her face.

'I had no idea what was going to happen,' she says quietly. 'How could I have known? I'm so, so sorry, I can't tell you . . .'

The room falls silent for a moment. In the distance they can hear the sound of the pool machinery.

'What's a Paganini contract?' Joona asks.

'Raphael owns several incredibly valuable violins,' Veronique says. 'He collects instruments that Paganini himself played over a century ago. He keeps some of the violins in his home, but he loans others to talented musicians and . . .'

She runs her hand nervously over her hair before she goes on.

'This business with Paganini . . . I've never really understood it, but Pontus says that Raphael somehow sees a connection to Paganini in his contracts, he says his contracts are eternal, that's what he means. There's never any documentation, but . . . Pontus told me that Raphael had really done his homework. He had all the figures in his head, he was familiar with the logistics, knew exactly how and when the deal could be put into practice. He told each and every one of them what was required of them, and how much they would earn from the deal. Once you've kissed his hand there's no way back. You can't run, you can't get anyone to protect you, you can't even die . . .'

'Why not?' Joona asks.

'Raphael is so . . . I don't know, he . . . this is so terrible,' she says, her mouth trembling. 'He manages to get everyone concerned to . . . to tell him what their worst nightmare is.'

'What?' Saga asks.

'Pontus said that, he said Raphael had the ability to do that,' she replies seriously.

'What did he mean by nightmare?' Joona asks.

'Obviously I asked Pontus if he had told him anything,' she says with a pained expression on her face. 'But he wouldn't tell me. I don't know what to think.'

Silence settles on the small library. There are large damp patches of sweat under the arms of Veronique Salman's white blouse.

'You can't stop Raphael,' she says after a while, and looks Joona in the eye. 'But you have to make sure that ammunition never reaches Darfur.'

'We will,' Saga says.

'You know . . . the fact that the unrest after the Sudanese election hasn't turned into a complete catastrophe is largely because of the lack of ammunition . . . and if it flares up again, the aid organisations will have to leave Darfur.'

Veronique Salman looks at her watch and tells Joona that she has to leave for the airport soon, then goes to the window and gazes out blankly through the coloured glass.

'My boyfriend is dead,' Penelope says, wiping tears from her cheeks. 'My sister is dead, and I don't know how many more people.'

Veronique Salman turns towards her.

'Penelope, I didn't know what to do, I had that photograph, and I thought that you, if anyone, would be able to identify those people,' she explains. 'I thought you'd understand the significance of Agathe al-Haji buying ammunition, because you've been in Darfur, you've got contacts there, you're a peace campaigner and . . .'

'You were wrong,' Penelope snaps. 'You sent the picture to the wrong person. I was aware of Agathe al-Haji, but I had no idea what she looked like.'

'I couldn't send the photograph to the police or the newspapers, they wouldn't have understood its significance, not without explanation, and I couldn't explain the circumstances, how could I have done? It was impossible, because if there was one thing I understood, it was that there had to be no way to link me to the person I sent it to. I wanted to get rid of it, and I wanted never to have to acknowledge my connection to the picture.'

'But now you have,' Joona says.

'Yes, because I . . . I . . .'

'Why?' he asks. 'What made you change your mind?'

'Because I'm leaving the country, and I needed to . . .'

She falls silent and looks down at her hands.

'What's happened?'

'Nothing,' she sobs.

'You can tell us,' Joona says.

'No, it . . .'

'It's okay,' Saga whispers.

Veronique wipes the tears from her cheeks and looks up.

'Pontus called me from our summerhouse in tears, and said he was sorry, and I don't know exactly what he meant, but he said he was going to do all he could to escape the nightmare.'

91

A final way out

A rowing boat made of varnished mahogany is bobbing on the water of Malmsjön in the shelter of a large headland. There's a very mild easterly breeze. It carries with it a faint smell of manure from the farms on the far side of the lake. Pontus Salman has drawn up the oars, but the boat has drifted no more than ten metres in the past hour. He's thinking that he would have brought something to drink if he'd realised it was going to take this long to shoot himself.

The double-barrelled shotgun is lying across his thighs.

The only sound is the water lapping against the hull, and the gentle rustling of the leaves in the trees.

He closes his eyes for a while, takes several deep breaths, then opens his eyes and rests the butt of the shotgun on the bottom of the boat, making sure it can't slip. He holds the sun-warmed barrel in his hand and tries pointing it at his forehead.

He feels sick at the thought of his head being blown off.

His hands are shaking so badly that he has to wait for a while. He pulls himself together, and aims the barrel at his heart instead.

The swallows are flying low now, hunting insects above the surface of the water.

There'll probably be rain tonight, he thinks.

A white streak appears across the sky as a plane passes, and Pontus starts to think about his nightmare again.

Suddenly it feels as if the whole lake were getting darker, as if the water were being turned black from below.

He looks back at the shotgun again, puts the barrel in his mouth, feels it scrape against his teeth, leaving a metallic taste.

He reaches for the trigger, but suddenly hears the sound of a car. His heart flutters in his chest. All manner of thoughts flash through his head in the space of a second, but he realises it must be his wife, seeing as she's the only person who knows where he is.

He puts the shotgun down again, and feels his pulse throb hard through his body. He's shaking as he tries to see through the trees towards the cottage.

A man is walking down the path towards the jetty.

It takes Pontus a few moments to realise that it's the detective who came to the office and showed him Veronique's photograph.

But when he does recognise him, an entirely different type of anxiety swells up inside him. Don't say it's too late, he thinks over and over again as he starts to row towards the shore. Don't say it's too late, don't say my nightmare's come true, don't say it's too late.

Pontus Salman stops rowing before he reaches the jetty. His face is white and he just shakes his head when Joona Linna asks him to come closer. He takes care to maintain the distance between them as he turns the rowing boat round so that the front is pointing away from the shore.

Joona sits down on the cracked, sun-bleached wooden bench at the end of the jetty. The land is radiating heat as the water laps gently.

'What do you want?' Pontus asks in a frightened voice.

'I've just been talking to your wife,' Joona says calmly.

'Talking?'

'Yes, and I . . .'

'You talked to Veronique?' Pontus asks anxiously.

'I need answers to some more questions.'

'There isn't time.'

'There's no hurry to do that,' Joona says, glancing at the shotgun in the boat.

'What would you know?' Pontus mutters.

The oars move gently in the water.

'What I do know is that the ammunition being shipped to Kenya is bound for Sudan,' Joona says.

Pontus Salman doesn't reply.

'And I know that it was your wife who took that photograph in the box at the concert hall.'

Pontus sits there with his face downturned, and lifts the oars, feeling the water run down to his hands.

'I can't stop the deal,' he says tersely. 'I was in too much of a hurry, I needed the order . . .'

'So you signed the contract.'

'It was watertight, even if it did get out. Everyone could claim to have acted in good faith, no one was to blame.'

'But it still went wrong,' Joona says.

'Yes.'

'I was planning to wait before arresting you . . .'

'Because you can't prove anything,' Pontus says.

'I haven't spoken to the prosecutor,' Joona goes on. 'But I'm sure we can offer a more lenient sentence if you give evidence against Raphael Guidi.'

'Evidence! I'm not going to give evidence!' Pontus says heatedly. 'I can see you really don't get this. I've signed a very specific type of contract, and if I weren't such a fucking coward I'd have done the same as Palmcrona by now.'

'We can protect you if you give evidence,' Joona says.

'Palmcrona got away with it,' Pontus whispers. 'He hanged himself and now his successor is going to have to sign the export licence. Raphael lost all interest in Palmcrona, so he didn't have to reap his nightmare . . .'

Pontus's lifeless face suddenly breaks into a smile. Joona looks at him and thinks that it isn't true that Palmcrona got away with it, because his nightmare must have been the death of his son.

'There's a psychologist on her way,' Joona says. 'And she's going to try to convince you that suicide isn't a way out of . . .'

Pontus Salman starts to row back out.

'Pontus, I need answers to some more questions,' Joona says, raising his voice. 'You say the new director of the ISP is going to to sign the export licence, but what happens if he refuses? Can't he just refuse to enter into one of these Paganini contracts? Can't he just refuse?'

Pontus Salman stops rowing, and the boat continues to glide away from shore, its oars trailing in the water.

'He could,' he replies calmly. 'But he won't want to do that . . .'

92

Axel wakes up when his phone starts to ring on the bedside table. It was almost morning when he finally got to sleep, tucked up next to Beverly's sweaty body.

Now he looks at her young face, and he can see traces of Greta again, in her mouth and eyelids.

Beverly whispers something in her sleep, then rolls onto her stomach. Axel feels a surge of tenderness inside at the sight of her fragile little body, her heartbreakingly young body.

He sits up in bed and is reaching for his book, A *Dangerous Game* by Friedrich Dürrenmatt, when there's a sudden knock on the bedroom door.

'Just a moment!' Axel calls at the same time as Robert comes into the room.

'I thought you'd be awake,' his brother says. 'I'd like your opinion on a new instrument that . . .'

Robert catches sight of Beverly and stops abruptly.

'Axel,' he stammers. 'What's going on, Axel?'

His voice wakes Beverly. When she sees Robert she hides under the covers. Axel gets up and puts his dressing-gown on, but Robert is backing towards the door.

'Fuck you,' he says quietly. 'Fuck you . . .'

'It's not what . . .'

'Have you been taking advantage of her?' Robert asks, almost yelling. 'A girl who's not well?'

'Let me explain,' Axel tries to say.

'You bastard,' Robert whispers, and grabs hold of him, dragging him sideways.

Axel loses his balance and throws his arm out, and manages to knock a lamp to the floor. Robert backs out of the room.

'Wait,' Axel says, following him. 'I know how it looks, but that's wrong. You can ask . . .'

'I'm taking her to the police,' Robert says angrily. 'I never would have believed that you . . .'

He chokes up and his eyes fill with tears.

'I'm not a paedophile,' Axel tries to explain in a subdued voice. 'You have to understand that. I just need . . .'

'You just need to abuse children,' Robert snaps, in a state of utter despair. 'You're taking advantage of someone you promised to care for and protect.'

Axel stops in front of him in the library. Robert sits down heavily on the sofa, looks at his brother, and tries to keep his voice steady:

'Axel, you do realise that I have to take her to the police, don't you?' he says.

'Yes,' Axel replies. 'I realise.'

Robert can't bear to look at his brother, and wipes his mouth and sighs.

'It would be just as well to go right away,' he says.

'I'll go and get her,' Axel says, and walks into the bedroom.

Beverly is sitting in bed, smiling and wiggling her toes.

'Get dressed,' he says seriously. 'You're going out with Robert.'

When he returns to the library Robert gets up at once from the sofa. The pair of them stand there in silence, staring at the floor as they wait.

'You're staying here,' Robert says quietly.

'Yes,' Axel whispers.

After a while Beverly comes out. She's wearing a pair of jeans and a T-shirt. She's not wearing any make-up and looks even younger than she usually does.

93

Greta's death

Robert drives in silence, pulls up gently at a set of traffic lights and waits for them to turn green.

'I'm so sorry, Beverly,' he says in a subdued voice. 'My brother said he was helping you with somewhere to stay while you were waiting for a student flat. I don't understand, I would never have believed that . . .'

'Axel isn't a paedophile,' she says quietly.

'I don't want you to defend him, he doesn't deserve that.'

'He doesn't touch me, just so you know. He never has.'

'What does he do, then?'

'He holds me,' Beverly replies.

'Holds?' Robert repeats. 'But you said . . .'

'He holds me so he can get to sleep,' she says in her high, frank voice.

'What do you mean?'

'It's nothing dirty – not as far as I've noticed, anyway.'

Robert sighs and says she'll be able to tell the police everything. A rumbling despair is swelling in his chest again.

'It's all about his sleep,' Beverly explains slowly. 'He can't sleep without pills, but I make him calm, he gets . . .'

'You're underage,' Robert interrupts.

Beverly stares out through the windscreen. The bright green leaves on the trees are dancing in the early summer breeze. A group of heavily pregnant women are chatting as they walk along the pavement. An old lady is standing completely still with her face turned towards the sun.

'Why?' Robert suddenly asks. 'Why can't he sleep at night?'

'He says it's been that way for a hundred years.'

'Yes, he ruined his liver with all those pills.'

'He talked all about that at the hospital,' Beverly says. 'There was something that happened to him, but . . .'

Robert stops at a pedestrian crossing. A little girl drops her dummy on the road, but her mother doesn't notice and just keeps walking. The child pulls free and runs back. The mother screams in horror, then sees that Robert was watching and guessed what was going to happen. She carries the struggling child back across the street.

'There was a girl who died,' Beverly says slowly.

'Who?'

'He never wants to talk about it. Only back then, at the hospital . . .'

She falls silent, knits her fingers together and drums her legs.

'Tell me what he said,' Robert says in a tense voice.

'They were together one night, and then she killed herself,' Beverly says, and glances at Robert. 'I look like her, don't I?'

'Yes,' Robert says.

'In the hospital he said he'd killed her,' Beverly whispers.

Robert starts and looks at her again.

'What do you mean?' he asks.

'He said he was responsible.'

Robert stares at her open-mouthed.

'He says . . . he says it was his fault?'

Beverly nods.

'It was his fault,' she goes on. 'Because they should have been practising on their violins, but instead they had sex and she thought he'd tricked her into doing it so he could win the violin competition.'

'It wasn't his fault.'

'Yes, it was,' she retorts.

Robert sinks lower in the driver's seat. He rubs his face with his hands several times.

'Dear God,' Robert whispers. 'I have to . . .'

The car swerves and someone behind blows their horn irritably, and Beverly gives him a worried look.

'What is it?' she asks.

'I . . . I have to tell him something,' Robert goes on, and does a U-turn. 'I was standing behind the stage when he went on, I know what happened. Greta was on before him, she was first, and . . .'

'You were there?'

'Hang on,' Robert says. 'I heard everything, I . . . Greta's death, that had nothing to do with Axel . . .'

He's so upset he has to stop the car again. His face is grey as ash and he turns towards Beverly and whispers:

'Sorry. But I just have to . . .'

'Are you sure?'

'What?' he asks, looking at her.

'Are you sure it wasn't Axel's fault?'

'Yes,' he replies.

'So what happened, then?'

Robert wipes tears from his eyes and opens the car door pensively.

'Just give me a moment, I have to . . . I have to talk to him,' he says quietly, and goes and stands on the pavement.

The large lime trees on Sveavägen are dropping clouds of pollen which dances in the sun before landing on the cars and pedestrians. Robert suddenly grins to himself, pulls out his phone and calls Axel's number. After three rings his smile vanishes and he returns to the car with the phone pressed to his ear. Only when he ends the call to try again does he realise that the car is empty. Beverly is gone. He looks round but can't see her anywhere. The city traffic is deafening, and he can hear students celebrating their high-school graduation down at Sergels torg. He closes the door, starts the engine and starts to drive slowly as he searches for Beverly.

94

White, rustling plastic

Axel Riessen isn't sure how long he's been standing looking out of the window since he watched Robert and Beverly disappear. His thoughts have wandered back to the past. He forces himself away from his memories and goes over to the music centre instead, and puts on the A-side of David Bowie's *The Rise and Fall of Ziggy Stardust and the Spiders from Mars*, and turns up the volume.

Pushing through the market square . . .

Axel walks over to the drinks cabinet and picks out one of the most expensive bottles in his whisky collection, a Macallan from the first year of the Second World War, 1939. He pours himself half a glass, then sits down on the sofa. He listens to the music with downcast eyes – the young voice and untidy piano, as he detects the scent of oak barrels and dark cellars, straw and lemon. He drinks, and the strong liquor burns his lips and fills his mouth. The whisky has been nurturing its flavour for generations, through changes of government, war and peace.

Axel is thinking that perhaps it's just as well that this is happening now, perhaps Beverly will get the help she needs after this. He gets an impulse to phone his brother and tell him that he loves him, then smiles at what a pathetic idea that is. He's not going to kill himself, he's going to meet what's coming towards him as best he can and try to stay upright.

He takes the whisky with him into the bedroom and looks at the unmade bed. He just has time to hear his mobile phone buzzing in the jacket hanging over the back of a chair when creaking footsteps in the sitting room make him turn round.

'Beverly,' he says in surprise.

Her face is dusty and she's holding a dandelion clock in her hand.

'I didn't want to talk to the police . . .'

'Where's Robert?'

'I got a lift back,' she says. 'Don't worry, it was all fine . . .'

'Why do you do things like this? You should have . . .'

'Don't be angry, I haven't done anything wrong, I just needed to tell you something really important . . .'

His phone starts to ring in his jacket pocket again.

'Hang on, Beverly, I need to get this . . .'

He hunts through his pockets, finds it and answers:

'Axel Riessen.'

He hears a distant voice.

'Hello?'

'Hello,' Axel replies.

'This is Raphael Guidi,' the voice says in heavily accented English. 'I'm sorry about the poor line, but I'm at sea at the moment.'

'Not a problem,' Axel replies politely as he watches Beverly sit down on the bed.

'I'll get straight to the point,' Raphael Guidi says. 'I'm calling to check if you've had time to sign the export licence for the Kenya shipment yet. I was counting on the ship having left harbour by now.'

Axel holds the phone to his ear, goes out into the sitting room, but can't hear anything but his own breathing. He thinks about the photograph of Raphael Guidi, Carl Palmcrona, Agathe al-Haji and Pontus Salman. The way Palmcrona was holding his glass of champagne and laughing so that his gums showed.

'Are you still there?' Raphael Guidi says over the crackly line.

'I'm not going to sign the export licence,' Axel replies curtly, and feels a shiver run down his spine.

'Perhaps I can persuade you to change your mind,' Raphael

says. 'You'll have to think if there's anything I could offer you that might . . .'

'You've got nothing I want.'

'I think you're mistaken there. When I enter into a contract . . .'

Axel ends the call and everything goes silent. He puts the phone back in his jacket and is filled with unease, almost like a premonition. He starts to walk towards the passageway leading to the stairs. When he looks out through the window he can see movement in the park, like a transparent shadow between the bushes heading towards the house. Axel moves to the other window, but can't see anything. There's a noise from downstairs, like a small pane of glass cracking in the sunshine. Axel can't help thinking that it's absurd, but still understands what's going on. His heart is beating very fast, his body fills with adrenalin and all his senses become extremely alert. He moves as fast as he can without running. He walks back into the bedroom to see Beverly. Gorgeous sunlight is streaming through the gap between the curtains, like a wall of uneven glass across the room, to Beverly's feet. She's got undressed again and is lying down on the unmade bed with the Dürrenmatt book on her stomach.

'Axel,' she says. 'I came back to tell you something good . . .'

'Don't be frightened,' he interrupts as calmly as he can. 'But you need to hide under the bed. Do it now, and stay there, for at least an hour.'

She responds at once, doesn't ask any questions, just crawls under the bed. He can hear rapid footsteps on the stairs. At least two people, he thinks. Beverly's jeans and T-shirt are on the armchair. He hurries over and throws the clothes under the bed. His heart is beating hard in his chest. He looks round, unsure of what to do. His mind is racing. He takes his phone out of his jacket and hurries into the sitting room from the bedroom. Behind him he can hear steps in the passageway heading towards the library. With trembling fingers he unlocks the phone, and hears the floor creak as someone runs in on soft feet. There's no time to make the call. He tries to reach the window overlooking the street to call for help when someone grabs hold of his right wrist and simultaneously presses something cool against his neck. He doesn't realise that it's a Taser. Sixty-nine thousand volts shoot into his body. There's an electrical crackle, but Axel just registers it as a series of heavy blows, as if someone was hitting his neck with an iron pipe. He doesn't know that he's screaming, because his brain shuts down and the world disappears.

The men have already taped his mouth when he regains consciousness, one fragment at a time. He's lying on the floor and his body is twitching spasmodically. His arms and legs are shaking. What feels like a burning insect bite on his neck overwhelms everything else in its sheer pain. There's no possibility of him defending himself, his muscles feel paralysed. With brusque familiarity, they tie his arms, thighs and ankles, then roll him up in white plastic. It rustles softly and he thinks he's going to suffocate, but the air doesn't run out. He tries to twist his body, but it's hopeless, he can't even control his own muscles. The two men carry him perfectly calmly down the stairs, out through the front door and into a waiting van.

95

Joona tries to call Pontus Salman back. The rowing boat slips further out on the lake. Joona runs back from the jetty and meets the psychologist and two police officers from Södertälje. He leads them down to the jetty and tells them to be careful, but that he doesn't believe that Pontus Salman is going to hurt either himself or anyone else.

'Just make sure you keep hold of him, and I'll be in touch as soon as possible,' he says, then hurries back to his car.

As Joona drives across the bridge over Fittjaviken he thinks about Pontus Salman, the way he sat in the boat saying that he was sure Axel Riessen would sign a Paganini contract.

Joona had asked if he could just refuse, but Pontus had said that he wouldn't want to.

As he dials Axel Riessen's number, he sees Veronique Salman, Pontus's wife, in his mind's eye. The disappointed set of her mouth and the fear in her eyes as she told them that once you've kissed Raphael Guidi on the hand, there's no way back.

The word nightmare keeps coming back, Joona thinks. Palmcrona's housekeeper had used it. Veronique Salman had said that Raphael managed to get everyone to talk about their worst nightmare, and Pontus Salman had claimed that Palmcrona managed to escape his nightmare by committing suicide.

He didn't have to see his nightmare come true, he had said.

Joona thinks about the fact that Stefan Bergkvist never found out that Carl Palmcrona was his father. He thinks about the intense heat that burned the flesh from his skeleton, that made his blood boil, that cracked the boy's skull.

You can't break a Paganini contract even with your own death.

Joona tries to call Axel Riessen on his mobile again, then tries the direct number for the Inspectorate for Strategic Products.

'Director general Axel Riessen's secretary,' a female voice answers.

'I'm trying to get hold of Axel Riessen,' Joona says quickly.

'I'm afraid he's not available at the moment,' she replies.

'I'm a detective superintendent, and I need to talk to him at once.'

'I understand, but . . .'

'Interrupt him if he's in a meeting.'

'He isn't here,' she says, raising her voice. 'He didn't turn up this morning and I haven't been able to reach him on his phone.'

'I see,' Joona says, and ends the call.

Joona parks his Volvo on Bragevägen outside the gate of Axel Riessen's house. He spots someone closing the door to his brother's part of the building. Joona runs over and rings the doorbell. The lock rattles and the door opens again.

'Oh,' Robert Riessen says when he sees Joona. 'Hello.'

'Is Axel home?'

'He should be, but I've only just got in,' he replies. 'Has something happened?'

'I've been trying to get hold of him.'

'Me too,' Robert says, letting Joona in.

They go up half a flight of stairs into a large lobby with a pink glass chandelier hanging from the ceiling. Robert knocks on a door and then walks into Axel's part of the house. They hurry up to his private apartment in silence.

'Axel!' Robert calls.

They look around, walk through the rooms. Everything is the same as usual, the music centre is lit up but quiet, and there's a volume of the *Encyclopaedia Britannica* on the library trolley.

'You don't know if he might have gone away somewhere?' Joona asks.

'No,' Robert says in a remarkably weary voice. 'But he does so many odd things.'

'What do you mean?'

'You think you know him, but . . . Oh, I don't know.'

Joona goes into the bedroom, looks round quickly, sees a large oil-painting resting on the floor facing the wall, a dandelion clock in a whisky glass, the unmade bed, and a book.

Robert has already started to go back downstairs, and Joona follows him down to the large kitchen.

96

Raphael Guidi

Joona parks the car by Kronoberg Park and walks quickly across the grass towards Police Headquarters as he calls the Södertälje Police. He's started to worry about the fact that he didn't have time to wait while they were dealing with Pontus Salman.

His unease only gets worse when the officer in Södertälje explains that he doesn't know where Pontus Salman is.

'I'll call you back,' the man in a Gotland accent. 'Just give me a couple of minutes.'

'But you've got him?' Joona asks.

'We're supposed to have him,' the man says hesitantly.

'I made it very clear that he was to be held.'

'You don't have to have a go at me,' the officer says. 'I'm sure my colleagues have done their job properly.'

He taps at a computer, mutters to himself, then taps some more before speaking again.

'Yes, we've got him, and we've seized his shotgun, a Winchester 400.'

'Good, hold him and we'll send a car to collect him,' Joona says, detecting a faint whiff of chlorine from the Kronoberg baths as he walks in through the big glass doors.

He takes the lift up, walks quickly along the corridor and has almost reached Carlos Eliasson's office when his phone rings.

It's Disa. He hasn't really got time to take the call, but he answers anyway.

'Hi,' Disa says. 'Are you coming tomorrow?'

'You said you didn't want to celebrate your birthday.'

'I know, but I was thinking . . . just you and me.'

'That sounds good,' Joona says.

'I've got something important to tell you,' she says.

'Okay,' Joona says as he reaches Carlos's door.

'I . . .'

'Sorry, Disa,' he interrupts. 'But I can't talk more now. I'm just on my way into an important meeting.'

'I've got a surprise,' she says.

'Disa, I've got to go now,' he says, opening the door.

'But . . .' Disa says.

'I'm really sorry, but I haven't got time.'

He walks into Carlos's office, closes the door behind him and goes and sits down on the sofa next to Saga Bauer.

'We can't get hold of Axel Riessen and we're worried it's connected with the export licence,' Joona says. 'We think Raphael Guidi is behind this, so we need an arrest warrant as soon as . . .'

'An arrest warrant?' Carlos interrupts in astonishment. 'Axel Riessen hasn't been answering his phone for two hours, he didn't arrive at work this morning, and you think he's been kidnapped by Raphael Guidi, a successful businessman who has never been charged with any offences at all.'

Carlos raises his hand and starts counting on his fingers:

'The Swedish police have nothing on him, Europol have nothing on him, Interpol have nothing, and I've also spoken to the police in France, Italy and Monaco.'

'But I've spoken to Anja,' Joona says with a smile.

'You've spoken to . . .'

Carlos falls silent as the door opens and Anja Larsson comes in.

'During the past ten years Raphael Guidi's name has cropped up in six preliminary investigations relating to arms offences, financial offences and deaths,' she says.

'But preliminary investigations,' Carlos interjects. 'They don't mean . . .'

'Can I just say what I've found out?' she interrupts.

'Yes, of course.'

'The suspicions against Raphael Guidi were dismissed at an early stage in almost every case, and nothing has ever gone to trial.'

'Nothing,' Carlos says.

'His business earned a hundred and twenty-three million dollars in Operation Desert Storm by supplying the Nighthawk attack planes with AGM-65 Maverick missiles,' Anja goes on after consulting her notes to check the details. 'But one of his subsidiaries also supplied Serbian forces with rocket munitions when they shot down the same planes during the Kosovo war.'

Anja shows them a photograph of Raphael in sunglasses with bright yellow lenses. He's wearing casual clothes, cornflower-blue trousers and an ironed but loose shirt the same colour. He's standing between two black-clad bodyguards in front of a smoke-coloured Lamborghini Diablo.

'Raphael's wife . . . she used to be a famous violinist, Fiorenza Colini,' Anja says. 'Only a year after the birth of their son Peter she got breast cancer. She underwent all the treatment available, but died when the boy was seven.'

A newspaper cutting from *La Repubblica* shows Fiorenza Colini holding a beautiful red violin to her shoulder, with the orchestra of La Scala behind her, and conductor Riccardo Muti beside her with his wavy hair glinting under the spotlights. Fiorenza Colini is wearing a slim, shimmering platinum-coloured dress with silver embroidery and tiny glass prisms stitched into it. She is smiling to herself with her eyes closed. Her elbow is held low, the bow on its way down, her left hand arching over the body of the violin as she plays a high note.

A front cover of *Newsweek* shows Raphael Guidi standing next to Alice Cooper showing off his new-born son, under the heading 'Billion Dollar Baby'.

Another cutting shows him wearing a pale suit and talking to Silvio Berlusconi. Behind the men are three blonde women in minuscule bikinis sitting around a heart-shaped, pink marble swimming pool.

'Raphael Guidi is a resident of Monaco, but it looks like you have to head out to sea if you want to meet him,' Anja goes on. 'These days he spends almost all his time on his mega-yacht *Theresa*. Which is understandable. It was built by Lürssen in Bremen fifteen years ago, the most expensive one in the world at the time.'

A small picture in the French edition of *Vogue* shows the white, dart-shaped vessel on the open sea, like a porcelain arrowhead. A double-page spread inside, with the headline 'Lion en Cannes', contains a number of pictures from a party held on board the luxury yacht during the film festival. All the men are wearing dinner jackets. Kevin Costner is shown talking to Salma Hayek, and Raphael Guidi is seen standing between his wife and famous Swedish *Playboy* model, Victoria Silvstedt. Behind him stand two blank-faced bodyguards. The harbour is visible through the many windows of the dining room. There are toucans in cages hanging from the ceiling, and in the middle of the dining room is a cage containing a large male lion.

They hand the cuttings back to Anja, who goes on calmly:

'Now, shall we all take a listen to this? The Belgian security service recorded a phone call between an Italian prosecutor and Salvatore Garibaldi, who used to be a brigadier in Esercito Italiano – the Italian army.'

She distributes a hasty translation, then slots a USB stick into Carlos's computer, leans forward and clicks on the audio-file. A voice begins to talk rapidly, explaining the circumstances of the call in French: location, date and time. There's a metallic click as a call goes through.

The file crackles for a moment, then a voice can clearly be heard:

'I'm listening, and I'm prepared to instigate a preliminary investigation,' the prosecutor says.

'I'd never give evidence against Raphael, not even under torture, not . . .'

Salvatore Garibaldi's voice disappears in static, then becomes audible again, weaker, as if through a closed door.

'. . . with recoil buffers and recoilless rocket launchers . . . and a hell of a lot of mines, landmines, anti-personnel mines, anti-tank mines . . . Raphael would never . . . like Rwanda, he didn't care. That was all clubs and machetes – there was no money in that. But when it changed and spilled over into Congo he wanted to be part of it, because that's when it became dynamic, in his opinion. First he armed the Rwandan RPF regime to put Mobuto under serious pressure, then he started to pump heavy weaponry to the Hutus again, so that they could fight back against the RPF.'

There's a weird whistling noise through the static, then a clicking sound, before his voice comes back again.

He's breathing quickly, muttering to himself, and then says, very clearly:

'This business about the nightmare, I didn't believe it was real. I had to stand alongside holding her sweating hand . . . My daughter, she was fourteen. So beautiful, so perfect . . . Raphael . . . he did it himself, he wanted to wield the knife, kept yelling that he owned my nightmare. It's beyond comprehension.'

The line crackles and they can hear shouting, glass breaking, and the recording stutters.

'Why would anyone want to do things that are . . . He got the fillet-knife from one of his bodyguards . . . my daughter's face, her beautiful, beautiful . . .'

Salvatore Garibaldi is sobbing loudly, moaning and shouting that he just wants to die.

The recording crackles again, then stops. Silence descends on Carlos Eliasson's office. Light filters into the room through the small windows overlooking the green slopes of Kronoberg Park.

'This recording,' Carlos says after a while. 'It doesn't prove anything . . . He said at the outset that he wasn't going to give evidence, so I presume the prosecutor dropped the preliminary investigation.'

'Three weeks after this phone call, Salvatore Garibaldi's head was found by a dog-walker,' Anja says. 'It was lying in a ditch beside the Viale Goethe in the Villa Borghese in Rome.'

'What was that about his daughter?' Joona asks in a low voice. 'What happened?'

'Fourteen-year-old Maria Garibaldi is still missing,' Anja says bluntly.

Carlos sighs, mutters something to himself, then goes over to the aquarium and looks at his paradise fish for a while before turning back towards the others.

'What am I supposed to do? You can't prove that the ammunition is going to Sudan, and you've got nothing to show that Axel Riessen's disappearance is in any way connected to Raphael Guidi,' he says. 'Give me just a shred of evidence and I'll talk to the prosecutor, but I need something definite, not just . . .'

'I know it's him,' Joona interrupts.

'Not just Joona telling me that he knows,' Carlos concludes.

'We need the authority and resources to arrest Raphael Guidi for crimes against Swedish and international law,' Joona persists stubbornly.

'Not without proof,' Carlos says.

'We'll get proof,' Joona says.

'You need to persuade Pontus Salman to give evidence.'

'We're picking him up today, but I think it's going to be hard to get him to give evidence, he's still too frightened . . . so frightened that he was prepared to kill himself,' Joona says.

'But if we arrest Raphael, he might dare to talk. I mean, if things calm down,' Saga says.

'We can't just arrest a man like Raphael Guidi without any evidence or witnesses,' Carlos says emphatically.

'So what the hell are we supposed to do?' Saga asks.

'We put pressure on Pontus Salman, that's all we can . . .'

'But I think Axel Riessen is in danger,' Joona says. 'There's no time to lose, because . . .'

The four of them stop talking and look towards the door when Senior Prosecutor Jens Svanehjälm walks into the room.

97

The air-conditioning has made the car feel cold. Pontus Salman feels his hands shaking on the steering wheel. He's already halfway across the Lidingö Bridge. One of the Finland ferries is on its way out from its berth, and beyond Millesgården someone is burning leaves.

Only a couple of hours have passed since he was sitting in his rowing boat trying to put the barrel of his shotgun in his mouth. He can still taste the metal and feel the way it scraped against his teeth as a terrifying memory.

A woman with spiky hair came down onto the jetty with the detective, and called to him to come closer. It looked like she had something important to tell him. She was about forty, with a bluish, punkish hairstyle and red lipstick.

When he was sitting opposite her in a small, grey room later on, he found out that her name was Gunilla, and that she was a psychologist.

She had spoken to him sternly and seriously about the shotgun, and about what he was thinking of doing out on the lake.

'Why did you want to die, Pontus?' Gunilla asked.

'I didn't,' he had replied truthfully.

The silence filled the little room. Then they went on talking, and he answered her questions and became more and more convinced that he didn't want to die, that he'd much rather run away, and he had started thinking about going somewhere. Just disappearing and starting a new life as a different person.

The car is across the bridge now. Pontus Salman looks at his watch and feels the warmth of relief spread through his chest. By now Veronique's plane must have left Swedish airspace.

He's talked to Veronique about French Polynesia, and can see her in his imagination, walking out of the airport with a pale blue fabric bag in her hand, and a wide-brimmed hat that she has to hold onto in the wind.

Why shouldn't he escape too?

All he has to do is hurry back to the house and fetch his passport from the desk drawer.

I don't want to die, Pontus Salman thinks, as he watches the traffic rush past.

He rowed out onto the lake to escape his nightmare, but was incapable of firing the gun at himself.

I'll take any flight, he thinks. I can go to Iceland, Japan, Brazil. If Raphael Guidi really wanted to kill me, I wouldn't be alive now.

Pontus Salman turns into the drive in front of his house and gets out of the car. He breathes in the smell of sun-warmed tarmac, exhaust fumes and greenery.

The street is deserted, everyone is at work and the children still have a few days of school left.

Pontus Salman unlocks the door and walks in. The house is dark, the blinds closed.

He keeps his passport in his office, so starts to go downstairs.

When he reaches the ground floor he suddenly stops and listens, and hears an odd dragging sound, like a wet rag being pulled over a tiled floor.

'Veronique?' he says, in a voice that's almost inaudible.

Pontus Salman sees the calm light of the pool reflected off the white stone wall. He walks slowly forward with his heart thudding.

98

The prosecutor

Senior Prosecutor Jens Svanehjälm says a muted hello to Saga Bauer, Joona Linna and Carlos Eliasson, then sits down. The material that Anja Larsson has uncovered is lying on the low table in front of him. Svanehjälm drinks his soya latte, looks at the top picture, then turns to Carlos.

'I think you're going to have a hard time trying to convince me,' he says.

'But we'll do it,' Joona says with a smile.

'Make my day,' the prosecutor says.

Svanehjälm's thin neck, with no visible Adam's apple, and his narrow, sloping shoulders beneath his carefully tailored suit only emphasise the impression that he's a boy dressed as a grown-up.

'It's pretty complicated,' Saga says. 'We believe that Axel Riessen from the ISP has been abducted, and that his disappearance is connected to everything that's happened in the past few days.'

She stops when Carlos's phone rings.

'Sorry, I thought I'd made it very clear that we weren't to be disturbed,' he says, then picks up the phone and answers. 'Yes, Carlos Eliasson . . .'

He listens, his cheeks flush, he mumbles that he understands, says thanks for the call and puts the phone down with a reserved gesture.

'I'm sorry,' Carlos says.

'No problem,' Jens Svanehjälm replies.

'I mean I'm sorry to have dragged you to this meeting,' Carlos explains. 'That was Axel Riessen's secretary at the ISP, I contacted her earlier today . . . She says she's just spoken to Axel Riessen.'

'What did she say – had he been kidnapped?' Svanehjälm asks with a smile.

'He's on Raphael Guidi's boat, to discuss the last issues relating to the export licence.'

Joona and Saga glance quickly at each other.

'Are you happy with that answer?' the prosecutor asks.

'Apparently Axel Riessen had requested a meeting with Raphael Guidi,' Carlos says.

'He should have talked to us first,' Saga says.

'His secretary says they've been in a meeting out on the boat all day to sort out the last details of a case that's been dragging on, and Axel Riessen is hoping to fax the signed export licence to the ISP this evening.'

'The export licence?' Saga repeats, getting to her feet.

'Yes,' Carlos smiles.

'What's he going to do after the meeting?' Joona asks.

'He . . .'

Carlos tails off and looks at Joona in surprise.

'How did you know he was going to do anything after the meeting?' he asks. 'The secretary said Axel Riessen had booked some holiday to sail along the coast, all the way to Kaliningrad. He's going to borrow a Forgus from Raphael Guidi.'

'Sounds lovely,' Svanehjälm says, standing up.

'Idiots,' Saga snaps, and kicks the waste-paper bin over. 'Surely you can see that he was forced to make that call?'

'Let's all try to behave like adults,' Carlos mutters.

He picks the bin up and starts to gather the rubbish that fell out.

'We're done here, aren't we?' Svanehjälm says seriously.

'Axel Riessen is being held captive on Raphael Guidi's boat,' Joona says. 'Give us the resources to get him back.'

'I might be an idiot, but I can't see a single reason to take any action at all,' Jens Svanehjälm says, then walks out of the room.

They watch him close the door behind him without any hurry.

'Sorry I lost it back then,' Saga says to Carlos. 'But this doesn't make any sense, we don't believe Axel Riessen would ever sign the export licence.'

'Saga, I've had two lawyers look at this,' Carlos explains calmly. 'All they could see is that Silencia Defence's application for an export licence is perfect, the analysis has been ambitious and . . .'

'But we've got that photograph where Palmcrona and Salman are meeting Raphael Guidi and Agathe al-Haji to . . .'

'I know that,' Carlos interrupts. 'That was the answer to the mystery, and now we have the answer, but there's nothing more we can do without evidence. We have to be able to prove what we know, and the photograph alone isn't enough.'

'So we're just going to sit back and watch this ship leave Sweden even though we know the ammunition is on its way to fuel the genocide in Sudan?' Saga asks angrily.

'Just bring in Pontus Salman,' Carlos replies. 'Persuade him to give evidence against Raphael, promise him anything, just get him to give evidence . . .'

'And what if he won't do it, if he refuses?' Saga says.

'Then there's nothing we can do.'

'We've got another witness,' Joona says.

'I'd be very interested in meeting this witness,' Carlos says sceptically.

'We just need to get hold of him before he's found drowned off the coast of Kaliningrad.'

'You're not going to get your way this time, Joona.'

'Yes, I am.'

'No.'

'Yes,' Joona says in a hard voice.

Carlos looks at Joona sadly.

'We'll never be able to convince the prosecutor about this,' he says after a short pause. 'But because I don't want to spend the rest of my life sitting here saying no when you say yes, then . . .'

He tails off, sighs, thinks for a while, then goes on.

'I'm giving you permission to look for Axel Riessen on your own, to reassure yourself that he's okay.'

'Joona needs backup,' Saga says quickly.

'This isn't an official police operation, it's just a way of getting Joona to shut up,' Carlos says, and throws one arm out.

'But Joona will . . .'

'Right now,' Carlos interrupts, 'I want the two of you to fetch Pontus Salman from Södertälje, as I've already said . . . Because if you can get a witness statement that stands up, I'll see to it that we go in with full force and bring in Raphael Guidi, once and for all.'

'There isn't time for that,' Joona says, walking towards the door.

'I can talk to Pontus Salman on my own,' Saga says.

'What about Joona? What are you . . .'

'I'm going to pay Raphael a visit,' he says, and leaves the room.

99

After having to lie still in the boot of a car, Axel Riessen is finally allowed out. He is at a private airfield. The concrete landing strip is surrounded by a high fence. In front of a barrack-like building with a tall mast a helicopter is waiting.

Axel can hear the plaintive cries of seagulls as he walks between the two men who abducted him. He's still wearing just his shirt and trousers. There's no point trying to talk, he just goes with them and climbs into the helicopter, sits down and fastens the safety harness round his waist and over his shoulders. The other two men get into the cockpit of the helicopter, the pilot flicks a switch, turns a shiny little key on the instrument panel, flicks another switch and presses a pedal down.

The man beside the pilot takes out a map and puts it on his lap.

There's a strip of tape on the windscreen that has started to come loose.

The engine starts to rumble, and after a while the rotor slowly begins to turn. The narrow blades sweep sluggishly through the air, and the hazy sunshine glints on the glass. The rotor spins faster and faster.

A paper cup gets blown away from the helicopter.

The engine is heating up. The noise of the blades is deafening. The pilot grips the joystick in his right hand, guiding it with slight, edgy movements, then suddenly they take off.

At first the helicopter rises almost vertically, very gently. Then it tilts forward and starts to gain speed.

Axel's stomach lurches as they fly over the fence and up over the trees, then turn left so sharply that it feels like the helicopter is going to roll onto its side.

They fly quickly across the green landscape below them, crossing the occasional road and a house with a shiny tin roof.

The noise is extreme and the rotor-blades are whirring past in front of the windscreen.

The mainland comes to an end and the choppy, lead-grey sea takes over.

Axel tries once more to understand what's happening to him. It started when he spoke on the phone to Raphael Guidi, who was on his boat in the Gulf of Finland, on his way out into the Baltic and down towards Latvia. It can't have been much more than a minute after Axel told Raphael that he wasn't going to sign the export licence before the two men broke into his home and zapped him in the neck with a Taser.

Since then they had treated him well, and handled him carefully.

After half an hour in the first car they stopped, and the men carried him to a second car.

About an hour later they let him out onto the landing strip and led him to the helicopter.

The monotonous sea disappears beneath them as quickly as a motorway. The sky above feels motionless, overcast and damply white. They are flying fast at an altitude of fifty metres. The pilot is in radio contact with someone, but it's impossible to hear what he's saying.

Axel dozes off for a while, and doesn't know how long he's been in the helicopter when he catches sight of a magnificent luxury yacht on the choppy sea. It's a huge, white boat with a pale blue swimming pool and several sundecks.

They're getting rapidly closer.

Axel reminds himself that Raphael Guidi is an incredibly wealthy man, and leans forward to get a better view of the yacht. It's the most astonishing boat he's ever seen. Slender and pointed like a flame, as white as icing. It must be a hundred metres long, with a grand two-storey bridge above the aft-deck.

With a thunderous roar they sink down to the circles on the helicopter pad on the foredeck. The rotor-blades make the swell from the boat change direction and flatten as it gets pushed away.

The landing is so gentle that he almost doesn't feel it: the helicopter hovers, then descends very slowly until it's standing on the platform, rocking gently. They wait until the rotors have stopped moving. The pilot remains in the cockpit while the other man leads Axel Riessen across the landing pad with its painted circles. They crouch down until they get past a glass door. The sound of the helicopter almost disappears behind the glass. The room they are in resembles an elegant waiting room, with a suite of armchairs, a coffee table and a dark television. A man dressed in white welcomes them and invites Axel to sit down with a gesture towards the armchairs.

'Would you like anything to drink?' the man asks.

'Water, please,' Axel replies.

'Still or carbonated?'

Before Axel has time to answer, another man comes in through a door.

He looks like the first man, the one who was sitting beside the helicopter pilot. Both of them are tall and broad-shouldered, with strangely similar and synchronised bodies. The new man has very fair hair and almost white eyebrows, and a nose that has clearly been broken. The first has grey hair and is wearing horn-rimmed glasses.

They move silently, efficiently and sparingly as they lead Axel to the suites of rooms below deck.

The luxury yacht feels peculiarly deserted. Axel notices that the pool is empty; it doesn't look like it's been used for years. There's some broken furniture at the bottom, a cushionless sofa and some damaged office chairs.

Axel notes that the elegant cane furniture on a small balcony has seen better days. The weaving has cracked and there are splinters sticking out from the armchairs and coffee table.

The further in they go, the stronger the impression that the boat is an empty, abandoned shell. Axel's footsteps echo on the deserted corridor's scratched marble floor. They go in through a pair of double doors with the words 'Sala da pranzo' carved into the dark wood in elaborate lettering.

The dining room is vast. Through the panoramic windows there is nothing in sight except open water. A wide staircase with a red carpet leads up to the next deck. Ornate crystal chandeliers hang from the ceiling. The room is made for grand dinners, but on the dining table stand a photocopier, a fax machine, two computers and a large collection of folders full of paper.

At the far end of the dining room a short man is sitting at a smaller table. His hair is flecked with grey, and he has a large bald spot in the middle of his scalp. Axel recognises him immediately as arms dealer Raphael Guidi. He is wearing a pair of baggy, pale blue jogging bottoms and a matching top with the number 7 on the chest and back. On his feet he is wearing a pair of white trainers without socks.

'Welcome,' the man says, in heavily accented English.

His pocket rings and he pulls out his mobile, checks the screen but doesn't answer. Almost at once Raphael Guidi receives a second call, and he takes it, says a few brief words in Italian, then looks at Axel Riessen. He gestures towards the picture windows looking out over the dark expanse of the sea.

'I'm not here voluntarily,' Axel says.

'I'm sorry about that, there wasn't time for . . .'

'So what do you want?'

'I want to earn your loyalty,' Raphael says curtly.

They fall silent and the two bodyguards smile down at the floor before becoming very serious. Raphael takes a sip of his yellow vitamin drink and belches quietly.

'Loyalty is all that counts,' he says in a low voice, and looks Axel right in the eyes. 'You said before that I have nothing you wanted, but . . .'

'It's true.'

'But I think I've got a very good proposal,' Raphael goes on, and his face contorts into a joyless grimace that's supposed to be a smile. 'To win your loyalty, I know I have to offer you something you really want, perhaps the thing that you wish for most of all.'

Axel shakes his head.

'I don't even know what I wish for most of all.'

'I think you probably do,' Raphael says. 'You wish you could sleep again, sleep all the way through the night without . . .'

'How did you know . . .?'

He tails off abruptly and Raphael gives him a chilly, impatient glance.

'Then you presumably already know that I've tried everything,' Axel says slowly.

Raphael waves his hand dismissively.

'You can have a new liver.'

'I'm already in the queue for a liver transplant,' Axel says with an involuntary smile. 'I call every time the doctors have had a board meeting, but the damage to my liver was self-inflicted and my tissue type is unusual, which means that there are almost no suitable donors . . .'

'I've got a liver for you, Axel Riessen,' Raphael says in his accented English.

Silence falls, and Axel can feel his face starting to flush, and his ears are feeling warm.

'And in return?' Axel asks, and swallows hard. 'You want me to sign the export licence for Kenya.'

'Yes, I want us to enter into a Paganini contract,' Raphael replies.

'What's . . .?'

'No rush, you can think it over, it's a big decision. You need to see the exact details of the organ donor, and so on.'

Thoughts are spinning through Axel's head at lightning speed. He tells himself he can sign the export licence, then if he gets a new liver he can give evidence against Raphael Guidi afterwards. He'd get police protection, he knows that, and he might be forced to have a new identity, but he'd able to sleep again.

'Shall we eat? I'm hungry – are you hungry?' Raphael asks.

'A little, maybe . . .'

'But before we eat, I want you to call your secretary at the ISP and let her know you're here.'

100

Pontus Salman

Saga holds the phone to her ear and stops in the corridor next to a large container for recycling paper. With a distant look in her eyes she sees the leaf-like remains of a butterfly trembling on the floor in the draught from the ventilation system.

'Haven't you got anything better to do in Stockholm?' a man with a strong Gotland accent says when she finally gets put through to the Södertälje Police.

'I'm calling about Pontus Salman,' she says, trying to contain the stress in her voice.

'Yes, well he's gone now,' the police officer says happily.

'What the hell do you mean?' she asks, raising her voice.

'Look, I've only spoken to Gunilla Sommer, the psychologist who went with him to the emergency mental health unit.'

'And?'

'She didn't think he was serious about threatening to commit suicide, so she let him go. Hospital beds aren't free, after all, and . . .'

'Put out an alert for him,' Saga says quickly.

'What for? A half-hearted suicide attempt?'

'Just make sure you find him,' Saga says, and ends the call.

She starts to walk towards the lifts but Göran Stone steps in front of her and stops her, holding his arms out.

'You wanted to question Pontus Salman, didn't you?' he asks in a teasing tone of voice.

'Yes,' she replies tersely, and starts walking again, but he doesn't let her past.

'All you have to do is wiggle your backside,' he says. 'And maybe flutter your eyelashes a bit, and you'll get promoted or . . .'

'Move,' Saga snaps as angry red dots flare up on her forehead.

'Okay, sorry for trying to help,' Göran Stone says, pretending to be affronted. 'But we've just sent four cars to Salman's home on Lidingö because . . .'

'What's happened?' Saga asks quickly.

'His neighbours called,' he smiles. 'Apparently they heard gunshots and screaming.'

Saga shoves him out of the way and starts to run.

'*Thanks very much, Göran,*' he calls after her. '*You're the best, Göran!*'

As she drives out to Lidingö Saga tries not to think about everything that's happened, but her mind keeps going back to the recording of the man sobbing as he talked about what had happened to his daughter.

Saga tells herself that she'll do a hard session in the gym that evening, then get an early night.

She can't get through on Roskullsvägen, there are so many people out in the road that she has to park a couple of hundred metres away from Salman's house. Curious onlookers and journalists are pressed against the blue and white tape of the cordon trying to get a glimpse of the house. Saga mutters apologies as she pushes her way through. The flashing blue lights of the emergency vehicles are pulsing across the trees. Her colleague, Magdalena Ronander, is leaning against the dark-brown brick wall being sick. Pontus Salman's car is parked in front of the garage. The bonnet and driveway are littered with tiny, bloody cubes of glass. A man's body is visible through the side window.

Pontus Salman.

Magdalena looks up wearily, wipes her mouth with a handkerchief, and stops Saga as she's on her way into the house.

'No, don't,' she says in a hoarse voice. 'You definitely don't want to go in there.'

Saga stops, looks into the large house, turns towards Magdalena as if to ask something, then thinks that she needs to call Joona to let him know that they no longer have a witness.

101

The girl with dandelions

Joona is running through the arrivals hall of Vantaa Airport outside Helsinki when his phone rings.

'Saga? What's happening?'

'Pontus Salman is dead, he's sitting in his car outside his house, looks like he shot himself.'

Joona heads outside, goes over to the first taxi in the queue, tells the driver he wants to go to the harbour, then gets in the back seat.

'What did you say?' Saga asks.

'Nothing.'

'We've got no witnesses at all,' Saga says, sounding agitated. 'What the hell are we going to do?'

'I don't know,' Joona says, and closes his eyes for a few moments.

He can feel the car's movements, the gentle roll of the suspension. The taxi leaves the airport and speeds up as it pulls out onto the motorway.

'You can't head out to Raphael's boat without backup . . .'

'The girl,' Joona says suddenly.

'What?'

'Axel Riessen was playing the violin with a girl,' Joona says, opening his grey eyes. 'She might have seen something.'

'What makes you think that?'

'There was a dandelion, a dandelion clock in a whisky glass . . .'

'What the hell are you talking about?' Saga asks.

'Just try to get hold of her.'

Joona leans back in the seat and remembers how Axel Riessen had been standing with his violin in his hand when the girl brought a bunch of dandelions that had gone to seed. Then he thinks again about the dandelion clock with the bent stem, leaning over the edge of a whisky glass in Axel's bedroom. She had been there, which means that she might just have seen something.

Joona goes on board the patrol vessel *Kirku*, which the Finnish navy took over from the coastguard six years before. When he shakes hands with the ship's commander, Pasi Rannikko, his mind goes automatically to Lennart Johansson at the marine police on Dalarö – the guy who loved surfing and called himself Lance.

Pasi Rannikko looks a lot like Lance, a young, suntanned man with bright blue eyes. But unlike Lance, he takes his job extremely seriously. This unexpected mission outside Finnish territorial waters clearly troubles him.

'Nothing about this makes me happy,' Pasi Rannikko says drily. 'But my commanding officer is friends with your boss . . . and apparently that was enough.'

'I'm counting on getting a decision from the prosecutor while we're underway,' Joona says, feeling the vibration of the boat as it pulls away from the quay and heads out to sea.

'As soon as you get your decision from the prosecutor I'll contact the FNS *Hanko*. That's a fast attack craft with twenty officers and seven national service cadets.'

He points out the attack craft on the radar.

'She can get up to thirty-five knots, it'll take her less than twenty minutes to catch up with us.'

'Good.'

'Raphael Guidi's yacht has passed the island of Hiiumaa and is still off the coast of Estonia . . . I hope you're aware that we can't go on board a vessel in Estonian waters unless it's an emergency or there's openly criminal activity taking place.'

'Yes,' Joona replies.

With its engines rumbling, the boat leaves the harbour.

'Here comes the entire crew,' Pasi Rannikko says ironically.

A huge man with a blond beard climbs up onto the bridge. He's the boat's first and only mate, and introduces himself as 'Niko Kapanen, like the ice-hockey player'. He glances at Joona, scratches his beard, then asks tentatively:

'So what's Guidi suspected of doing?'

'Kidnap, murder, murdering police officers, arms smuggling,' Joona says.

'And Sweden's sending just one police officer?'

'Yes,' Joona smiles.

'And we're contributing an unarmed old barge.'

'As soon as we get a decision from the prosecutor we'll have almost a whole platoon,' Pasi Rannikko says in a monotone. 'I'll call Urho Saarinen on the *Hanko*, and he'll be with us in twenty minutes.'

'What about an inspection?' Niko says. 'Surely we have the right to conduct a damn inspection?'

'Not in Estonian waters,' Pasi Rannikko says.

'Fucking hell,' Niko mutters.

'It'll be okay,' Joona says curtly.

102

The other side of the picture

Axel Riessen is lying, fully dressed, on the bed in the five-room suite he has been given on Raphael Guidi's mega-yacht. Beside him is the folder containing detailed notes about the liver-donor, a man in a coma after an unsuccessful operation. All the test results are perfect – his tissue type is an exact match for Axel.

Axel stares up at the ceiling and feels his heart beat hard in his chest. He jumps when there's a sudden knock on the door. It's the man in white, the one who met him after the helicopter landed.

'Dinner,' the man says curtly.

They walk together through the spa area. Axel notes the large green tubs set into the deck, which are full of empty bottles and beer cans. There are still plastic-wrapped towels on the elegant white marble shelves along the walls. He can see a gym behind frosted glass walls. A double door made of matt metal slides silently open when they pass the relaxation area with its beige fitted carpet, sofas and low table made of polished limestone. The room is suffused with oddly dark light, casting slippery shadows and patches of light across the walls and floor. Axel looks up and realises that they are beneath the swimming pool. The bottom of the pool is made of glass, and the pale sky is visible through the rubbish and broken furniture.

Raphael Guidi is sitting on a sofa dressed in the same jogging bottoms as before, and a white T-shirt that's stretched across his stomach. He pats the seat beside him, and Axel walks over and sits down. The two bodyguards are standing behind Raphael like shadows. None of them speaks. Raphael Guidi's phone rings, he answers, and conducts a long conversation.

After a while the white-clad man returns with a serving trolley. He silently lays the low limestone table with plates and glasses, a large dish of fried hamburgers, bread and fries, a bottle of ketchup and a large plastic bottle of Pepsi.

Raphael doesn't look up, just carries on with his phone call. He is discussing details of production rates and logistics in a neutral voice.

No one says anything as they all wait patiently.

After fifteen minutes Raphael Guidi ends the call and looks calmly at Axel Riessen. Then he starts to talk, softly and gently.

'Perhaps you'd like a glass of wine?' he says. 'You can have a new liver in a couple of days.'

'I read through the information about the donor several times,' Axel says. 'He's perfect, I'm impressed, it all matches . . .'

'It's interesting, this business of wishes,' Raphael says. 'The things people wish for most of all. I wish my wife was still alive, and that we could be together.'

'I can understand that.'

'But for me, wishes are closely connected to their opposites,' Raphael says.

He helps himself to a hamburger and basket of fries, then passes the dish to Axel.

'Thank you.'

'A wish on one side of the scales balances a nightmare on the other,' Raphael goes on.

'Nightmare?'

'I just mean . . . we live our lives, getting caught up in all sorts of trivialities, we carry wishes that never get fulfilled, and nightmares that never come true.'

'Maybe,' Axel replies, taking a bite of his burger.

'Your wish to be able to sleep again can be fulfilled, but . . . I wonder how you imagine the other side of the scales, what your nightmare looks like?'

'I don't actually know,' Axel smiles.

'What are you afraid of?' Raphael asks, putting salt on his fries.

'Illness, death . . . pain.'

'Of course, pain, I agree,' Raphael says. 'But, speaking for myself, I've started to realise that it's all about my son. He's almost an adult now, and I've started to worry that he's going to move on, leave me behind.'

'Loneliness?'

'Yes, I think so,' Raphael says. 'Complete loneliness is probably my nightmare.'

'I'm already alone,' Axel smiles. 'The worst has already happened.'

'Don't say that,' Raphael jokes.

'No, but the idea of it happening again . . .'

'How do you mean?'

'Forget it, I don't want to talk about it.'

'You mean, causing another girl to commit suicide?' Raphael says slowly, putting something down on the table.

'Yes.'

'Who would kill herself?'

'Beverly,' Axel whispers, and sees that the object Raphael has put on the table in front of him is a photograph.

It's facing the table.

Axel reaches out his hand without really wanting to. His fingers are shaking when he turns the picture over. He snatches his hand away and gasps for breath. The photograph shows Beverly's quizzical face caught by the flash of a camera. He stares at the picture and tries to understand what's going on. He realises that it's meant as a warning, because the photograph was taken several days ago, inside his house, in the kitchen, when Beverly had been trying to play the violin, then went indoors to find a vase for the bunch of dandelion clocks.

103

Closer

After two hours on board the Finnish naval patrol vessel Joona catches his first glimpse of Raphael Guidi's luxury yacht as it glides gracefully across the horizon. In the bright sunlight it looks like it's made of sparkling crystal.

Captain Pasi Rannikko comes over to join him, and nods towards the huge yacht.

'How close do we go?' he asks tersely.

Joona gives him a look with his ice-grey eyes.

'Close enough to see what's happening on board,' he says calmly. 'I need . . .'

He falls silent when he feels a sudden stab of pain in his temples. He reaches for the railing and tries to breathe slowly.

'What's the matter?' Pasi Rannikko asks with a trace of laughter in his voice. 'Sea-sick?'

'Nothing to worry about,' Joona says.

The pain throbs again, and he clings on and only just manages to stay upright. He knows he can't possibly take his medication now, because it might leave him unfocused and tired.

Joona feels the chill wind cool the beads of sweat on his forehead. He thinks about the way Disa looked at him, her serious, transparent face. The sun glints off the surface of the water and he suddenly sees the bridal crown before him, shimmering in its display case in the Nordic Museum, its woven points glowing softly. He thinks about the scent of wild flowers and a church decked out for the summer wedding, and his heart is beating so fast that at first he doesn't realise that the captain is talking to him.

'What do you mean?'

Joona looks confusedly at Pasi Rannikko standing beside him, then over towards the big, white yacht.

104

Axel can't eat any more, he feels sick. His eyes keep going to the photograph of Beverly.

Raphael is dipping fries in a little pool of ketchup at the side of his plate.

Axel suddenly sees a young man standing in the doorway watching them. He looks tired and anxious. He's holding a mobile phone in his hand.

'Peter,' Raphael calls. 'Come here!'

'I don't want to,' the young man says in a weak voice.

'It wasn't a question,' Raphael smiles irritably.

The youth walks over and shyly says hello to Axel Riessen.

'This is my son,' Raphael explains, as if this were a perfectly ordinary dinner.

'Hello,' Axel says amiably.

The man who had sat next to the pilot in the helicopter is standing by the bar, tossing peanuts to a large, shaggy dog. His grey hair looks almost metallic and his white glasses are glinting.

'Nuts aren't good for him,' Peter says.

'After dinner can you fetch the violin?' Raphael asks with sudden weariness in his voice. 'Our guest is interested in music.'

Peter nods; he's pale and sweating, and the rings under his eyes look almost purple.

Axel makes an effort to smile.

'What sort of violin have you got?'

Peter shrugs his shoulders.

'It's far too good for me, it's an Amati. My mum was a musician, it's her Amati.'

'An Amati?'

'Which instrument is best?' Raphael asks. 'Amati or Stradivarius?'

'That depends who's playing,' Axel replies.

'You're from Sweden,' Raphael says. 'In Sweden there are four violins made by Stradivarius, but none that Paganini played on . . . and I daresay . . .'

'That sounds about right,' Axel says.

'I collect string instruments that still remember how . . . No,' he interrupts himself. 'Let me put it another way . . . If these instruments are handled correctly, you can hear the longing of a lost soul.'

'Possibly,' Axel says.

'I make it my business to provide a reminder of that longing when it's time to sign a contract,' Raphael goes on, smiling mirthlessly. 'I gather the interested parties, we listen to music, to this unique, mournful tone, and then we sign a contract in the air, with our wishes and nightmares as our stake . . . that's a Paganini contract.'

'I understand.'

'Do you?' Raphael says. 'It can't be broken, not even by one's own death. Anyone who tries to breach the terms of the agreement or take their own life should know that they will reap the fruits of their worst nightmare if they do so.'

'What do you want me to say?' Axel says.

'I'm just saying . . . This isn't the sort of contract you can break, and I . . . how can I put it?' he asks himself hesitantly. 'I can't see how it would benefit my enterprise if you were to mistake me for a kind person.'

Raphael goes over to the large television mounted on the wall. He takes a shiny disk from his inside pocket and inserts it in the DVD player. Peter sits down on the edge of one of the sofas. The boy looks awkwardly at the men in the room. His hair is fair, he doesn't look anything like his father. His frame isn't broad-shouldered and compact, but long-limbed, and his features are sensitive.

The screen flickers, then grey streaks appear. Axel feels a tangible, physical dread when he sees three people walk out through the door of a brick villa. He instantly recognises two of them: Detective Inspector Joona Linna and Saga Bauer. The third person is a young woman with Latin-American features.

Axel looks at the screen and watches as Joona Linna takes out a phone and makes a call. He doesn't appear to get an answer. The three of them look anxious and stressed as they get into a car and drive away.

The camera moves slowly towards the door, which opens, and the screen goes momentarily dark from the change in light, before being adjusted by the automatic focus. There are two large suitcases in the hall. The camera carries on into the kitchen, then turns left and goes down a flight of stairs, along a tiled passageway and into a large room containing a swimming pool. A woman in a bathing suit is sitting on a sun-lounger, and a second woman with a boyish haircut is standing and talking on her phone.

The camera moves back furtively, waits for the woman to finish her call, then moves forward again. The sound of footsteps is very audible and the woman with the phone turns her weary, frightened face towards the camera and stiffens. An expression of utter dread fills her face.

'I don't think I want to watch any more, Dad,' Peter says in a thin voice.

'It's only just starting,' Raphael replies.

The screen suddenly goes dark as the camera is switched off, then the picture comes back again, and flickers as the light-level stabilises. The camera is now fixed to a stand, and the two women are sitting next to each other on the floor with their backs to the tiled wall. On a chair in front of the women sits Pontus Salman. He looks like he's breathing fast, and his body keeps shuffling nervously on the chair.

The clock in the corner of the screen indicates that the recording was only made an hour ago.

A black-clad man with his face covered by a balaclava walks

over to Veronique, grabs hold of her hair and forces her face towards the camera.

'Sorry, sorry, sorry,' Raphael says in a squeaky voice.

Axel looks at him quizzically, then hears Veronique Salman's voice:

'Sorry, sorry, sorry.'

Terror makes her voice sound clipped.

'I had no idea,' Raphael squeaks, and points at the television.

'I had no idea,' Veronique pleads. 'I took the photograph, but I didn't mean any harm, I didn't know how stupid it was, I just thought . . .'

'You have to choose,' the man in the balaclava says to Pontus Salman. 'Who do I shoot in the knee? Your wife . . . or your sister?'

'Please,' Pontus whispers. 'Don't do this.'

'Who should I shoot?' the man asks.

'My wife,' Pontus replies, almost inaudibly.

'Pontus,' his wife begs. 'Please, don't let him . . .'

Pontus starts to cry, his body wracked with loud sobs.

'It's going to hurt if I shoot her,' the man warns.

'Don't let him do it!' Veronique screams in panic.

'Have you changed your mind? Shall I shoot your sister instead?'

'No,' Pontus replies.

'Ask me.'

'What?' he asks, his face distraught.

'Ask me to do it nicely.'

Silence, then Axel hears Pontus Salman say:

'Please . . . shoot my wife in the knee.'

'Seeing as you asked so nicely, I'll shoot her in both her knees,' the man says, and holds his revolver to Veronique Salman's leg.

'Don't let him do it!' she screams. 'Please, Pontus . . .'

The man fires, there's a sharp bang and her leg jerks. Blood sprays across the tiles. A cloud of percussive gas spreads out from the pistol. Veronique screams so hard that her voice breaks. He fires again. The recoil makes the barrel of the pistol jump. Her other leg bends at an impossible angle.

Veronique screams again, hoarse, almost inhuman, her body jerks with pain and blood spreads out across the tiled floor beneath her.

Pontus Salman throws up, and the man in the balaclava watches him with a bemused, detached look in his eyes.

Veronique leans sideways, breathing hard as she tries to reach her wounded legs with her hands. The other woman looks like she's in shock, her face is pale and her eyes just big black holes.

'Your sister's mentally ill, isn't she?' the man asks curiously. 'Do you think she knows what's going on?'

He pats Pontus Salman's head consolingly then says:

'Shall I rape your sister or shoot your wife?'

Pontus doesn't answer, he looks like he's going to pass out. His eyes start to roll back in his head, and the man slaps him across the face.

'Answer me: shall I shoot your wife or rape your sister?'

Pontus Salman's sister shakes her head.

'Rape her,' Veronique whispers between gasped breaths. 'Please, Pontus. Please! Tell him to rape her.'

'Rape her,' Pontus whispers.

'What?'

'Rape my sister.'

'Okay, soon,' the man says.

Axel looks down at the floor between his feet. He tries hard to hear anything apart from the moaning from the television, the pleading, the raw, terrified screams. He tries to fill his head with memories of music, tries to conjure up the spaces Bach creates, spaces full of radiant beams of light.

In the end the television goes silent. Axel looks up at the screen. The two women are lying dead against the wall. He sees the man in the balaclava stand there breathing heavily with a knife in one hand and the pistol in the other.

'The nightmare has been reaped – now you can kill yourself,' the man on the screen says, tossing the pistol to Pontus and then walking away, behind the camera.

105

Saga Bauer walks away from Magdalena Ronander and steps back over the cordon. The crowd has got even bigger, and a large truck from Swedish Television has arrived. A uniformed police officer is trying to get people to move so that an ambulance can get through.

Saga leaves it all behind her and takes a detour, up a paved path into someone's garden and past a large philadelphus. She speeds up and runs the last stretch towards the car, across a lawn.

'The girl,' Joona had said out of the blue on the phone. 'You have to find the girl. There was a girl in Axel Riessen's house. He called her Beverly. Talk to his brother, Robert. She's about fifteen years old, it must be possible to trace her.'

'How long have I got to get the prosecutor on side with this?'

'Not long,' Joona had said. 'But you'll do it.'

As Saga drives into Stockholm she tries calling Axel Riessen, but there's no answer. She calls the main number for the National Crime Unit and asks to be put through to Joona's assistant, the rather plump woman who once won an Olympic medal in swimming, and who insists on wearing elaborately painted finger-nails and bright lipstick.

'Anja Larsson,' a voice replies after just half a ring.

'Hi, this is Saga Bauer from the Security Police, we met earlier in . . .'

'I know,' Anja replies coolly.

'I was wondering if you could track down a girl who might be called Beverly, and . . .'

'Shall I invoice the Security Police for that, then?'

'Do whatever the hell you like, as long as you get me a fucking phone number before . . .'

'Mind your language, young lady.'

'Forget I asked.'

Saga swears and blows her horn loudly at a car that's not moving even though the lights have turned green. She's about to end the call when Anja suddenly speaks.

'How old is she?'

'Around fifteen.'

'There's only one Beverly of that age, Beverly Andersson. She's not got a phone number registered . . . but she's listed as living at the same address as her father, Evert Andersson.'

'Okay, I'll call him. Can you text me his number?'

'I already have.'

'Thanks – thank you, Anja . . . Sorry I was impatient, I'm just worried about Joona, about him doing something stupid if he doesn't get backup.'

'Have you spoken to him?'

'He's the one who asked me to look for the girl. I've never even met her, I don't know . . . He's relying on me to sort this out, but . . .'

'Call Beverly's dad, and I'll carry on looking,' Anja says, and hangs up.

Saga pulls over to the verge in Hjorthagen and pulls up the number Anja has sent her. The dialling code, 0418, tells her it's a Skåne number, in the far south of Sweden. Maybe Svalöv, she thinks as the phone rings.

106

In a pine kitchen in the middle of Skåne, a man starts when his phone rings. He's just come in from spending over an hour trying to disentangle one of the heifers that got through the electric fence and got itself caught on the neighbour's barbed wire. Evert Andersson has blood on his fingers, blood that he's wiped off on his blue overalls.

His dirty fingers aren't the only things stopping him from answering when the phone rings – there isn't really anyone he feels like talking to right now. He leans over and looks at the screen, and sees that it's a withheld number. Probably one of those marketing calls from a salesman with a phony-sounding voice.

He waits until it stops ringing. But then it starts again. Evert Andersson takes another look at the screen, and eventually answers:

'Andersson.'

'Hello, my name is Saga Bauer,' a stressed female voice says. 'I'm a police officer, a superintendent with the Security Police. I'm trying to contact your daughter, Beverly Andersson.'

'What's happened?'

'She hasn't done anything, but we believe she may have important information that could help us.'

'And now she's gone missing?' he asks weakly.

'I thought you might have a phone number I can reach her on,' Saga says.

Evert thinks of how he once saw his daughter as his heir, someone to carry on the family business, and take over the running of the house, barns, offices and fields. She would walk across the farm the way her mother had, in a sheepskin coat and with her hair in a plait over one shoulder.

But even as a small child there had been something different about Beverly, something that frightened him.

As she grew up, she became more and more different. Different to him, different to her mother. One time he walked into one of the barns when she was eight, nine years old. She was sitting in an empty pen on an upturned bucket, singing to herself with her eyes closed. She was lost in the sound of her own voice. He had been about to yell at her to stop, and not to be so silly, but the joyous expression on her face bewildered him. From that moment he knew there was something inside her that he would never understand. And he stopped talking to her. As soon as he tried to say anything, all his words would vanish.

When her mother died the silence on the farm became absolute.

Beverly started to wander, she could be missing for hours at a time, even whole days. The police had to bring her home from places she had no idea how she had reached. She would go with anyone if they spoke to her kindly.

'There's nothing I want to say to her. So why would I have a phone number?' he says in his brusque, dismissive Skåne accent.

'Are you sure you . . .'

'It's not the sort of a thing a Stockholmer would understand,' he snaps, and puts the phone down.

He looks at his fingers on the phone, sees the blood on his knuckles, the dirt under and around his fingernails, in every crease and crack. He walks slowly to the green armchair, picks up the entertainment supplement of the evening paper and starts to leaf through it. That evening they are broadcasting a tribute to the former television personality Ossian

474

Wallenberg. Evert lets the paper fall to the floor when his tears catch him by surprise. He had suddenly remembered that Beverly used to sit and watch *Golden Friday* on the sofa next to him.

107

The empty room

Saga Bauer swears loudly to herself as she sits in the car. She closes her eyes and slams her hand on the steering wheel several times. Slowly she tells herself that she needs to focus, and find a way to make progress before it's too late. She's so immersed in thought that she starts when her phone rings.

'It's me again,' Anja Larsson says. 'I'm putting you through to Herbert Saxéus at the Sankta Maria Hjärta clinic.'

'Okay, what . . .?'

'Saxéus looked after Beverly Andersson for the two years she lived at the clinic.'

'Thanks, that's . . .'

But Anja has already connected Saga to another line.

Saga waits as the phone rings. Sankta Maria Hjärta, she thinks, recalling that the hospital is in Torsby, east of Stockholm.

'Hello, Herbert here,' a warm voice says in her ear.

'Hello, my name is Saga Bauer, I'm a police officer, a super-intendent with the Security Police. I need to get in touch with a girl who used to be one of your patients, Beverly Andersson.'

The line goes quiet.

'Is she okay?' the doctor asks after a pause.

'I don't know, I need to talk to her,' Saga says quickly. 'It really is urgent.'

'She's still lodging with Axel Riessen, who . . . well, he's her informal guardian.'

'So she lives there?' Saga asks, turning the key in the ignition and driving off.

'Axel Riessen is letting her stay there until she finds a place of her own,' he replies. 'She's only fifteen, but it would have been a mistake to try to force her to move back home again.'

The traffic is relatively light and Saga is able to drive fast.

'Can you tell me what Beverly Andersson is being treated for?' she asks.

The doctor takes a deep breath, then says in his deep, friendly voice:

'I don't know if it's of any real interest . . . As her doctor, I'd say she was suffering from a serious personality disorder when she first came here, Cluster B.'

'What does that mean?'

'Nothing,' Herbert Saxéus replies, and clears his throat. 'But if you were to ask me as a human being, I'd say that Beverly is healthy, probably healthier than most people . . . I know it sounds like I'm talking rubbish, but she isn't the one who's sick.'

'The world is.'

'Yes,' he sighs.

Saga thanks him and ends the call, and turns into Valhallavägen. The back of the driver's seat is sticky with sweat. Her phone rings and she accelerates past the traffic lights at the Olympic Stadium just as they're turning red before she answers.

'I thought I'd have a word with Beverly's dad as well,' Anja says. 'He's a very nice man, but he's had a rough day looking after a wounded cow, trying to make it feel better. His family's always lived there. Now there's just him left on the farm. We talked about Nils Holgersson's Wonderful Journey, and in the end he went and got some letters that Beverly had sent him. He hadn't even opened them. Can you imagine such a stubborn man? Beverly had written her phone number in every letter.'

Saga Bauer thanks Anja several times, then calls the number. She pulls up outside Axel and Robert Riessen's house as her call to Beverly Andersson's mobile phone goes through.

Ring after ring disappears into the void. The sun shines through the dust in the air in front of the church. Saga can feel her body trembling from exertion as time starts to run out: Joona is going to end up completely alone when he confronts Raphael Guidi.

With the phone clutched to her ear, she walks up to Robert Riessen's door and rings the bell. Suddenly there's a click on the phone and she hears a faint rustling sound.

'Beverly?' Saga says. 'Is that you?'

She can hear someone breathing.

'Answer me, Beverly,' Saga says, in the gentlest voice she can muster. 'Where are you?'

'I . . .'

The line goes quiet again.

'What did you say? What did you say, Beverly, I couldn't quite hear you?'

'I mustn't come out yet,' the girl whispers, and ends the call.

Robert Riessen is silent and pale as he leaves Saga in Beverly Andersson's room and asks her to lock up behind her when she's done. The room looks almost uninhabited. The only things in it are some basic items of clothing in the wardrobe, a pair of wellington boots, a padded jacket and a phone charger.

Saga locks the door behind her, then goes into Axel Riessen's apartment to try to figure out what Joona had meant about the girl being able to give evidence. She passes through the silent reception rooms, the sitting room and library. The door to Axel Riessen's bedroom is ajar. Saga walks over the thick Chinese rug, past the bed and into the adjoining bathroom, then returns to the bedroom. Something has put her on edge. There's an anxious atmosphere in the room and Saga puts one hand on the Glock in her shoulder holster. On the table is a whisky glass with the wilted remains of a dandelion.

Dust is moving slowly in the sunlight, the furniture and other belongings are pregnant with silence. Her heart suddenly beats faster as a branch outside scrapes the window.

She goes over to the unmade bed, looks at the pattern of the sheets, the two pillows.

Saga imagines she can hear careful footsteps from the library and is about to creep in that direction when a hand grabs hold of her ankle. There's someone lying under the bed. She pulls free, moves backward, draws her pistol and accidentally knocks over the table holding the glass.

Saga gets down on her knees, pointing the gun, but quickly lowers it again.

From the darkness under the bed a girl is looking at her with big, frightened eyes. Saga puts her pistol back in its holster again, then lets out a deep sigh.

'You're glowing,' the girl whispers.

'Beverly?' Saga asks.

'Can I come out now?'

'I swear, you can come out now,' Saga says calmly.

'Has an hour passed? Axel told me not to come out until an hour had passed.'

'Much more than an hour has passed, Beverly.'

Saga helps her out of the cramped space. The girl is wearing nothing but her underwear, and is stiff from having lain still for so long. Her hair is very short, and her arms are covered in drawings and writing.

'What were you doing under Axel Riessen's bed?' Saga asks, trying to keep her voice steady.

'He's my best friend,' Beverly replies quietly, pulling on a pair of jeans.

'I think he's in danger – you have to tell me what you know.'

Beverly stands there with her T-shirt in her hand. Her face turns red and her eyes fill with tears.

'I haven't . . .'

Beverly falls silent and her mouth begins to quiver.

'Hey, don't get upset,' Saga says, trying again to stifle the anxiety in her voice.

'I was lying in bed when Axel came in,' Beverly says in a thin voice. 'I realised at once that something had happened, because his face was really pale. I thought he was sad because I'd hitched a lift, because I'm not supposed to do that.'

She stops and turns her face away.

'Please, go on, Beverly. We're in a bit of a hurry.'

Beverly whispers an apology, wipes her cheeks quickly with the T-shirt, then looks at Saga with moist eyes.

'Axel came into the room,' Beverly goes on, more composed now. 'He told me to crawl under the bed and stay hidden for a whole hour . . . then he rushed out into the living room and I don't know . . . I only saw their legs, but two men went in behind him. They did something terrible to him. He screamed and they threw him on the floor and wrapped him in white plastic, then they carried him out. It all happened really fast. I didn't see their faces . . . I don't even know if they were people . . .'

'Hold on a moment,' Saga says, taking her phone out. 'You need to come with me and tell the same thing to a man called Jens Svanehjälm.'

Saga calls Carlos Eliasson with her hands shaking with stress.

'We've got a witness who saw Axel Riessen being abducted against his will. We've got a witness,' she repeats. 'The witness saw Riessen being attacked and taken away, that has to be enough.'

Saga looks into Beverly's eyes as she listens to the response.

'Good, we're coming in at once,' she says. 'Get Svanehjälm, and make sure he's got Europol prepared.'

108

Raphael Guidi walks through the dining room with a black leather folder in his hand. He puts it down on the table and pushes it across to Axel Riessen.

'Pontus Salman's nightmare, as you may have guessed, was being forced to choose between his wife and his sister,' he explains. 'I don't know, I've never found it necessary to be so explicit before, but I have . . . How can I put it? I have found that some people imagine that they can escape their nightmare by dying. Don't misunderstand me, most of the time everything is perfectly pleasant and civilised, I'm a very generous man towards people who are loyal.'

'You're threatening to hurt Beverly.'

'You can choose between her and your brother, if you'd prefer that?' Raphael says, swallows some of his vitamin drink, wipes one corner of his mouth and then asks Peter to fetch the violin.

'Have I told you I only own instruments that Paganini himself played?' he asks. 'That's the only thing I care about. It's said that Paganini hated his face . . . personally I believe he sold his soul to the devil to be worshipped. He called himself an ape . . . but when he played, women threw themselves at him. It was worth the cost. He would play and play until he seemed to be on fire.'

Axel looks out through the huge windows, where the great

expanse of water is lying quite still. Through the smaller windows facing the foredeck he can make out the white helicopter in which he arrived on the luxury yacht. Axel's thoughts keep alternating between the hideous film and possible escape routes.

He feels incredibly tired, and just sits and listens to Raphael talking about violins, Stradivarius's fixation on the higher notes, the hardness of the wood, the slow growth of maple and fir trees.

Raphael pauses, smiles lifelessly once again, and says:

'As long as you are loyal, you can enjoy everything on the beneficial side of the scales – you can have a healthy liver, sleep well, live your life. All that would require is that you don't forget your contract with me.'

'And you want the export licence signed.'

'I would want that in any case, but I don't want to force you, I don't want to kill you, that would be a waste, I want . . .'

'My loyalty,' Axel concludes.

'Is that foolish, do you think?' Raphael asks. 'Think for a moment, then count the number of people in your life whom you know to be completely loyal.'

Silence settles between them. Axel stares in front of him.

'Exactly,' Raphael says after a while with a sad look on his face.

109

Axel opens the leather folder on the table and sees that it contains all the documentation needed for the M/S *Icelus* to be granted permission to leave Gothenburg harbour with its cargo of ammunition.

The only thing missing is his signature.

Raphael Guidi's son Peter comes back into the room, his face pale and blank. He's holding an extremely beautiful violin, a reddish-brown instrument with a bowed top plate. Axel can see at once that it's an Amati, and an extremely well-preserved Amati at that.

'As I think I mentioned, I believe certain music is suited to what we're about to do,' Raphael says softly. 'That violin belonged to his mother . . . and much further back, Nicolò Paganini played it.'

'It was made in 1657,' Peter says, taking his keys and mobile phone out of his pockets and putting them on the table before raising the violin to his shoulder.

The boy places the bow on the strings, and hesitantly starts to play. Axel immediately identifies the opening notes of Paganini's most famous work, *24 Caprices*. It's reputed to be the most difficult violin piece in the world. The boy plays like he's underwater, far too slowly.

'It's a generous contract,' Raphael says quietly.

It's still light outside, the big picture windows are spreading a grey shimmer over the room.

Axel thinks about Beverly, and the way she had crept up onto his bed at the psychiatric clinic and whispered: *You're glowing, I could see it from out in the corridor.*

'Have you had enough time to think?' Raphael asks.

Axel can't bring himself to look into Raphael's desolate eyes, and looks down as he picks up the pen in front of him. He can hear his own heart beating and tries to hide the fact that he's breathing very fast.

This time he isn't going to draw a stick-figure saying hello, he's going to sign his name and pray to God that Raphael Guidi will be content with that and let him return to Sweden.

Axel feels the pen shake in his hand. He puts his other hand on top of it to hold it still, takes a deep breath, then puts the tip of the pen to the empty line on the page.

'Wait,' Raphael says. 'Before you sign anything, I want to know if you're going to be loyal.'

Axel looks up and meets his gaze.

'If you really are prepared to reap your nightmare if you breach the contract, you need to show it by kissing my hand.'

'What?' Axel whispers.

'Do we have a contract?'

'Yes,' Axel replies.

'Kiss my hand,' Raphael says in a distorted voice, as if he were playing the idiot in an old play.

His son is playing slower and slower, trying to get his fingers to obey him, to change position, but keeps getting the difficult transitions wrong. He loses his place and suddenly just gives up.

'Keep going,' Raphael says without looking at him.

'It's too hard for me, it doesn't sound good.'

'Peter, it's very immature to give up before you've even . . .'

'Play it yourself,' his son says.

Raphael's face becomes completely rigid, like a rock-face.

'Do as I say,' he says, forcing himself to remain calm.

The boy stands perfectly still, looking at the floor. Raphael's right hand goes to the zip of his tracksuit top.

'Peter, I thought it sounded good,' he says in a composed voice.

'The bridge is crooked,' Axel says, almost in a whisper.

Peter looks at the violin with blushing cheeks.

'Can it be repaired?' he asks.

'Adjusting it is easy, I can do it if you like,' Axel says.

'Will it take long?' Raphael asks.

'No,' Axel replies.

He puts the pen down, takes the violin and turns it over, feeling how light it is. He's never held a genuine Amati before, and certainly never one that Paganini himself played.

Raphael Guidi's phone rings. He takes it out and looks at it, then stands up and moves away as he listens to someone at the other end.

'That can't be right,' he says with an odd expression on his face.

A strange smile plays across his lips, then he says something in a tense voice to the bodyguards. They leave the dining room and hurry up the steps after Raphael.

Peter watches Axel as he loosens the strings. The instrument creaks. The dry sound caused by the movement of his fingers is amplified by the body. Axel carefully moves the bridge, then stretches the strings across it.

'Is it okay?' Peter whispers.

'Yes,' Axel replies as he tunes the violin. 'Try it now and you'll see.'

'Thanks,' Peter says, taking the violin.

Axel notices that Peter's mobile is still on the table, and says:

'Keep playing. You'd just finished the first progression and were about to play the pizzicato.'

'Now I'm even more embarrassed,' Peter says, turning away.

Axel leans on the table, carefully reaches his hand out behind him and touches the phone, but manages to nudge it in a way that makes it spin round silently on the tabletop.

With his back to Axel, Peter puts the violin to his shoulder and raises his bow.

Axel takes the phone, holds it hidden in his hand, and moves a little way to the side.

Peter lowers the bow to the strings, then stops, turns round and tries to see past Axel.

'My phone,' he says. 'Is it behind you?'

Axel lets the phone slide out of his hand and onto the table again before turning round and picking it up.

'Can you see if I've got a text message?' Peter asks.

Axel looks at the phone and notes that it's got full reception, even though they're in the middle of the sea. Then he realises that of course the boat must have a satellite connection.

'No messages,' he says, and puts the phone back on the table. 'Thanks.'

Axel stays by the table as Peter continues playing *Caprice* No. 24, slowly and increasingly awkwardly.

Peter isn't talented, and even though he clearly practises a lot there's no way he's going to be able to master this piece. Even so, the timbre of the violin is so wonderful that Axel would have enjoyed it if a small child had just been plucking at the strings. He leans back against the table and listens, trying to reach the phone again.

Peter struggles to find the right settings for his fingers, but he loses the tempo, stops and starts again while Axel tries to reach the phone. He moves sideways but doesn't have time to grab it. Peter plays a wrong note, stops and turns towards Axel again.

'It's hard,' he says, and makes another attempt.

He starts again, but quickly goes wrong.

'It's impossible,' he says, lowering the violin.

'If you keep your ring-finger on the A-string, it'll be easier to make . . .'

'Can you show me?'

Axel glances at the phone lying on the table. There's a glint of light from outside and Axel turns to look at the picture windows. The sea is oddly still and empty. There's a rumble from the engine room, a persistent noise that he hasn't noticed until now.

Peter hands Axel the violin, and he puts it to his shoulder, tenses the bow slightly, then starts to play the piece from the beginning. The flowing, melancholic introduction spreads through the room as Axel plays it at a high tempo. The tone of the instrument isn't powerful, but wonderfully soft and clean.

Paganini's music coils around itself, increasingly faster and higher.

'God . . .' Peter whispers.

The pace is suddenly dizzying, prestissimo. It's playful and beautiful, and simultaneously suffused with abrupt note changes and sharp jumps between octaves.

Axel has all the music in his head, and just has to let it out. Not every note is perfect, but his fingers can still find their way over the neck of the violin, darting across the wood and strings.

Raphael shouts something from the bridge, and something hits the floor, making the chandelier tinkle. Axel goes on playing – the twittering progressions sparkle like sunlight on water.

Suddenly there are footsteps on the stairs, and when Axel sees Raphael walk in with a sweaty face and a bloody military knife in his hand, he stops playing abruptly. The grey-haired bodyguard is walking beside Raphael with a yellowish-green assault rifle raised, a Belgian Fabrique Nationale SCAR.

110

Joona Linna is standing with a pair of binoculars next to Pasi Rannikko and the bearded first mate. They're watching the enormous luxury yacht that's sitting motionless on the sea. The wind has dropped during the day. The Italian flag is hanging limply. There's no visible sign of activity on the boat. It's as if the passengers and crew have been lured into enchanted sleep. The Baltic Sea is calm, the water reflecting the clear blue sky. The gentle swell that occasionally lifts the water seems to be easing still further.

Suddenly Joona's phone rings in his pocket. He hands the binoculars to Niko, pulls out his phone and answers.

'We've got a witness!' Saga yells. 'The girl's our witness, she saw everything. Axel Riessen was kidnapped, the prosecutor has already acted, you can go on board to look for him!'

'Good work,' Joona says tersely.

Pasi Rannikko looks at him as he puts his phone away.

'We've got a decision from the prosecutor to arrest Raphael Guidi,' Joona says. 'He's suspected of abduction on reasonable grounds.'

'I'll contact the FNS *Hanko*,' Pasi Rannikko says, and hurries over to the comms unit.

'They'll be here in twenty minutes,' Niko says animatedly.

'This is a request for assistance,' Pasi Rannikko says into the microphone. 'We have authorisation from a prosecutor to go on board Raphael Guidi's boat immediately and arrest him . . . Yes, that's correct . . . Yes . . . Get moving! Get fucking moving!'

Joona looks through the binoculars again, from the painted white steps from the platform at the rear, across the lower decks and up to the aft-deck with its folded parasols. He looks for movement through the dark windows of the dining room, but can see nothing but black. He looks along the railing, then up to the next deck, with the main terrace.

The air emerging from the funnels above the bridge is vibrating. Joona points the binoculars at the dark windows, then stops. He thinks he can see movement through the glass. Something white sliding across the inside of the pane. As first it reminds him of a huge wing, furled feathers pressed against the glass.

Then, a moment later, it looks like a piece of fabric or white plastic being folded up.

Joona squints to see better, and suddenly finds himself looking at a face staring back at him, raising a pair of binoculars to his eyes.

The steel door to the bridge of the yacht opens and a fair-haired man in dark clothes comes out, climbs quickly down some steps and hurries across the foredeck.

It's the first time Joona has seen anyone on board Raphael's boat.

The dark-clad man walks over to the helicopter on the landing pad, loosens the straps over the runners and opens the cockpit door.

'They're listening to our communications,' Joona says.

'We can change channel,' Pasi Rannikko calls out.

'Doesn't matter now,' Joona says. 'They're not staying on the boat, it looks like they're going to use the helicopter.'

He passes the binoculars to Niko.

'We'll have reinforcements in fifteen minutes,' Pasi Rannikko says.

'That'll be too late,' Joona declares quickly.

'There's someone in the helicopter,' Niko says.

'Raphael knows we've got a prosecutor's authorisation to go

on board,' Joona says. 'He must have got the information the same time as us.'

'Can the two of us go on board?' Niko asks.

'Looks like that's the only option,' Joona says, glancing at him.

Niko inserts a magazine into his assault rifle, a pitch-black, short-barrelled Heckler & Koch 416.

Pasi Rannikko pulls his pistol from his holster and passes it to Joona.

'Thanks,' Joona says, checking the ammunition and then looking it over to familiarise himself with it. It's an M9A1, semi-automatic. It's similar to the M9, which was used in the Gulf War, but the magazine looks a bit different, and has fittings for a light and laser-sights.

Without saying anything, Pasi Rannikko steers the patrol vessel towards the platform at the aft of the yacht, which is just above the waterline. When they get closer the yacht feels huge, like a tower block. The engine slips into reverse and the boat brakes with a surge of foam. Niko slings the fenders over the railing, and the hull nudges the platform with a creak.

Joona climbs on board, then the boats start to glide apart and water squelches up between them. Niko jumps and Joona catches his hand. His assault rifle clatters against the railing. Their eyes meet briefly, then they head towards the steps, squeezing past some broken cane furniture and old wine-boxes, and continue heading upwards.

Niko turns and waves to Pasi Rannikko, who is already steering the patrol vessel away from the yacht.

111

Raphael Guidi is standing on the bridge with the bodyguard with the cropped grey hair and horn-rimmed glasses. The captain stares at them anxiously, and rubs his stomach with his hand.

'What's happening?' Raphael asks quickly.

'I gave the order to warm up the helicopter,' the captain says. 'I thought . . .'

'Where's the boat?'

'There,' he says, pointing towards the stern.

The unarmed patrol vessel is clearly visible, beyond the decks of the yacht, the swimming pool and lifeboats. Swell is lapping against the speckled grey hull as the propellers turn the vessel.

'What did they say? What exactly did they say?' Raphael asks.

'They were in a hurry, asked for backup, said they had an arrest warrant.'

'None of it makes sense,' Raphael says, looking round.

Through the window they can see the helicopter pilot already sitting in the cockpit. The rotors have just started to move. Suddenly the sound of Paganini's *Caprice* No. 24 can be heard from the dining room below.

'There's their backup,' the captain says, pointing at the radar.

'I see it. How long have we got?' Raphael asks.

'They're maintaining a speed of just over thirty-three knots, so they'll be here in ten minutes.'

'No problem,' the bodyguard says, glancing at the helicopter. 'We can get you and Peter away in time, at least three minutes before . . .'

The other, fair-haired bodyguard rushes in through the glass door of the bridge. His pale face looks worried.

'There's someone here. There's someone on the boat,' he cries.

'How many?' the grey-haired bodyguard asks.

'I only saw one, but I don't know . . . he was carrying an assault rifle, but no special equipment.'

'Stop him,' the grey-haired man tells his colleague tersely.

'Give me a knife,' Raphael snaps.

The bodyguard pulls out a knife with a narrow grey blade. Raphael takes it and walks closer to the captain with a tense look on his face.

'So they were going to wait for backup?' he yells. 'You said they were going to wait for backup!'

'As I understood it, they . . .'

'What the hell are they doing here? They've got nothing on me,' Raphael says. 'Nothing!'

The captain shakes his head and takes a step back. Raphael moves closer.

'What the hell are they doing here if they haven't got anything on me?' he screams. 'There's nothing . . .'

'I don't know, I don't know,' the captain replies with tears in his eyes. 'I just repeated what I heard . . .'

'What did you say?'

'Say? I don't understand . . .'

'I haven't got time for this,' Raphael yells. 'Just tell me what the fuck you said to them!'

'I haven't said anything to them.'

'Weird. Fucking weird, isn't it? Isn't it?'

'I've been monitoring their channels, just like I should, I haven't . . .'

'Is it really so hard to confess?' Raphael roars, then darts forward and drives the knife straight into the captain's stomach.

Almost without any resistance it glides through his shirt and into fat and guts. Blood sprays out like steam above a bath, spattering Raphael's hand and the sleeve of his tracksuit top. With an incredulous expression on his face the captain tries to take a step back to get away from the knife, but Raphael follows him, and stands there for a few moments looking him in the eye.

Violin music is still coming from the dining room, its light notes dancing and bubbling.

'It could be Axel Riessen,' the grey-haired bodyguard suddenly says. 'He could be bugged, he might be in contact with the police via . . .'

Raphael pulls the knife from the captain's stomach and rushes down the steep flight of steps.

The captain stands there clutching his stomach as the blood drips onto his black shoes. He tries to take a step, but slips over, and lies there staring up at the roof.

The grey-haired bodyguard follows Raphael with his assault rifle raised, staring out through the picture windows of the dining room.

Axel stops playing when Raphael comes in and points the bloody knife at him.

'Traitor!' he roars. 'How could you be so fucking . . .'

The grey-haired bodyguard suddenly fires his assault rifle with a series of ear-splitting shots. The bullets pass straight through the windows, and the shells fall onto the steps with a clatter.

112

Joona and Niko head carefully up the steps, past the lower deck and up to the expanse of the aft-deck. The silent sea spreads out in all directions like a vast pane of glass. Suddenly Joona hears violin music. He tries to see through the big glass doors. He can make out dark shapes through the reflective surface. He can only see a small portion of the dining room. There's no one in sight. The music continues feverishly, as distant as a dream, muffled by the glass.

Joona and Niko wait a few seconds, then run quickly across an open space beside a waterless swimming pool and in under the projecting roof to the next flight of metal steps.

They hear footsteps on the deck above and Niko points at the steps. They press up against the wall beside the ladder.

The rapid, playful violin music is clearer now. The violinist is obviously very talented. Joona glances cautiously into a huge dining room with office equipment on various tables, but he still can't see anyone. Whoever is playing the music must be hidden by the wide, red staircase.

Joona gestures to Niko to follow him and cover his back, and points to the bridge above them.

Suddenly the violin stops playing in the middle of a beautiful passage.

Very suddenly.

Joona throws himself behind the ladder just as he hears the muffled sound of automatic fire. Sharp, hard bangs. The jacketed bullets hit the ladder where he was standing a moment before and ricochet off in different directions.

Joona pulls back further behind the steps, feeling adrenalin course through his body. Niko has taken cover behind the lifeboat winch and is returning fire. Joona crouches down and moves round, and sees the row of bullet-holes across the dark window, like rings of frost around black pupils.

113

The knife-blade

The grey-haired bodyguard carries on down the stairs with his gun aimed at the picture windows and the row of bullet-holes. The barrel of the assault rifle is smoking, and the empty shells clatter down the steps.

Peter has curled up with his hands over his ears.

Without a sound, the bodyguard leaves the dining room through a side door.

Axel moves away between the tables, with the violin and bow in his hand. Raphael points at him with the knife.

'How could you be so fucking stupid?' he screams, moving after Axel. 'I'm going to cut your face, I'm going to . . .'

'Dad, what's happening?' Peter cries.

'Fetch my pistol and get to the helicopter – we're leaving the boat!'

The boy nods. His face is pale and his chin is trembling. Raphael starts to walk through the tables towards Axel again. Axel moves backwards, toppling chairs in front of him to block Raphael's path.

'Load it with Parabellum, hollow-tipped,' Raphael says.

'One magazine?' the boy asks, sounding more focused.

'Yes, that'll be enough – but get moving!' Raphael replies, kicking a chair out of the way.

Axel tries to open the door on the other side of the room. He twists the lock, but the door won't budge.

'We're not finished, you and me,' Raphael roars.

Axel yanks at the handle with his free hand, then notices the bolt at the top of the door. Raphael is only metres away now. As he gets ever closer with the knife, Axel acts instinctively. He turns round and throws the beautiful violin at Raphael. It spins through the air, red and shimmering. Raphael darts to the side and stumbles over a fallen chair in order to save the instrument. He almost catches it, drops it, but manages to break its fall.

The violin slides onto the floor with a dull clang.

Axel gets the door open and rushes into a cluttered corridor. So many things have been abandoned in it that it's hard to move. He climbs over a pile of sun-loungers and slips on a heap of goggles and wetsuits.

'I'm coming to get you,' Raphael says, following him with the violin in one hand and the knife in the other.

Axel falls over a rolled tennis net, catches his foot in the broken netting, and crawls away from Raphael, who's marching towards him through the passageway. He kicks wildly to free himself.

Outside there's the sound of automatic gunfire, a series of short, hard shots.

Raphael is breathing heavily and lunges with the knife, but doesn't have time to do anything before Axel pulls free. He stumbles to his feet, backs away and pulls a large table-football game over in front of Raphael. He rushes to the next door, his hands fumble with the lock and handle – there's something blocking the door, but he manages to open it a little.

'There's no point,' Raphael calls.

Axel tries to squeeze through the gap, but it's too tight. There's a large cupboard full of stacked clay pots in the way. He throws himself at the door again and the cupboard shifts a few centimetres. Axel can feel Raphael behind him, getting closer and closer. A chill runs down his spine as he shoves the door again and forces his body through the gap. He cuts himself on the lock but doesn't care, he just has to get away.

Raphael tries to reach him with the knife, he swipes and the point of the blade cuts into Axel's shoulder.

He feels a sudden flare of pain.

Axel tumbles into a light room with a glass roof. It looks like an abandoned greenhouse. He carries on, feels his shoulder with his hand and looks at the blood on his fingers as he knocks into a withered lemon tree.

He hurries on, crouching down between the benches of dry plants with shrivelled leaves.

Raphael is kicking the door hard, grunting loudly with each kick. The pots rattle and the cupboard slowly moves.

Axel knows he has to hide, and quickly crawls under one of the benches and shuffles sideways, beneath a dirty plastic sheet. He carries on, in amongst a clutter of buckets and tubs. He's hoping that Raphael is going to give up soon and just leave the boat with his son.

There's a thunderous noise from the door and several pots fall to the deck and shatter.

Raphael comes into the room, panting for breath, and leans against a trellis covered in withered vines.

'Come out and kiss my hand!' Raphael calls.

Axel does his best to breathe silently, and tries to move further back, but he can't get any further. His path is blocked by a large metal cabinet.

'I promise to keep my promises,' Raphael says with a smile, looking round at the benches and dry stumps of dead plants. 'Your brother's liver is waiting for you, and all you have to do to get it is kiss my hand.'

Axel feels sick, and sits there shaking with fear with his back against the metal cabinet. His heart is beating fast. He does his best to be completely silent. There's a roaring sound inside his head. He stares around him, trying to find a way out, and realises that there's a sliding door leading to the yacht's foredeck just five metres away from him.

He can hear the sound of the helicopter as its engines warm up.

Axel thinks he could crawl under the table laden with soil-filled clay pots, and then run the last bit. He starts to move sideways, very cautiously. The door only seems to be held by a clasp.

He raises his head to get a better view, and just about manages to think that he could be out on the foredeck in a few seconds when he suddenly feels as if his heart has stopped. The cold blade of a knife is being held to his throat. The touch of the metal stings slightly. Raphael has found him and crept up on him behind his back. His body is pulsing with adrenalin, it's like being chilled from inside. Only now does he hear Raphael's breathing and smell his sweat. The knife-blade is resting against his throat, and feels like it's burning him.

114

The final struggle

The grey-haired bodyguard leaves the dining room silently, slipping out between the doors and running quickly along the side of the deck with his sand-coloured assault rifle held to his shoulder. The light glints off his glasses. Joona sees that the bodyguard is heading towards Niko from behind, and will reach him in just a few seconds.

Niko is completely unprotected from that direction.

The bodyguard raises the gun and moves his finger to the trigger.

Joona quickly stands up, aims, takes a step forward to clear his line of sight, and shoots the bodyguard with two shots directly in the chest. The grey-haired man staggers backward, reaches out his hand and grabs the railing to stop himself falling. He looks round, sees Joona rushing towards him and raises the assault rifle.

Only now does Joona see that he's wearing a bulletproof vest under his black jacket.

Joona is already upon him, pushes the barrel of the rifle away with one hand and slams his pistol into his face with the other. It hits his nose and glasses hard. The bodyguard's legs buckle, the back of his head hits the railing with a dull clang, and sweat and snot spray from his face as his body collapses.

Joona and Niko make their way towards the front of the yacht on either side of the dining room. The helicopter's rotors are clattering faster and faster.

'Come on! Get in!' someone shouts.

Joona runs as close to the wall as he can. He slows down and cautiously walks the last bit, and looks out across the open foredeck. Raphael Guidi's son is already sitting in the helicopter. The shadows of the rotor-blades flutter across the deck and railings.

Joona hears voices from the bridge above him, and has just taken a step forward when he realises that Raphael Guidi's other bodyguard has spotted him. The fair-haired man is standing twenty-five metres away, and his pistol is aiming straight at Joona. There's no time to react before the shot goes off. There's a blunt bang. It feels like the crack of a whip in Joona's face, and then everything goes white. He crashes over some sun-loungers and lands hard on the metal deck, hitting the back of his head against the railing of the terrace. The hand holding the pistol slams into the bars holding the railing. His wrist almost breaks and the gun falls from his grasp. The pistol echoes as it falls through the bars and hits the metal panelling.

Joona blinks and his sight starts to come back. He crawls in behind the wall. His hands are shaking, and he can't really understand what happened. Warm blood is running down his face as he tries to get to his feet – he needs to get to Niko to help him, needs to figure out where the bodyguard went.

He quickly feels his cheek, and a flash of pain when his fingers move further up tells him that the bullet merely grazed his temple.

It's left only a superficial wound.

He can hear a strange ringing sound in his left ear.

His heart is beating fast, thudding hard in his chest.

When he stands up again with the help of the metal wall his head becomes even more painful.

The ringing tone of the migraine is getting louder.

Joona presses one thumb against his forehead, between his eyebrows, and closes his eyes, forcing the flaring pain away.

He glances over at the helicopter, trying to see Niko as he looks along the foredeck and railings.

The Finnish navy's fully equipped vessel is approaching from behind like a black shadow across the calm sea.

Joona twists off a long strip of metal from the broken sun-lounger so that he has some sort of weapon when the bodyguard comes for him.

He presses himself against the wall, then suddenly sees Raphael and Axel on the foredeck. They're standing close together, backing slowly towards the helicopter. Raphael has his right arm around Axel and is holding a knife to Axel's throat with one hand. In his other hand he is clutching a violin. Their clothes and hair are blowing in the downdraught from the rotor-blades.

The bodyguard who shot Joona is slipping smoothly sideways to get a clear view of him behind the wall. He isn't sure if he hit the intruder in the head, it all happened too quickly.

Joona knows the bodyguard is looking for him, and tries to pull back, but his headache is slowing his movements.

He has to stop.

Not now, he thinks, as he feels the sweat running down his back.

The bodyguard rounds the corner, raises his weapon, and gradually Joona's shoulder comes into view, followed by his head and neck.

Suddenly the bearded figure of Niko Kapanen rushes out from the other side with his assault rifle raised. The bodyguard is fast, spins round and fires his pistol, a series of four shots. Niko doesn't even notice the first bullet hit his shoulder, but stops when the second hits him in the stomach, penetrating his small intestine. The third shot misses, but the fourth hits him in the chest. Niko's legs buckle and he falls sideways, behind the bulkhead at the base of the helipad. He's seriously wounded, and probably unaware that he's squeezing the trigger of the assault rifle as he falls. The bullet fly off aimlessly. He empties the entire magazine in two seconds, straight out over the water, until it just clicks.

Niko gasps, his eyes roll into his head as he slides onto his back, leaving a bloody stain across the bulkhead, and he drops the rifle. His chest is horribly painful. He closes his eyes for a few seconds, then looks up groggily and sees the massive bolts beneath the helipad. He notes that rust has penetrated the white paint surrounding the huge nuts, but doesn't notice his right lung filling with blood.

He coughs weakly, and is on the brink of losing consciousness when he suddenly sees Joona, hidden against the dining room wall with a length of metal in his hand. Their eyes meet, Niko summons the last of his strength and kicks the assault rifle over towards Joona.

Axel is terrified. His heart is racing, the sound of the shots is ringing in his ears and his body is trembling. Raphael is dragging him along like a shield. They both stumble, and the blade of the knife is cutting into the skin on his neck. He feels warm blood start to trickle down his chest. He sees the last bodyguard approaching Joona Linna's hiding place but can do nothing about it.

Joona reaches forward quickly and snatches up the hot assault rifle. The bodyguard in front of the helicopter fires two shots at him. They ricochet off the walls, floor and railing. Joona removes the empty magazine, and sees Niko feeling in his pockets for more ammunition. Niko gasps, he's very weak and has to pause for a moment with his hand pressed against his bloody stomach. The bodyguard shouts to Raphael to get in – the helicopter is ready to take off. Niko feels in one of his trouser pockets and pulls his hand out again. A sweet-wrapper flies off in the wind, but in his palm is one bullet. Niko coughs weakly, looks at the single bullet and then rolls it across the deck towards Joona.

The jacketed bullet spins across the metal floor, its brass case and copper tip glinting in the light.

Joona grabs it and quickly pushes it into the magazine.

Niko's eyes are closed now, a bubble of blood appears between his lips. He's still breathing, but very shallowly.

The bodyguard's heavy steps resound across the deck.

Joona slides the magazine into the assault rifle, feeds the only bullet into the chamber, raises the gun, waits a moment, then leaves his hiding place.

Raphael is still backing away, holding Axel in front of him. His son is shouting from the helicopter, and the pilot is beckoning Raphael to get in.

'You should have kissed my hand when you had the chance,' Raphael whispers in Axel's ear.

The strings of the violin ring out as Axel's arm brushes against them.

The bodyguard walks quickly towards Niko, leans over the bulkhead and points the pistol at his face.

'Jonottakaa,' Joona says in Finnish.

He sees the bodyguard raise the gun to point it at him instead and darts sideways, trying to find the right line – he has to make his only shot count.

It all happens in a matter of seconds.

Raphael is standing immediately behind the bodyguard, holding the knife to Axel's throat. Their clothes are being blown about by the downdraught from the helicopter. Drops of blood fly through the air. Joona crouches down slightly, lowers the sights a few millimetres, then fires the assault rifle.

Jonottakaa, he thinks. Get in line.

There's a bang and he feels the hard recoil against his shoulder. The jacketed bullet leaves the barrel at a speed of 800 metres per second. Without any sound at all, the bullet goes in through the bodyguard's throat and out the back of his neck, and continues with very little loss of velocity, straight through Raphael Guidi's shoulder and on across the sea.

His arm flails from the impact and the knife clatters across the deck.

Axel Riessen sinks to the deck.

The bodyguard stares at Joona in surprise as blood streams down his chest. He tries to raise the pistol with his wavering arm, but hasn't got the strength. He makes a weird gurgling sound and coughs, and a surge of blood pours down his chin.

He sits down, fumbles for his throat with one hand, blinks twice, then his eyes stay wide open.

Raphael's lips are pale. He's standing in the pulsing downdraught pressing the hand holding the violin to his bleeding shoulder, staring at Joona.

'Dad!' his son cries from the helicopter, and tosses a pistol towards him.

It lands on the deck with a clatter, bounces and stops in front of Raphael's feet.

Axel is sitting dazed against the railing, trying to stop the flow of blood from his neck with his hand.

'Raphael! Raphael Guidi!' Joona shouts loudly. 'I'm here to arrest you.'

Raphael is standing five metres away from his helicopter with the pistol between his feet. His tracksuit is flapping around his body. With an immense effort he bends down and picks up the pistol.

'You're suspected of arms smuggling, kidnap and murder,' Joona says.

Raphael's face is sweaty and the pistol is shaking in his hand.

'Put the gun down,' Joona calls.

Raphael holds the heavy pistol in his hand, but his heart starts to beat faster when he looks Joona in the eye.

Axel is staring at Joona, and tries to tell him to run.

Joona stands still.

Everything happens at the same time.

Raphael raises the pistol towards Joona and squeezes the trigger, but the pistol just clicks. He tries again, and takes a deep breath when he realises that his son didn't fill the magazine as he promised. Raphael feels a terrible loneliness embrace him. He realises that it's too late to drop the gun and surrender at the same moment his body is rocked by three gentle thuds, one after the other. Then the sound of the shots rings out across the sea. To Raphael it feels like someone is punching him hard in the chest, followed by shrill pain as he staggers backwards and loses all feeling in his legs.

The helicopter doesn't wait any longer, it takes off without Raphael Guidi, rising into the air with a roar.

The Finnish navy's fast attack vessel FNS *Hanko* is alongside the yacht. The three snipers fire again. All three bullets hit Raphael's torso, but the sound of the shots merges into one.

Raphael takes a few steps back and falls. He tries to sit up, but can no longer move.

His back feels hot, but his feet are already ice-cold.

Raphael stares up at the helicopter rising quickly into the hazy sky.

Peter sits in the helicopter gazing down at the shrinking luxury yacht. His father is lying on the helipad, in the centre of the circles, at the middle of a target.

Raphael Guidi is still clutching Paganini's violin in his hand. A pool of dark blood is spreading out rapidly around him, but the look in his eyes is already dead.

Joona is the only person still standing on the foredeck of the boat.

He stands still as the white helicopter disappears.

The sky is illuminated by a desolate, crystalline light. Three vessels lie still on the expanse of calm water, drifting alongside each other as if they've been abandoned.

Soon the rescue helicopters from Finland will arrive, but right now it's quiet and remarkably still, like the moment after the last note of a concert, while the audience are still enchanted by the music and the silence that follows it.

115

Conclusion

Joona Linna, Axel Riessen, Niko Kapanen and the grey-haired bodyguard are transported by emergency helicopter to the HCUS surgical hospital in Helsinki. At the hospital Axel couldn't help asking Joona why he didn't move when Raphael picked up the pistol from the deck.

'Didn't you hear me shouting?' Axel asked.

Joona just looked him in the eye and explained that he had already seen the snipers on the boat, and expected them to fire their weapons before Raphael had time to fire his.

'But they didn't,' Axel pointed out.

'You can't be right all the time,' Joona replied with a smile.

Niko was awake when Joona and Axel went in to say goodbye. He joked about feeling like Vanhala in the novel *The Unknown Soldier*.

'Say hello to Sweden,' he told them. 'But . . . tough little Finland came in a very good second!'

Niko's injuries were very serious, but no longer life-threatening. He would have to undergo a number of operations over the next few days, then would be allowed home to his parents in a wheelchair within a couple of weeks. It would be almost a year before he would be able to play ice-hockey with his sister again.

Raphael Guidi's bodyguard was arrested and taken to Vantaa

Prison while his extradition was processed, and Joona Linna and Axel Riessen went home to Stockholm.

The large container vessel, M/S *Icelus*, never left Gothenburg harbour. Its cargo of ammunition was unloaded and taken to the warehouses of the Swedish Customs Office.

Jens Svanehjälm was put in charge of the protracted legal proceedings, but with the exception of Raphael Guidi's nameless bodyguard, all the guilty parties were already dead.

It wasn't possible to determine if anyone else at Silencia Defence Ltd had been involved in criminal activity. The only person who had committed an offence at the Inspectorate for Strategic Products was its former director general, Carl Palmcrona.

A case was prepared against Jörgen Grünlicht, for suspected bribery and as an accessory to arms offences, but none of the charges was deemed strong enough to go to trial. The conclusion was that the Export Control Committee and any Swedish politicians involved in the deal had all been deceived and had been acting in good faith.

The material gathered during the preliminary investigations relating to two Kenyan politicians was handed over to Roland Lidonde, Minister for Governance and Ethics, but it looked likely that even the Kenyan politicians would also be found to have acted in good faith.

The freight company, Intersafe Shipping, were unaware that the cargo was to be taken from Mombasa harbour to south Sudan, and the Kenyan transport company, Trans Continent, didn't know that the goods they had been commissioned to carry to Sudan consisted of ammunition. Everyone had acted in good faith.

Axel Riessen feels the stitches pull at his neck as he gets out of the taxi and walks the last bit of the way up Bragevägen. The tarmac looks pale, almost white, in the blazing sunlight. The moment he puts his hand on the gate the front door swings open. Robert has been looking out for him from the window.

'What on earth have you been up to?' Robert says, shaking his head. 'I've spoken to Joona Linna, and he told me some of it, it sounds insane . . .'

'You should know by now that your big brother's pretty tough,' Axel smiles.

They hug each other hard, then start to walk towards the house.

'We've laid the table in the garden,' Robert says.

'How's your heart? Hasn't stopped yet, then?' Axel asks, following his brother through the front door.

'I was actually booked in for an operation next week,' Robert replies.

'I didn't know that,' Axel says, and feels the hairs on the back of his neck stand up.

'To have a pacemaker fitted, I don't think I mentioned it . . .'

'An operation?'

'It got cancelled.'

Axel looks at his brother and it feels as if his soul is going

509

through contortions in the darkness. He realises that Raphael had booked Robert's operation, that it was predestined to go horribly wrong, and that Robert was supposed to die on the operating table and donate his liver to him.

Axel has to stop in the hallway and calm down before he goes any further. His face feels hot, and a sob is welling up in his throat.

'Are you coming?' Robert asks breezily.

Axel stays where he is for a moment before following his brother through the house and into the back garden. The table on the marble floor under the large tree is standing ready.

He's on his way towards Anette when Robert takes hold of his arm and stops him.

'We had fun when we were kids,' Robert says, with a serious look on his face. 'Why did we stop talking? How did that happen?'

Axel looks at his brother in surprise, at the wrinkles at the corners of his eyes, the ring of hair around his bald scalp.

'Things happen in . . .'

'Wait a moment . . . I didn't want to say over the phone,' Robert interrupts.

'What is it?'

'Beverly said that you think it was your fault that Greta took her own life, but I . . .'

'I don't want to talk about that,' Axel says instantly.

'You have to,' Robert says. 'I was there on the day of the competition, I heard everything, I heard Greta and her father talking, she couldn't stop crying, she'd made a mistake and her dad was horribly upset and . . .'

Axel pulls free from his brother's hand.

'I already know everything that . . .'

'Just let me say what I have to say,' Robert interrupts.

'Go on, then.'

'Axel . . . if only you'd said something, if only I'd known you thought it was your fault that Greta died. I heard her dad. It was his fault, and his fault alone . . . They had a terrible row, I heard him say the most appalling things, that she'd made a fool of him in public, that she was no longer his daughter. That he didn't want her in the house, she'd have to leave college and move in with her junkie mother in Mora.'

'He said that?'

'I'll never forget the way Greta's voice sounded,' Robert goes on steadily. 'She was so frightened when she tried to tell her dad that everyone makes mistakes, that she'd tried her hardest, that it wasn't such a disaster, there'd be more competitions . . .'

'But I've always . . .'

Axel looks round, doesn't know what to do with himself. All the energy goes out of him and he just sits down heavily on the marble floor and covers his face with both hands.

'She was crying, and told her dad she'd kill herself if she wasn't allowed to stay and carry on with her music.'

'I don't know what to say,' Axel whispers.

'Thank Beverly,' Robert replies.

It starts to rain heavily as Beverly is standing on the platform of the Central Station in Stockholm. Her journey south takes her through a summer landscape shrouded in grey mist. The sun doesn't appear again before the train reaches Hässleholm. She changes trains in Lund, and then takes the bus from Landskrona to get to Svalöv.

It's been a long time since she was last home.

She thinks about how Dr Saxéus has assured her that it's going to be okay.

'I've talked to your dad,' the doctor said. 'He's serious.'

Beverly walks across the dusty square and sees an image of herself lying in the middle of the square being sick two years ago. Some boys had persuaded her to drink hooch. They took photographs of her and then they let go of her in the square. That was the incident that made her dad decide he didn't want her in the house any more.

She walks on. Her stomach clenches when she sees the road open up outside the town. The farm is three kilometres away. It was along this stretch of road that drivers used to pick her up. Now she can't remember why she thought going with them was a good idea. She thought she could see something in their eyes. A glow, she used to think.

Beverly switches her heavy bag to her other hand.

In the distance a car is approaching.
She recognises it, doesn't she?
Beverly smiles and waves.
Her dad's coming. Dad's coming.

Penelope Fernandez

Roslags-Kulla Church is a small, red wooden church with a big, beautiful bell-tower. The church is situated in a tranquil location out in the countryside near Vira bruk, some distance from the region's busiest roads. The sky is bright blue and the air is clear, and the scent of wild flowers is being carried on the wind across the churchyard.

Yesterday Björn Almskog was buried in Stockholm's Northern Cemetery, and now four men in black suits are carrying Viola Maria Liselott Fernandez to her final resting place. Penelope and her mother Claudia are walking with the priest behind the pall-bearers, two uncles and two cousins from El Salvador.

They stop at the open grave. One of Penelope and Viola's cousin's children, a nine-year-old girl, looks at her father. He nods, and she takes out her recorder and starts to play Psalm 97 as the coffin is lowered into the ground.

Penelope Fernandez holds her mother's hand, and the priest reads from the Book of Revelations.

God shall wipe away all tears from their eyes, and there shall be no more death.

Claudia looks at Penelope, adjusts her collar, then pats her cheek as if she were a small child.

As they are walking back towards the cars, Penelope's phone buzzes in her little black handbag. It's Joona Linna. Penelope gently detaches herself from her mother and goes into the shade of one of the large trees before she answers.

'Hello, Penelope,' Joona says in his unmistakable voice, sing-song but sombre.

'Hello, Joona,' Penelope says.

'I thought you'd like to know that Raphael Guidi is dead.'

'And the ammunition for Darfur?'

'We stopped it.'

'Good.'

Penelope looks over at her family and friends, and her mother, who's still standing where she left her, not taking her eyes off Penelope.

'Thank you,' she says.

She returns to her mother, who takes her hand again and together they walk towards the people waiting by the cars.

Penelope.

She stops and turns round. She thought she heard her sister's voice, very close by. A shiver runs down her spine as a shadow crosses the fresh green grass. The little girl who played the recorder is standing among the gravestones looking at her. She's lost her hairband and her hair is blowing in the summer breeze.

Saga Bauer and Anja Larsson

The summer days never seem to end: the night shines like
mother-of-pearl until dawn.

The Swedish Police Force is holding a staff party in the
baroque garden in front of Drottningholm Palace.

Joona Linna is sitting with his colleagues at a long table
under a large tree.

On a stage beside a red dance-floor a group of musicians are
playing 'Hårgalåten', a traditional Swedish folksong.

Petter Näslund is dancing with Fatima Zanjani from Iraq.
With a broad smile on his face, he says something that makes
her look happy.

The song tells how the devil played the violin so well that
the young folk didn't want to stop dancing. They danced all
night, and when they made the mistake of not respecting the
church-bells they were physically unable to stop dancing. They
were so tired that they were crying. Their shoes got worn down,
their feet got worn down, until in the end only their heads were
bouncing around to the violin music.

Anja is sitting on a folding chair. She's wearing a flowery blue
dress, and is glaring at the couples dancing. Her round face is
sullen, disappointed. But her cheeks flush when she sees Joona
leave his seat at the table.

'Happy Midsummer, Anja,' he says.

Saga Bauer is skipping across the grass between the trees. She's chasing soap-bubbles with Magdalena Ronander's twins. Her billowing blonde hair with its colourful braids is shimmering in the sunlight. Two middle-aged women have stopped to look at her in admiration.

'Ladies and gentlemen,' the singer says after the applause. 'We've had a special request . . .'

Carlos Eliasson smiles to himself and glances at someone behind the stage.

'My roots are in Oulu, in Finland,' the singer says with a smile. 'So I'm delighted to be asked to sing you a classic Finnish tango called "Satumaa".'

Magdalena Ronander has a garland of flowers in her hair as she walks over to Joona and tries to catch his eye. Anja is staring down at her new shoes.

The band start to play the sad, melodic tango. Joona turns to Anja, bows slightly and asks quietly:

'May I have the pleasure?'

Anja's forehead, cheeks and neck turn bright red. She looks up at his face and nods seriously.

'Yes,' she says. 'Yes, you may.'

She takes his arm, casting a proud glance at Magdalena, and walks onto the dance-floor with Joona, her head held high.

At first Anja dances with great concentration, with a slight frown on her brow. But her round face soon relaxes into a smile. Her carefully sprayed hair is arranged in a complicated knot at the back of her head. She lets herself be guided round the dance-floor by Joona.

As the sentimental song approaches its end, Joona suddenly feels Anja nip his shoulder with her teeth, but it doesn't really hurt.

She bites again, a bit harder, and he feels obliged to ask:

'What are you doing?'

Her eyes are sparkling like glass.

'I don't know,' she replies honestly. 'I just thought I'd see what would happen, you never know unless you try . . .'

At that moment the music comes to an end. He lets go of her and thanks her for the dance. Before he has time to escort her back to her chair, Carlos glides over and asks Anja to dance.

Joona steps back and looks on as his colleagues dance, eat and drink, then starts to walk to his car.

People dressed in white are sitting on picnic blankets or strolling through the trees.

Joona walks over to the car park and opens the door of his Volvo. On the back seat is a huge bouquet of flowers. He gets in the car and calls Disa. Her voicemail clicks in on the fourth ring.

Disa Helenius

Disa is sitting in front of her computer in her apartment at Karlaplan. She's wearing her reading glasses and has a rug wrapped round her shoulders. Her mobile phone is lying on the desk next to a mug of cold coffee and a cinnamon bun.

On the screen is a picture of an overgrown and eroded pile of stones: the remains of the cholera cemetery at Skanstull in Stockholm.

She types some notes into the document on the computer, then stretches her back and picks up the mug of coffee, but changes her mind. She gets up to make some fresh coffee as her phone buzzes on the desk.

Without checking to see who it is, she switches it off and then stands there staring out of the window. Motes of dust dance in the sunlight. Disa's heart beats faster and harder as she sits back down in front of the computer. She's never going to talk to Joona Linna again.

Stockholm is in holiday mode and the traffic is thin as Joona walks slowly down Tegnérgatan. He's given up trying to contact Disa. Her phone is switched off and he assumes she wants to be left alone. Joona walks round the Blue Tower and carries on down the stretch of Drottninggatan that's lined with second-hand booksellers and shops. An old woman is standing in front of the new-age bookshop, Vattumannen, and pretending to look in the window. When Joona passes her she gestures towards the glass, then starts to follow him at a distance.

It takes him a while to realise he's being followed.

He turns round when he reaches the black railings outside Adolf Fredrik's Church. Just ten metres behind him is a woman in her eighties. She looks at him seriously, then holds out some cards.

'This is you, isn't it?' she says, showing him one of the cards. 'And here's the crown, the bridal crown.'

Joona walks up to her and takes the cards. They're from a pack of 'cuckoo' cards, one of the oldest card games in Europe.

'What do you want?' he asks calmly.

'I don't want anything,' the woman says. 'But I've got a message from Rosa Bergman.'

'There must be some mistake, because I don't know anyone called . . .'

'She's wondering why you're pretending that your daughter's dead.'

It's early autumn in Copenhagen, and the air is clear and cold by the time a discreet company arrives at the Glyptotek in four separate limousines. The men go up the stairs, through the entrance, and walk through the Winter Garden with its lofty glass roof, and along corridors lined with ancient sculptures before they arrive in the ornate banqueting hall.

The audience is already in place, and the Tokyo String Quartet are sitting on the low stage with their legendary Stradivarius instruments at rest, the same instruments that were once played by Nicolò Paganini himself.

The guests take their places at a table in the pillared aisle, slightly separate from the rest of the audience. The youngest of them is a fair, long-limbed man by the name of Peter Guidi. He is little more than a boy, but the expressions on the other men's faces say otherwise, because they will shortly be kissing his hand.

The musicians nod to each other and start to play Schubert's String Quartet No. 14. The piece opens with great pathos, a sense of emotion and energy being held back. One violin responds with excruciating beauty. The music pauses for breath one last time, and then just pours forth. The tune is joyful, but the instruments still convey a sense of the grief at the loss of more souls.

*   *   *

Every day 39 million bullets are made for various projectile weapons. A conservative estimate of the amount spent globally on the military each year is 1,226 billion dollars. Despite the fact that vast quantities of military material is being produced without pause, demand is still insatiable. The nine largest exporters of conventional weapons in the world are: the USA, Russia, Germany, France, Great Britain, the Netherlands, Italy, Sweden and China.